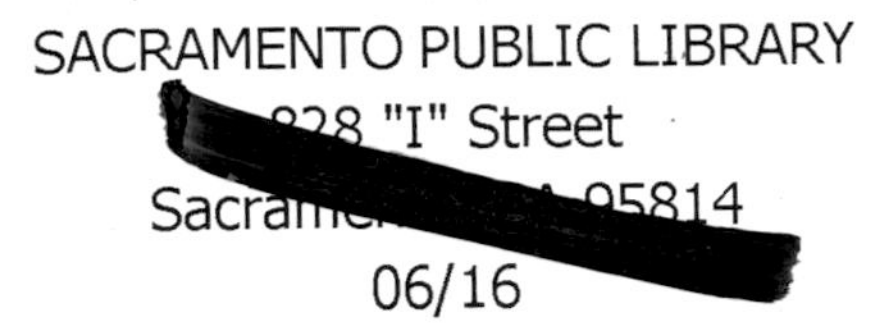

Paper Princess

The Royals Book 1

erin watt

COPYRIGHT

Cover Design by Meljean Brook
ISBN: 978-1682304563

For Margo, whose enthusiasm for this project matched our own.

ACKNOWLEDGEMENTS

WHEN WE DECIDED TO PULL a mind meld and collaborate on this book, we had no idea how cracktastic it would end up being, and how obsessed we would become with the characters and the world we created. This project has been a joy to write from moment one, but we wouldn't have been able to get it from our brains and into your hands without the help and support of some pretty amazing people:

Early readers Margo, Shauna and Nina, who still like us despite the brutal cliffhanger we left them with.

Our publicist Nina, for her contagious enthusiasm and constant cheerleading for this project.

Meljean Brooks, for coming up with a cover concept that fit this series so ridiculously well!

And of course, we are forever indebted to all the bloggers, reviewers and readers who took the time to read, review and rave over this book. Your support and feedback makes this whole process worthwhile!

CHAPTER 1

"ELLA, YOU'RE WANTED IN THE principal's office," Ms. Weir says before I can step inside her precalculus classroom.

I check my watch. "I'm not even late."

It's one minute before nine and this watch is never wrong. It's probably the most expensive item I own. My mom said that it was my dad's. Besides his sperm, it's the only thing he left behind.

"No, it's not about tardiness...this time." Her normally flinty gaze is soft around the edges, and my gut relays a warning to my sluggish morning brain. Ms. Weir is a hard ass, which is why I like her. She treats her students like we're here to learn actual math instead of some life lesson on loving your neighbor and crap like that. So for her to be giving me sympathetic looks means something bad is cooking down at the principal's office.

"Fine." It's not like I can give any other response. I offer a nod and redirect myself to the school office.

"I'll email you the course assignment," Ms. Weir calls after me. I guess she thinks I won't be returning to class, but there isn't anything Principal Thompson could throw at me that's worse than what I've faced before.

Before enrolling in George Washington High School for my junior year, I'd already lost everything of importance. Even if Mr. Thompson has somehow figured out I'm not technically living in the GW school district, I can lie to stall for time. And if I have to transfer, which is the worst thing that could happen to me today, then no big deal. I'll do it.

"How's it going, Darlene?"

The mom-haired school secretary barely looks up from her *People* magazine. "Take a seat, Ella. Mr. Thompson will be right with you."

Yep, we're on a first-name basis, me and Darlene. One month at GW High, and I've already spent way too much time in this office, thanks to my ever-growing stack of late slips. But that's what happens when you work nights and don't see the smooth side of the sheets until three a.m. every night.

I crane my neck around to peek through the open blinds of Mr. Thompson's office. Someone's sitting in the visitor's chair, but all I can make out is a hard jaw and dark brown hair. Total opposite of me. I'm as blonde and blue-eyed as they come. Courtesy of my sperm donor, according to Mom.

Thompson's visitor reminds me of the out-of-town businessmen who would tip my mom mega bucks for her to pretend to be their girlfriend for the night. Some guys got off on that even more than actual sex. This is per my mom, of course. I haven't had to go down that path...yet. And I hope I never have to, which is why I need my high school diploma so I can go to college, get a degree, and be normal.

Some kids dream of traveling the world, owning fast cars, big houses. Me? I want my own apartment, a fridge full of food, and a steady paying job, preferably one that's as exciting as paste drying.

The two men talk and talk and talk. Fifteen minutes pass and they're still shooting the shit.

"Hey, Darlene? I'm missing precalc right now. Okay for me to come back when Mr. Thompson isn't busy?"

I try to state it as nicely as possible, but years of having no real adult presence in my life—my flighty, lovely mom doesn't count—makes it hard for me to summon up the necessary submissiveness adults prefer from anyone who isn't allowed to legally drink.

"No, Ella. Mr. Thompson will be right out."

This time she's right, because the door opens and the principal steps out. Mr. Thompson is about five ten and looks like he graduated from high school last year. Somehow he manages a certain air of capable responsibility.

He gestures me forward. "Miss Harper, please come inside."

Inside? While Don Juan is in there?

"You already have someone in your office." I point out the obvious. This looks suspicious as hell and my gut is telling me to get out of here. But if I run, I'll be giving up on this careful life I've spent months planning.

Thompson turns around and looks toward Don Juan, who rises from his chair and waves at me with his large hand. "Yes, well, he's why you're here. Please come in."

Against my better judgment, I slip past Mr. Thompson and stand just inside the door. Thompson closes the door and flips the blinds to the office shut. Now I'm really nervous.

"Ms. Harper, if you'd sit down." Thompson points at the chair Don Juan just vacated.

I cross my arms and look at both of them mutinously. The seas could flood the earth before I take a seat.

Thompson sighs and settles in his own chair, knowing a lost cause when he sees one. That makes me even more uneasy, because if he's giving up this fight it means there's a bigger one coming.

He picks up a set of papers on his desk. "Ella Harper, this is Callum Royal." He pauses as if that means something to me.

Meanwhile, Royal is staring at me like he's never seen a girl before. I realize that my crossed arms are pushing my boobs together and so I drop my hands to my sides where they dangle awkwardly.

"Nice to meet you, Mr. Royal." It's apparent to everyone in the room that I'm thinking the exact opposite.

The sound of my voice jolts him out of his hypnosis. He strides forward and, before I can move, has my right hand clasped between two of his.

"My God, you look just like him." The words are whispered so only he and I can hear them. Then, as if remembering where he is, he shakes my hand. "Please, call me Callum."

There's an odd tone to his words. Like they're hard to get out. I tug my hand from his, which requires some effort because the creep does not want to let go. It takes Mr. Thompson clearing his throat to get Royal to drop my hand.

"What's this all about?" I demand. As a seventeen-year-old in a room full of adults, my tone is out of place, but no one even bats an eyelash.

Mr. Thompson runs an agitated hand through his hair. "I don't know how to say this so I'll just be straightforward. Mr. Royal tells me that your parents are both deceased and that he's now your guardian."

I falter. Just for a beat. Just long enough to let the shock filter into indignation.

"Bullshit!" The curse word bursts out before I can stop it. "My mother signed me up for classes. You have her signature on the registration forms."

My heart is beating a million miles a minute, because that signature is actually mine. I forged it to maintain control over my own life. Even though I'm a minor, I've had to be the adult in my family since the age of fifteen.

To Mr. Thompson's credit, he doesn't chastise me for the profanity. "The paperwork indicates that Mr. Royal's claim is legitimate." He rattles the papers in his hands.

"Yeah? Well, he's lying. I've never seen this guy before, and if you let me go with him, the next report you'll see is how some girl from GW disappeared into a sex trafficking scheme."

"You're right, we haven't met before," Royal interjects. "But that doesn't change the reality here."

"Let me see." I jump to Thompson's desk and pluck the papers out of his hands. My eyes run over the pages, not really reading what's there. Words pop out at me—*guardian* and *deceased* and *bequeath*—but they mean nothing. Callum Royal is still a stranger. Period.

"Perhaps if your mother could come in, we could clear everything up," Mr. Thompson suggests.

"Yes, Ella, bring your mother and I'll withdraw my claim." Royal's voice is soft, but I hear the steel. He knows something.

I turn back to my principal. He's the weak link here. "I could create this in the school computer lab. I wouldn't even need Photoshop." I toss the sheaf of papers in front of him. Doubt is forming in his eyes, so I press my advantage. "I need to get back to class. The semester is just starting and I don't want to fall behind."

He licks his lips uncertainly and I stare him down with all the conviction in my heart. I don't have a dad. I certainly don't have a guardian. If I did, where was this jackass all my life while my mom was struggling to make ends meet, when she was in god-awful pain from her cancer, when she was weeping on her hospice bed about leaving me alone? Where was he *then*?

Thompson sighs. "All right, Ella, why don't you go to class? Clearly Mr. Royal and I have more matters to discuss."

Royal objects. "These papers are all in order. You know me and you know my family. I wouldn't be here presenting this to you if it were not the truth. What would be the reason?"

"There are a lot of perverts in this world," I say snidely. "They have lots of reasons to make up stories."

Thompson waves his hand. "Ella, that's enough. Mr. Royal, this is a surprise to all of us. Once we contact Ella's mother, we can clear this all up."

Royal doesn't like the delay and renews his argument about how important he is and how a Royal wouldn't tell a lie. I half expect him to invoke George Washington and the cherry tree. As the two bicker, I slip out of the room.

"I'm going to the bathroom, Darlene," I lie. "I'll head back to class right after."

She buys it easily. "Take your time. I'll let your teacher know."

I don't go to the bathroom. I don't go back to class. Instead, I hustle to the bus stop and catch the G bus to the last stop.

From there it's a thirty-minute walk to the apartment I lease for a measly five hundred a month. It has one bedroom, a dingy bathroom, and a living/kitchen area that smells like mold. But it's cheap and the landlord is a woman who was willing to accept cash and not run a background check.

I don't know who Callum Royal is, but I do know that his presence in Kirkwood is bad, bad news. Those legal papers hadn't been Photoshopped. They were real. But there's no way I'm placing my life in the hands of some stranger who appeared out of the blue.

My life is *mine*. I live it. I control it.

I dump my hundred-dollar textbooks out of my backpack and fill the newly emptied bag with clothes, toiletries, and the last of my savings—one thousand dollars. Crap. I need some quick money to help me get out of town. I'm seriously depleted. It cost me over two grand to move here, what with bus tickets and then first and last month's rent along with a rental deposit. It sucks that I'm going to be eating the unused rent money, but it's clear I can't stick around.

I'm running again. Story of my life. Mom and I were always running. From her boyfriends, her pervert bosses, social services, poverty. The hospice was the only place we stayed in for any substantial amount of time, and that's because she was dying. Sometimes I think the universe has decided I'm not allowed to be happy.

I sit on the side of the bed and try not to cry out of frustration and anger and okay, yes, even fear. I allow myself five minutes of self-pity and then get on the phone. Screw the universe.

"Hey, George, I've been thinking about your offer to work at Daddy G's," I say when a male voice answers the call. "I'm ready to take you up on that."

I've been working the pole at Miss Candy's, a baby club where I strip down to a G-string and pasties. It's good, but not great, money. George has been asking me to graduate to Daddy G's, a full nudity place, for the last few weeks. I've resisted because I didn't see the need. I do now.

I'm blessed with my mother's body. Long legs. Nipped-in waist. My boobs aren't double-D spectacular, but George said he liked my perky B-cup because it gives the illusion of youth. It's not an illusion, but my identification says I'm thirty-four and that my name isn't Ella Harper but Margaret Harper. My dead mom. Super creepy if you stop to think about it, which I try not to.

There aren't many jobs a seventeen-year-old can actually do part time and still pay the bills. And none of them are legal. Run drugs. Turn tricks. Strip. I chose the last one.

"Damn, girl, that's excellent news!" George crows. "I have an opening tonight. You can be the third dancer. Wear the Catholic schoolgirl uniform. The guys are gonna love that."

"How much for tonight?"

"How much what?"

"Cash, George. How much cash?"

"Five hundred and any tips you can make. If you want to do some private lap dances, I'll give you one hundred per dance."

Shit. I could make a grand easy tonight. I shove all my anxiety and discomfort to the back of my mind. Now isn't the time for an internal morality debate. I need money, and stripping is one of the safest ways for me to get it.

"I'll be there. Book as many as you can for me."

CHAPTER 2

DADDY G'S IS A SHITHOLE, but it's a lot nicer than some of the other clubs in town. Then again, that's like saying, "Take a bite of this rotten chicken. It's not as green and moldy as these other pieces." Still, money is money.

Callum Royal's appearance at the school has been eating at me all day. If I had a laptop and an Internet connection, I would've Googled the guy, but my old computer is broken and I haven't had the cash to lay out for a replacement. I didn't want to trek to the library to use theirs, either. It's stupid, but I was scared if I left the apartment, Royal might ambush me on the street.

Who *is* he? And why does he think he's my guardian? Mom never once mentioned his name to me. For a moment earlier, I wondered if he might be my father, but those papers said my dad was deceased, too. And unless Mom lied to me, I know my dad's name wasn't Callum. It was Steve.

Steve. That always felt made-up to me. Like, when your kid says, "Tell me about my daddy, Mama!" and you're on the spot so you blurt out the first name that comes to mind—"Uh, his name was, um, Steve, honey."

But I hate to think that Mom was lying. We'd always been honest with each other.

I push Callum Royal out of my mind, because tonight is my debut at Daddy G's, and I can't let some middle-aged stranger in a thousand-dollar suit distract me. There are already enough middle-aged men in this joint to occupy my thoughts.

The club is packed. I guess Catholic schoolgirl night is a big draw at Daddy G's. The tables and booths on the main floor are all occupied, but the raised level that holds the VIP lounge is deserted. Not a surprise. There aren't many VIPs in Kirkwood, this small Tennessee town outside of Knoxville. It's a blue-collar town, mostly lower class. If you make more than 40K a year, you're considered filthy rich. That's why I chose it. The rent's cheap and the public school system is decent.

The dressing room is in the back, and it's full of life when I walk inside. Half-naked women glance over at my entrance. Some nod, a couple smile, and then they refocus their attention on securing their garter belts or applying their makeup at the vanity tables.

Only one rushes over to me.

"Cinderella?" she says.

I nod. It's the stage name I've been using at Miss Candy's. Seemed fitting at the time.

"I'm Rose. George asked me to show you the ropes tonight."

There's always one mother hen in every club—an older woman who realizes she's losing the fight against gravity and decides to make herself useful in other ways. At Miss Candy's, it had been Tina, the aging bleached blonde who took me under her wing from moment one. Here, it's the aging redhead Rose, who clucks over me as she guides me toward the metal rack of costumes.

When I reach for the schoolgirl uniform, she intercepts my hand. "No, that's for later. Put this on."

Next thing I know, she's helping me into a black corset with crisscrossed laces and a lacy black thong.

"I'm dancing in this?" I can barely breathe in the corset, let alone reach in front of me to unlace it.

"Forget what's up top." She laughs when she notices my halted breathing. "Just wiggle that bottom of yours and ride Richie Rich's pole, and you'll be fine."

I give her a blank look. "I thought I was going on stage?"

"George didn't tell you? You're doing a private dance in the VIP lounge now."

What? But I just got here. From my experience at Miss Candy's, normally you dance on stage a few times before any of the customers request a private show.

"Must be one of your regulars from your former club," Rose guesses when she notices my confusion. "Richie Rich just waltzes in here like he owns the place, hands George five hundies, and tells 'im to send you over." She winks at me. "Play it right and you'll squeeze a few more Benjamins outta him."

Then she's gone. Flouncing off to one of the other dancers, while I stand there debating if this was a mistake.

I like to play it off like I'm tough, and yeah, I am, to some extent. I've been poor and hungry. I was raised by a stripper. I know how to throw a punch if I have to. But I'm only seventeen. Sometimes that feels too young to have lived the life I have. Sometimes I look around at my surroundings and think, *I don't belong here.*

But I *am* here. I'm here, and I'm broke, and if I want to be that normal girl I'm desperately trying to be, then I need to walk out of this dressing room and ride Mr. VIP's pole, as Rose so nicely phrased it.

George appears as I step into the hallway. He's a stocky man with a full beard and kind eyes. "Did Rose tell you about the customer? He's been waiting for you."

Nodding, I swallow awkwardly. "I don't have to do anything fancy, right? Just a regular lap dance?"

He chuckles. "Get as fancy as you like, but if he touches you, Bruno'll haul him out on his ass."

I'm relieved to hear that Daddy G's enforces the no-touching-the-merchandise rule. Dancing for slimy men is a lot easier to swallow when their slimy hands don't get anywhere near you.

"You'll do fine, girl." He pats my arm. "And if he asks, you're twenty-four, okay? No one over thirty works here, remember?"

What about under twenty? I almost ask. But I keep my lips pressed tight. He has to know I'm lying about my age. Half the girls here are. And I may have lived a hard life, but no way do I look thirty-fricking-four. The makeup helps me pass for twenty-one. Barely.

George disappears into the dressing room, and I take a breath before heading down the hallway.

The sultry bass line greets me in the main room. The dancer on stage just unbuttoned her white uniform shirt, and the men go wild at the first sight of her see-through bra. Dollar bills rain on the stage. That's what I focus on. The money. Screw everything else.

Still, I'm so bummed at the thought of leaving GW High and all those teachers who actually seem to care about what they're teaching. But I'll find another school in another town. A town where Callum Royal won't be able to find—

I halt in my tracks. Then I spin around in a panic.

It's too late. Royal has already crossed the shadowy VIP lounge and his strong hand encircles my upper arm.

"Ella," he says in a low voice.

"Let me go." My tone is as indifferent as I can make it, but my hand shakes as I try to pry his off me.

He doesn't let go, not until another figure steps out of the shadows, a man in a dark suit and with the shoulders of a linebacker. "No touching," the bouncer says ominously.

Royal releases my arm as if it's made of lava. He spares a grim look at Bruno the bouncer, then turns back to me. His eyes stay locked on my face, like he's making a pointed effort not to look at my skimpy outfit. "We need to talk."

The whiskey on his breath nearly knocks me over.

"I have nothing to say to you," I answer coolly. "I don't know you."

"I'm your guardian."

"You're a stranger." Now I'm haughty. "And you're interfering with my work."

His mouth opens. Then closes. Then he says, "All right. Get to work then."

What?

There's a mocking gleam in his eyes as he drifts backward toward the plush couches. He sits, spreading his legs slightly, still mocking me. "Give me what I paid for."

My heart speeds up. No way. I'm not dancing for this man.

From the corner of my eye I see George approaching the steps of the lounge. My new boss stares at me expectantly.

I gulp. I want to cry, but I don't. Instead, I sashay over to Royal with confidence I don't feel.

"Fine. You want me to dance for you, Daddy? I'll dance for you."

Tears prick the insides of my eyelids, but I know they won't spill over. I've trained myself never to cry in public. The last time I cried, it was by my mother's deathbed, and that was after all the nurses and doctors left the room.

Callum Royal has a pained look on his face as I move in front of him. My hips roll to the music, as if on instinct. Actually, it *is* instinct. Dancing is in my blood. It's part of me. When I was younger, Mom was able to scrape money together to send me to ballet and jazz classes for three years. After the funds ran out, she took up the teaching part herself. She would watch videos, or crash classes at the community center before they kicked her out, and then she'd come home and teach me.

I love to dance, and I'm good at it, but I'm not stupid enough to think it'll ever be a career, not unless I want to strip for a living. Nope, my career will be practical. Business or law, something that will earn me a good living. Dancing is a little girl's foolish dream.

As I run my hands seductively down the front of my corset, Royal lets out a groan. It's not the groan I'm used to hearing, though. He doesn't look turned on. He looks…sad.

"He's rolling over in his grave right now," Royal says hoarsely.

I ignore him. He doesn't exist to me.

"This isn't right." He sounds choked up.

I toss my hair back and jut my boobs out. I can feel Bruno's eyes on me from the shadows.

A hundred bucks for a ten-minute dance, and I've already gyrated away two minutes. Eight more to go. I can do this.

But evidently, Royal can't. One more sway and both his hands clamp down on my hips. "*No*," he growls. "Steve wouldn't want this for you."

I don't have time to blink, to register his words. He's on his feet and I'm flying through the air, my torso slamming into his broad shoulder.

"Let me go!" I scream.

He's not listening. He carries me over his shoulder like I'm a rag doll, and not even Bruno's sudden appearance can stop him.

"Get the hell out of my way!" When Bruno takes another step, Royal booms at him. "This girl is seventeen years old! She's a minor, and I'm her guardian, and so help me God, if you take one more step, I will have every cop in Kirkwood swarming this place and you and all these other perverts will be thrown in jail for endangering a minor."

Bruno might be beefy, but he's not dumb. With a stricken look, he moves out of the way.

Me, I'm not so cooperative. My fists pound against Royal's back, my nails clawing at his expensive suit jacket. "Put me down!" I shriek.

He doesn't. And nobody stops him as he marches toward the exit. The men in the club are too busy leering and hooting at the stage. I see a flash of movement—George coming up beside Bruno, who furiously whispers in his ear—but then they're gone and I'm hit by a gust of cool air.

We're outside, but Callum Royal still doesn't put me down. I see his fancy shoes slapping the cracked pavement of the parking lot. There's a jingle of keys, a loud beep, and then I'm propelled through the air again before landing on a leather seat. I'm in the back of a car. A door slams. An engine roars to life.

Oh my God. This man is kidnapping me.

CHAPTER 3

MY BACKPACK!

It has my money and my watch in it! The backseat of the behemoth Callum Royal calls a car is more luxurious than anything my butt has ever touched in my entire life. Too bad I won't have time to appreciate it. I dive for the door handle and pull on it but the stupid thing won't open.

My eyes shift to the driver. It's reckless as hell but I don't have any choice—I lunge forward and grab the shoulder of the driver whose neck is as big as my thigh. "Turn around! I have to go back!"

He doesn't even flinch. It's like he's made out of brick. I tug a few more times, but I'm pretty sure that short of stabbing this guy in the neck—and maybe not even then—he's not doing anything unless Royal tells him to.

Callum hasn't moved an inch from his side of the rear passenger seat, and I resign myself to the fact that I won't be exiting the car until he okays it. I test the window just to be sure. It remains stubbornly closed.

"Child safety locks?" I mutter, even though I'm sure of the answer.

He nods slightly. "Among other things, but suffice it to say that you're in the car for the duration of our trip. Are you looking for this?"

My backpack lands in my lap. I resist the urge to rip it open and check if he's taken my cash and identification. Without either, I'm completely at his mercy, but I don't want to reveal a thing until I figure out his angle.

"Look, mister, I don't know what you want but it's obvious you have money. There are plenty of hookers out there who will do whatever you want and won't cause you the legal trouble that I could. Just drop me off at the next intersection and I promise you'll never hear from me again. I won't go to the cops. I'll tell George that you were an old client but that we hammered out our issues."

"I'm not looking for a hooker. I'm here for you." After that ominous statement, Royal shrugs out of his suit coat and offers it to me.

Part of me wishes I was just a little bolder, but sitting here in this super fancy car in front of the man I'd just used as a pole is making me feel awkward and exposed. I'd give anything for a pair of granny panties right now. Reluctantly, I slip the jacket on, ignoring the uncomfortable pain the corset is causing me, and clutch the lapels tight against my chest.

"I have nothing you want." Surely the small amount of cash shoved into the bottom of my bag is peanuts to this dude. We could trade this car for all of Daddy G's.

Royal raises one eyebrow in a wordless rebuttal. Now that he's in his shirtsleeves, I can see his watch and it looks…exactly like mine. His eyes follow my gaze.

"You've seen this before." It's not a question. He shoves his wrist toward me. The watch has a plain black leather band, silver knobs and an 18-carat gold housing around the domed glass of the watch face. The numbers and hands are glow-in-the-dark.

Dry-mouthed, I lie, "Never seen it before in my life."

"Really? It's an Oris watch. Swiss, made by hand. It was a gift when I graduated BUD/S. My best friend, Steve O'Halloran, received the same exact watch when he graduated from BUD/S, too. On the back it's engraved—"

Non sibi sed patriae.

I looked up the phrase when I was nine years old, after my mom told me the story of my birth. *Sorry, kid, but I slept with a sailor. He left me with nothing more than his first name and this watch.* And me, I'd reminded her. She'd playfully ruffled my hair and told me I was the best thing ever. My heart lurches again at her absence.

"—It means 'not for self, but for country.' Steve's watch went missing eighteen years ago. He said he lost it, but he never replaced it. Never wore another watch." Royal releases a rueful snort. "He used that as an excuse for why he was late all the time."

I catch myself leaning forward, wanting to know more about Steve O'Halloran, what the heck 'buds' is, and how the men knew each other. Then I give myself a mental face slap and slouch back against the door.

"Cool story, bro. But what does that have to do with me?" I glance at Goliath in the front seat and raise my voice. "Because both of you just kidnapped a minor, and I'm pretty sure that's a felony in all fifty states."

Only Royal responds. "It's a felony to kidnap anyone regardless of age, but since I'm your guardian and you were engaging in illegal acts, it's within my right to remove you from the premises."

I force out a mocking laugh. "I'm not sure who you think I am, but I'm thirty-four." I reach into the backpack to find my ID, pushing aside the watch that's a perfect match to the one Royal has on his left wrist. "See? Margaret Harper. Age thirty-four."

He plucks the identification from my fingers. "Five foot seven inches. One hundred and thirty pounds." His eyes flick over me. "Felt more like a hundred, but I suspect you've lost weight since you've been on the run."

On the run? How the hell does he know that?

As if he can read my expression, he snorts. "I've got five sons. There's no trick in the book that one of them haven't tried on me, and I know a teenager when I see one, even beneath a foot of makeup."

I stare back stonily. This man, whoever he is, is getting nothing from me.

"Your father is Steven O'Halloran." He checks himself. "Was. Your father was Steven O'Halloran."

I turn my face against the window so this stranger doesn't see the flash of pain that crosses my expression before I can bury it. Of course my dad is dead. Of course.

My throat feels tight and the awful sensation of tears pricks at the back of my eyes. Crying is for babies. Crying is for weaklings. Crying for a dad I never knew? Totally weak.

Over the hum of the road, I hear a clink of glass against glass and then the familiar sound of liquor splashing into a tumbler. Royal starts talking a moment later.

"Your father and I were best friends. We grew up together. Went to college together. Decided to enlist in the Navy on a whim. We eventually joined the SEALs, but our fathers wanted to retire early so instead of re-upping for duty, we moved home to take up the reins of our family business. We build airplanes, if you were wondering."

Of course you do, I think sourly.

He ignores my silence or takes it as approval to continue. "Five months ago, Steve died during a hang-gliding accident. But before he left…it's eerie, almost like he had some kind of premonition"—Royal shakes his head—"he gave me a letter and said it might be the most important piece of correspondence he'd ever received. He told me we'd go over it together once he got back, but a week later, his wife returned from the trip and informed me Steve was dead. I set the letter aside to deal with…complications regarding his death and his widow."

Complications? What did that mean? You die and then that's it, no? Plus, the way he said *widow*, like it was a nasty word, makes me wonder about her.

"A couple of months later, I remembered the letter. Do you want to know what it said?"

What a horrible tease. Of course I want to know what the letter said but I'm not going to give him the satisfaction of a response. I fix my cheek against the window.

Several blocks whiz by before Royal gives in.

"The letter was from your mother."

"What?" I whip my head around in shock.

He doesn't look smug that he's finally gained my attention—only tired. The loss of his friend, of my dad, is etched all over his face, and for the first time I see Callum Royal as the man he professes to be: a father who lost his best friend and received the surprise of a lifetime.

Before he can say another word, though, the car comes to a stop. I look out the window and see we're out in the country. There's a long flat strip of land, a large one-story building made of metal sheeting, and a tower. Near the building is a large white airplane with the words "Atlantic Aviation" emblazoned on it. When Royal said he built airplanes, I didn't expect *this* kind of airplane. I don't know what I expected, but a huge ass jet large enough to carry hundreds of people across the world was not it.

"Is that yours?" I have a hard time not gaping.

"It is but we're not stopping."

I pull my hand away from the heavy silver door latch. "What do you mean?"

For the time being, I shelve the shock of being kidnapped, of the existence—and death—of the sperm donor who helped make me, of this mysterious letter, to watch in open-mouthed amazement when we drive past the gates, past the building, and onto what I presume to be the airfield. At the rear of the plane, a hatch lowers and once the ramp hits the ground, Goliath motors up the incline and right into the belly of the plane.

I twist around to look out the back windshield as the hatch closes loudly behind us. As soon as the door of the plane shuts, the locks to the car doors make a soft snick. And I'm free. Sort of.

"After you." Callum gestures toward the door Goliath is holding open for me.

With the jacket clutched tightly around me, I try to gather my composure. Even the plane is in better condition than me with my borrowed stripper corset and uncomfortable heels.

"I need to change." I'm grateful I manage to sound halfway normal. I've had a lot of experience being shamed, and over the years I've learned that the best defense is a good offense. But I'm at a low point right now. I don't want anyone, not Goliath or the flight people, looking at me in this getup.

This is my first time on a plane. Before it was always buses and, in some really terrible spots, rides with truck drivers. But this is a giant thing, big enough to house a car. Surely there's a closet somewhere for me to change.

Callum's eyes soften and he gives a brisk nod to Goliath. "We'll wait upstairs." He points to the end of the garage-like room. "Through that door is a set of stairs. Come up when you're ready."

The minute I'm alone, I quickly exchange my stripper clothes for my most comfortable undies, a pair of baggy jeans, a tank top, and a flannel button-down top that I'd normally leave open but tonight fasten all the way up, leaving only the top button undone. I look like a hobo, but at least I'm covered.

I stuff the stripper gear in the bag and check to see if my money is there. It is, thankfully, along with Steve's watch. My wrist feels naked without it, and since Callum already knows, I might as well wear it. The second the latch is affixed around my wrist, I feel instantly better, stronger. I can face whatever Callum Royal has in store for me.

Slinging the backpack over my shoulder, I start plotting as I walk toward the door. I need money. Callum has that. I need a new place to live, and fast. If I get enough money from him,

I'll fly to my next destination and start over again. I know how to do that.

I'm going to be okay.

Everything is going to be okay. If I tell myself that lie long enough, I'll believe it to be true…even if it isn't.

When I reach the top of the stairs, Callum is there waiting for me. He introduces me to the driver. "Ella Harper, this is Durand Sahadi. Durand, Steven's daughter, Ella."

"Nice to meet you," Durand says in a ridiculously deep voice. Jeez, he sounds like Batman. "I'm sorry for your loss."

He bows his head slightly and he's just so fricking nice that it'd be rude to ignore him. I push my backpack out of the way and shake his outstretched hand. "Thank you."

"Thank you as well, Durand." Callum dismisses his driver and turns to me. "Let's take our seats. I want to get home. It's an hour plane ride to Bayview."

"An hour? You brought a plane to go an hour?" I exclaim.

"It would have taken me six hours to drive and that was far too long. It's already taken me nine weeks and an army of detectives to find you."

Since I don't have any other options right now, I follow Callum toward a set of plush cream leather seats facing each other, with a fancy black wooden table inlaid with silver situated between them. He settles into one, then gestures for me to take my place opposite him. A glass and a bottle are already set out, as if his staff knows he can't function without a drink.

Across the aisle from Callum is another set of cushy chairs, and a sofa lies beyond that. I wonder if I could get a job as a flight attendant for him. This place is even nicer than his car. I could live here, no question.

I sit down and set my backpack between my feet.

"Nice watch," he comments dryly.

"Thanks. My mom gave it to me. Said it was the only thing my dad left her besides his name and me." There's no point in lying anymore. If his army of private detectives led him to me in Kirkwood, he probably knows more about me and Mom than I do. He certainly seems to know a lot about my dad, and I find, against my better judgment, I'm starving for that information. "Where's the letter?"

"At home. I'll give it to you when we arrive." He reaches for a leather portfolio and pulls out a stack of cash—the kind you see in movies with a white wrapper around it. "I want to make a deal with you, Ella."

I know my eyes are as huge as saucers but I can't help it. I've never seen so many hundred-dollar bills in my entire life.

He pushes the stack across the dark surface until the pile of bills sits in front of me. Maybe this is a game show or some kind of reality television competition? I snap my mouth shut and try to stiffen up. No one plays me for a fool.

"Let's hear it," I say, crossing my arms and looking at Callum with narrowed eyes.

"From what I can tell, you're stripping to support yourself and get a high school diploma. From there, I presume you'd like to go to college and give up stripping and perhaps do something else. Maybe you'd like to be an accountant or doctor or lawyer. This money is a good faith gesture." He taps the bills. "This stack contains ten thousand dollars. For every month you stay with me, I'll give you a new stack—in cash—for the same amount. If you stay with me until you graduate from high school, you'll receive a bonus of two hundred thousand. That will pay for your college education, housing, clothing, and food. If you graduate with a degree, you'll receive another substantial bonus."

"What's the catch?" My hands itch to grab the money, find a parachute and escape from Callum Royal's clutches before he can even say *stock market*.

Instead, I stay seated, waiting to hear what kind of sick deed I'll have to do to get this money—and debating internally what my limits are.

"The catch is that you don't fight. You don't try to run away. You accept my guardianship. You live in my home. You treat my sons as your brothers. If you do that, you can have the life you've dreamed of." He pauses. "The life Steve would have wanted you to have."

"And what do I have to do for *you*?" I need the terms spelled out exactly.

Callum's eyes widen and his face takes on a green cast. "Nothing for *me*. You're a very pretty girl, Ella, but you *are* a girl and I'm a forty-two-year-old man with five sons. Rest assured, I have an attractive girlfriend who meets my every need."

Ewww. I hold up a hand. "Okay, I don't need any more explanation."

Callum laughs with relief before his tone goes serious again. "I know I can't replace your parents, but I'm here for you in any way that you would need them. You may have lost your family, but you're not alone anymore, Ella. You're a Royal now."

CHAPTER 4

WE'RE LANDING, BUT EVEN WITH my nose pressed right up to the window, it's too dark to see anything. Blinking lights from the runway below are all I can make out, and once we touch down, Callum doesn't give me time to examine my surroundings. We don't take the car that's in the belly of the plane. No, that must be the "travel" car because Durand ushers us to another sleek black sedan. The windows are tinted so dark I have no idea what kind of scenery is flashing past us, but then Callum rolls the window down a bit, and I smell it—salt. The ocean.

We're on the coast then. One of the Carolinas? Six hours from Kirkwood would place us somewhere along the Atlantic, which makes sense given the name of Callum's company. It doesn't matter, though. All that matters is the stack of crisp bills in my backpack. Ten grand. I still can't fathom it. Ten grand a *month*. And a helluva lot more after I graduate.

There has to be a catch. Callum might have assured me that he doesn't expect…*special favors* in return, but this isn't my first rodeo. There's always a catch, and eventually it will make itself known. When it does, at least I'll have ten grand in my pocket if I need to run again.

Until then, I'm playing along. Making nice with Royal.

And his sons…

Crap, I forgot about the sons—five of them, he'd said.

How bad could they really be, though? Five spoiled rich boys? Ha. I've dealt with a lot worse. Like my mom's gangster boyfriend, Leo, who tried to feel me up when I was twelve, then taught me the right way to form a fist after I punched him in the gut and nearly broke my hand. He'd laughed and we were fast friends after that. The self-defense tips definitely helped me with Mom's *next* boyfriend, who was just as handsy. Mom really knew how to pick winners.

But I try not to judge her. She did what she had to do to survive, and I never doubted her love for me.

After thirty minutes of driving, Durand slows the car in front of a gate. There's a divider between us and the driver's seat, but I hear an electronic beep, then a mechanical whir, and then we're driving again. Slower this time, until finally the car stops altogether and the locks release with a click.

"We're home," Callum says quietly.

I want to correct him—there's no such thing—but I keep my mouth shut.

Durand opens the door for me and extends a hand. My knees wobble slightly as I exit. Three other vehicles are parked outside a huge garage—two black SUVS and a cherry-red pickup truck that looks out of place.

Callum notices where my gaze has gone and smiles ruefully. "Used to be three Range Rovers, but Easton traded his for the pickup. I suspect he wanted more room to screw around with his dates."

He doesn't say it with reproach, but resignation. I assume Easton is one of his sons. I also sense an undercurrent of… *something* in Callum's tone. Helplessness maybe? I've only known him a few hours, but somehow I can't imagine this man ever being helpless, and my guard shoots up again.

"You'll have to catch a ride to school with the boys for the first few days," he adds. "Until I get you a car." His eyes narrow. "That is, if you have a license under your own name and which doesn't say you're thirty-four?"

I nod grudgingly.

"Good."

Then I realize what he said before. "You're buying me a car?"

"It'll be easier that way. My sons…"—he seems to be choosing his words carefully—"…aren't quick to warm up to strangers. But you need to go to school, so…" He shrugs and repeats himself. "It will be easier."

I can't fight my suspicion. Something is off here. With this man. With his kids. Maybe I should have fought harder to get out of his car back in Kirkwood. Maybe I—

My thoughts die as I shift my gaze and get my first glimpse of the mansion.

No, the palace. The Royal Palace. Literally.

This isn't real. The house is only two stories tall but it stretches out so far I can barely see the end of it. And there are windows *everywhere*. Maybe the architect who designed this place was allergic to walls or had a deep fear of vampires.

"You…" My voice hitches. "You live here?"

"*We* live here," he corrects. "This is your home now, too, Ella."

This will never be my home. I don't belong in splendor, I belong in squalor. That's what I know. It's what I'm comfortable with, because squalor doesn't lie to you. It's not wrapped in a pretty package. It is what it is.

This house is an illusion. It's polished and pretty, but the dream Callum is trying to sell is as flimsy as paper. Nothing stays shiny forever in this world.

The interior of the Royal mansion is as extravagant as the exterior. White slabs of tile veined with gray and gold—the kind that banks and doctors' offices have—span the foyer, which seems to go on for miles. The ceiling never ends either, and I'm tempted to shout something just to see how deep the echo goes.

Stairs on either side of the entrance meet at an actual balcony that overlooks the foyer. The chandelier above my head must contain a hundred lights and so much crystal that if it fell on my head, all they'd be able to find is glass dust. It looks like it belongs in a hotel. I wouldn't be surprised if it was taken from one.

Everywhere I look I see *wealth*.

And through it all, Callum watches me with wary eyes, as if he's stepped inside my mind and realizes how close I am to freaking out. To running hard and fast, because I don't fucking belong here.

"I know it's different from what you're used to," he says gruffly, "but you'll get used to this, too. You're going to like it here. I promise you."

My shoulders stiffen. "Don't make promises, Mr. Royal. Not to me, not ever."

His face goes stricken. "Call me Callum. And I intend to keep any promise I make to you, Ella. Same way I kept every promise I made to your father."

Something softens inside me. "You...uh..." The words come out awkwardly. "You really cared about my—about Steve, huh?"

"He was my best friend," Callum says simply. "I trusted him with my life."

Must be nice. The only person I've ever trusted is gone. Dead and buried. I think of Mom, and suddenly I miss her so much my throat closes up.

"Um..." I struggle to sound casual, as if I'm not on the verge of tears or a breakdown. "So do you have a butler or something? Or a housekeeper? Who takes care of this place?"

"I have staff. You won't be required to scrub floors to earn your keep." His grin dies off at my unsmiling stare.

"Where's my letter?"

Callum must sense how close I am to losing it, because his tone softens. "Look, it's late, and you've had a lot of excitement for one day. Why don't we save this conversation for tomorrow? Right now I just want you to get a good night's sleep." He eyes me knowingly. "I get the feeling it's been a long time since you've had one of those."

He's right. I take a breath, then exhale slowly. "Where's my room?"

"I'll take you up—" He halts when footsteps sound from above us, and I glimpse a flicker of approval in his blue eyes. "Here they are. Gideon is at college, but I asked the others to come down and meet you. They don't always listen—"

And still don't, apparently, because whatever orders he issued to the junior Royals are being ignored. And so am I. Not a single gaze flicks in my direction as four dark-haired figures appear at the curved railing of the balcony.

My jaw falls open, just slightly, before I slam it shut, steeling myself against the show of aggression from above. I won't let them see how much they've rattled me, but holy shit, I'm rattled. No, I'm intimidated.

The Royal boys are not what I expected. They don't look like rich pricks in preppy clothes. They look like terrifying thugs who can snap me like a twig.

Each one is as big as his father, easily six feet tall, and with varying degrees of muscle—the two on the right are leaner, the two on the left are broad-shouldered with sculpted arms. They must be athletes. Nobody is that ripped without working hard for it, bleeding and sweating for it.

I'm nervous now, because nobody has said a word. Not them, not Callum. Even standing far below them, I can see that all his sons have his eyes. Vivid blue and piercing in their intensity—all of it focused on their father.

"Boys," he finally says. "Come meet our guest." He shakes his head as if correcting himself. "Come meet the new member of our family."

Silence.

It's eerie.

The one in the middle smirks, just a tiny tug on the corner of his mouth. Mocking his father as he rests his muscled forearms on the railing and says nothing.

"Reed." Callum's commanding voice bounces off the walls. "Easton." Another name rattles out. "Sawyer." Then another. "Sebastian. Get down here. Now."

They don't move. The two on the right are twins, I realize. Identical in looks, and in their insolent poses when they cross their arms over their chests. One of the twins glances to the side, casting a barely noticeable look toward the brother on the far left.

A chill runs through me. *He's* the one to worry about. He's the one I need to watch out for.

And he's the only one who tilts his head toward me in a calculated slant. As our gazes lock, my heart beats a little bit faster. Out of fear. Maybe under different circumstances, my heart would be pounding for another reason. Because he's gorgeous. They all are.

But this one scares me, and I work hard to hide the response. I meet his eyes in challenge. *Come down here, Royal. Bring it on.*

Those dark blue eyes narrow slightly. He senses the unspoken challenge. He sees my defiance and he doesn't like it. Then he turns from the railing and walks away. The others follow as if on command. They dismiss their father from their gazes. Footsteps echo in the cavernous house. Doors close.

Next to me, Callum sighs. "I'm sorry about that. I thought I got through to them before—they've had time to prepare for it—but clearly they still need more time to absorb all this."

All this? He means me. My presence in their home, my tie to their father that I never knew I had before today.

"I'm sure they'll be more welcoming in the morning," he says. It sounds like he's trying to convince himself.

He sure as hell hasn't convinced me.

CHAPTER 5

I WAKE UP IN AN unfamiliar bed and I don't like it. Not the bed. The bed is the shit. It's soft but firm at the same time and the sheets are buttery smooth, not like the scratchy pieces of crap that I'm used to, when I actually slept on a bed with sheets. Lots of times it was just a sleeping bag, and those nylon sacks get smelly after a while.

This bed smells like honey and lavender.

All this luxury and niceness feels threatening, because in my experience, nice is usually followed by a real nasty surprise. One time, Mom came home from work and announced that we were moving into a better place. A tall, thin man came and helped us pack our meager belongings, and several hours later we were in his tiny house. It was adorable, with plaid curtains on the windows, and despite the small size, I even had my own bedroom.

Later that night I woke up to the sound of shouting and glass breaking. Mom rushed into my room and pulled me out of bed, and we were out of the house before I could take a breath. It wasn't until we'd stopped two blocks away that I saw the bruise forming on her cheekbone.

So nice things doesn't equal nice people.

I sit up and take in my surroundings. The whole room is designed for a princess—a really young one. There's a gag worthy amount of pink and ruffles. It's really only missing Disney posters, although I'm sure posters are too low-class for this place, just like my backpack sitting on the floor near the door is.

Yesterday's events flick through my mind, halting at the stack of hundred dollar bills. I leap out of bed and grab the backpack. Ripping it open, I sigh with relief when I see the stack of Benjamins on the top. I thumb the bills and listen to the sweet sound of the paper shuffling, replacing the silence of the room. I could take this right now and leave. Ten grand would keep me afloat for a long time.

But…if I stay, Callum Royal has promised me so much more. The bed, the room, ten grand each month until I graduate…just for going to school? For living in this mansion? For driving my own car?

I tuck the money into the secret pocket at the bottom of the bag. I'll give it a day. There's nothing stopping me from leaving tomorrow or next month or the month after. The minute things go bad, I can jet.

With my money secured, I dump the rest of the bag's contents out on the bed and take stock. For clothes, there are two pairs of skinny jeans, the baggy pair I wore home from the strip joint to avoid attention, five T-shirts, five pairs of undies, one bra, the corset I danced in last night, a G-string, a pair of stripper heels, and one nice dress that was my mother's back in the day. It's black, short, and makes me look like I have more upstairs than what God gave me. There's a makeup case, again mostly things my mom used, but also castaways from various strippers we met along the way. The kit is probably worth at least a grand.

I've also got my book of Auden poetry, which I guess is the most romantic and unnecessary part of my belongings, but I found it lying on a coffee shop table and the inscription matched the one on my watch. I couldn't leave it there. It was kismet, even though I generally don't believe in that stuff. Fate is for the weak—those people who don't have enough power or will to shape life into what they need it to be. I'm not there yet. I don't have enough power, but I will some day.

I rub my hand over the cover of the book. Maybe I can get a part-time job somewhere waiting tables. A steakhouse would be good. That'd give me some spending money so I wouldn't have to dip into the ten grand, which I've now deemed untouchable.

A knock at the door startles me.

"Callum?" I call.

"No, it's Reed. Open up."

I glance down at my oversized T-shirt. It belonged to one of my mom's old boyfriends and mostly covers me, but I'm not facing the accusing and angry glare of one of the Royal boys unless I'm fully armed. Which means dressed up and with a complete layer of bad girl makeup on.

"I'm not decent."

"Like I give a shit. You've got five seconds and then I'm coming in." The words are flat and forceful.

Jerk. With the guns on that guy, I have no doubt he could break down the door if he wanted to.

I stomp over and fling it open. "What do you want?"

He gives me a rude onceover, and even though my shirt hangs down far enough to cover anything racy, he makes me feel like I'm completely naked. I hate that, and the distrust that planted itself last night grows into genuine dislike.

"I want to know what your game is." He steps forward and I know it's meant to intimidate me. This is a guy who uses his physicality as both a weapon and a lure.

"I think you should be talking to your father. He's the one who kidnapped me and brought me here."

Reed takes another step until we're so close each breath we take makes our bodies rub against each other.

He's hot enough that my mouth dries up and tingles start dancing in places I'd like to think an asshole like him would never awaken. But another lesson I learned from my mom is that your body can like things that your head hates. Your head just has to be the one in charge. That was one of her "do as I say, not as I do" admonishments.

He's a jerk and he wants to hurt you, I scream at my body. My nipples pucker despite my warning.

"And you fought real hard, didn't you?" He looks down with disdain at the peaks that have formed under my thin shirt.

There's nothing for me to do but pretend my nips are always at attention.

"Again, you should be talking to your father." I turn away and pretend Reed Royal isn't firing every nerve ending in my body. I stroll to the bed and pick up a pair of plain bikini panties. As if I don't have a care in the world, I step out of my old ones and leave them lying on the cream-colored carpet.

Behind me I hear a swift intake of breath. Score one for the away team.

As nonchalantly as possible I pull on the new pair, carefully working them up my legs and under the long hem of my nightshirt. I can feel his eyes run over my body like it's a physical touch.

"You should know whatever game you're playing, you can't win. Not against all of us." His voice has deepened and roughened. My show is affecting him. Score two. I'm so glad my back is to him so he doesn't see that I'm affected, too, by just his voice and his gaze. "If you leave now, you won't be hurt. We'll let you keep whatever Dad's given you and none of us will bother you. If you stay, we'll break you so bad that you'll be crawling away."

I tug my jeans on, and then, with my back still turned, start to whip off my shirt.

A harsh chuckle follows and I hear swift footsteps. His hand clamps on my shoulder, keeping my shirt intact. He twists me to face him. Then he leans in close, his lips inches from my ear.

"Newsflash, baby—you can do a striptease in front of me every day and I still wouldn't do you, got that? You may have my dad wrapped around your underage ass, but the rest of us have your number."

Reed's hot breath skates down my neck and it takes every ounce of willpower not to shiver. Am I scared? Turned on? Who the hell knows. My body is so confused right now. Crap. Am I ever my mother's daughter or what? Because liking men who treat you badly is—was, dammit—Maggie Harper's calling card.

"Let me go," I say coldly.

His fingers tighten on my shoulder a moment before he pushes back from me. I stumble forward, catching myself on the edge of the bed.

"We're all watching you," he says ominously and then stomps out.

My hands shake as I hurriedly finish dressing. Starting now, I'm *always* going to have clothes on in this house, even in the privacy of my bedroom. There's no way I'm letting that jerk Reed catch me off-guard ever again.

"Ella?"

I jump in surprise and whirl around to see Callum standing at my open door.

"Callum, you scared me," I squeak, slapping my hand across my thundering heart.

"Sorry." He walks in holding a worn piece of notebook paper. "Your letter."

My surprised gaze flies up to his. "I, ah, thanks."

"Didn't think I'd give it to you, did you?"

I make a face. "Truthfully? I wasn't sure it existed."

"I won't lie to you, Ella. I've got a lot of flaws. My sons' antics could probably fill a book longer than *War and Peace* with all of them, but I won't lie. And I'm not going to ask you for anything more than a chance." He presses the paper into my hand. "When you're done, come down and have breakfast. There's a back staircase at the end of the hall and it leads to the kitchen. Whenever you're ready."

"Thanks, I will."

He smiles warmly at me. "I'm so glad you're here. For a while there I thought I'd never find you."

"I—I don't know what to say." If it was just Callum and me, I think I would be relieved to be here, maybe even grateful, but after the encounter with Reed, I'm halfway between afraid and terrified.

"That's okay. You'll get used to all of this. I promise." He gives me what is supposed to be a reassuring wink and disappears.

I sink onto the bed and unfold the letter with trembling fingers.

Dear Steve,

I don't know if you'll ever get this letter or if you'll even believe it when you read it. I'm sending it to the Little Creek naval base with your ID #. You dropped a piece of paper here with it, along with your watch. I kept the watch. Somehow remembered that damned number.

Anyway, straight to the point—you knocked me up in that frenzy we had the month before you shipped out to God knows where. By the time I figured out I was preggo, you were long gone. The guys at the base weren't interested in hearing my story. I suspect you aren't interested in it now.

But if you are, you should come. I'm sick with cancer. It's eating up my colon. I swear I can feel it inside me like some parasite. My baby girl's going to be alone. She's resilient. Tough. Tougher than me. I love her. And while I don't fear death, I dread that she's going to be alone.

I know we weren't more than two warm bodies knocking uglies, but I swear to you we created the best damn thing in the world. You'll hate yourself if you don't at least meet her.

Ella Harper. I named her after that corny music box you won for me in Atlantic City. Thought you might appreciate that.

Anyway, hope you get this in time. She doesn't know you exist but she has your watch and your eyes. You'll know it the first time you lay eyes on her.

Sincerely,

Maggie Harper.

I duck into my private bathroom—also bubble-gum pink—to press a washcloth against my face. *Don't cry, Ella.* There's no point in crying. I lean over the sink and splash my face, pretending that all the water dripping into the porcelain bowl is from the faucet and not my eyes.

Once I have myself under control, I yank a brush through my hair and sweep it up into a high ponytail. I slather on some BB cream to cover up my red eyes and call it a day.

Before I leave, I stuff everything into the backpack and then swing it over my shoulder. This is going with me everywhere until I find a place to hide it.

I pass four doors before I find the back staircase. The hallway outside my room is so wide I could drive one of Callum's cars down it. Okay, this place *must* have been a hotel at one time, because it just seems ridiculous that a house for one family is this big.

The kitchen at the bottom of the stairs is ginormous. There are two stoves, an island with a marble countertop, and a huge bank of white cabinets. I spot a sink but no refrigerator or dishwasher. Maybe there's another working kitchen in the bowels of the house and I'll be sent there to scrub floors, despite what Callum said earlier. Which would actually be okay. I'd be more comfortable doing real work for the money than just going to school and being a normal kid, because who gets paid for being normal? No one.

At the far end of the kitchen, an enormous table overlooks the ocean through floor-to-ceiling windows. The Royal brothers sit at four of the sixteen seats. They're all wearing uniforms—white dress shirts with the untucked tails resting over flat front khakis. Blue blazers hang over the backs of a few chairs. And somehow each boy manages to pull off looking gorgeous with a side of brutishness.

This place is like the Garden of Eden. Beautiful but full of danger.

"How do you like your eggs?" Callum asks. He stands at the stove with a spatula in one hand and two eggs in the other. It doesn't look like a comfortable pose for him. A quick glance at the boys confirms my suspicions. Callum rarely cooks.

"Scrambled is good for me." No one can screw that up.

He nods and then points the spatula at a large cabinet door close to him. "There's fruit and yogurt in the fridge and bagels behind me."

I walk over to the cabinet and pull it open as four sets of sullen, angry eyes track me. It's like the first day at a new school and everyone has decided they hate the new girl—just for the hell of it. A light turns on and cold air hits my face. Hidden refrigerators. Because why would you want anyone to see that you own a refrigerator? Weird.

I pull out a container of strawberries and set it on the counter.

Reed throws down his napkin. "I'm done. Who wants a ride?"

The twins scrape back their chairs but the other one—Easton, I think—shakes his head. "I'm picking up Claire this morning."

"Boys," their father says warningly.

"It's fine." I don't want to start a fight or be the source of tension between Callum and his sons.

"It's fine, *Dad*," Reed mocks. He turns to his brothers. "Ten minutes and we leave."

They all follow like baby ducks. Or maybe the better analogy is soldiers.

"I'm sorry." Callum heaves a sigh. "I don't know why they're so upset. I planned on driving you to school regardless. I just hoped they'd be more…welcoming."

The smell of burning eggs has us both turning toward the stove. "Shit," he curses. I move next to him and see a dark congealing mess. He smiles ruefully. "I never cook but I figured I couldn't screw eggs up. Guess I was wrong."

So he never cooks but he does for some strange girl he brought home? Not hard to see the source of resentment.

"Are you hungry? Because I'm okay with fruit and yogurt." Fresh fruit is something I haven't had the privilege of eating often. Fresh anything is a sign of privilege.

"Starving actually." He gives me a pitiful look.

"I can cook some eggs"—before I can even finish, he pulls out a package of bacon—"and bacon if you have it."

As I cook, Callum leans against the counter.

"So five boys, huh? That's a handful."

"Their mother died two years ago. They've never really recovered. None of us have. Maria was the glue that held us together." He shoves a hand through his hair. "I wasn't around much before she died. Atlantic Aviation was going through a rough time and I was chasing deals around the globe." He lets out a gusty sigh. "The business, I've managed to turn around… the family is still a work in progress."

Based on what I saw of his sons, I don't think they're even close to the bend in the road, but Callum's parenting skills aren't any of my business. I make a noncommittal noise at the back of my throat that Callum takes as encouragement to continue.

"Gideon's the oldest. He's away at college but comes home on the weekends. I think he must be seeing someone around town but I don't know who. You should meet him tonight."

Goodie. Not. "That'd be nice." In the way an enema is nice.

"I'd like to take you over to the school, get you enrolled. After we get you squared away, Brooke—that's my girlfriend—has offered to take you shopping. I figure you can start school on Monday."

"How far behind am I?"

"Classes started two weeks ago. I've seen your grades, so I think you'll be fine," he reassures me.

"Your PIs must be pretty good if you have my school records." I frown into the eggs.

"You've moved around a lot, but yes, eventually when I found out your mother's full name, it wasn't too hard to backtrack and obtain everything I needed."

"Mom did the best she could with me." I jut out my chin.

"She stripped. Did she force you to do that, too?" Callum reacts angrily.

"No, I did that all on my own." I slap his eggs onto a plate. He can cook his own stupid bacon. No one gets to run down my mom in front of me.

Callum grabs my arm. "Look, I—"

"Am I interrupting something?" A cold voice sounds from the doorway.

I whip around and see Reed. His voice is icy but his eyes are full of fire. He doesn't like me standing close to his dad. I know it's a total dick move, but something drives me to step even closer to Callum, almost under his arm. Callum's paying attention to his son, so he doesn't realize the reason for my sudden closeness. But Reed's narrowed eyes tell me he gets the message.

I raise my hand and place it on Callum's shoulder. "No, I was just making your dad some breakfast." I smile sweetly.

If possible, Reed's expression gets even stormier. "I forgot my jacket." He stalks over to the table and pulls it off the chair.

"See you at school, Reed," I taunt.

He spears me with another glare before turning and leaving. My hand falls away. Callum looks down at me, bemused. "You're poking a tiger."

I shrug. "He poked me first."

Callum shakes his head. "And I thought raising five boys was an adventure. I haven't seen anything yet, have I?"

CHAPTER 6

CALLUM DRIVES ME TO THE school I'll be attending for the next two years. Well, Durand drives. Callum and I sit in the backseat, and he's shuffling through a stack of what looks like blueprints while I stare out the window, trying not to think about what went down in my bedroom earlier with Reed.

Ten minutes pass before Callum finally looks up from his work. "I'm sorry, I'm playing catch-up. I took some time off after Steve's death, and the board is on my ass to get on top of things."

I'm tempted to ask him what Steve was like, if he was nice, what he did for fun, why he screwed my mom and never looked back. I keep my mouth shut instead. A part of me doesn't want to know about my father. Because if I know about him, he becomes real. He might even become *good*. It's easier to think of him as the jerk who abandoned my mom.

I gesture to the papers. "Are those plans for your airplanes?"

He nods. "We're designing a new fighter jet. Army commissioned it."

Jesus. He doesn't just build planes. He builds military-grade planes. That's big money. Then again, considering their house, I shouldn't be surprised.

"And my fath—Steve. He designed planes, too?"

"He was more involved in the testing sector. I am, too, to some extent, but your father had a real passion for flying."

My dad liked to fly planes. I file away that information.

As I fall silent, Callum's voice softens. "You can ask me whatever you want about him, Ella. I knew Steve better than anyone."

"I'm not sure I'm ready to know about him yet," I answer vaguely.

"Understood. But whenever you *are* ready, I'm happy to tell you about him. He was a great man."

I bite back the retort that he couldn't have been that great if he abandoned me, but I don't want to get into it with Callum.

All thoughts of Steve disappear when the car reaches a set of gates that must be twenty feet high, at least. Is this how the Royals live? Driving from one gate to another? We pass through them and follow a paved road that ends in front of a massive Gothic-looking building covered in ivy. I look around when we step out of the car and note similar buildings dotting the pristine campus of Astor Park Prep Academy, along with acres of grass. I guess that's why *park* is in the name of the school.

"Stick around," Callum tells Durand through the open driver's window. "I'll ring you when we're ready to leave."

The black car disappears toward a parking gate at the far end of the drive. Callum turns to me and says, "Headmaster Beringer is expecting us."

It's hard to keep my jaw off the ground as I follow him up the wide set of steps toward the front doors. This school is bonkers. It oozes money and privilege. The manicured lawn and massive courtyard are deserted—I guess everyone is already in class—in one of the far fields I see a blur of uniform-clad boys playing soccer.

Callum follows my gaze. "Do you play any sports?"

"Uh, no. I mean, I'm athletic, kind of. Dance, gymnastics, that stuff. But I'm not very good at sports."

He purses his lips. "That's too bad. If you join a team or squad, you're exempt from taking the phys ed class. I'll ask if there's an opening on one of the cheerleading squads—you might be a good fit there."

A cheerleader? Yeah right. You need pep for that, and I'm the least peppy person you'll ever meet.

We step into a lobby that belongs in a college movie. Large portraits of alumni hang on the oak-paneled walls, and the hardwood floor beneath our feet is polished. A few guys in blue blazers saunter by, their curious gazes landing on me briefly before they continue on.

"Reed and Easton play football—our team is number one in the state. And the twins play lacrosse," Callum tells me. "If you earn a spot on a pep squad, you might end up cheering for one of their teams."

I wonder if he realizes he's just building an even bigger case for me *not* becoming a cheerleader. No way am I bouncing around and waving my arms in the air for an asshole Royal.

"Maybe," I mutter. "I'd rather concentrate on my studies."

Callum strides into the waiting room of the headmaster's office as if he's been there hundreds of times before. He probably has, because the white-haired secretary behind the desk greets him like they're old friends.

"Mr. Royal, it's lovely to see you here under positive circumstances for a change."

He offers a crooked grin. "Tell me about it. Is Francois ready for us?"

"He is. Go right in."

THE MEETING WITH THE HEADMASTER goes smoother than I expect. I wonder if Callum threw some money at the guy so he wouldn't ask too many questions about my background. But he must have been told *some* things, because at the start of the meeting, he asks if I want to be called Ella Harper or O'Halloran.

"Harper," I answer stiffly. I'm not giving up my mother's name. *She* raised me, not Steve O'Halloran.

I'm given my class schedule, which includes a gym class. Against my protests, Callum tells Headmaster Beringer that I'm interested in trying out for a pep squad. Jeez. I have no idea what this man has against PE.

Once we're done, Beringer shakes my hand and tells me that my student guide is waiting in the lobby to take me on a quick tour. I shoot a panicky glance at Callum, but he's oblivious—too busy talking about the ninth green being tricky. Apparently he and Beringer are golf buddies, and he waves me off, telling me Durand will bring the car around in an hour.

I bite my lip as I leave the office. I don't know how I feel about this school. Academically, I'm told it's top-notch. But everything else...the uniforms, the fancy campus...I don't fit in. I already know this, and my thoughts are confirmed the moment I meet my tour guide.

She's wearing the navy-blue skirt and white dress shirt that make up the school uniform, and everything about her screams *money*, from her perfectly styled hair to the French-tip nails. She introduces herself as Savannah Montgomery—"Yes, *those* Montgomerys," she says knowingly, as if that's supposed to clue me in. I still have no fricking idea who she is.

She's a junior like me, and she spends a good twenty seconds sizing me up. Her nose wrinkles at my tight jeans and tank top, the scuffed combat boots on my feet, my hair, my unmanicured nails and hastily applied makeup.

"Your uniforms will be shipped to your house this weekend," she informs me. "The skirt's non-negotiable, but there are ways around the hem length." She winks and smooths out the bottom of her skirt, which barely grazes her lower thighs. The other girls I glimpsed in the hallway had their skirts down to their knees.

"What, blow the teachers, get a shorter skirt allowance?" I ask politely.

Her ice-blue eyes widen in alarm. Then she laughs awkwardly. "Um, no. Just slip a hundie to Beringer if one of the teachers complains, and he looks the other way."

Must be nice living in a world were you can slip people "hundies." I'm a dollar-bill kinda girl. Because that was the denomination usually tucked into my G-string.

I decide not to share that with Savannah.

"Anyway, let me show you around," she says, but we're barely a minute into the tour before I realize she's not interested in playing tour guide. She wants intel.

"Classroom, classroom, ladies' room." Her fancy fingernails flick at various doors as we head down the hall. "So Callum Royal is your legal guardian?—classroom, classroom, junior faculty lounge—How did that happen?"

I'm stingy with my response. "He knew my father."

"Callum's business partner, right? My parents were at his funeral." Savannah flips her chestnut brown hair over her shoulder and pushes open a set of doors. "Freshman classrooms," she says. "You won't be spending much time here. Sophomore classes are in the east wing. So you're living with the Royals, huh?"

"Yes." I don't elaborate.

We whiz past a long row of lockers, which look nothing like the narrow, rusty lockers in the public schools I went to over the years. These are navy-blue and the width of three regular lockers. They gleam in the sunlight streaming in from the wall of windows in the hall.

We're outside before I can blink, walking down a cobblestone path lined with gorgeous shade trees on each side. Savannah points to another ivy-covered building. "That's the junior wing. All your classes will be in there. Except PE—the gym's on the south lawn."

East wing. South lawn. This campus is ridiculous.

"You meet the boys yet?" She stops in the middle of the path, her shrewd dark eyes fixed on my face. She's sizing me up again.

"Yep." I meet her gaze head-on. "Wasn't too impressed."

That gets me a startled laugh. "You're in the minority then." Her face sharpens again. "First thing you need to know about Astor—the Royals run this place, Eleanor."

"Ella," I correct.

She waves her hand. "Whatever. They make the rules. They enforce them."

"And you all follow them like good little sheep."

A slight sneer touches her lips. "If you don't, then the four years you spend here will be miserable."

"Well, I don't give a damn about their rules," I say with a shrug. "I might live in their house, but I don't know them, and I don't want to know them. I'm just here to get my diploma."

"All right, I guess it's time for another lesson about Astor." She shrugs back. "Only reason I'm being so nice to you right now—"

Wait, this is her way of being *nice*?

"—is because Reed hasn't issued the Royal decree yet."

I raise a brow. "Meaning?"

"Meaning all it takes is one word from him and you'll be nothing here. Insignificant. Invisible. Or worse."

Now I laugh. "Is this supposed to scare me?"

"No. It's just the truth. We've been waiting for you to show up. We were warned, and we've been told to stand down until otherwise ordered."

"By who? Reed? The King of Astor Park? Gee, I'm trembling in my panties."

"They haven't reached a decision about you. They will soon, though. I've known you for five minutes and I can already tell you what their decision will be." She smirks. "Women have a sixth sense. It doesn't take us long to know what we're dealing with."

I smirk back. "No. It doesn't."

The stare-off that follows only lasts a few seconds. Long enough for me to convey with my eyes that I don't give a shit about her, or Reed, or this social hierarchy she clearly abides by. Then Savannah flips her hair again and beams at me.

"Come on, Eleanor, let me show you the football stadium. It's state-of-the-art, you know."

CHAPTER 7

SAVANNAH'S TOUR WRAPS UP AFTER a view of the indoor Olympic-size swimming pool. If there's one thing she approves of, it's my figure. The barely fed look is popular, she informs me with a brusqueness I'm beginning to believe is just her personality and not a reflection of what she thinks of me.

"You might think I'm a bitch, but I'm just honest. Astor Park is an entirely different kind of school. I'm assuming you went to public?" She gestures toward my thrift store skinny jeans.

"Yeah, but so what? School is school. I get it. There are different cliques. The popular kids, the rich kids—"

She flips her hand up to stop me. "No. This isn't like anything you've ever experienced before. The gym we saw earlier?" I nod at the question. "It was originally supposed to be for the football team, but Jordan Carrington's family threw a fit and it was re-designated as open access except during specific times. Between five and eight in the morning and two and eight in the afternoon, it's football only. The rest of the time, normals can use it. Nice, hmmm?"

I'm not sure if she's joking, because the limited access sounds ridiculous.

"Why did the Carringtons object?" I ask curiously.

"Astor Park is a prep school with a P." Savannah keeps walking. There's no quit button on her. "Every family in the state wants their kids to go here, but it's exclusive. You can't just have money to get in. Everyone that attends, even the scholarship students, are here because they have something special to offer. It might be that they're great on the football field or can elevate the science team to win national awards, which means national press. In Jordan's case, she's the captain of the dance team, which in my opinion, is one step up from stripping—"

Crap, that better not be why Callum suggested that this morning.

"—but they win, and Astor likes to see its name in the paper next to the W."

"Then why am I here?" I mutter under my breath.

But Savannah has superhero hearing because as she pushes open the front door, she says, "You're a Royal of some sort. What kind of Royal remains to be seen. This school will eat you up if you're weak, so my suggestion is to take advantage of everything the Royal name offers you, even if it means taking it by force."

A car door slams and a very thin, platinum blonde in skintight jeans and sky-high stilettos totters towards us.

"Hello…um…" The stranger holds a hand to her forehead as if she's shading her eyes from the sun, which is completely unnecessary given that she has enormous sunglasses covering her face.

My tour guide mutters softly. "That's Callum Royal's girlfriend. You don't have to be nice to her. She's just an extra."

And with that last bit of sage advice, Savannah disappears, leaving me with this wisp of a woman.

"You must be Elaine. I'm Brooke, Callum's friend. I'm here to take you shopping." She claps her hands together as if this is the most exciting thing ever.

"Ella," I correct.

"Oh, I'm sorry! I'm *so* terrible with names." She beams at me. "We're going to have so much fun today!"

I hesitate. "Um. We don't have to go shopping. I'm good just hanging out here at the school until the bus comes."

"Oh dear," she titters. "There are no buses. Besides, Callum told me to take you shopping so that's what we're going to do."

She grips my arm with surprising strength and drags me toward the Town Car. And inside is Durand. I'm beginning to love him.

"Hey, Durand." I wave, before glancing back at Brooke. "How about I sit up front with Durand and let you relax in the back?" I offer.

"No. I want to get to know you." She pushes me into the backseat and climbs in beside me. "Tell me everything."

I stifle a sigh, not exactly looking forward to making small talk with Callum's girlfriend. Then I chastise myself for it, because Brooke hasn't done anything but be nice to me. I'm not usually so judgy, and I force myself to lower my guard a little. If anything, it sounds like Brooke is more my type thanthe Royals, if random classmates of the boys call her an *extra*.

She looks young, though. Really young. As in Callum could be her father young.

"There's not much to tell," I reply with a shrug. "I'm Ella Harper. Callum says that Steve O'Halloran is my father."

Brooke nods. "Yes, he told me this morning. Isn't that amazing? He told me how he found you just a few hours away and he was so upset to discover your mom had passed away." She reaches for my hand, her bright smile dimming at the corners slightly. "My mother died when I was thirteen. A brain aneurysm. I was heartbroken, so I know just how you feel."

When she squeezes my hand, I feel a lump develop in my throat. I have to swallow twice before I can answer. "I'm sorry for your loss."

Her eyelids flutter closed for a moment, as if she's also struggling for control over her emotions. "Well, we're both in a better place now, aren't we? Callum saved me as well, you know."

"You were stripping, too?" I blurt out.

Brooke's eyes widen and a little laugh trips out before she can cover her mouth. "Is that what you were doing?"

"It wasn't full nudity." I cringe in the face of her giggles, wishing I never brought it up in the first place.

She composes herself and reaches out to pat my hand again. "I'm sorry I'm laughing. It's not at you, but at Callum. He was probably mortified. He's trying so hard to be a good father for his boys right now and I'm sure finding his young charge in a strip club had to be shocking."

Flushed and embarrassed, I look out the window. This day couldn't have gone worse. From the weird feelings Reed's aggressive hate brought out, to the condescending tour guided by Savannah, to my embarrassing confession to Callum's girlfriend. I *hate* feeling like I don't belong. The first day at a new school. The first ride on a bus. The first—

A tap on my forehead interrupts my thoughts. "Hey, don't get lost in there, sweetie."

I glance over my shoulder at Brooke. "I'm not," I tell her.

"Bullshit." She speaks the curse word softly and tenderly. Her hand rises to cup my cheek. "I didn't strip, but that's because I chose to do worse things to get by. You get no judgment from me. None. The important thing is that you're not there anymore and you won't ever have to be again. If you play your cards right, you'll be set for life." Then she pulls her hand back and smacks me lightly. "Now, put on a smile because we're going shopping."

Not gonna lie, that sounds good to me. "How much will it cost?" I've been to the mall before. Things can add up fast, even if they're on sale, but if I have a school uniform then I only need one or two items. Another pair of pants. Maybe a shirt or two. The beach is nearby so a swimsuit makes sense. I could part with a few hundred dollars.

Brooke's face lights up. She pulls out a card and waves it in front of my face. "You're asking the wrong question. This is all on Callum and trust me, no matter what he says about his business being in the toilet a few years ago, that man could buy and sell the entire shopping complex and still have enough left over to make even the most expensive hooker orgasm."

I don't even know how to respond to that.

WE END UP AT AN outdoor mall that features tiny shops with tiny clothes and enormous price tags. When I can't bring myself to pull the trigger on any purchase—$1500 for a pair of shoes? Are they made out of actual gold?—Brooke takes over and shoves item after item at the sales clerk.

There are so many bags and boxes, I'm scared Durand is going to have to trade in the Town Car for a U-Haul. After the tenth store, I'm exhausted, and from the sigh she heaves out, I'm guessing Brooke isn't far behind.

"I'm going to sit here and enjoy some refreshments while you finish up." She sinks down in a velvet chair and gestures for a salesgirl, who comes over immediately.

"What can I get for you, Ms. Davidson?"

"A mimosa." She waves a hand at me, clutching the black credit card she's been using so hard I'm surprised it hasn't melted between her fingers. "Go forth and buy. Callum will be disappointed if you come home with less than a trunk full of bags. He specifically told me that you needed everything."

"But…I…" I'm completely out of my element. Drop me in a Walmart or heck, even a Gap, and I think I could do just fine. But here? None of these clothes look like they should even be worn, but Brooke's done talking to me. She and the sales clerk are having an intense conversation about whether gray flannel or gray tweed is a better fall trend.

I reluctantly take the credit card, which is heavier than any card I've ever felt. I wonder if there's another card sandwiched between this one and that's how Brooke manages to charge half the store and not be turned away. I leave and buy a few more things, trembling at the cost of them, and am frankly relieved when Durand shows up to take us back to the Royal Castle.

On the drive home, Brooke chatters my ear off and offers tips about how to pair up some of my purchases to create the perfect designer "ensemble." Some of her suggestions make me giggle, and I'm startled to realize I didn't have such a bad time with Brooke today. Her enthusiasm is a bit much, sure, and she's kind of over the top, but maybe I was being unfair when I questioned Callum's taste in women. If anything, Brooke is at least entertaining.

"Thanks for the ride, Durand," I say when we pull up to the front door of the mansion. He stops the car here instead of driving around to the side like he did yesterday when we arrived from Kirkwood.

Durand helps Brooke out of the car and up the stairs. I trail behind like the *extra* that Savannah referred to Brooke as.

"I'll bring in the bags," he tells me over his shoulder.

All of it makes me feel awkward and useless. I really should get a job. Maybe if I had my own money and some real friends, I could start feeling normal again.

When I dreamed of my future, it didn't include limos and mansions and mean girls and designer labels. The pendulum of my life has swung too far in the opposite direction.

Callum is waiting in the foyer as Durand carries my bags inside, Brooke and I trailing behind him.

"Thanks for your help," Callum tells his driver.

"Darling!" Brooke comes alive at Callum's voice and throws herself at him. "We had so much fun!"

Callum nods in approval. "I'm glad." He glances my way. "Gideon is home. I want you to meet him...without other distractions. After that, why don't we grab a late lunch?"

"Gideon?" Brooke's eyes light up. "It's been too long since I've seen that darling boy." She rises on her tiptoes and pecks at Callum's cheek. "Your lunch plans sound delightful. I can't wait."

The throaty delivery nearly makes me blush. Callum coughs awkwardly.

"Come on, Ella. I want you to meet my oldest." There's a lot of pride in his voice and I follow him curiously to the back of the house, where a gorgeous blue-and-white tiled pool decorates a perfectly manicured lawn.

Inside the pool is a human arrow, slicing through the water with clean, even strokes. Next to me Brooke sighs. Or maybe that's a moan. Either sound makes sense because even in the water you can appreciate the sculpted muscles of the eldest Royal. And if the other Royal sons are anything to go by, he's probably not hard to look at out of the water, too.

I guess I can see why Brooke was excited to hear his name, but it's a little creepy given that she's dating his dad. Adults are complicated, I decide. It's not my place to judge their relationship.

After two more laps, Gideon stops and hauls himself out of the pool. In his Speedo it's easy to see there's no shrinkage problem for this guy.

"Dad." He rubs a towel over his wet face and then drapes it around his neck. He doesn't seem to notice or care that he's dripping water all over the deck.

"Gideon, this is Ella Harper, Steve's daughter."

His son flicks his eyes over me. "So you found her."

"I did."

They talk about me like I'm a lost puppy.

Callum's hand lands on my shoulder and propels me forward.

"Nice to meet you, Gideon." I wipe my hand on my jeans and then stick it out.

"Likewise." He shakes my hand and despite the coolness in his tone, I find him to be friendlier than anyone else in this house, other than his father. "I've got some calls to make." He turns to his dad. "But first I need to shower. I'll see you later."

He brushes by us. As we turn to watch him walk away, I happen to catch a glimpse of Brooke's face and the hunger there shocks me. Her eyes have that greedy look—the one my mom would wear when she saw something extravagant she wanted but couldn't have.

Callum seems oblivious. He's turned his attention to me, but I can't stop thinking about Brooke's expression. She totally has the hots for Callum's son. Am I the only one who can see that?

Stop it, Ella. This is none of your business.

"How about we get some lunch now?" Callum suggests. "There's a great little café just about five minutes from here. Serves amazing farm to table stuff. Very fresh. Light."

"Sure." I'm ready to escape.

"I'll come, too," Brooke says.

"Actually, Brooke. If it's all right with you, I want to have Ella to myself for now." His tone says it doesn't matter if she's okay with the arrangement because that's how it's going to be.

CHAPTER 8

LUNCH WITH CALLUM IS SURPRISINGLY pleasant. He tells me more about Steve even though I didn't ask about him, but he confesses that just being able to talk about Steve is a relief. Callum admits he hadn't always been there for either his sons or his wife, but whenever Steve needed him, he'd drop everything. Apparently that SEAL bond was unbreakable.

He doesn't make fun of me when I ask if that's where they became buds, but he looks like he's fighting a smile as he explains that BUD/S is a navy training program. By the time we're done eating, I have a better sense of the senior Royal—devoted, a little single-minded, and not entirely in control of his own life. We stay away from the topic of his sons but I tense up when the gates swing open.

"They'll come around," Callum says encouragingly.

We find the guys huddled in a large room at the end of the right wing of the house. The game room, Callum calls it.

Despite the black walls, the place is enormous, so it doesn't look like a cave. The boys meet us with stone-cold silence, and Callum's earlier reassurances suddenly sound unconvincing.

"Where are you all going tonight?" Callum asks in a conversational tone.

At first, no one says anything. The younger ones all look to Reed, who's leaning against a bar stool, one foot on the floor and one foot braced on the lowest rung of the chair. Gideon stands behind the bar, his hands braced on the top, watching it all.

"Gideon?" Callum prompts.

His eldest shrugs. "Jordan Carrington's having a party."

Reed swings around and scowls at Gideon as if he's a traitor.

"You're taking Ella to the party," their father orders. "It will be good for her to get to know her new classmates."

"There'll be booze, drugs, and sex," Reed mocks. "You really want her there?"

"I'd rather just stay in tonight," I volunteer but no one is listening to me.

"Then you five will watch out for her. She's your sister now." Callum folds his arms over his chest. This is a contest of wills and he wants to win it. He also seems completely unconcerned about the "booze, drugs, and sex" part. Awesome. This is really fantastic.

"Oh, did you adopt her?" Reed says sarcastically. "Guess we shouldn't be surprised. Doing shit without telling us is your MO, right, Dad?"

"I don't want to go to the party," I cut in. "I'm tired. I'm happy just to stay at home."

"Good idea, Ella." Callum unfolds his arms and places one around my shoulder. "You and I will watch a movie then."

A muscle ticks in Reed's jaw. "You win. She can come with us. We leave at eight."

Callum drops his arm. He isn't as clueless as I thought. The boys don't want me alone with him, and Callum knows it.

Reed's steely blue eyes shift to me. "Better go upstairs and make yourself presentable, *sis*. Can't ruin your big debut by showing up looking like that."

"Reed…" Callum warns.

His son's expression is the epitome of innocence. "Just trying to be helpful."

From his perch near the pool table, Easton looks like he's fighting a grin. Gideon is resigned and the twins are studiously ignoring us all.

A tremor of panic ripples through me. The high school parties I'd gone to in the past—all one of them—had been a jeans-and-T-shirt affair. The girls slutted it up, sure, but in a casual-smut kind of way. I want to ask how fancy this party will be, but I don't want to give the Royal brothers the satisfaction of knowing just how out of my element I feel.

Since eight o'clock is fifteen minutes from now, I book it upstairs where I find all my shopping bags placed in a neat row at the end of the bed. Savannah's warnings hang in the back of my mind. If I'm going to be here for two years, then I need to make a good impression. And now at the forefront of my mind is another thought—why the hell do I care? I don't need these people to like me, I just need to graduate from high school.

But I do care. I hate myself for it, but I can't fight this desperate need to *try*. Try to fit in. Try to make this school experience different than all the previous ones.

It's warm out, so I choose a short navy-blue skirt and an ice-blue and white top made of silk and cotton. It cost as much as the entire clothing section at Walmart but it's so fricking pretty, and I sigh when it falls into place.

In another bag, I find a pair of navy flats with a wide retro silver buckle. I brush my hair and gather the long strands to tie it in a ponytail, then decide to leave it down. I throw on a silver-colored headband that Brooke made me purchase—"accessories are a *must*," she'd insisted, which is why I also have an entire shopping bag full of bracelets, necklaces, scarves, and purses.

In the bathroom, I dig into my makeup kit and apply it with the lightest hand possible. I try for the dewy look, hoping that my time spent in strip clubs and bars doesn't show in my application. I'm not used to high school parties. I'm used to working with thirty-year-olds trying to pass as ten years younger, whose motto is if you're not wearing makeup three layers deep, you're not trying.

Once I'm done, I examine my reflection in the mirror and see a stranger. I look prim and proper. I look like a Savannah Montgomery, not an Ella Harper. But maybe that's a good thing.

Except there's nothing encouraging about the response I get when I meet the Royal brothers in the driveway a few minutes later. Gideon looks startled by my appearance. The twins and Easton snort. Reed smirks.

Did I mention they're all wearing low-riding jeans and snug T-shirts?

The assholes played me.

"We're going to a party, *sis*, not tea with the queen." Reed's deep voice doesn't give me any tingles this time. He's mocking me again, *and* he's enjoying himself.

"Can you wait five minutes while I change?" I ask tightly.

"Naah. Time to go." He strides toward one of the Range Rovers without a backward look.

Gideon glances at me again, then at his brother. Then he sighs and follows Reed to the car.

THE PARTY IS AT A house inland, away from the ocean. Easton drives me. The rest of the guys have gone ahead, and he doesn't look thrilled being the one stuck with me. He doesn't say much during the drive. He doesn't turn on the radio either, so the silence makes for an uncomfortable ride.

It isn't until he drives through the main gate of a three-story mansion that he looks my way. "Nice headband."

I resist the urge to smack that smug smile off his smug face. "Thanks. It cost a hundred and thirty bucks. Courtesy of your dad's magic black card."

That brings a dark look to his eyes. "Watch yourself. *Ella*."

I smile and reach for the door handle. "Thanks for the ride. *Easton*."

At the columned entrance of the house, Reed and Gideon are standing with their backs turned, engaged in hushed conversation. I hear an annoyed curse from Gideon, then, "Not smart, bro. Not during the season."

"The fuck do you care?" Reed mutters. "You made it clear where you stand—and it's no longer at our side."

"You're my brother and I'm worried about—" He halts when he notices me approaching.

They both tense up, and then Reed turns to greet me, and by greet me, I mean give me a laundry list of things I can and cannot do.

"This is Jordan's place. Her parents deal in hotels. Don't get sloppy drunk. Don't embarrass the Royal name. Don't hang around us. Don't use the Royal name to get anything. Act like a whore and we toss you out on your ass. Gid says your mom was a prostitute. You don't try that shit here, got it?"

The infamous Royal decrees.

"Screw you, Royal. She was *not* a prostitute, unless dancing is your version of sex and if so, your sex life must suck." I meet Reed's hard eyes with defiant ones. "Do your worst. You're an amateur compared to what I've been through."

I waltz past the Royal brothers and hike inside like I own the place, then regret it instantly, because everyone in the front parlor turns to stare at me. Pounding bass music thuds through the house, shaking the walls and vibrating beneath my feet, and loud voices and laughter echo from beyond an arched doorway to my left. A couple of girls in skimpy tops and skin-tight jeans eye me in disdain. A tall polo-shirt-wearing guy smirks at me as he raises a beer bottle to his lips.

I fight the urge to race back out into the night, but I can cower and be a target for the next two years, or I can brazen it out. The best I can do is be bold-faced when necessary and blend in whenever I have the opportunity. I'm no one's bitch, but I don't need to make waves either.

So I just smile politely in the face of their stares, and when their gazes shift behind me toward the incoming Royals, I take the opportunity to duck into the nearest corridor. I keep going until I find the quietest corner, a shadowy little nook tucked at the end of a hallway. While it seems like the perfect make-out spot, it's empty.

"It's still early," a female voice says, and I jump back in surprise. "But even if it was later, this part of the house is always empty."

"Oh God, I didn't see you there." I clasp a hand over my racing heart.

"I get that a lot."

As my eyes adjust to the dark, I see that there's an armchair situated in the corner. The girl on the chair pushes to her feet. She's really short, with chin-length black hair and a tiny mole over her top lip. And she's got curves I'd kill for.

"I'm Valerie Carrington."

Jordan's sister?

"I'm—"

"Ella Royal," she interrupts.

"Harper actually." I peer around her. Was she reading with a flashlight? I spot a phone lying on the small table next to the chair. Texting with her boyfriend? "You hiding?"

"Yup. I'd offer you a chair, but there's only one here."

"I know why I'm hiding," I say with sheepish honesty, "but what's your excuse? If you're a Carrington, don't you live here?"

She snickers. "I'm Jordan's poor cousin twice removed. A complete charity case."

And I bet Jordan doesn't let her forget it. "Hiding's not a bad thing. If you run away, you live to fight another day. That's my theory at least." I shrug.

"Why are you hiding? You're a Royal now." There's a slight sneer in her voice that makes me strike back.

"Like you're a Carrington?"

She frowns. "Gotcha."

I run a hand over my forehead, feeling like a complete jerk. "I'm sorry. I didn't mean to snap. It's been a long couple of days and I'm dead tired and completely out of my element."

Valerie's head tilts and she contemplates me for a few seconds. "Okay then, Ella *Harper*"—she emphasizes that as if it's an olive branch—"let's find something to wake you up. You know how to dance?"

"Yeah, sort of, I guess. I took lessons when I was younger."

"This will be fun then. Come on."

She leads me down the hall, past the nook, toward a set of stairs.

"Please don't tell me you have to sleep in a cupboard under the stairs."

"Ha! No. I have a proper bedroom upstairs. This is the staff quarters, and the housekeeper's son is a friend of mine. He went to college and left his old gaming equipment here. We played all the time, including DDR."

"I have no idea what that is," I confess. Mom and I didn't even own a TV when we were living in that last place in Seattle.

"Dance Dance Revolution. You copy the movements on the screen and get scored for how well you can dance. I'm pretty good at it, but if you have some past dance experience, then it shouldn't be a total annihilation."

When she grins at me, I nearly hug her, because it's been so long since I've had a friend. I didn't even realize I needed one until this minute.

"Tam was terrible," she confesses.

The wistful note in her voice tells me she misses him. A lot.

"Does he come home often?" I think of Gideon, who's home after only two weeks of college.

"No. He doesn't have a car so we won't see each other until Thanksgiving. That's when his mom will drive up. I'm going with her." She nearly skips with excitement at the mention of the trip. "But someday he'll have one."

"Is he your boyfriend?"

"Yeah." She looks at me in accusation. "Why? You got a problem with that?"

I hold up my hands in surrender. "Of course not. I was just curious."

She nods and opens the door to a small room with a neatly made bed and a normal sized television.

"So how are the Royals at home?" she asks as she sets up the game.

"Nice," I lie.

"Really?" She looks skeptical. "Because they haven't been nice to you. Or about you."

Some misplaced sense of loyalty to those jerks makes me shut her down. "Naah, they're coming around." I echo Callum's earlier words, but they don't sound any more believable from my mouth. Trying to change the subject, I tap the television. "Ready to dance?"

"Yep." Valerie accepts my topic switch with ease. She grabs two wine coolers from a mini fridge and hands me one. "Here's to hiding and still having fun."

The game is a breeze. It's way too easy for both of us. Valerie is a great dancer, but I grew up in this environment and there's no shift of the hips or flip of the arm that I can't make. Valerie decides we need handicaps and so she pauses the game and we start chugging our wine coolers. As we drink, her moves become increasingly terrible, but the alcohol is like magic for me and the music just takes over.

"Damn, girl, you've got *moves*," she teases. "You should try out for one of those TV dance shows."

"Nope." I take another swig of my drink. "I've got no interest in being on television."

"Well, you should. I mean, look at you. You're hot even in that rich bi-otch getup you're rocking, and with those moves? You'd be a star."

"Not interested," I say again.

She laughs. "Fine, be that way. Gotta pee!"

I laugh, too, as she bounds away from the screen mid-song to use the bathroom. She's got a crazy amount of energy, and I like her. I make a mental note to ask her if she goes to Astor Park Prep too. It'd be nice to have a friend there when I start on Monday. But then the song on the screen changes, and the music pulls me in again.

While Valerie is in the bathroom, the Divinyls' "Touch Myself" starts playing and I start dancing—not to the game, but my own moves. A slick sultry dance. One that makes my blood pound and my hands grow sweaty.

The unwelcome image of Reed's hot body and blue eyes appears in front of me. Dammit, the asshole Royal has invaded my thoughts and I'm helpless to shut him out. I close my eyes and imagine his hands running along my hips and wrenching me close. It's his leg thrust between mine—

The lights turn on and I stop abruptly.

"Where is he?" the devil himself demands.

"Who?" I ask dumbly. I can't believe I was fantasizing about Reed Royal, the guy who thinks I'm screwing his father.

"The meathead you're dancing for." Reed crosses the room and grabs my upper arms. "I told you that you can't turn tricks with my friends."

"There's no one here." My drunk mind is too slow to catch on to what he's saying. The toilet flushes.

"Oh yeah?" He flings me away and yanks open the bathroom door. A squeal of dismay rings out and he bites out an apology as he slams the door shut.

I can't help the smug smile from forming.

"Did I mention I was a lesbian?"

He doesn't think I'm funny. "Why didn't you tell me you were with Valerie?"

"Because it's funnier watching you to jump to conclusions. And even if I told you who I was with, you wouldn't have believed me. You've already decided who and what I am and nothing is going to change that."

He scowls but doesn't contradict me. "Come with me."

"Let me think on that." I tap a finger against my bottom lip as if I'm really contemplating his crappily delivered invitation. His eyes drop to watch the movement. "Okay. I've decided. *No.*"

"You don't like it here," he says flatly.

"Thank you, Mr. Perceptive."

He ignores the sarcasm. "Yeah, well I don't like it either. But here's the deal. If you don't come with me and make a fucking effort, then my father will keep forcing you to go to these parties. But if you get your ass out there and everyone reports back to their parents that they saw you, then Dad will lay off. Got it?"

"Not really."

Reed moves closer again, and I'm once again floored by the size of him. He's so tall. Tall enough that if he were skinny, his nickname would be "beanpole" or something. But he's not skinny. He's *built.* He's big and muscular and the alcohol is making me feel all hot and achy around him.

He's still talking, oblivious to my inappropriate train of thought. "If my dad thinks you're a lost, lonely lamb, he'll keep pushing us all together. Or maybe that's what you want. Is that it? You want to be seen with us. You want to be at these parties."

The accusations snap me out of my haze. "Because I've spent *so* much time around you tonight."

His expression doesn't change, not even to acknowledge that I'm right. Whatever. Fine.

"Come on, Valerie, let's go party," I call out.

"I can't. I'm mortified. Reed Royal saw me in the bathroom," she moans through the door.

"The asshole is gone. Besides, you're probably the most attractive and decent thing he's seen tonight."

Reed rolls his eyes but leaves as I motion him out the door.

Valerie finally comes out. "Why are we leaving our little haven?"

"To see and be seen," I answer honestly.

"Ugh. Sounds terrible."

"I never said it wasn't."

CHAPTER 9

THE FIRST PERSON I SEE when Valerie and I enter the living room is Savannah Montgomery. She's wearing tight jeans that are ripped at the knees and a halter top that bares her midriff. Her eyes are glued to Gideon, whose back is turned as he leans against the wall chatting with another guy.

As if she can see me making a mental connection between her and Gideon, Savannah swivels her head toward me. She doesn't wave or say hello, but her eyes meet mine briefly before she turns to talk to her friend.

The music is blaring, and everyone is drinking or dancing or making out in various corners of the room. Beyond the French doors I glimpse a large kidney-shaped pool, its bluish light casting shadows on the faces of the teenagers standing around it. There are people everywhere. It's loud and hot and I already miss the quiet safety of the staff quarters.

"Do we really have to be here?" Valerie murmurs.

I catch Reed watching us from the oak bar across the room. He's with Easton, and they both nod in warning when I meet their gaze.

"Yeah, we do."

She looks resigned. "Fine. Then we might as well get the bullshit out of the way."

Valerie is a godsend. She links her arm through mine and takes me around the party, introducing me to random people, then whispering details in my ear.

"That chick Claire? She's screwing Easton Royal. She likes telling people she's his girlfriend, but everyone knows Easton doesn't do girlfriends."

"Thomas? Raging cokehead, but Daddy's a senator so Thomas's messes are always cleaned up."

"Definitely stay away from Derek. Chlamydia central over there."

I swallow a choked laugh as she guides me toward another group, a trio of girls in assorted pastel minidresses.

"Lydia, Ginnie, Francine, this is Ella." Valerie waves a hand between us, then leads me away from the Pastels before they can even open their mouths. "You ever wonder if some people are born without brains?" she asks me. "Proof of it right there. Girls give new meaning to the word *airhead*."

I'm not going to lie—I'm enjoying the introductions, or rather, the gossip that comes with them. I do notice that nobody says much more than a muttered "hello" to me, before shifting their gazes to the Royal brothers to check their reactions.

"All right, easy part is over," Valerie says with a sigh. "It's time to slay the dragon."

"The dragon?"

"My cousin. AKA the Queen Bee of Astor Park Prep. Be warned—she's crazy possessive about the Royals. I'm pretty sure she's hooked up with all of them, even the twins."

Speaking of the twins, we pass Sawyer on our way to the pool area. I know it's Sawyer because he's wearing a black T-shirt, and earlier I heard Gideon call the white T-shirt-wearing twin Sebastian. A petite redhead is draped around Sawyer, trailing kisses along his neck, but his gaze stays fixed on me as we walk past.

"Little Royal's girlfriend," Valerie tells me. "Lauren or Laura, something like that. Sorry, I'm not knowledgeable about the sophomore circles."

But she's knowledgeable about almost everyone else, it seems. For a girl who likes to hide in the corner, Valerie is a bottomless well of gossip, but I guess that's the best way to gather information, watching from the shadows.

"Brace yourself," she warns. "The claws might come out."

The claws in question belong to a gorgeous brunette in a silky green dress that barely covers her thighs. She's draped on a plush lounge chair like she's Cleopatra or some shit. Her friends take up similar poses, each one in similarly skimpy dresses.

The hairs on the back of my neck stand on end, and I turn my head to find Reed and Easton sliding through the French doors. Reed's eyes lock with mine. His tongue comes out briefly to moisten his bottom lip, and my heart does an irritating flip. I hate this guy. He's too attractive for his own good.

"Jordan," Valerie greets her cousin. "Awesome party, as always."

The brunette smirks. "I'm surprised to see you out and about, Val. Don't you usually like to cower in the attic?"

"I decided to live on the edge tonight."

Jordan studies her cousin's flushed cheeks. "I see you have. Drunk much?"

Valerie rolls her eyes, then tugs me forward. "This is Ella. Ella, Jordan." She points a finger at each of the other girls and rattles off names. "Shea, Rachel, Abby."

Only one of the friends spares me a look—Shea. "You met my sister earlier," she says coolly. "Savannah."

I nod. "Yeah. Cool chick."

Shea narrows her eyes. I think she's trying to figure out if I'm being sarcastic or not.

Jordan speaks up, her almond-brown eyes gleaming. "So. Ella. Callum Royal is your new daddy, huh?"

I notice the entire backyard has grown silent. Even the music pouring out of the living room seems to have quieted. I feel everyone's eyes on us. No, on Jordan. Her friends' expressions are almost gleeful.

I brace myself for an attack, because obviously that's where this is leading.

Jordan sits up and crosses her long legs seductively. "What's it like, sucking old man cock?" she asks.

Someone snorts. A few titters tickle my back.

My throat tightens with embarrassment. These people are laughing at me. I realize the Royals had gotten to their friends, probably long before I showed up. Nobody here ever planned on giving me a real chance.

I'm horrified to feel tears stinging my eyes. No. Screw that. Screw Jordan and screw all of them. I might not come from a family who "deals in hotels," but I'm better than this bitch. I've survived more than she ever could.

I blink, pasting on an indifferent expression. "Your dad's not bad, if that's what you're asking, but I find it super creepy that he wants to pull my hair and have me call him *Daddy*. Is everything okay at home?"

Valerie snickers.

A shocked gasp comes from one of Jordan's friends.

Jordan's eyes blaze for one brief moment before the mocking glint returns and she lets out a husky laugh.

"You were right," she calls out to someone behind me. "She's trash."

I don't need to turn around to know she's talking to Reed.

Beside me, Valerie's features tighten. "You're a real bitch, you know that?" she tells her cousin.

"Better a bitch than a casual," Jordan answers with a grin. Then she waves a hand at us. "Get out of my sight. I'm trying to enjoy my party."

We've been dismissed. Valerie turns on her heel and I follow, but when we reach the doors, I veer away from her and march up to Reed.

His blue eyes reveal nothing, but his jaw twitches slightly when he sees me.

"There. I've done my Royal duty," I mutter to him. "Come find me when it's time to go."

I brush past him without looking back.

IT'S AFTER ONE A.M. WHEN we leave the party. Easton finds me in Valerie's room upstairs, the two of us sprawled on her bed watching *So You Think You Can Dance*. Valerie downloaded an entire season and forced me to watch a bunch of episodes, insisting I need to try out for the show. I declined yet again.

Easton announces we're leaving, then stands there rolling his eyes while I hug Valerie goodbye and tell her she'd better find me at school on Monday.

Outside, I realize Gideon and the twins already left in one of the Range Rovers, which means I'm stuck riding back with Easton and Reed. Reed gets behind the wheel, his brother slides in the passenger seat, and I sit in the back while they carry on a whole conversation like I'm not even there.

"We're gonna crush Wyatt Prep," Easton is saying. "Half their O-line graduated last year, so it's pretty much a straight path to Donovan."

Reed grunts in agreement.

"Then we're looking at Devlin High—easy fuckin' peasy. Their QB's hung-over half the time, and that butterfingers receiver corps of theirs is a joke." Easton babbles away, his voice animated, his shoulders free of the tension I'm used to seeing. Either he's drunk, or he's finally starting to accept my presence in his life.

I try to join the conversation. "What positions do you guys play?"

Just like that, his shoulders are stiff again.

"Linebacker," Reed says without turning around.

"Defensive end," Easton mutters.

They go back to ignoring me. Easton is now telling his brother about the blowjob he got tonight.

"It's like she's only giving forty percent now," he gripes. "Used to be a solid hundred, y'know? Going to town on my dick like it's made of chocolate, and suddenly it's a few licks and then *let's cuddle*? Eff that."

Reed snickers. "She thinks she's your girlfriend. Girlfriends don't need to put in an effort."

"Yeah, might be time to cut that one loose."

"You guys are pigs," I say from the backseat.

Easton twists around, his blue eyes mocking me. "Well, aren't we all high and mighty, Ms. Sex Worker."

I grit my teeth. "I'm not a sex worker."

"Hmmm." He turns back in his seat.

"I'm not." A helpless feeling lodges in my throat. "You know what? Screw you both. You don't know me."

"We know everything we need to know," Reed says.

"You know shit." I bite my lip and focus my gaze out the window.

We're only about halfway to the Royal mansion when Reed abruptly stops the car on the side of the road. I meet his eyes in the rearview mirror, but his face has zero expression as he snaps, "Last stop. Get out."

Shock smacks into me. "What?"

"East and I have somewhere else to be. We're going that way—" He points to the left. "The house is that way—" He points straight ahead. "Time for you to start walking."

"But—"

"It's only two miles, you'll be fine." He seems to be enjoying himself.

Easton is already out of the car and opening the back door for me. "Get a move on, sis. We don't want to be late."

I'm a tad dazed as he yanks me out of the car and pushes me toward the side of the road. Are they seriously ditching me here? It's one o'clock in the morning, and it's *dark*.

Neither of them care. Easton hops in the passenger seat, slams the door and gives me a little wave. The SUV zooms forward and Reed makes a speedy left turn, leaving me in his dust. I can hear their laughter from the open window.

I don't cry. I just start walking.

CHAPTER 10

I EAT BREAKFAST IN THE kitchen alone the next morning. My legs ache and my feet are sore from walking two miles in new shoes that hadn't been broken in yet. I dreamed that Reed Royal was chasing me in a pitch-black tunnel, his deep voice taunting me in the darkness, his breath hot on my neck. I woke up before he was able to catch me, but I like to think that when he did, I strangled him to death.

I'm not looking forward to school on Monday, and that ten thousand dollars in my backpack is calling out to me. *Leave. Run. Start over*. But there's so much more money on the line…

Maybe the Royals are right. Maybe I am a whore. I might not be sleeping with anyone for money, but I am taking it from Callum for favors unspecified in the future. Brooke said he saved her, but I'm guessing from the way they act around each other that she's definitely sleeping with him.

Footsteps thud in the hall, and Easton walks into the kitchen. He's bare-chested and wearing gray sweatpants that ride low on his hips. I try not to stare at the hard ridges of his abs. But I do take a long look at the cut on his right temple. It must have bled at some point, but now it's just a red line, an inch long and marring his perfect skin.

Without acknowledging me, he grabs some orange juice from the fridge and drinks straight from the carton.

Note to self: don't drink from that carton unless you want oral herpes.

I focus on eating my yogurt and pretend he's not here. I have no idea where he and Reed went last night or when they got home, and I'm not sure I want to know.

I can feel him watching me. When I turn my head, I find him leaning against the counter. His blue-eyed gaze tracks the movement of my spoon as I raise it to my lips, then lowers to the hem of my short sleep shirt.

"See something you like?" I crack as I take another bite.

"Not really."

I roll my eyes and gesture to his head with my spoon. "So what happened? Bump your head on the dashboard when you were blowing your brother last night?"

He laughs, then glances at the doorway behind me. "Hear that, Reed? Our new sister thinks I blew you last night."

Reed enters the kitchen, also shirtless and in sweatpants. He doesn't even look my way. "See if she'll give you some pointers. She looks like she knows her way around dick."

I flip up my middle finger but he has his back turned to me. Easton sees it, though, and a slow grin stretches his mouth.

"Nice. I like a chick with a little fight in her," he drawls. He pushes off the counter and comes closer, his thumbs tucked in his waistband. "What do you say, *Ella*?" He voices my name as if it's a curse word. "Want to show us what you've got?"

My heart stops. I don't like the feral look in his eyes. He stands in front of me. Then his smile widens and he slides one hand inside his pants to cup his junk.

"You're our sister now, right? So come on." He rubs himself. "Help a brother out."

I can't breathe. I'm…scared.

I shoot a glance at Reed, but he's leaning against the counter now, arms crossed. He looks amused.

Easton's blue eyes go smoky. "What's the matter, sis? Cat got your tongue?"

It's impossible to answer. My eyes dart toward the doorway that leads upstairs. The other door is behind me, but I don't want to turn my back to Easton if I need to run for help.

He catches the fear in my eyes and starts to laugh. Just like that, his hand slides out of his pants. "Aw, look at that, Reed. She's scared of us. Thinks we're gonna hurt her."

Reed laughs, too. From his perch on the counter, he smirks at me. "Not our MO. We have no problem getting laid."

Sexual assault isn't about getting laid, it's about power, I want to say, but I can see now that I was afraid for nothing. They don't need to hurt me. They already have power. This… whatever this was…it was intimidation. A game. They wanted to make me uncomfortable, and they succeeded.

As our gazes lock in a three-way stare-down, Callum walks into the room. He frowns when he notices Easton standing so close to me and his other son lurking at the counter. "Is everything all right?"

The Royal brothers watch me, waiting for me to tattle on them.

I don't. "Everything's awesome." I take another bite of yogurt but my appetite is gone. "Your sons and I are just getting to know each other. Did you know they have a stellar sense of humor?"

Easton's lips twitch. When his dad turns away, Easton's palm grazes his crotch again.

"Did you enjoy the party last night?" Callum asks.

Reed cocks an eyebrow at me. Waiting again, this time to see if I'll tell their father about the way they deserted me on the side of the road. I keep that to myself, too.

"It was great," I lie. "Super fun."

Callum joins me at the table, trying to provide a buffer between me and the guys, but his attention only draws sneers from Reed and Easton, who make no effort to hide their feelings.

"What would you like to do this weekend?"

"I'm fine. You don't have to entertain me," I answer.

He swivels in his chair. With an upward tip of his chin, he asks, "What about you two?"

The subtext is *what are we going to do with Ella*. It makes me cringe and a tightness that I'm beginning to call the Royal Pain appears between my shoulder blades.

"We got plans," Reed mutters and walks out of the room before Callum can even open his mouth again. He turns to Easton, who raises both palms and blinks innocently.

"Don't ask me. I'm the middle child. I do what everyone else tells me."

Callum rolls his eyes and despite the tension, I snort softly into my bowl. Easton does what Easton wants. No one made him put his hand down his pants and proposition me. That's a game he enjoyed playing and one he did without prompting.

It's convenient for him to pretend like Reed is his leader, absolving Easton of responsibility.

"Well, maybe you can let me know what Reed's plans are for you later," Callum grinds out.

Easton flushes. It's one thing for him to cast Reed as a leader and another thing for their father to imply Easton's a puppet.

"You never cared what I did on the weekends before." He shoves the OJ carton back into the fridge. With a glare at his father that is hot enough to turn the hair on Callum's head entirely gray, he walks off as well.

Callum sighs. "I'm not winning any father of the year awards, am I?"

I tap my spoon against the table a few times because I know better than to stick my nose where it doesn't belong. But in this case, Callum is dragging me right into the middle of a messed-up dynamic and the collateral damage could get real bad if he doesn't rein it in.

"Look, don't take this the wrong way, Callum, and obviously you know your kids better than I do, but does it really make sense shoving me down their throats? Honestly, I'd rather they ignored me. It doesn't hurt my feelings that they aren't happy I'm here, and the house is big enough we could all go for days and not see each other."

He scrutinizes me as if he's trying to figure out if I'm being sincere. Finally, he smiles sheepishly. "You're right. It wasn't always like this. We used to get along fine, but ever since their mother's death, the whole family hasn't been right. Unfortunately, these boys are spoiled. They need a dose of real life."

And I'm that dose?

I scowl. "I'm not an afterschool lesson. And you know what? I've experienced real life and it sucks. I wouldn't force *real life* on the people I love the most. I'd try to protect them from that."

I push away from the table and leave him behind.

Outside the kitchen, I find Reed lurking in the hall.

"Waiting for me?" I'm not even remotely sorry for the snide edge that's crept into my voice.

Reed gives me the onceover, his gorgeous blue eyes lingering on my bare legs. "Just wondering what your game is."

"I'm trying to survive," I tell him honestly. "All I want to do is to make it to college."

"And take a chunk of Royal money with you?"

I bristle. This guy just won't let up. "Maybe with a few Royal hearts in my pocket, too," I say sweetly.

And then, with a forced boldness, I lift a finger and trail it slowly across his naked pecs, my nail scraping across his smooth skin. His breath hitches, almost imperceptibly, but it's there.

My heart leaps to my throat and blood begins to pound in places that I absolutely do not want to be associated with Reed Royal.

"You're playing a dangerous game," he rasps out.

Don't I know it. Still, I can't let Reed see he's gotten to me. I pull my hand away, folding the fingers into a fist. "I don't know any other way to play it."

That bit of truth stuns him and I slip away. I'd like to think I won that round, but I feel like every encounter with Reed chips away at something vital inside me.

I SPEND THE DAY EXPLORING the house and the grounds. Beside the pool is a pool house made almost entirely of glass, which holds a sofa, some chairs, and a tiny kitchen. A stairway leads to the shore, but with all the rocks, there really isn't anything you could call a beach, at least not unless you walk farther down the shoreline. Still, it's beautiful, and I can see myself sitting down here with a book and a mug of hot cocoa.

It's hard to believe this is my life now. If all I have to do is endure two years of insults from the Royal boys, it'll still be a cakewalk compared to everything I've gone through in the past. No worrying about having enough to eat or wondering where I'm going to sleep. No moving from town to town, looking for a quick score. No sitting by my mom's bedside watching her shake and cry from pain but being too poor to afford the medication that would put her out of her misery.

A sharp bolt of grief slices through me at those memories. Like Callum, Mom wasn't the best parent in the world, but she tried hard and I loved her. When she was alive, I wasn't completely alone.

Here, with the big endless ocean rolling away from me and not another person as far as I can see, the solitude hits me hard. No matter what Callum says or tries to do, I'm never going to be a Royal.

Maybe I'll do my reading inside.

The big house is quiet. The guys are gone. Callum has left a note that says he's working and provides me with the Wi-Fi password, his cell phone number, and Durand's number. Under the piece of paper is a small white box. Cue heavy breathing. I lift out the smart phone like it's made of sugared crystals. My old phones were disposable flip phones that sent and received calls. This one…I feel like I could hack a database with it.

I spend the rest of the afternoon playing with the phone, looking up random shit and watching really terrible YouTube videos. It's wonderful.

Around seven, Callum calls to tell me that dinner is ready. I find him and Brooke out on the patio.

"Mind if we eat out here?" he asks.

I stare at the delicious-looking food and the beautifully lit patio area, and try not to roll my eyes because who in their right mind would hate this? "It's perfect."

During dinner, I get a chance to see a different side of Brooke. A strange, vulnerable one where she ducks her head and bats her eyelashes at Callum. And Callum? The man who heads up a corporation that builds planes for the military? He eats it up like candy.

"Can I get you more wine, honey?" Brooke offers. Callum's glass is almost overflowing already.

"No. I'm perfect." He smiles easily. "I've got the two most beautiful ladies sitting down to dinner with me. The steak is cooked perfectly and I just closed a deal with Singapore Air."

Brooke clasps her hands together. "You are just amazing. Have I told you how amazing you are?"

She leans close, her breasts squashing against his arm, and plants a wet kiss against his cheek. He casts a quick glance in my direction before gently moving away. Brooke makes a small noise of disappointment but settles into her chair.

I dig into my steak. I don't know if I've ever had a piece of meat so juicy before.

"Steak is very fattening. All red meat is," Brooke informs me.

"Ella doesn't need to worry about that," Callum says brusquely.

"Not now, but later you'll regret it," Brooke warns.

I look down at the succulent piece of meat and then over at Brooke's willowy frame. I think I get where she's coming from. Like me, she's poor. She relies on Callum's generosity and probably fears that if she's less beautiful tomorrow, he'll be done with her. I don't know if she's wrong or right, but it doesn't make her concerns less valid. Still, I'm hungry and I want this steak. "Thanks for your input."

Callum smothers a chuckle as Brooke frowns. An expression I can't make out flits across her face. Something like disappointment or disapproval. Her pouty lips firm and she turns to Callum, engaging him in conversation about some party they went to before I arrived.

Guilt makes my next bite of meat a little less delicious than the first one. I hurt her feelings and now she's shutting me out. Other than Valerie, she was the one friendly face around in this new place and now I've offended her.

"Should we plan a party to welcome Ella into the family?" Callum suggests, trying to include me in the conversation.

And Callum. He's been nothing but perfect since he dragged me out of Daddy G's, but a party with the assholes from school? I'd rather have my fingernails pulled out one by one.

I place my fork beside my plate. "I don't need a party. You've already given me everything I need."

Brooke lays her head against Callum's stiff shoulder. "Callum, don't worry about it. Ella will make friends in her own time, won't you, darling?"

I nod in agreement. "That's right."

I summon up my best smile, and it must work because the tension in his body disappears. "All right, then. No party."

"Callum's the best, isn't he?" Brooke reaches up to toy with the top button of his shirt. Her actions are possessive, almost as if she's trying to defend her territory. I want to tell her I'm not a threat, but I don't know if she'd believe me. "We're his soiled doves. Hopefully once we're cleaned up, he doesn't send us away."

"No one's sending Ella away. She's a Royal," Callum declares.

My gaze shifts to Brooke, and by the tight expression on her face, she doesn't miss that her name wasn't included in his pronouncement.

"Really? I thought she was Steve's daughter. Is there something you're not telling us?" Brooke trills.

He rears back as if she hit him. "What? No. Of course she's Steve's. But he's"—Callum swallows hard—"he's gone, and so Ella is part of my family now just as the boys would have been Steve's if anything had happened to me."

"Of course. I didn't mean anything other than you're generous." Her voice drops to a purr. "So very generous."

With each word, she moves closer and closer to Callum until she's virtually on his lap. He switches his fork to his left hand and drapes an arm around the back of Brooke's chair. His eyes plead with me to understand. *I'm using her just as she's using me.*

I get it, I really do. This is a man who lost his wife and best friend in a short span of time. I know what loss feels like, and if Brooke fills up those empty spaces for Callum, then good for him.

But I don't need to watch them in action.

"I'm going inside to get a—" I don't even bother finishing because Brooke has climbed on top of Callum. I watch wide-eyed as she straddles him, pulling on his ears like he's a hobby horse.

"Not here, Brooke." His eyes flicker toward me.

I start walking—quickly—toward the kitchen. Behind me, I hear her reassure Callum.

"She's seventeen, darling. She probably knows more about sex than the two of us put together. And if she doesn't, your boys will expose her innocent eyes soon enough."

That makes me cringe, but whatever spell Brooke has cooked up is doing its thing because I hear Callum groan.

"Wait. Wait. Brooke."

She giggles breathily and then Callum's chair starts squeaking. Damn, this is a big patio.

Easton is coming out of the kitchen as I make my escape inside. He peers past me, totally unfazed by what's happening on the patio.

"Welcome to the Royal Palace," he says. An impish grin spreads across his face and he yells, "Don't forget to wrap it before you tap it. We don't need more money-grubbing illegitimate kids in this family."

My smile dies off immediately. "Did someone teach you how to be a jerk or does it come naturally?"

Easton hesitates for a moment, but then, as if Reed is sitting on his shoulder, he drops his hand to his crotch. "Why don't you come upstairs and I'll show you just how good I am in my natural state?"

"Pass." I walk by as calmly as possible, and I don't start running until I hit the stairs.

Once I'm in the privacy of my bedroom, I list all the reasons why I shouldn't leave immediately. I remind myself that I'm not hungry. I have ten grand in my backpack. I'm not stripping for greedy men with dollar bills clutched in their sweaty hands. I can handle two years of sexual come-ons and personal putdowns from the Royal boys.

But for the rest of the night I stay in my room, where I spend the time looking for part-time jobs using the shiny new MacBook that magically appeared on my desk. There's no public transport outside the house, but I passed a bus stop last night that wasn't too far away. Maybe a quarter of a mile.

The next day, I make the walk, and according to my watch it takes ten minutes at a brisk pace, which is more like a half mile. The Sunday bus schedule is snoozy—only one every hour and it stops at six. Whatever job I get would need to be over early on Sundays.

On my way home, Gideon drives by in a shiny SUV. His hair is sticking up and he's got red marks on his neck. If it were anyone else, I'd say he just had sex, but he looks too angry for that. Maybe he fought with a raccoon.

"What are you doing?" he barks.

"Walking."

"Get in." He stops and shoves open the door. "You shouldn't be out here alone."

"Seems like a nice place." The houses are big. The lawns are bigger. Besides, his brothers had no problem ditching me on this road the other night. "The most danger I've encountered this morning is a big bad man trying to lure me into his truck. Good thing I know better."

A reluctant smile lurks on the corner of his mouth. "I don't have any candy or ice cream, so by default I should be considered safe."

"Nah, just a shitty kidnapper."

"You coming or are we going to block the Sunday traffic all day?"

I glance behind him and see another car coming. Why the hell not? It's a short trip to the house.

Gideon doesn't say anything during the drive, only rubs his arm a couple of times. A few minutes later, he stops in front of the entrance and puts the car in park.

"Thanks for the ride, Gideon." When he doesn't follow me inside, I glance over and call out to the SUV. "Not coming?"

He looks up at the house. "No. I need a swim. A long one."

Then he rubs his arm again like there's dirt on it that he simply can't get off. He catches me watching him and frowns.

I want to ask if there's anything wrong but the *no trespassing* look that shutters over his face makes me swallow back the words. I give him a worried look instead, an invitation. *I've seen shit*, I try to telegraph. I only get a clenched jaw in return.

ON MY BED IS ANOTHER note from Callum. I climb onto the cloud of pink and white and curl up next to the headboard to read.

Sorry about last night's dinner. Won't happen again. Durand will drive you to school in the morning. Let him know the time.

P.S. Your car is coming. Wanted to get exactly the right one and the only one with the correct color was in California.

Oh God, please don't let it be pink. I think I'll die if I'm supposed to drive Malibu Barbie's dream car.

I bolt upright from the bed. I can't believe those words even passed through my head. A car is a car. I should be grateful just to be driving one. Who cares what color it is? If it's pink, I'll get down and kiss the bubble-gum-colored fender.

Jeez. One weekend and I'm already turning into a spoiled brat.

CHAPTER 11

THE NEXT MORNING, I'M UP at dawn. I'm not going to repeat my mistakes from the party. I push aside all the pretty shoes that Brooke bought and find some white canvas sneakers. I pair them with skinny jeans and a T-shirt.

I nibble on my lip. Do I leave the backpack here or take it with me? If I take it with me, some punk ass kid might steal it. If I leave it, one of the Royals might go through it. I decide to take it with me, although carrying around ten large makes me feel paranoid and jumpy.

I run into Callum in the kitchen—he's leaving for work, and he's surprised to find me up so early. I lie and tell him I'm meeting Valerie for breakfast, and he looks so excited I made a friend that I think he's going to pee his pants.

After chugging down a cup of coffee, I meet Durand outside the house two hours before school starts. "Thanks for agreeing to drive me."

He merely gives a dip of his head.

I have him drop me off at a bakery that's just minutes away from the prep school, and the moment I step inside, I'm greeted by the most heavenly smell. Behind the counter is a woman about my mom's age, with wheat-blond hair swept up in a tight, ballet-style bun.

"Hi there, sweetie, what can I get for you?" she asks with her hands poised over the register.

"I'm Ella Harper and I'd like to apply for the assistant job. The ad said there were school friendly hours? I go to Astor Park."

"Hmm, a scholarship student?" I don't correct her because it's mostly true. I'm a Callum Royal scholarship beneficiary. I hold my breath as she inspects me. "Do you have any experience baking?"

"None," I admit, "But I'm a quick learner and I'll work harder than anyone else you've ever hired. I don't mind long days or early mornings or late nights."

She purses her lips. "I'm not a fan of hiring high school students. But…we could give it a try. Say a week. You'll have to serve your peers. Will that be a problem?"

"Absolutely not."

"Some of those Astor Park kids can be a real handful."

Translation: the school is full of assholes.

"Again, the clientele is not a problem for me."

She sighs. "All right. I really do need another hand. If you show up for the next six days on time and work all your scheduled hours, the job is yours." I flash her a smile, and she slaps a hand to her heart. "Honey, you should have smiled before. It completely transforms your face. In fact, the more you smile, the more tips you'll get. Remember that."

Smiling is not my natural state. In fact, it kind of hurts. My face is so unused to it but I keep smiling because I want this nice lady to like me.

"I start baking at four but I won't expect you until five-thirty. I'll need you every morning during the week—you'll work until classes start. And on Thursdays and Fridays you'll need to come back after school and work until close, which is eight p.m. Will that interfere with any after-school activities?"

"Nope."

"Not even Friday?"

"I'm more interested in this job than anything the school has going on Friday nights."

She gives me another smile. "All right. Pick out a scone then and I'll make you up a coffee. My name's Lucy, by the way. And the rush starts in about an hour. You might change your mind after you see what a madhouse this can be."

LUCY IS RIGHT—THE BAKERY IS jam-packed, but I don't mind the rush. Bustling behind the counter and serving baked goods for two hours distracts me from worrying about what will happen when I get to school.

I feel weird wearing a uniform, but I'm sure I'll get used to it soon. I notice the other girls at school have found ways to sexy up their attire. Like Savannah said, skirt lengths have been altered, and a lot of the girls leave nearly half their shirt buttons undone so you can see the lacy tops of their bras. I'm not interested in drawing attention to myself, so my hem stays at my knee and my shirt stays buttoned almost to the collar.

I have precalc, Entrepreneurial Studies, and English in the morning. Valerie isn't in any of those classes, but Savannah is in all three, and Easton is in the English class, but he sits in the back of the room with his buddies and doesn't say a word to me. I don't care. I kind of hope he ignores me all semester.

Being ignored seems to be the theme of the day. Nobody says a word to me except my teachers, and after making several attempts at smiling at kids in the hallway and getting no response, I eventually give up and pretend they don't exist either.

It isn't until lunch that I finally see a familiar face. "Harper! Get your butt over here." Valerie waves me over from the salad bar in the cafeteria.

Actually, *cafeteria* might not be the right word to describe this cavernous room. The walls are wood paneled, the chairs are leather upholstered, and the food area looks like the buffet setup of a luxury hotel. At the far edge of the room are endless sets of French doors, all open and spilling onto an outdoor eating area for students who want to sit outside when the weather's nice. It's not even the end of September, so the sun is shining and I suppose we could sit outside, but I spot Jordan Carrington and her friends out there, as well as Reed and Easton, and opt to stay inside.

Valerie and I load our trays with food and find an empty table in the corner of the room. I glance around, realizing that all the students look older. "No freshmen?" I ask.

She shakes her head. "Their lunch is an hour earlier."

"Gotcha." I stick my fork in my pasta and keep looking around. Nobody meets my eyes. It's like Valerie and I don't exist.

"Get used to your cloak of invisibility," Valerie says knowingly. "Actually, you should wear it like a badge of honor. That just means the rich bitches don't care enough to torment you."

"What's their idea of torment?"

"The usual. Spray-painting rude shit on your locker, tripping you in the hall, trashing you online. Jordan and her minions aren't very creative."

"So she's the female-equivalent of Reed, huh?"

"Yeppers. And if it were up to her, she'd be on his arm every day and screwing him every night, but alas, my poor cousin can't seem to land her man."

I snicker. "How is it you know everything about everyone?"

Valerie shrugs. "I watch. I listen. I remember."

"All right. Then tell me more about the Royals." I feel awkward asking, but after all my run-ins with the Royal brothers, I've come to the conclusion that I need to arm myself with ammo against them.

My new friend groans. "Oh no, don't tell me you've got the hots for one of them already."

"Ew. Never." I force myself not to think about the way my heart pounds whenever Reed Royal enters a room. I'm not crushing on the guy, dammit. He's an asshole and I want nothing to do with him. "I just want to know what I'm up against."

She relaxes. "Okay. Well. I already told you about Easton and Claire. One twin has a girlfriend, the other is a slut like his big brothers. Reed, I'm not sure about. Half the chicks in this school claim to have slept with him, but who knows if that's true. Only one I know about for sure is Jordan's friend Abby—trust me, my cousin wasn't happy about *that* hookup."

"What else? Scandals? Rumors?" I feel like a detective questioning a suspect.

"Their dad has a trashy girlfriend. I think that's been going on for a couple years."

The memory of Callum and Brooke's dinner shenanigans flashes in my mind. "I know all about the girlfriend," I say with a sigh.

"Okay…what else…their mom died a while ago." Valerie lowers her voice. "From an overdose."

My breath hitches. "Really?"

"Oh yeah. It was all over the news and in all the papers. I guess she'd been prescribed sleeping pills or something, but it interfered with some other medication she was taking. I don't really know the details, but I think her doctor was under investigation for screwing up the prescription."

Despite myself, my heart aches for the Royals. There are pictures of their mom on the fireplace mantel in the living room. She was a pretty brunette with kind-looking eyes. Every time Callum mentions her in passing, grief fills his eyes, which tells me he must have truly loved her.

I wonder if she was close to her sons, and I suddenly feel really bad for Reed and his brothers. Nobody should ever have to lose their mom.

Since I've tapped out Valerie's Royal knowledge, we change the subject and I tell her about my new job. She promises to come by after school twice a week to annoy me, and we spend the rest of the lunch period laughing and getting to know each other more. By the time we drop off our trays, I've decided I'm definitely keeping her as a friend.

"I can't believe we have *zero* classes together," she complains as we leave the cafeteria. "What the hell, girl? Who forced you to sign up for all those math and science and business classes? You should be taking Life Skills with me. We're learning to apply for credit cards."

"I chose them. I'm here to learn, not waste time."

"Nerd."

"Brat."

We part ways outside my chemistry class. We already exchanged numbers at lunch, and she promises to text me later, then flounces off.

When I enter the chem lab, the teacher rises from his desk as if he's been waiting for me. He's hobbit-sized, with a bushy beard that looks like it's trying to devour his face. He introduces himself as Mr. Neville.

I try not to look at the other students, but my gaze has already picked out Easton at one of the tables. He's the only student without anyone sitting beside him. Shit. That's not good.

"It's a pleasure to meet you, Ella," Mr. Neville says. "I peeked at your transcript earlier and was impressed by your previous science grades."

I shrug. Math and science come easy for me. I know I got my talent for dance from my mother, but since she could barely calculate a tip percentage in her head when we went out to eat, I always wondered if I got my aptitude for numbers from my father. Steve, the Navy SEAL slash pilot slash multi-millionaire.

"Anyway, Mr. Royal contacted the headmaster this weekend and requested we pair you up with Easton this semester." Neville lowers his voice. "Easton could learn some discipline, and it makes sense for you two to be lab partners. You'll be able to study together at home."

Oh joy. I stifle a sigh and head for Easton's table, where I drop my backpack under the desk and slip into the chair next to his. He doesn't look happy to see me.

"Fucking hell," he mutters.

"Hey, don't look at me," I mutter back. "This was your father's idea."

He stares straight ahead, a muscle ticking in his jaw. "Of course it was."

Unlike my morning classes, chemistry seems to drag on forever, but that's probably because Easton sits there scowling at me for ninety-nine percent of the time. For the other one percent of it, I get a cocky grin from him as he leans back in his chair and orders me to mix the solution we need to grow the crystals.

The second the bell rings, I'm out of my chair and eager to escape my sulking "brother."

I race out of the classroom, ready to get to my next class, but then I remember I need to make a quick stop at my locker to grab my textbook. All the courses I'm taking are advanced and come with thousand-page texts. I wasn't able to fit them all in my backpack.

Fortunately, my locker is nearby and so is the World History classroom.

Unfortunately, Jordan Carrington and her friends round the corner before I can reach my locker.

The four of them stop and smirk when they notice me. None of them say hello. Whatever. I don't say hello either, and I try not to feel self-conscious as I walk past them. They might be bitches, but they're beautiful bitches. Every guy in the hallway is checking them out, including Easton, who lazily strides out of chem class and walks over to the girls.

The group stops by the locker bank, and Jordan whispers something in Easton's ear, her manicured nails resting on his upper arm.

He shrugs, causing his navy-blue blazer to tighten across his broad shoulders. He's undeniably the hottest guy in a five-mile radius, though the two guys who join him aren't hard to look at either.

I ignore them all as I reach my locker and spin the combination lock. Two more classes and then school will be over and the stares will stop. I'll go back to the mansion and do my homework, then go to sleep. Keep myself busy and block out the bullshit. That's my new motto and I'm sticking to it.

I'm relieved when the lock clicks on the first try. I wasn't sure I got the combination, but the locker door opens easily and—

A mountain of garbage falls out.

I'm so startled I squeak out loud, then curse myself for it. Laughter rings out behind me, and I close my eyes, willing the heat in my cheeks to subside.

I don't want them to see me blushing.

I don't want them to know that this stinking, heaping mess of trash at my feet has affected me in any way.

I kick a stray banana peel and breathe through my mouth so the stench of rotting food doesn't make my eyes water. The floor is littered with even more disgusting items than the spoiled produce—used napkins, tissues, a bloody tampon…

I will not cry.

The laughter doesn't die down. I ignore it. I just scoop up the World History textbook from the bottom shelf of my luxury-sized locker. Then I flick away the wad of crumbled newspapers that's sticking to the latch and slam the door shut.

When I turn around, all eyes are on me. I only seek out one pair—Jordan's, almond-brown and gleaming evilly. She gives me a regal little wave.

I square my shoulders and tuck my book under my arm. A tall guy with brown curls snickers as I start to walk. Oh my God. There's a sanitary pad stuck to my shoe. I swallow my embarrassment, kick the pad away, and keep walking.

Easton wears a bored expression as I approach.

I pause in front of Jordan, one eyebrow arched, my own smirk forming on my lips. "Is that all you've got, Carrington? I'm trash? Tsk-tsk. I'm disappointed in your lack of creativity."

Her eyes flash, but I'm already sauntering past her like I have no care in the world.

Another score for the away team. Kind of. Because I'm the only one who knows just how close I am to bursting into tears.

CHAPTER 12

I MAKE IT THROUGH THE rest of the day without crying, but part of me wants to go all *Carrie* on these kids until they look back at trash in the locker as the easiest day of their lives.

Valerie texts me during class. *Are U OK? Heard abt locker. Jordan is an ass.*

I'm fine, I respond. *It was stupid and like u said. No creativity. Trash? Did she steal that from a Disney show?*

Ha! Don't say that tho. She'll B forced 2 think of something worse

2 late.

I'll throw flowers on ur grave!

Gee thanks. I tuck the phone away when the teacher glances in my direction. Once the fancy chimes ring to let us know class is over, I shove everything into my pack and hoof it outside, hoping that Durand is waiting and I can escape to the princess bedroom. The pink and white is growing on me.

The parking lot is filled with noise, people, and expensive cars, but no Durand.

"Harper." Valerie appears over my right shoulder. "Your ride isn't here?"

"No, I don't see him."

She clicks her tongue sympathetically. "I'd offer you a ride but I don't think you want to get in the same car as Jordan."

"You'd be right about that."

"You should go, though. Once school is out, it can get rough."

"Out here in broad daylight?" That's alarming.

Valerie's forehead wrinkles with concern. "Jordan has moments of cunning. Don't underestimate her."

I tighten my grip on the backpack and give myself an internal slap for carrying around so much cash. There has to be a place in the Royal pile of bricks where I can hide this.

"Why does she get away with it? Savannah Montgomery told me that everyone here is special. So why is Jordan the leader if everyone has something unique to offer?"

"Connections," Valerie replies bluntly. "The Carringtons aren't part of the ten-figure club like the Royals, but they know everyone. They've done business with celebs, royalty. Jordan's aunt on her dad's side is married to some Italian count. We actually have to refer to her as Lady Perino if she shows up for Christmas."

"That's unreal."

"So Jordan is, by extension—" She breaks off. "Hold on. Here she comes."

I brace myself as Jordan strolls toward us. Like all alphas, she has a pack trailing behind her. They look like a toothpaste commercial—acres of white shining teeth and long straight hair swishing behind them.

"If it makes you feel any better, Jordan's hair has a lot of wave to it and she has to spend an hour flat-ironing it every morning," Valerie mutters under her breath.

Doesn't Valerie have any decent shit on Jordan? Because *she spends too much time on her hair* really isn't a great put-down.

"I'm feeling really superior now," I say dryly.

Valerie gives me a quirky smile and slides her hand around my arm in moral support.

Jordan halts about two feet from me and makes a couple of obvious sniffs with her nose. "You smell," she informs me. "And it's not from the trash in your locker. It's just you."

"Thanks for the heads up. I guess I'll start showering twice a day instead of just once," I say sweetly, but inside I'm worried, because what if I really do smell? That would be about just as bad as toting around a used maxi pad on my shoe.

She sighs and flips her hair over one shoulder. "It's the type of smell no amount of showering will ever wash away. You see, you're a casual."

I look at Valerie with a question. She rolls her eyes in response.

"Okay then," I reply cheerfully. "Good to know." Jordan wants me to look stupid, so the best I can do is not get drawn into her game. But my non-reaction doesn't turn her away. She just keeps shooting her mouth, probably because she likes hearing herself talk.

"Casuals will always reek of desperation."

Well, she's got me there. That's pretty much the perfume of a strip club.

I force myself to shrug. "I don't know what *casual* means in Bitch, but I'm assuming it's bad. What I don't get is why you think I give a rat's ass about your opinion of me. The world is really big, Jordan. You throwing trash in my locker or calling me names isn't going to matter in two years. Hell, it hardly matters today."

Her mouth drops open and Valerie turns her face into my arm to smother a laugh.

I don't know what Jordan's comeback would have been, because there's a commotion behind me. People move, and I know who's standing behind me before Jordan's perfect red lips form his name.

"Reed," she breathes. "I didn't see you there."

There's an uncertainty in her voice that surprises me. I wonder what the exact text of Reed's anti-Ella decree is, and I make a mental note to ask Valerie.

"You done?" he asks, and I'm not sure if he's talking to me, or Jordan. By the way her eyes flick from me to some place about a foot above my head, she's not sure either.

"I was wondering if you wanted to go over our AP English assignment," she says finally.

"Finished it," he replies tersely.

Jordan rubs her lips together. That's a slap at her and we all know it. I almost feel sorry for her…almost.

"Hey, Reed," a different, softer voice chimes in. It comes from a delicate looking girl whose golden blonde hair is caught up in braids that wrap around her head like a crown. Her cornflower blue eyes are covered in ridiculously long lashes, which wave like feathers as she waits for Reed's response.

"Abby," he says, his entire face softening. "Nice to see you."

Half the chicks in this school claim to have slept with him, but who knows if that's true. Only one I know about for sure is Jordan's friend Abby.

So this is the girl who caught Reed, at least once. I can see why. She's gorgeous. So is Jordan, but Abby is soft in a way that Jordan—and me—are not. This is what Reed likes? Soft girls who talk to their feet? No wonder he isn't interested in—wait, what am I even thinking? I don't care if Reed is interested in me. He's welcome to all the pale, starry-eyed girls like Abby he wants.

"I've missed you," she says, and the longing in her voice makes us all shift uncomfortably.

"It's been a busy summer," Reed replies, shoving both hands in his pockets. He's not meeting Abby's eyes, and his tone has an air of finality to it.

She hears it, too, and her eyes glisten. It might be over for Reed, but it's painfully obvious that Abby hasn't moved on. I kind of feel sorry for her.

When Reed lays his heavy hand on my shoulder, I almost jump out of my skin. And I don't miss the spiteful glares from the toothpaste girls or the wounded dove expression on Abby's face. If Reed Royal touches anyone, it's not supposed to be me.

"You ready, Ella?" he mutters.

"Ahhh, I guess?"

This whole confrontation makes my shoulders itch, so I don't argue when Reed steers me toward Easton's truck. When we reach it, I jerk out of Reed's grip. "Where's Easton?"

"He's driving the twins."

"Did you just use me to get away from your ex?" I ask as he opens the door and pushes me inside.

"She's not my ex." He slams the door.

As Reed rounds the front of the truck, I see Valerie waving to me with a huge-ass grin on her face. Behind her, Jordan is glowering. Abby looks like a kicked puppy.

"Buckle up," Reed orders as he starts the truck.

I do what he says because it's safe, not because he told me to.

"Where's Durand?" I wave back to Valerie, who gives me the thumbs up. I hope Jordan didn't see that or Valerie may find herself moving from her proper bedroom to some closet in the basement. "And why are you driving me?"

"I wanted to talk to you." He pauses for a beat. "Are you trying to embarrass the family?"

Shocked, I turn in my seat to look at him and try not to notice how sexy his strong forearms look as he grips the steering wheel in frustration.

"Do you think I threw garbage in my own locker?" I ask incredulously.

"I'm not talking about that juvenile bullshit Jordan is pulling. I mean your job at the bakery."

"First, how do you know about that, Mr. Stalker? And second, how is that even remotely embarrassing?"

"First, I have football practice in the mornings. I saw Durand drop you off there," he bites out. "And second, it implies that we aren't taking care of you. At lunch someone asked if Callum bought the bakery and that's why the new Royal is working there."

I fall back against the seat and cross my arms. "Well, golly gee, I'm so sorry that you had to answer an awkward question at lunch. That must have been *so* inconvenient. *Much* more inconvenient than getting hit in the face with a tampon flying out of your locker."

When he grins, I totally lose it. All the frustration and hurt comes rolling out of me. I'm tired of playing the good, calm girl. I rise up on my knees, reach over and hit him across the top of his head.

"Fuck," he curses. "What the hell was that for?"

"That's for being an asshole!" I hit him again, thumb tucked away and knuckles out, just like my mom's old boyfriend taught me.

Reed pushes me back, hard, against the passenger door. "Sit the fuck down! You're gonna make us crash."

"I'm not going to sit down!" I swing at him again. "I'm tired of you and your insults and your awful friends!"

"Maybe if you're straight with me, then I'll call off the dogs. What's your game?" He glowers at me, one long arm still pushing me away from him.

I try to fight my way to him, flinging my arms but catching nothing but air. "You want to know what my game is? My game is to get a diploma and go to college! That's my game!"

"Why'd you come here? I know you took money from my dad."

"I never asked for your father to bring me here!"

"You didn't fight it very hard," he snaps. "If you even fought at all."

The accusation stings, partly because it's true but also because it's unfair.

"Yeah, I didn't fight it—because I'm not an idiot. Your father offered me a future, and I'd be the stupidest person on the planet not to take him up on that. If that makes me a money grubber or a gold digger, then fine, I guess I am. But at least I'm not the type of person who makes someone walk two miles in the dark, in a strange place."

I watch with satisfaction as a flicker of remorse flashes through his eyes.

"So you admit you have no shame," he spits out.

"Yes, I don't have any problem admitting I have no shame," I shoot back. "Shame and principles are for people who don't have to worry about the little things, like how much can I buy for a dollar to feed myself all day or do I pay my mom's medical bills or buy some weed so she can go for an hour without pain. Shame is a luxury."

I fall back, exhausted. I stop trying to fight him. It's impossible anyway. He's too strong. Dammit.

"You haven't cornered the market on grief. You're not the only one who lost his mother. Oh poor Reed Royal," I mock, "he's turned into an asshole because he lost his mommy."

"Shut up."

"No, you shut up."

Before the words even come out of my mouth, I realize how ridiculous we're being and start laughing. A minute ago, we were yelling at each other like five-year-olds. I laugh so hard I start crying. Or maybe I was crying all along and it just sounded like laughter. I bend over and put my head between my legs because I don't want Reed to see he's broken me.

"Stop crying," he mutters.

"Stop telling me what to do," I sob.

He finally shuts up and I manage to get myself back in control by the time we drive past the gate and into the side driveway. Did I really say I had no shame? That's not at all true. And I'm mortified that I cried for five minutes in front of Reed Royal.

"You done?" he asks after he brakes and cuts the engine.

"Screw you," I say tiredly.

"I want you to stop working at the bakery."

"I want Jordan to grow a heart overnight. But we don't always get what we want, do we?"

He makes a frustrated noise. "Callum won't like it."

"Oh my God! You're constantly changing the rules. Stay away from me, Ella. Get in the car, Ella. Don't bleed my father dry, Ella. Don't get a job, Ella. I don't know what you want from me."

"That makes two of us," he says darkly.

I don't even want to touch that. So I open the truck door and stumble out.

The devil inside of me stirs, I guess so I can save a little face, and I turn abruptly. "Oh, and Reed? Don't use me as a cover because you don't want to face up to an ex."

"She's not an ex," he roars after me.

I shouldn't find those words so satisfying, but I do.

CHAPTER 13

THE SECOND I GET INSIDE, I hurry upstairs and lock myself in my bedroom. I dump my schoolbooks on the bed and grab the first assignment I see, but it's hard to concentrate on my homework when I'm still so angry and embarrassed about what just happened between Reed and me.

The rational part of my brain understands where my outburst came from. Less than a week ago my entire life was uprooted. Callum wrenched me out of Kirkwood and brought me to this strange town and his fancy house to face off with his asshole sons. The Royal brothers have done nothing but antagonize me since I got here. Their friends shamed me at that stupid party and humiliated me at school today. And through it all, Reed Royal is spouting his golden rules and then changing them every other second.

What normal seventeen-year-old girl *wouldn't* lose her shit?

But that other part of me, the one that tries to protect me at all costs by shielding my emotions…that part yells at me for allowing myself to cry in front of Reed. For letting him see just how uncertain and vulnerable I feel in this new world I've been thrust into.

I hate myself for being weak.

Somehow I manage to finish my assignments, but now it's six o'clock and my stomach is grumbling.

God, I don't want to go downstairs. I wish I could just order room service. Why doesn't this place have room service? It's pretty much a hotel already.

Stop hiding from him. Don't give him the satisfaction.

If I skip dinner, Reed will know he won, and I can't let him win. I won't let him break me.

Still, even after I decide to face the jerk, I continue to stall. I take a long shower and wash my hair, then change into a pair of tiny black boxers and a loose red tank top. Then I brush my wet hair. Then I check my phone to see if Valerie texted. Then—

Okay, enough procrastinating. My empty stomach agrees, rumbling the entire way down the spiral staircase.

In the kitchen, I find one of the twins at the stove, stirring a spatula in what looks like a wad of noodles. The other twin is poking his head in the fridge, griping to his brother.

"What the hell, man. I thought Sandra was back from vacation."

"Tomorrow," the other twin answers.

"Thank fuck. Since when do housekeepers go on vacay? I'm tired of cooking our own meals. We shoulda gone out for dinner with Dad 'n Reed."

My forehead wrinkles as I absorb the information. One, these boys are *so* spoiled—they can't even cook their own meals? And two, Reed went out for dinner with Callum? Did Callum hold a gun to his head?

The twin at the stove notices me lurking in the doorway and frowns. "What are you looking at?"

I shrug. "Just watching you burn your dinner."

His head whirls to the pan, and he groans when he notices the smoke rising from it. "Goddammit! Seb, grab an oven mitt!"

Jeez, these boys really are useless. What the heck does he plan on doing with the oven mitt?

The question answers itself when Sawyer slips on the mitt his brother tosses him and lifts the pan by its handle, which, unless it's a defective pan, wouldn't have a hot handle. I get a kick out of watching the boys try to salvage their dinner, and I can't fight a snicker when hot oil splashes out of the pan and burns Sawyer's non-oven-mitt-covered wrist.

He howls in pain as his brother shuts off the burner. Then they both stare at the burnt chicken and noodles in dismay.

"Cereal?" Sebastian says.

Sawyer sighs.

Even with the terrible burning smell in the air, my stomach is still growling, so I saunter over to the wall of cupboards and start grabbing ingredients while the twins watch me warily.

"I'm making spaghetti," I tell them without turning around. "Do you want any?"

There's a long silence before one of them mumbles "yes." The other follows suit.

I cook in silence while they sit at the table like the lazy, entitled Royals that they are, neither one offering to help me.

Twenty minutes later, the three of us are eating our dinner. Not a single word passes between us.

Easton walks in at the tail end of the meal, his eyes narrowing when he spots me shoving my plate in the dishwasher. Then he looks at the table, where his brothers are on their second helping of spaghetti.

"Sandra back from vacation?"

Sebastian shakes his head and shovels more pasta into his mouth.

His twin jerks his head toward me. "She cooked."

"*She* has a name," I say curtly. "And you're welcome for dinner. Ungrateful jerks." I mutter that last part under my breath as I stalk out of the kitchen.

Instead of going back to my room, I find myself wandering into the library. Callum showed it to me the other day, and I'm still in awe of the sheer amount of books in the room. The built-in bookshelves go all the way up to the ceiling, and there's an old-timey ladder you can use to reach the top shelves. On the other side of the room is a cozy sitting area with two overstuffed chairs positioned in front of a modern fireplace.

I don't feel like reading, but I flop down in one of the chairs anyway, breathing in the scent of leather and old books. As my gaze moves to the fireplace mantle, my heart speeds up. Photographs line the stone ledge, and one in particular snags my attention. It's a shot of a young-looking Callum in a Navy uniform, with his arm slung over the shoulder of a tall, blond man also in uniform.

I think it's Steve O'Halloran. My father.

I stare at the man's chiseled face, the blue eyes that seem to twinkle with mischief as they meet the camera lens. I have his eyes. And my hair is the same shade of blond.

When footsteps echo behind me, I turn to see Easton stride into the library.

"I heard you tried to kill my brother today," he drawls.

"He had it coming." I turn my back to him again, but he comes up beside me, and from the corner of my eye I see that his profile is harder than stone.

"Let's be straight with each other. Did you really think you'd show up here on our father's arm and we'd all be cool with it?"

"I'm not on your father's arm. I'm his ward."

"Yeah? Look me in the eye and tell me you're not fucking my dad."

For God's sake. Gritting my teeth, I meet his surly gaze head-on and say, "I'm not fucking your dad. And ew for even suggesting it."

He shrugs. "It's not a stretch. He likes 'em young."

That's obviously a reference toward Brooke, but I don't comment on it. My gaze travels back to the picture on the mantle.

Easton and I go silent, for so long I wonder why he's even still here.

"Uncle Steve was a baller," he finally says. "Chicks dropped their panties when that dude walked into a room."

Double ew. That is *not* something I ever wanted to know about my father.

"What was he like?" I ask reluctantly.

"He was all right, I guess. We didn't spend much time with him. He was always holed up in my dad's study. The two of them would sit there talking for hours." Easton sounds bitter.

"Aw, your daddy liked my daddy better than you? Is that why you hate me so much?"

He rolls his eyes. "Do yourself a favor and stop provoking my brother. If you keep getting in his face, you're just gonna get hurt."

"Why bother with the warning? Isn't that what you want, for me to get hurt?"

He doesn't answer. He just steps away from the mantle and leaves me in the library, where I continue to stare at my father's picture.

I WAKE UP AT MIDNIGHT to the sound of hushed voices in the hallway outside my bedroom door. I'm groggy as hell, but alert enough to recognize Reed's voice, and even though I'm lying down, my knees actually feel weak.

I haven't seen him since our fight in the car earlier. When he got back from dinner with Callum, I was already locked up in my room again, but judging by the angry footsteps and slamming door, I'm pretty sure dinner didn't go so well.

I don't know why I slide out of bed, or why I tiptoe toward my door. Eavesdropping isn't really my style, but I want to know what he's saying and who he's saying it to. I want to know if it's about me, and maybe that's really conceited, but I still need to know.

"...practice in the morning." It's Easton talking now, and I press my ear to the door to try to hear more clearly. "...agreed to cut down during the season."

Reed mutters something I can't make out.

"I get it, okay? I'm not crazy about her being here either, but that's no reason to..." Easton's sentence cuts out.

"It's not about her." I hear that loud and clear, and I don't know whether I'm relieved or disappointed that whatever they're discussing doesn't involve me.

"...then I'm coming with you."

"No," Reed says sharply. "...going alone tonight."

He's going somewhere? Where the hell is he going this late, and on a school night? Worry tugs at my gut, which almost makes me laugh, because all of a sudden I'm *worrying* about Reed Royal, the guy I attacked in the car earlier?

"Now you sound like Gid," Reed accuses.

"Yeah, well, maybe you..."

Their voices go hushed again, which is so fricking frustrating because I know I'm missing something important.

I'm tempted to fling open the door and stop Reed from doing whatever he's about to do, but it's too late. Two sets of footsteps echo in the hall, and a door clicks shut. Then it's just one set of footsteps, barely audible as they descend the stairs.

A few minutes later, a car engine rumbles from the courtyard, and I know Reed is gone.

CHAPTER 14

THE NEXT MORNING I FIND Reed in the driveway leaning against Easton's truck. He's dressed in sneakers, long gym shorts, and a muscle tee that is open at the sides, and looking hotter than any jerk has the right to. A baseball cap is pulled low over his forehead.

I look around, but the black Town Car is nowhere in sight. "Where's Durand?"

"You planning on going to the bakery?"

"You planning on burning it down so I don't tarnish the Royal name by working there?"

He grumbles in annoyance.

I grumble back.

"Well?" he mutters.

I scowl at him. "Yes, I'm going to work."

"I've got football practice, so if you want a ride, I suggest getting in the car because otherwise you're going to be walking." He opens the passenger door and then stomps to the driver's side.

I look for Durand again. Dammit, where is he?

When Reed guns the engine, I start moving. What harm can he really do in a twenty-minute ride?

"Buckle up," he snaps.

"I just got in. Give me a minute." I cast my eyes upward and say a tiny prayer for patience. Reed doesn't take off until I'm all buckled in. "Do you have male PMS or are you just in a shitty mood twenty-four/seven?"

He doesn't answer.

I hate myself for it, but I can't stop looking at him. Can't stop sweeping my eyes over the side of his movie-star face, his perfect ear that is framed by his dark hair. All the Royals have varying shades of brown hair. Reed's runs closer to chestnut.

In profile, his nose has a tiny bump on it and I wonder which of his brothers broke it for him.

It's really not fair how hot this guy is. And he's got this whole bad boy vibe that I'm not usually into, but for some reason it makes him even hotter. I guess I like bad boys.

Wait, what the hell am I thinking? I don't like bad boys, and I don't like *Reed*. He's the biggest asshole I've ever—

"Why are you staring at me?" he asks in annoyance.

I push away all my crazy thoughts and counter, "Why not?"

"Like the way I look, do you?" he taunts.

"Nope, just committing to memory the profile of a jackass. You know, so if I'm ever called upon to draw one in art, I'll have some inspiration," I reply airily.

He grunts and it sounds suspiciously like a laugh. For the first time in his presence, I start to relax.

The rest of the trip passes quickly, almost too quickly. I feel a tiny kernel of disappointment when the bakery comes into view, which is all sorts of fucked up because I *don't like this guy.*

"You driving me every day or just this morning?" I ask when he brakes in front of the French Twist.

"Depends. How long you planning on keeping up the charade?"

"It's not a charade. It's called earning a living."

I get out of the truck before he can manage another stupid and mean retort.

"Hey," he calls after me.

"What?" I turn around, and that's when I get my first full look at his face this morning. My hand flies up to cover my mouth. The left side of his face, a part that I now realize he kept shaded from me the entire ride, is bruised. His lip is puffy. There's a gash over his eye and a bruise on the upper edge of his cheek. "Oh my God, what happened to you?"

I raise my fingers to his face, not realizing that my feet carried me from the bakery back to the truck.

He jerks away from my touch. "Nothing."

My hand falls uselessly to my side. "It doesn't look like nothing."

"It is to you."

Grim faced, he speeds off, leaving me behind to wonder what he did last night and why he called me over just now if he wasn't planning on saying anything important. I do know one thing. If I got hit that hard in the face, I'd be pissy the next morning, too.

Despite my better judgment, I worry about Reed throughout my morning shift at the bakery. Lucy casts me some concerned looks but since I work hard like I'd promised, she doesn't say anything.

After my shift, I hurry off to school, but I don't see Reed. Not on the path leading to the gym, not in the halls, and not even at lunch. It's like he doesn't even go to Astor Park.

And when classes are over, it's the big Town Car that's waiting for me. Durand's holding the door impatiently, so I can't even loiter in the parking lot. *It's better this way*, I tell myself. *No good can come from thinking about Reed Royal.*

I lecture myself all the way home, but as we pull through the wrought-iron gates, Durand gives me something else to think about.

"Mr. Royal would like to see you," his double bass voice informs me when the car comes to a stop at the front steps.

I sit there like a dummy as I process that Mr. Royal means Callum. "Um, okay."

"He's in the pool house."

"The pool house," I repeat. "Am I being called to the principal's office, Durand?"

His eyes meet mine in the rearview mirror. "Don't think so, Ella."

"That's not very encouraging."

"Want me to drive you around some more?"

"Will he still want to see me?"

Durand nods.

"Then I better go." I sigh dramatically.

The corner of his eyes lift slightly in what is considered a broad smile for him.

I drop my backpack at the base of the sweeping staircase and then make the trek to the back of the house, across the long patio, and to the end of the yard. The pool house is glassed in on three sides. There must be some trick to the walls because sometimes the side nearest the pool is reflective rather than see-through.

As I get closer, I realize that the walls are really a series of doors on a slider and they've been opened, allowing the ocean breeze to drift from the shore up to the house.

Callum is sitting on a sofa facing the ocean. He turns around when my shoes scrape on the tiled floor.

He nods in greeting. "Ella. You have a good day at school?"

No trash in my locker? No pranks in the girls' room? "Could have been worse," I reply.

He gestures for me to come sit with him.

"This was Maria's favorite place," he tells me. "When all the doors are open, you can hear the ocean. She liked getting up early to watch the sunrise. She told me once it was like a magic show every morning. The sun draws back the curtain of inky black to reveal a palette of colors more gorgeous than even the greatest masters could conjure."

"Are you sure she wasn't a poet?"

He smiles. "She was rather poetic. She also said the rhythmic push and pull of the waves against the shore is a musical score as pure as the most brilliant orchestration."

We listen to it, the tinkle and wash as the tides creep up to the sand and then slide back as if pulled by an invisible hand. "It's beautiful," I admit.

A low moan slips from Callum's throat. In one hand, he clutches his usual glass of whiskey, but in the other, gripped so tight his knuckles are white, he holds a picture of a dark-haired woman with eyes so bright it's like sun shining from the frame.

"Is that Maria?" I gesture to the frame.

He swallows and nods. "Beautiful, isn't she?"

I nod back.

Callum tips his head and empties the glass in one swift gulp. He barely sets the glass down before reaching for a refill. "Maria was the glue that held our family together. Atlantic Aviation hit a bad patch about ten years ago. A series of reckless decisions coupled with the recession placed my sons' legacy in jeopardy, and I threw myself into saving it, which took me away from the family. I missed seeing Maria. She always wanted a daughter, you know?"

I can only nod again. It's kind of hard to follow along this weird disjointed speech. I have no idea where he's going with all of this.

"She would have loved you. She would have taken you from Steve and raised you as her own. She wanted a girl so badly."

I sit still as a stone. None of this sad story can be leading anywhere good.

"My sons blame me for her death," he says suddenly, startling me with the unexpected confession. "They're right to do so. Which is why I let them get away with all kinds of shit. Oh, I know all about their little rebellions, but I can't bring myself to raise a harsh word. I'm trying to pull the threads together now, but I'll be the first to admit that I'm a mess. And I've made a mess of this family." He draws a shaky hand through his hair, still managing to hold his glass, almost like the crystal object is the only thing keeping him tethered to this earth.

"I'm sorry," is all I can think to say.

"You're probably wondering why I'm telling you this."

"A little."

He gives me a crooked, rough smile that reminds me so much of Reed that my insides flip over.

"Dinah wants to meet you."

"Who's Dinah?"

"Steve's widow."

My pulse speeds up. "Oh."

"I've been putting her off because you just got here, and, well, I wanted you to come to me about Steve. She and Steve toward the end there..." He trails off. "It wasn't good."

My guard snaps up. "I get the feeling that I'm not going to like whatever you're about to say."

"You're pretty perceptive." He hastily finishes off his second glass. "She's demanding you come alone."

So I'm supposed to meet my dead dad's wife, who Callum dislikes so much that he's mainlining whiskey, without anyone at my back?

I sigh. "When I said my day could be worse, it wasn't meant as a challenge."

He snorts at this. "Dinah reminded me that my connection to you is more tenuous than hers. She's your father's widow. I'm just his friend and business partner."

A chill skates across my skin. "Are you saying that your guardianship isn't legit?"

"It's temporary until Steve's will has been probated," he admits. "Dinah could contest it."

I can't sit. I jump up and walk to the edge of the room, staring out at the water. I suddenly feel so stupid. I let myself believe I could make a home here even though Reed hates me, even though the students at Astor Park delight in tormenting me. Those things are supposed to be temporary nuisances. Callum has promised me a future, dammit. And now he's telling me this Dinah woman can take that future away?

"If I don't go," I say slowly, "then she'll start making trouble, won't she?"

"That's a fair assessment."

Mind made up, I turn back to Callum. "Then what are we waiting for?"

DURAND TAKES US INTO THE city and stops in front of a high-rise. Callum tells me he's going to wait for me in the car, which only makes me more nervous.

"This sucks," I say flatly.

He reaches out to touch my arm. "You don't have to go."

"What other choice do I have? I can either go up and keep living with the Royals, or stay in the car and get taken away? That's messed up."

"Ella," he calls as I step onto the curb.

"What?"

"Steve wanted you. When he found out he had a daughter, it tore him up. I swear to you, he would have loved you. Remember that. No matter what Dinah says."

With those not-so-encouraging words in my ear, I let Durand escort me inside. The lobby of Dinah's building is gorgeous, but the effect of the pretty stone walls, crystal lights, and deep wood trim doesn't stun me like it would have pre-Royals.

"She's here to see Dinah O'Halloran," Durand tells the desk clerk.

"You can go right up."

Durand gives me a little push. "Last elevator. Press "P" for penthouse."

The carpeted, wood-paneled elevator is almost completely silent. There's no music, only a slight mechanical whir to accompany its movement upward. It stops way too soon.

The elevator doors slide open and I step into a wide, short hallway. At the end is one set of double doors. Holy shit. Does she live on the entire floor?

A woman dressed in a maid's outfit opens one of the doors as I get close. "Mrs. O'Halloran is waiting for you in the sitting room. May I get you a beverage?"

"Water," I croak. "I'd like a water, please."

My sneakers sink into the heavy carpet as I follow the maid down the hall and into the sitting room. I feel like a little lamb walking to her slaughter.

Dinah O'Halloran is seated beneath a large painting of a nude woman. The model's golden hair is down and she's looking over her shoulder, green eyes narrowed seductively at the viewer. It…oh my God. The woman's face is Dinah's.

"Do you like it?" Dinah asks with raised eyebrows. "I have others in the house but this is the most conservative."

Conservative? *Lady, I can see your ass crack in the picture.* "It's nice," I lie. Who has a bunch of nude paintings of themselves hanging around their house?

I start to lower myself into the other chair in the room, but Dinah's sharp voice stops me.

"Did I tell you to sit down?"

Cheeks flaming, I stiffen. "No. I'm sorry." I remain standing.

Her eyes rake over me. "So you're the girl who Callum says is Steve's daughter. Have you taken a paternity test yet?"

A paternity test? "Um. No."

She laughs, a hollow, awful sound. "Then how do we know you're not Callum's bastard that he's trying to pass off as Steve's? That would be convenient for him. He always claimed he was faithful to his little wife, but you would be direct evidence that he wasn't."

Callum's daughter? Brooke had implied the same thing, but Callum looked offended when she'd said it. And my mother said that my dad was a man named Steve. I have his watch.

Still, I feel sick to my stomach, even as I straighten my shoulders with false confidence. "I'm not Callum's daughter."

"Oh, and you know that how?"

"Because Callum's not the type of man to ignore that he has a kid."

"You've been with the Royals for all of a week and you think you know them?" She sneers, then leans forward, hands pressed into the arms of her chair. "Steve and Callum were old SEAL buddies. They shared more women than a kindergarten class shares toys."

I stare in open-mouthed shock.

"I have no doubt that your whore mother screwed them both," she adds.

The slur against Mom wrenches me out of a stunned stupor. "Don't talk about my mother. You know nothing about her."

"I know enough." Dinah leans back. "She was dirt poor and tried to shake Steve down for money by attempting to blackmail him. When that didn't work, she pretended she had his kid. Only what she didn't know is that Steve was sterile."

Dinah's accusations are starting to sound like she's flinging a bunch of wet spaghetti at the wall and hoping something sticks, kind of like Jordan and her tampons. I'm getting kind of sick of this crap. "Then let's order up the paternity test. I don't have anything to lose. If I'm a Royal, then I'll be able to claim a sixth of the Royal fortune. Seems like a better deal than just being the ward of Callum Royal."

My bravado doesn't go over well with Dinah, because she redoubles her attack. "You think Callum Royal cares about you? That man couldn't keep his wife alive. She killed herself, rather than be with him. *That's* the kind of person you're cozying up to. And his boys? They're drunk with money and privilege and he lets them run wild. I hope you lock your door at night."

Unwittingly, my mind jumps to that first morning when Easton stuck his hand down his pants and casually threatened me. I grit my teeth. "Why did you ask me to come here?" I'm still not seeing the point of this visit. It seems like she's only interested in taunting me and making me uncomfortable.

Dinah offers a cool smile. "I just wanted to see what I'm dealing with." One eyebrow flicks up. "And I must say, I'm not too impressed."

That makes two of us.

"Here's my advice," she continues. "Take whatever Callum has given you and leave. That house is cancer for women, and someday soon it'll be nothing but dust. I suggest you get out while you still can."

She reaches over and grabs a bell. After one brisk ring, the maid appears like an obedient dog. She holds a tray with a single glass of water on it.

"Ms. Harper is ready to leave," Dinah announces. "She doesn't need the water."

I can't get out of there fast enough.

Callum is waiting in the lobby when I stumble out of the elevator. "Are you okay?" he asks immediately.

I rub my hands over my arms. I can't remember the last time I've felt this cold.

"Is Steve really my dad?" I blurt out. "Tell me."

He doesn't look at all shocked by the question. "Yes, of course," he says quietly.

Callum leans in, arms open as if he wants to embrace me, but I rock backward, still completely shaken by Dinah's revelations. I don't need his comfort right now. I need the *truth*.

"Why should I believe you?" I think of Dinah's cynical words. "You never gave me proof of paternity."

"You want proof? Fine, I'll give you proof." He looks tired. "The DNA results are locked in my safe at home. And Dinah, by the way, has already seen them. Her lawyers have a copy."

I'm shocked. Did she lie to me? Or is he the liar in the bunch? "You did a DNA test?"

"I wouldn't have brought you here unless I knew for sure. I took a piece of hair from Steve's bathroom at the office, and my PI got a sample of yours to compare it to."

How did… forget it, I don't even want to know how he got his hands on my DNA. "I want to see the test results," I demand.

"Suit yourself, but believe me when I say that you're Steve's daughter. I knew you were his the moment I saw you. You have his stubborn jaw. His eyes. I could have picked you out of any lineup as Steve O'Halloran's child. Dinah's angry and scared. Don't let her get to you."

Don't let her get to me? The woman just dropped enough bombshells and made enough insinuations to make my head spin.

I can't deal with this right now. Any of it. I just…

"I'm ready to go," I say numbly.

In the car, I can't bring myself to meet Callum's concerned eyes. Dinah's words play themselves over and over in my mind.

"Ella, when I lost my wife I went through a dark time." It's a bare acknowledgment of what he thinks Dinah told me.

I answer without looking at him. "That dark time? I think you're still there."

He pours himself another glass. "Maybe I am."

The rest of the ride is full of silence.

CHAPTER 15

MY MEETING WITH DINAH STAYS with me for three days, running through my mind like it's on some sick loop. Lucy probably thinks she hired a robot for all the emotion that I display. I'm afraid if I move my face, though, I'll start crying. But she keeps me on because I show up every morning and the assigned evenings on time and work without complaint.

It's a relief to work. When it's busy, I manage to forget how screwed up my life has become. And that's saying something, considering I fled Seattle to avoid Social Services trying to push me into foster care and then spent a week on the road before settling in Kirkwood. I thought forging my dead mother's signature on school forms was nuts, but that was nothing compared to the Royals and their entourages.

It's harder to avoid the topic at school because Val keeps asking me what's wrong. As much as I adore Val, I don't think she's ready to hear all this crap, and even if she is…I'm not ready to share it.

It doesn't matter that Callum showed me the DNA results when we got home that night—the doubt kept eating at me for three whole days, until this morning, when I dragged myself out of bed after another sleepless night, and forced myself to remember one undeniable fact: My mother was not a liar.

I can count everything Mom told me about my father on one hand. His name was Steve. He was blond. He was a sailor. He gave her his watch.

All of that lines up with everything Callum told me, and when you add in the very obvious resemblance I have to the man in the picture in the library, I have to believe that Dinah O'Halloran, simply put, is full of shit.

"You banging someone?"

Reed's gruff demand jolts me from my thoughts. I'm in the passenger seat of his Range Rover, trying to stop yawning. "What? Why would you ask me that?"

"You've got dark circles under your eyes. You've been walking around the house like a zombie since Tuesday, and it looks like you haven't slept in days. So. Are you banging someone? Sneaking out to see him?" His jaw is tight.

"No."

"No," he echoes.

"Yes, Reed. *No*. I'm not dating anyone, okay? And even if I was, it's none of your business."

"Everything you do is my business. Every move you make affects me and my family."

"Wow. It must be nice to live in a world where everything revolves around you."

"What's going on with you then?" he demands. "You haven't been yourself."

"I haven't been myself? Like you know me well enough to make that kind of statement." I scowl at him. "Tell you what, I'll fill you in on all my secrets—*after* you tell me where you sneak off to every night and why you come home with cuts and bruises."

His eyes flash.

"Yeah. That's what I thought." I cross my arms and try not to yawn again.

Reed fixes his irritated gaze on the windshield, his big hands gripping the wheel tight. He's been driving me to work every morning at five-thirty, then continuing on to school for his six a.m. football practice. Easton is on the team, too, but he drives to practice on his own. I think it's because Reed wants alone time with me. So he can cross-examine me, the way he's done every morning since this annoying carpool began.

"You're not going away, are you?" There's a note of defeat in his voice, along with the usual dose of anger.

"Nope. I'm not going away."

He stops in front of the bakery and shoves the gearshift to park.

"What?" I mutter when those piercing blue eyes turn to me.

His lips tighten for a moment. "The game tonight."

"What about it?" The clock on the dash says it's five twenty-eight. The sun isn't even up yet, but the French Twist's front window is lit up. Lucy's already inside, waiting for me.

"My dad wants you to go."

The Royal Pain forms between my shoulder blades. "Goodie for him."

Reed looks like he's trying not to strangle me. "You're coming to the game."

"Pass. I don't like football. Besides, I have to work."

I reach for the door handle, but he leans over the seat and grabs my arm. A rush of heat travels from his fingers, down my arm, and settles between my legs. I order my traitorous body to stand down, and try not to breathe in the spicy, masculine scent that reaches my nostrils. Why does he have to smell so good?

"I don't care what you like or don't like. I know you get off at seven. Kick off is at seven thirty. You're coming." His voice is low, rippling with…it's not anger anymore, but thick with…I don't know with what. All I know is that he's too close for comfort, and my heart is beating dangerously fast.

"I'm not going to some stupid high school football game to cheer for you and your meathead friends," I snap, shrugging his hand off my arm. The loss of his warmth sends an instant shiver through me. "Callum will just have to deal."

I slide out of the SUV and slam the door, then hurry down the dark sidewalk toward the bakery.

I BARELY MAKE IT TO school before the first bell. I only have time for a quick stop in the bathroom to change into my Astor Park uniform, and then I sit through my morning classes and fight to stay awake. At lunch, I chug so much coffee that Val finally has to cut me off, but at least I feel alert now.

I take my seat next to Easton's in chem class and greet him with a reluctant hello.

"You were snoring in English class this morning," he says with a grin.

"I was not. I was wide awake the whole time." Was I, though? Now I'm not so sure.

Easton rolls his eyes. "Aw, sis. You work too hard. I'm worried about you."

I roll my eyes back. I know the Royal brothers aren't happy about my job. Neither is Callum, who wouldn't quit frowning when I told him about it. He insisted that I should be concentrating on my studies and not splitting my focus between school and work, but I hadn't budged. After I told him working was important to me and that I needed more than school to occupy my time, he'd backed off.

Or so I'd thought. It isn't until the bell rings for my last class of the day that I realize Callum has made another power play behind my back.

A tall, lithe woman comes up to me as I'm leaving my math class. She moves with the grace of a ballerina, so when she introduces herself as the coach of the dance team, I'm not surprised.

"Ella," Ms. Kelley says, her sharp eyes studying me. "Your guardian tells me you've been dancing since you were a child. What kind of training have you had?"

I shift in discomfort. "Not much training at all," I lie. "I'm not sure why Mr. Royal told you otherwise."

I think she sees right through me, because she arches a brow. "Why don't you let me be the judge of that? You're trying out for the team after school today."

Alarm bells ring in my head. What? No way. I don't want to join the dance team. Dancing is just a silly hobby. And...oh crap, didn't Savannah mention that Jordan is the captain of the team? Now I *really* don't want to try out.

"I work after school," I say curtly.

Ms. Kelley blinks. "Work?" She says the word as if it's a foreign concept to her. But I guess when it comes to having a part-time job, I'm in the minority here at Astor Park. "What time is that?"

"Three-thirty."

She frowns. "All right. Well, my session doesn't let out until four. Hmmm." She thinks it over. "You know what, my captain will handle it—Carrington knows what we're looking for. You can try out for her at three, and that leaves you plenty of time to get to your job."

My panic triples. I'm going to be trying out for *Jordan*? Hell to the *no*.

Ms. Kelley notices my expression and frowns again. "Mr. Royal and I expect you to be there, Ella. Every student at Astor Park Prep Academy is encouraged to contribute something to this school. Extra-curriculars are a healthy and productive way to occupy your time."

Damn Callum. The fact that she used the same phrase I gave him—occupy my time—tells me that he's definitely behind this.

"Come to the practice gym after your last class. You can wear your PE uniform." She pats me on the arm, then walks off before I can protest.

A groan rises in my throat, but I choke it down. Is there anything the Royals aren't capable of doing? I'm not interested in joining the dance team, but I know that if I don't show up to the tryout, Ms. Kelley will report back to Callum, and if he's pissed enough, he might actually force me to quit my job. Or worse, the school might decide I have nothing "special" to offer, and Beringer will kick me out, which Callum *definitely* won't like.

Truthfully, I wouldn't like it either. This school is light-years ahead academically from the public schools I attended in the past.

I can't concentrate at all during my last class. I'm filled with dread about the tryout, and when I make my way to the south lawn after the bell rings, I feel like an inmate walking the green mile. I should have asked Val how she got out of this sort of thing, because she can dance and I don't see anyone forcing her to a tryout.

The girls' locker room is empty when I walk in, but there's a rectangular box sitting on the long gleaming bench between the rows of lockers.

ELLA is scrawled on the top, and there's a folded piece of paper taped next to my name.

My stomach churns. With shaky hands, I snatch the note and unfold it.

Sorry, sweetie, we don't allow dirty strippers on the team. But I'm sure The XCalibur Club in town would LOVE to let you try out. In fact, I have so much faith in you that I even bought you an audition outfit. The club's located at the corner of Trash St. and Gutter Ave. Break a leg!

Jordan

Her name is signed in a feminine scrawl, and the glee behind each letter is unmistakable.

My hands tremble even harder as I open the box and shove the tissue paper aside. When I see what's inside, embarrassment floods my stomach.

The box contains a teeny pair of red panties, five-inch spiked stilettos, and a lacy red bra with black tassels. The lingerie is ugly and trashy and not unlike what I wore at Miss Candy's back in Kirkwood.

I wonder which Royal told them about my stripping. Callum must have confided in his sons, so who talked? Reed? Easton? I'm betting on Reed.

Another emotion eclipses my embarrassment—rage. White-hot rage that surges through my blood and makes the tips of my fingers tingle. I'm sick of this. I'm sick of the judgment and the insults and the sneers. I'm sick of it all.

I crumple Jordan's note in my fist and whip it across the room. Then I spin on my heel and march toward the exit.

Halfway to the door, I halt. My gaze travels back to the skanky underwear on the bench.

You know that?

They think I'm trash? I'll *show* them trash.

Maybe it's the anger, or the frustration, or the lump of sheer helplessness lodged in my throat, but I don't feel in control of my own body. My hands rip at my clothes as if on autopilot, and I'm so mad I can taste the fury. My mouth is even watering. God, I'm foaming at the mouth.

I yank the scrap of lace up my hips, snap the bra into place, and march toward the door. Not the door that leads outside, but the one that will take me to the gym.

I leave the stilettos on the bench. I'm going to need my balance.

My bare feet slap the floor, each step I take fueled by anger and a sense of injustice. These people don't know me. They have no right to judge me. I throw open the door and enter the gym. Head high, hands at my sides.

Someone notices me and gasps.

"Holy fuck." A male voice echoes from the other end of the gym, where the partition separating the weights and exercise equipment from the court is pushed open.

A clanging sound echoes through the gym, as if someone dropped a barbell.

My step stutters. The entire football team is over there lifting weights and working out. I sneak the briefest peek in their direction and feel my cheeks heat up. Every pair of male eyes is glazed over. Every jaw is unhinged. Except one. One jaw stays locked tight, as Reed's blue eyes blaze at me.

I tear my gaze off him and continue toward the group of girls who are stretching on a pile of blue mats. I add a little sway to my hips, and they all stop mid-stretch, wide-eyed.

Jordan's shock only registers for a moment. Then it fades to wariness. When she sees the look on my face, I swear she trembles. A second later, she hops to her feet and crosses her arms over her chest.

She's wearing bootie shorts and a tight tank top, her dark hair pulled back in a ponytail. Her body is long and toned. Strong. But so is mine.

"You really have no dignity, do you?" She smirks at my get-up.

I stop in front of her. I don't say a word. Every single person in the gym is looking at us. No, they're looking at *me*. I'm half-naked, and I know I look good even in this sleazy outfit. I might not have billionaire parents like these kids do, but I inherited my mother's looks.

These girls know it, too. A few envious glances flit my way before they're shielded with scowls.

"What do you want?" Jordan demands when I still don't utter a word. "I don't care what Coach Kelley says. You're not trying out."

"No?" I feign an innocent look. "But I was *so* looking forward to it."

"Well, it's not happening."

I smile at her. "That's too bad. I was dying to show you how we do it in the gutter. But I guess I still can."

Before she can respond, I wind my arm back and send my fist crashing into her face.

Instant pandemonium breaks out. Jordan's head jerks back from the blow, and her shriek of outrage gets lost in the sea of male hoots all around us. One of the guys shouts, "Catfight!" but I don't have time to see who it is, because Jordan launches herself at me.

The bitch *is* strong. We crash to the mats and suddenly she's on top of me, her fists coming at me. I deflect and roll us, elbowing her in the stomach before yanking on her ponytail and pulling hard. My vision is an angry blur. I land another blow to her cheek, and she retaliates by raking her nails down my left arm.

"Get off me, you stupid bitch!" she screams.

I ignore the pain shooting up my arm and raise my other fist. "Make me."

I let the fist fly, but before it can connect with her smug face, I'm sailing backward through the air. Muscular arms lock around my chest and yank me away from Jordan.

I pound at my captor's forearms. "Let me go!"

He growls in my ear. I don't need to turn around to know it's Reed. "Calm the fuck down," he spits out.

Three feet away, Jordan's friends are helping her to her feet. She touches her red cheek and glares at me. She looks ready to lunge again, but Shea and Rachel hold her back.

The adrenaline sizzling through my veins is making me jumpy. But I know I'm about to crash hard. I'm already starting to feel weak and loopy, my upper body trembling against Reed's strong chest.

"Let me at her, Reed," Jordan bursts out. Her hair has come loose from her ponytail and falls into her enraged eyes, and a bruise is already forming on one high cheekbone. "This bitch deserves a—"

"Enough." His sharp voice cuts her off.

Her menacing expression wavers when Reed releases me. He rips his sweaty T-shirt off, and now half the girls are ogling his ripped abs while the other half continue to stare at me in contempt.

Reed shoves the shirt at me. "Put this on."

I don't think twice. I yank the shirt over my head. When my head pops out of the neckhole, I see Jordan glaring bloody murder at me.

"Now get the hell out of here," Reed snaps at me. "Get dressed and go home."

A thirty-something man with balding hair marches forward. He's wearing a coach's uniform and a whistle around his neck, but I know he's not the head coach, because I saw Easton in the hall once talking to Coach Lewis. This one must be the team trainer or something, and he looks livid.

"These girls aren't going anywhere but the headmaster's office," he announces.

With a bored look, Reed turns to the man. "No, my *sister* is going home. Jordan can go wherever you tell her."

"Reed," the man warns. "You're not in charge here."

Reed sounds impatient. "It's done. Over. They're calm now." He shoots us a pointed look. "Right?"

I nod curtly.

So does Jordan.

"So let's not waste Beringer's time." Reed's voice is commanding and forceful with a hint of amusement, as if he's getting off on telling this older man what to do. "Because we both know he won't take any action. My father will pay him off and Ella will get nothing but a slap on the wrist. Jordan's father will do the same."

The trainer's jaw tightens, but he knows Reed is right, because he doesn't argue. After a long beat, he spins around and blows his whistle, the piercing sound making all of us jump.

"I don't see any lifting, ladies!" he booms.

The players who were egging on our catfight hurry back to their exercise stations like their asses are on fire.

Reed stays with me. "Go," he orders. "We've got a game tonight, and now my guys are distracted because you're dressed like a slut. Just get out of here."

He stalks off, shirtless, his muscular back gleaming in the sun streaming in from the skylights. Someone tosses him another shirt and he slips into it on his way to his brother. Easton meets my eyes for a moment, his expression impossible to decipher, but then he turns to Reed, and the Royals talk in hushed tones to each other.

"Bitch," a voice hisses.

I ignore Jordan and stalk away.

CHAPTER 16

I DON'T GO TO THE football game. Wild horses couldn't drag me to school tonight, not after everything that happened today. At least I was lively at the bakery. Still steaming from the fight, I tore around the little shop like a whirlwind. As Lucy was leaving, she made some comment about youth and energy and how she missed it.

I almost yelled after her that unless she liked assholes and bitches, she missed nothing, but I figured I shouldn't be shouting at my boss.

I still can't believe I physically assaulted Jordan Carrington.

I'd do it again, though. In a heartbeat. The bitch had it coming.

All I want to do tonight is hide in my room and pretend the rest of the world doesn't exist. That the Royals and their snobby friends don't exist. But even in my self-imposed sentence of solitude, I can't resist turning on the radio to the local station that's covering the game.

Of course, the Royal brothers get plenty of coverage. Reed gets a sack against the opposing quarterback. Easton makes a play that causes the announcers to groan.

"Now *that's* a hit."

"Both of them are gonna be icing their ribs tonight," the other announcer agrees.

Astor Park wins, and I sarcastically mutter, "Go team!" as I turn off the radio.

I do my homework as a distraction, but I'm interrupted by a text from Valerie. There's a party tonight, she informs me, this time at someone named Wade's house. She asks if I want to come over to her place instead and dance the night away. I decline. I'm not in the mood to pretend that everything is okay in my life.

I hate this school. I hate the people. Except Valerie, but I'm not sure even my quirky, energetic friend—my *only* friend—can make any of this torture worthwhile.

Eventually I wander downstairs to the kitchen, where I find Brooke sipping a glass of wine at the counter. She's wearing a silky red dress, strappy heels, and an impatient expression.

"Hi," I say tentatively.

She nods in greeting.

"Everything okay?" I grab a bag of corn chips from the pantry, then stand there awkwardly, wondering why I feel compelled to strike up a conversation with her.

"Callum's late," she answers, her voice tight. "We're flying to Manhattan for dinner, but he's not home yet."

"Oh. Ah. I'm sorry." They're flying to Manhattan just to have *dinner*? Who does that? "I'm sure he'll be back soon. He probably got held up at the office."

She snorts. "Of course he got held up at the office. He fucking *lives* there, in case you haven't noticed."

Her harsh expletive makes me squirm.

Brooke's expression softens when she notices my discomfort. "I'm sorry, sweetie. Ignore me. I'm a cranky bitch today." She smiles, but it doesn't quite reach her eyes. "Why don't you distract me while I wait? How was school?"

"Next question," I say immediately.

That gets me a genuine-sounding laugh. Eyes twinkling, Brooke taps the empty stool beside her. "Sit," she orders. "And tell Brooke all about it."

I sit down, though I'm not entirely sure why.

"What happened at school, Ella?"

I gulp. "Nothing, really. I, ah, may have beat the crap out of someone."

A shocked laugh flies out of her mouth. "Oh dear."

For some inexplicable reason, I end up telling her the whole story. How Jordan was determined to humiliate and shame me. How I turned the prank around to my own advantage. How I slammed my fist into the bitch's jaw. When I'm done, Brooke surprises me by patting my arm.

"You had every right to lose your temper," she says firmly. "And good for you, putting that nasty girl in her place."

I wonder if Callum would have the same oddly proud reaction if he knew what I did to Jordan, but somehow I doubt it. "I feel bad," I admit. "I'm not usually a violent person."

Brooke shrugs. "Sometimes a show of force is necessary, especially in this world. The *Royal* world. Do you think the

Carrington girl is going to be the only person who gives you grief about where you come from? She won't. Resign yourself to the fact that you now have enemies, Ella. A lot of them. The Royals are a powerful family, and you're one of them now. That's bound to inspire hate and jealousy in the people around you."

I bite my lip. "I'm not a real Royal. Not by blood."

"No, but you're an O'Halloran by blood." She smiles. "Trust me, that's equally enticing. Your father was a very rich man. Callum is a very rich man. Ergo, you're a very rich girl." Brooke takes a delicate sip of her wine. "Get used to the gossip, darling. Get used to walking into a room and having everyone in it whisper that you don't belong. Get used to it, but don't let those whispers defeat you. Strike back when they strike you. Don't be weak."

She's like a war chief delivering a speech before battle, and I'm not sure if I agree with her advice or not. But I can't deny I feel a bit better about rearranging Jordan's smug face today.

We hear the front doors open, and a moment later Callum strides into the kitchen. He's wearing a tailored suit and looks frazzled.

"Don't say it," he orders before Brooke can even speak. Then his tone goes softer. "I'm sorry I'm late. The board decided to call a meeting just as I was on my way out the door. But let me just get dressed and then Durand will take us to the airfield. Hi, Ella. How was school?"

"Great," I lie, hopping off the stool. I avoid Brooke's amused eyes. "Have fun at dinner. I've got homework to finish."

I dart out of the kitchen before Callum realizes I didn't go to the football game like he wanted.

I head back to my princess room and spend the next two hours tackling boring math equations, and it's a little past eleven when my door swings open and Easton strides inside without knocking.

I jump in surprise. "Why the hell didn't you knock?"

"We're family. Family doesn't knock." His dark hair is wet as if he's showered recently, and he's wearing sweats, a tight T-shirt, and a surly expression. In his right hand is a bottle of Jack Daniel's.

"What do you want?" I demand.

"You weren't at the game."

"So?"

"Reed told you to be there."

"So?" I say again.

Easton frowns. He takes a step toward me. "So you have to keep up appearances. Dad wants you involved in shit. He'll stay off our backs as long as you play along."

"I don't like games. You and your brothers don't want to be around me. I don't want be around you. Why pretend otherwise?"

"Naah, you want to be around us." He moves even closer and brings his mouth to my ear. His breath brushes my neck, but I don't smell alcohol on it. I don't think he's dipped into the bottle yet. "And maybe I want to be around you."

I narrow my eyes. "Why are you in my room, Easton?"

"Because I'm bored and you're the only one home." He flops down on my bed and lies back on his elbows, the whiskey bottle tucked at his side.

"Valerie said there's a post-game party. You could've gone to that."

Grimacing, he lifts his shirt, revealing a nasty looking bruise on his side. "I took a beating on the field. Don't feel like going out."

Suspicion rolls through me. "Where's Reed?"

"At the party. Twins, too." He shrugs. "Like I said, it's just you and me."

"I'm about to go to bed."

His eyes linger on my bare legs, and I know he also doesn't miss the way my threadbare shirt clings to my chest. Rather than comment, he slides up the bed and rests his head on my pillows.

I grit my teeth as he grabs the remote from the side table, flicks on the TV, and changes it to ESPN.

"Get out," I order. "I want to go to sleep."

"It's too early for bedtime. Stop being a little bitch and sit down." Surprisingly, there's no malice in his tone. Just humor.

But I'm still suspicious. I sit down as far away from him as possible without falling off the mattress.

With a grin, Easton glances around my pink bedroom and says, "My dad is a clueless fucker, huh?"

I can't help but return the grin. "I guess he's not used to raising girls."

"Not used to raising boys either," Easton mutters under his breath.

"Aw, is this where you tell me all about your daddy issues? Daddy wasn't home, Daddy ignored me, Daddy didn't love me."

He rolls his eyes again and ignores the taunt. "My brother's pissed at you," he says instead.

"Your brother is always pissed about something."

Easton doesn't respond. He raises the bottle to his lips.

My curiosity gets the better of me. "Fine, I'll bite. Why's he pissed?"

"Because you threw down with Jordan today."

"She had it coming."

He takes another sip. "Yeah, she did."

My eyebrows shoot up. "What, no lecture? No 'you're tarnishing the Royal name, Ella. You're a disappointment to us all.'"

His lips quirk. "Naah." Another grin surfaces, impish this time. "That was the hottest thing I've seen in a long time. The two of you rolling around on the floor like that….*damn*. You gave me enough material to feed the spank bank for years."

"Gross. I don't want to hear about your spank bank."

"Sure you do." One more sip, and then he holds out the Jack's. "Drink."

"No thanks."

"For fuck's sake, stop being so difficult all the time. Live a little." He shoves the bottle in my hand. "Drink."

I drink.

I'm not sure why. Maybe I do it because I want the buzz. Maybe I do it because this is the first time any Royal other than Callum has been somewhat nice to me since I moved in.

Easton's eyes shine with approval as I take a deep swig. He runs a hand through his hair, then winces at the movement. I feel sorry for him. That's a heck of a bruise.

We sit in silence for a while, passing the bottle back and forth. I stop drinking the moment I feel buzzed, and he pokes me in the side, even as his gaze stays glued to the TV.

"You're not drinking enough."

"I don't want any more." I lean back on the headboard and close my eyes. "I don't like being drunk. I stop at tipsy."

"Have you ever even been drunk?" he challenges.

"Yes. Have you?"

"Never," he says innocently.

I snort. "Uh-huh. You were probably an alcoholic at the age of ten." The moment the words leave my mouth, I let out a sigh.

"What?" He watches me curiously. He's a lot more attractive when he's not scowling or smirking.

"Nothing. Just a stupid memory." I should change the subject—talking about my past is something I usually avoid—but the memory has taken root, and I can't help but laugh now. "It's kind of messed up, actually."

"Well, now I'm intrigued."

"I was ten the first time I got drunk," I confess.

He grins. "For real?"

"Yeah. My mom was dating this guy. Leo." Who had mob ties, but I don't share that with Easton. "We were living in Chicago at the time, and he took us to a Cubs game one weekend. He was drinking beer, and I kept begging to try a sip. My mom was all, no way in hell, but Leo convinced her that one sip wouldn't hurt."

I close my eyes, transported back to that warm June day. "So I tried it, and it tasted awful. Leo thought the face I made when I drank it was hilarious, so every time Mom turned her back, he'd pass me the bottle and then piss his pants laughing at my expression. I couldn't have drunk more than a quarter of that bottle, but I got *wasted*."

Beside me, Easton bursts out laughing. I realize this is the first time I've heard genuine laughter in the Royal palace. "Did your mom freak?"

"Oh yeah. God. You should've seen it. I was stumbling up and down the aisle, this ten-year-old girl, slurring like a wino—'whadda you mean you won' buy me a hot dog?'"

We're both laughing now, the mattress shaking beneath us. It's nice. So of course that means it doesn't last long.

Easton abruptly goes silent for a moment, then twists his head to meet my eyes. "Were you really a stripper?"

I stiffen. The word *no* bites at my tongue. But what does it matter at this point? The kids at school are going to say I stripped, regardless of whether or not it's true.

So I nod.

He looks impressed. "That's kind of badass."

"No. It's not."

He shifts, and his shoulder grazes mine. I don't know if it's intentional on his part, but when his face turns toward mine again, I know he's totally aware of the contact between our bodies.

"You know, you're hot when you're not snarling." His gaze fixes on my mouth.

I'm frozen in place, but it's not fear that's making my heart pound. Easton's eyes are dark with need. They're the same shade of blue as Reed's.

"You should go." I swallow. "I want to go to bed now."

"No, you don't."

He's right. I don't. My thoughts are jumbled. I'm thinking of Reed, and his strong jaw and perfect face. Easton has the same jaw. Before I can stop myself, my hand reaches out to touch it.

A husky noise escapes his lips. He leans into my fingers. His stubble scrapes along my soft skin.

I'm stunned to feel a rush of heat between my legs.

"You just had to come and screw everything up, didn't you?" he mutters.

And then his lips press against mine.

My heart beats faster, in time to the pulse of the alcohol flowing through me. Sucking in a breath, I ease our mouths apart before the kiss can go any further.

I exhale in a rush, fully prepared to pretend that it didn't happen, but I underestimated Easton Royal's sex appeal. He's gorgeous. His eyes are heavy-lidded, his jaw strong like his brother's. His stupid brother. Why can't I get Reed out of my head?

Easton shoves his fingers through my hair and tugs me toward him again. His lips brush mine, just briefly, before he pulls back. His gaze holds an invitation.

I touch his cheek and close my eyes. A clear signal. I didn't realize how badly I've been craving human contact. A boy's warm lips on mine, his hands stroking my hair. I might be a virgin, but I've fooled around before, and my body remembers how good that feels. I sag against Easton's chest as our mouths meet again.

The next thing I know, he's on top of me, the heavy weight of his body pressing me into the mattress. He moves his hips, and pleasure sweeps through me, making me tremble with need.

Easton kisses me again. Deep and hungry.

His tongue enters my mouth at the same time an incredulous voice says, "Are you fucking kidding me?"

Easton and I break apart, both our heads swiveling toward the open doorway where Reed stands, staring at us in disbelief.

"Reed—" Easton starts, but it's no use. His brother turns around and stalks off.

Reed's footsteps are as loud as my pounding heart.

Beside me, Easton rolls onto his back. He stares up at the ceiling and whispers, "Shit."

CHAPTER 17

A SECOND TICKS BY. TWO. Three. And then Easton jackknives out of bed and runs out after Reed.

"I was drunk," I hear him exclaim in the hallway.

And the burn of humiliation—the shame I swore I never felt—scorches me. He only kissed me because he was drunk.

"Whatever, East. You do what you want. You always do." Reed sounds tired, and my stupid heart, the hungry and lonely one that allowed Easton to kiss me, aches for Reed.

"Screw you, Reed. You wanted me off painkillers and I am, but I got stomped by a three-hundred-pound heifer out there and my ribs hurt like a motherfucker. It's either beer or oxy. Pick one."

Easton's voice trails off and I don't hear Reed's response. Against my better judgment, I creep over to my door and peek out into the hall. I'm just in time to see them both disappear into Reed's room. My bare feet don't make a sound as I tiptoe down the hall to the now closed door.

"Why aren't you still at the party? Abby was all over you after the game," Easton says. "Easy ass, dude."

Reed snorts. "That's why I'm here. I can't go back to that well."

"Why'd you go out with her in the first place?"

I hold my breath because it's an answer I'd like to know, too. What exactly is Reed's type?

There's a thump and then another one, like something being throw at the wall.

"She…she reminded me of Mom. Soft. Quiet. Not pushy."

"Like Ella." Easton laughs sarcastically. Another thump, this time slightly muffled. "Hey, you almost hit me with that ball, fucker."

They both laugh. Are they laughing at me?

"Stay away from her, East. You don't know who she's been with," Reed warns, and now it sounds like they're playing catch, just casually discussing my sexual history.

"Is she really a stripper?" Easton asks after a bit. "She told me she was, but it could've been a lie."

"That's what Brooke said. Plus it was in Dad's report."

Brooke told them that I stripped? So much for trusting her! And what the hell does he mean that Callum has a *report* on me?

"I never read it. Were there pictures?"

I roll my eyes at the eagerness in Easton's voice.

"Yeah."

"Of her stripping?" He's even more excited.

"Naah. They were just of her doing normal shit." Reed pauses. "She worked three jobs last summer. She clerked at a truck stop in the morning, did retail in the afternoon, and stripped at this kiddy bar at night."

"Damn. That's rough," Easton sounds almost impressed. Not Reed, though. Reed comes off disgusted. "How'd Jordan find that out?"

"One of the twins blurted it out, probably while he was getting head."

"Sawyer then. Can't keep his mouth shut when there's a bitch around his dick."

"Truth." A drawer slams shut. "You know, you could use this. I mean, hell, if she's attracted to you, then use her. Stick with her. Find out what she really wants. I'm still not convinced that her and Dad don't have something going on."

"She said she wasn't doing him."

"And you believed that?"

"Maybe." Reed's disbelief infects Easton. "How many guys you think she's been with?"

"Who knows. Gold diggers like her will open their legs to anyone who waves a few dollars in front of 'em."

I'm not a gold digger! I want to shout. And these jerks couldn't be more wrong about my active "sex life." I haven't even given a blowjob before. On the sex scale, I veer closer to *prude* than *pro*.

"Think she could teach me something?" Easton wonders.

"How an STD feels. But if you want to fuck her, then do it. I don't care."

"Really? Because you're throwing that football hard enough that it sounds like you care."

The thumping stops. "You're right. I do care."

My hand creeps up to my throat. Thud. Thud. Thud. They toss the ball back and forth. Or maybe that's the hope in my heart.

"I care about you. I care if you get hurt, sick, whatever. I don't give two shits about her, though."

I look down at my hand, expecting to see blood from the wound he just slashed open. But there's nothing there.

MY ALARM GOES OFF AT five. My eyes are crusty and I feel sore all over. I might have cried a little before I fell asleep but this morning I feel a renewed sense of determination. There's no point in wanting the Royals to like me, especially Reed. Steve's widow is a bitch, but at least it's obvious so I know what to watch for. That goes double for Easton. If he tries to use me, then I'll use him right back.

After all, I don't have any secrets. They're all written out in some *report* of Callum's.

I lace up my sneakers and shoulder my backpack that is ten grand lighter. I decided it was too stressful to be carrying around that load of cash, so I taped it to the underside of the sink in the bathroom. Hopefully it'll be safe there.

Being up this early on a Saturday morning is so disorienting, but Lucy asked me to come in today and help her with a cake order, and I didn't feel right saying no. Besides, I could use all the extra cash I can get.

In the hallway, I try to be as quiet as possible so I don't wake up the Royals. I'm so focused on tiptoeing down the stairs that I almost topple over when I hear Reed's low voice behind me.

"Where are you going?"

Hmm, that'd be none of your business. I figure if I don't engage him then he'll just go back to his room.

"Whatever," he mutters when my silence drags on. "I don't give a shit."

After his bedroom door clicks shut, I give myself a pat on the back for alienating another person in my life and slip out through the front door. It's still dark out as I walk to the bus stop. When I reach it, I tuck myself inside the little bus shelter and try to shut out every bad thing in my life.

My skill, if I have one, isn't dancing. It's my ability to believe that tomorrow can be a better day. I don't really know where I got this optimism. Maybe it was from Mom. Somewhere along the line, I started thinking that if I just got through this bad experience, this bad day, that tomorrow I'd have something better, brighter, newer.

I still believe that. I still believe that there's something good out there for me. I just have to keep going until my time comes, because surely, *surely*, none of this would happen if there wasn't a reward down the line.

I take a deep breath. The salt of the sea makes the air taste fresh and tangy. As terrible as the Royals are, as awful as Dinah O'Halloran is, today *is* better than a week ago. I have a warm bed, nice clothes, plenty of food. I'm attending a really amazing school. I have a girlfriend.

It's all going to be okay.

Really.

I arrive at the bakery feeling better than I have in days. It must show because Lucy compliments me immediately.

"You look gorgeous this morning. Oh, to be young again." She clucks in mock dismay.

"You look amazing yourself, Luce," I tell her as I tie on an apron. "And something smells delicious. What are those?" I point to the little domes of glazed goodness.

"Mini monkey bread. It's tiny pieces of cinnamon-flavored bread dough mixed with caramel and butter. Want one?"

I nod so enthusiastically that my head nearly falls off. "I think I orgasmed just smelling them."

Lucy laughs in delight, her short curls bouncing around her head. "Then have one and I'll show you how to make four dozen more."

"I can't wait."

The mini monkey breads are a hit. We sell out of them before eight o'clock and Lucy sends me into the back to make more before my shift is over. At eleven forty-five, Valerie shows up and I'm in such a good mood, I practically tackle-hug her.

"What are you doing here?" I ask happily, squeezing her tight before releasing her.

"I was in the neighborhood. What's up with you?" Valerie laughs. "Did you get laid last night?"

"No, but I did have pastry-induced orgasms all morning." I pull a just-baked goodie from the shelf and hand it to her.

Valerie picks off a piece of the bread and starts moaning when the sugar hits her tongue. "Oh my God."

"Right?" I giggle.

"Is Durand picking you up or do need a ride home? I have a car today!" Valerie says between shoving her mouth full of carbs.

"I'd love a ride." I pull off the apron and hurry to get my things. "Okay if I go, Luce?"

She waves me off, busy with another customer.

Valerie's car is an older model Honda and it looks out of place amongst the Mercedes, Land Rovers, and Audis that fill the parking spots outside.

"It's Tam's mom's car," she explains. "I offered to pick up a few things for her."

"That's cool." Shyly, I share, "Callum says I'm getting a car, so once that arrives, you can borrow it whenever you want."

"Aw, thanks. You're the bestest friend ever." She laughs, then looks over at me. "Anyway, I actually stopped by to see if you wanted to go somewhere tonight."

My happy mood dims a little. I hope she's not asking me to go to a party, because the idea of spending time with Astor Park kids outside of school isn't too appealing. "Well, I have some homework…"

Valerie reaches over and pinches me.

"Ow! What was that for?" I rub my arm and scowl at her.

"Give me a little credit. I'm not taking us to an Astor party. I mean, there might be Astor peeps there, but it's a club downtown that sometimes allows in under twenty-one year olds, and tonight is one of those nights. There'll be kids from all over and not just from Astor Park."

"I'm not eighteen." I slump down in my seat. "And the only ID I have says I'm thirty-four."

"Doesn't matter. You're hot. They'll let you in," Valerie says confidently.

SHE'S RIGHT. THEY DON'T CARD either of us at the door when we arrive at the club later that night. The bouncer runs his flashlight over Val and then me, taking in our blown-out hair, skimpy dresses and high heels, and lets us in with a wink.

The place appears to be a renovated warehouse. The bass is shaking the walls and there are strobe lights illuminating the dance floor. Up toward the front is a stage and there are girls dirty dancing on it.

"We're dancing in that tonight," Valerie shouts in my ear.

I follow the line of her arm. Above the dance floor, suspended at different levels, are four human-sized birdcages. In each one there are dancers. One has a girl and a guy who are grinding against each other, and the other three feature solo girls.

"Why?" I ask suspiciously.

"To make ourselves feel good. I'm missing Tam and I want to dance and have fun."

"Can't we just dance on a stage?"

Val shakes her head. "No. Half of dancing is the crowd appreciation." She grins at me.

I stare back at her in amazement. "This seems so unlike you."

She laughs and shakes her cloud of hair. "I'm not a mouse. I love to dance and show off and this is a place I can do it. Tam brought me here and we tore up the floor. And after, we tore up the sheets." She bites her lip and her eyes get a little glassy as she recalls a post party romp with her boyfriend.

So Val's a little exhibitionist. Who knew? I guess it's always the quiet ones. I've never minded dancing in front of people, but I don't get off on it like Val apparently does. Once I start dancing, I get lost in the music and forget that anyone is even watching.

Maybe it's a protective reflex—one I learned early when I was stripping at the age of fifteen. But whatever the reason, when the beat seeps into my blood, there could be no one or there could be a hundred people around. I move to the music, not the audience.

"Sure. I'm up for that."

She looks thrilled. "Awesome. One cage or two?"

"How about together? We'll really give everyone a show."

The men at Miss Candy's loved it when two girls danced together. Just like the football players the other day enjoyed watching Jordan and me fight.

Valerie claps her hands. "Wait here. I'll be right back."

I watch as she trots over to a guy in a booth. I assumed he was a DJ, but I guess he's the one who controls access to the cages. They exchange words and then the guy holds up one finger. Valerie reaches over the barrier and gives him a hug.

Once she's done convincing him that we're a better act, she runs back to me. "One song," she says, "and then we're up." She grabs two sodas from a waitress passing by with a tray full of drinks and hands me one.

Val's not real patient. She shifts from one foot to another. Taps her palm against her leg. Finally, she turns to me. "Why does Jordan call you a stripper?"

"Because I was," I admit. "I stripped to pay my mom's medical bills and when she died I stripped to pay for the roof over my head."

Her mouth drops open. "Holy shit. Why didn't you just go to a relative?"

"I didn't know I had any." I shrug. "It's been me and Mom for as long as I can remember. And once she was gone, I just didn't want to go into foster care. I heard all these nightmares about the system and I figured I'd been taking care of her and me for so long that just taking care of myself for two years would be a breeze."

"Wow. You are entirely too impressive for me," Val declares.

I snort. "In what way? Taking my clothes off for money isn't a skill most people admire." My mind involuntarily skips back to Reed. He definitely doesn't think it's a skill I should be bragging about.

"You've got a lot of moxie," Val says. "And that's what's admirable."

"Moxie? Who says moxie?"

"I do!" She smiles and pulls on my hand. "Moxie. Moxie. Moxie." I start to laugh because Val is adorable and her smiles are infectious. She grabs my hand. "Let's go. It's our turn."

I let her drag me over to the base of the stairs. The couple has already left and the door to the cage is open. We run up the stairs and climb inside. Val shuts the door behind us.

"Let's have some fun!" she shouts over the music.

And we do. We start out dancing side by side, doing our own thing. It's like the video game only a live action one. Guys below us stop dancing and start watching, and their admiring gazes start working on me in a way I thought would be impossible. I've had dozens of men stare at me before, but this is the first time I've actually enjoyed the attention. I run my hands down my sides and shimmy low to the floor of the cage. Val is pressed up against the bars, bracing against them as she writhes to the music.

It's when I start to rise that I spot him—Reed. He's slouched against the bar, a beer bottle dangling from his fingers. His lips are parted—in surprise? Desire? I'm not sure, but even from this distance I can feel the heat from his eyes as they rake over me.

He's the hottest guy in the club, hands down. Taller than almost everyone, more muscular, more everything. I can't help but admire the way his black T-shirt clings to his perfect chest, and I feel a tingle shoot up my spine. Licking my lips, I push to my feet. Val's hands land on my waist. In our heels, we're about the same height. I feel her boobs push into my back as she uses my body as a pole to show off her own moves.

The cheers of the crowd below us are growing stronger, but for me, the only thing that exists is Reed Royal. I stare at him.

He stares back.

I stick my finger in my mouth and then slowly draw it out. He doesn't look away.

I drag the finger down my neck, down the valley between my breasts, down to my stomach. The noise is getting louder and louder. My hand is getting lower.

Reed's eyes are glued to me. His mouth moves. *Ella…Ella…*

"Ella."

Valerie grabs my waist and leans her head on my shoulder. "Song's over. Ready?"

I look back toward the bar, but Reed's gone. I shake my head. Had I imagined that whole thing? Was he ever even there?

"Yeah," I mumble. "I'm ready."

My whole body is throbbing. I'm not so inexperienced that I don't know what the ache between my legs means. It's just that…I don't know that touching myself is going to give me the relief I need.

"Nice, girls. Real nice," the bouncer yells at us when we exit. "Cage is yours anytime tonight."

"Thanks, Jorge!" Val says.

He hands her two bottles of water. "Any time, babe. Any time."

"He wants you," I tell her when we move away.

"Yeah, but I don't want anyone but Tam." She guzzles the water and rolls the cold bottle against her forehead. "But I'm feeling it right now. Know what I mean?"

To my miserable dismay, I do.

"Anyway, I gotta pee. You want to come?"

I shake my head. "I'll wait here."

While she disappears into the mob, I finish my bottle of water and then glance around the club. It's a lot more crowded now, and I notice quite a few interested looks aimed in my direction.

I make eye contact with a cute guy with a punk haircut. He's wearing jeans, a tight fitting T-shirt, and Converse tennis shoes. A strobe light highlights the piercing over his eyebrow and in his upper lip.

He looks…comfortable. Like I know him. Like we're cut from the same cloth. I give him a tentative smile, which he returns. I watch as he murmurs something to one of his friends and then starts across the floor toward me. I straighten—

"Hey, little sis. Let's dance." Easton pops up out of nowhere, his big body towering over me.

The boy headed my way stops. Crap. "I'm taking a breather." Should I wave to him to let him know it's okay? That Easton won't bite?

Easton tracks my gaze and glares at pierced guy until the pierced guy raises his hands in surrender and returns to his table. "So where were we?" Easton asks innocently. "Oh yeah, we're dancing."

I sigh and give in. Easton just made it clear he'll chase off any other guy tonight. He grabs me by my waist and virtually carries me to the dance floor.

"You look hot tonight. If you weren't my sister, I'd be all over you."

"You were already all over me." I cock a brow at his blank look. "Last night?"

He grins. "Oh right. That. C'mon, let's dance."

A few guys slap him on the back as we sway past and shout something like "you the man." I ignore it because if Easton's here, then it must be Reed I saw before. Reed who I danced for. Reed who devoured me with his eyes and made me feel so hot my body still feels like it's on fire.

"I'm pretty sure you'd be all over anyone in the state you're in," I remark.

Easton's hands run up my sides, skimming over my dress and settling on the bare skin exposed by the cut outs. "I've got a few standards. Not many but a few."

"Glad I make the cut," I say dryly.

He tugs me closer but surprisingly his hands don't wander. I twine my arms around his neck and wonder what game we're playing now.

"You put on a good show. I would've liked to have seen you strip."

"You go first and maybe, if you're good enough, I'll return the favor."

His eyes fill with glee. He loves the idea of a spectacle. "Little sis, I can't show you my goods. I'm so fine, just the sight of me would ruin you for all other men."

I laugh against my will. "You're too much, Easton."

"I am." He nods solemnly. "It's why I sleep around. Because no one girl can handle all of me."

This declaration makes me roll my eyes. "If telling yourself that story makes you feel better, then have at it."

"Oh I do, don't worry." He dips his head near mine and the wave of alcohol nearly knocks me off my feet.

"Jeez, you smell like a brewery." I shove him a little to put some distance between us.

He smiles, but it isn't pretty. "I'm an alcoholic, don't you know? I've got addiction problems. I inherited those from my mommy just like your mom passed sluttiness down to you. Aren't those grand gifts?"

If it wasn't for the hurt in his eyes, I would've told him that I'd rather dress like a slut than drown in a bottle, but his pain is one I recognize, so instead of making some flippant comment in response, I drag his head to my shoulder.

"Oh Easton, I miss my mom, too," I whisper into his sweat-dampened hair.

He shudders and clutches me tighter. His face turns into my neck and he presses his lips against a vein. It's not really erotic. It's more...he's seeking comfort from someone who isn't judging him.

Over his hunched frame, I spot a pair of blazing eyes.

Reed.

And I'm so tired of it. Easton may want to use me but I'm not against using him either.

We both want something...comfort, affection, a way to strike out at the world. I tug Easton's head up.

"What is it?" he murmurs.

"Kiss me like you mean it," I tell him.

His eyes darken and his tongue pokes out to run across his lower lip and it's sexy as hell.

My gaze flicks over to Reed, who hasn't stopped glowering. "Kiss me," I repeat.

He lowers his head and whispers, “It doesn’t matter that you’re pretending I’m Reed. I’m pretending you’re someone else, too.”

His words become lost when his mouth hits mine. His lips are so warm. And his body, strong and firm, so much like his brother’s, presses against mine. I give myself over to it. We kiss and kiss and sway to the music until someone breaks us up and we’re dragged off the dance floor.

An unhappy bouncer crosses his arms. “No sex on the dance floor. Time to go.”

Easton throws his head back and laughs hysterically. The bouncer doesn’t crack and instead points to the exit. I look around but Reed has pulled his disappearing act.

“Where’s Reed?” I stupidly ask.

“Probably screwing Abby in the parking lot.”

Thankfully Easton’s distracted by a search for something in his pockets so he doesn’t see how much his words hurt. He finds what he was looking for and hands me a key fob.

“I’m too drunk to drive, sis.”

I track down Valerie, who says she’ll be able to get home by herself. She’s on her way up the stairs for another cage dance. Resigned, I take Easton outside. The alcohol must have caught up with him, because he leans heavily against me.

“Where’d you park?”

He points left. “There. No wait.” He shifts to his right. “There.”

I see his truck and we hobble over to it. Three spots down is Reed’s SUV. It’s…moving.

Easton spots the Rover, too, and slaps the hood. He lets out a sharp bark of laughter. “If the truck’s a rocking, don’t come a knocking.”

The knowledge of what might be going on in that SUV burns me all the way home. At least I don't have to trade barbs with Easton, since he passes out about five minutes after we get rolling.

At the mansion, I help him out of the truck and up the stairs. He makes a turn into my bedroom and stumbles over to my bed, falling face down. After a couple of unsuccessful tries at moving him, I give up and go to the bathroom. By the time I get back, he's snoring and drooling on my comforter.

I debate going to his room and sleeping in his bed, then decide I'll just cover him up and sleep under the covers. I find an afghan and throw it over him. A yawn shakes my entire body as I pull off the scrap of fabric Val called a dress and let it drop to the floor. In just my undies, I crawl under the blankets and let sleep take over.

WHEN I WAKE UP, IT'S to Reed's angry face. I glance over to the side of the bed where Easton was, but he's gone.

"I told you to stay away from my brothers," Reed growls.

"I'm not a good listener." I start to sit up and then clasp the bedsheets against my chest. I forgot I took my dress off and all I'm wearing are panties.

"Sex is sex," he replies darkly. "If I have to fuck you so you don't ruin my family, I'll do it."

Then he's gone, shutting my door with a resounding *click*. I'm left sitting there in shock.

What the hell did he mean by that?

CHAPTER 18

AFTER *THAT* RUDE AWAKENING, I have no shot at falling back asleep. I don't bother hurrying after Reed to ask him to explain himself, because I know he won't, but now it's—I check the alarm clock—seven a.m. and I'm wide awake. Awesome.

I don't work on weekends, so I'm dreading this day already. Knowing Callum, he'll suggest a bunch of bonding activities for us to do and force his sons to come along. Kill me now.

I drag myself out of bed and take quick shower then throw on a bright yellow sundress I bought the day Brooke and I went shopping. From the sunlight streaming in through the curtains, I can tell it's going to be a gorgeous day, and when I open the window, a warm breeze filters in and surprises me. It's almost the end of September. The weather shouldn't be this nice.

Is Gideon coming home today? Last week he came back on a Friday, so it's unlikely he'll show up at the end of the weekend, but I kind of wish he would. Maybe he'll distract his dad and brothers and they won't remember I'm here.

I leave my bedroom at the same time that Sawyer's door swings open. The tiny redhead he'd been making out with at Jordan's party steps out, and he follows her, his hands on her waist as he leans down to kiss her.

She giggles quietly. "I have to go. Gotta get home before my parents figure out I didn't come home last night."

He whispers something in her ear and she laughs again.

"Love you."

"Love you too, babe," he answers. The kid's only sixteen and his voice is as deep and raspy as his older brothers'.

"Call me later?"

"Definitely." Grinning, Sawyer reaches out his hand, tucks a strand of red hair behind her ear and—

Oh my God. That's not Sawyer.

My jaw falls open. The nasty burn on his hand, the one he got earlier this week when he'd bungled dinner, is gone. But it had been there yesterday—I remember seeing it.

Which means the guy with Sawyer's girlfriend isn't Sawyer. It's Sebastian. I wonder if the girl knows.

She laughs in delight when he kisses her neck again. "Stop it. I have to go!"

Maybe she does know.

As they break apart, they both notice me standing there, and the girl looks uncertain for a moment. She murmurs a hasty, "Hello" and hurries down the stairs.

Sawyer—no, *Sebastian*—glowers at me, then disappears into his—no, his *brother's*—bedroom.

Okay then. Just minding my own business.

In the kitchen, I find the other twin eating cereal at the table. My gaze immediately goes to his left hand. Yep, the burn is there. Just to test the theory, I say, "Morning, Sebastian."

"Sawyer," he grinds out before shoveling more cereal into his mouth.

I swallow a gasp. Oh man. Are these boys pulling twin switches on Sawyer's girlfriend? That's ballsy. And twisted.

I pour my own bowl of cereal and lean against the counter to eat it. A few minutes later, Sebastian walks into the kitchen. As he passes the table, Sawyer murmurs, "Thanks, bro," to his twin.

I can't help it. The laugh pops out.

They both turn to glare at me. "What?" Sawyer mutters.

"Does your girlfriend know she slept with your brother last night?" I ask him.

His features harden, but he doesn't deny it. Instead, he issues a warning. "Say one word about this and—"

I cut him off with another laugh. "Relax, little Royals. Play all the creepy sex games you want. My lips are sealed."

Callum enters the kitchen, dressed in a white polo shirt and khakis. His dark hair is gelled away from his face, and, for once, he doesn't look like he's hit the liquor cabinet yet.

"Good, you boys are up," he tells the twins. "Where are the others? I told them to be downstairs at seven-fifteen." He turns to me. "You look lovely, but you might want to change into more proper sailing attire."

I stare at him blankly. "Sailing?"

"Didn't I tell you last night? We're all going sailing this morning."

What? No, he *hadn't* told me, and if I'd known this, I would have snuck right out of the house with Sawyer's girlfriend and stowed myself in the trunk of her car.

"You're going to love the *Maria*," Callum tells me, sounding excited. "There's not much of a breeze out so I don't think we'll use the sails, but it'll still be a fun time."

Me and the Royals on a boat? In open water? I don't think Callum understands what the word *fun* means.

Easton staggers into the kitchen then, decked out in wrinkled cargo shorts and a wife-beater, with a baseball cap hanging low on his forehead. He's no doubt hung-over from last night, and I suddenly have visions of the boat bouncing on the waves while Easton pukes over the side all morning.

"Reed!" Callum yells in the direction of the doorway. "Get a move on! Ella, get changed. And wear the deck shoes Brooke bought you—she got you deck shoes, right?"

I have no idea because "deck shoes" aren't a part of my vocabulary. I make a stab at getting out of this nightmare-scape he's just painted for me. "Callum, I have a lot of homework—"

"Bring it with you." He waves a hand and shouts "Reed!" again.

Dammit. I guess I'm going sailing.

THE *MARIA* IS EVERYTHING YOU'D expect from a gazillionaire's boat. *Boat*. Ha. It's a yacht, of course, and I feel like I'm starring in a rap video as I stand at the railing and sip on the flute of Cristal that Brooke slipped into my hand when Callum wasn't looking. She winked as she did it, whispering that I should say it's ginger ale if Callum asks, which he never does.

Callum was right—it's gorgeous out on the water, and the Atlantic stretches out all around us, calm and beautiful.

I drove to the marina with Callum and Brooke, while the boys took Reed's SUV. Which was a relief, because the thought of sitting in Reed's car after seeing it rocking in the parking lot last night made me sick to my stomach.

I wonder who he was with. His sweet, pure Abby, I bet. I'm not sure it satisfied him, though. I've heard sex is supposed to leave you all loose and relaxed, but Reed's entire body has been coiled with tension since we boarded the yacht.

He stands on the other side of the railing, as far as humanly possible from me and Callum without falling overboard. On the upper deck—which houses a dining area and a hot tub—Brooke is sunbathing in the nude, her golden hair gleaming in the sunshine. The weather's not warm enough for bathing suits, let alone birthday suits, but she doesn't seem to mind.

"So what do you think?" Callum gestures to the water. "Peaceful, huh?"

Not really. There's no such thing as peace when Reed Royal is staring at you. No, *glaring* at you, and he's been doing it for the past hour.

Easton is still downstairs doing God knows what, and the twins are fast asleep in a pair of nearby loungers, so Callum's the only company I've got, and Reed clearly isn't happy about it.

"Darling!" Brooke calls from the sundeck. "Come rub lotion on my back!"

Callum avoids my gaze, probably because he doesn't want me to see his sex eyes. "You okay down here alone for a bit?" he asks.

"It's fine. Go ahead."

I'm relieved to be left alone, but the relief doesn't last. The tension rises all over again when Reed moves toward me with predatory strides. He rests his forearms on the railing and keeps his gaze straight ahead.

"Ella."

I can't tell if it's a greeting or a question. I roll my eyes. "Reed."

He doesn't continue. Just keeps staring at the water.

I sneak a peek at him, and my heart does that irritating flip it always does when Reed is around. He's masculinity personified. Tall and broad, his gorgeous features chiseled to perfection. My mouth grows dry as I admire his arms, sleek with muscle, rippling with power.

He's a good foot taller than me, so when he finally turns to look at me, I have to tilt my head to meet his gaze.

Those blue eyes flick over me, resting briefly on my tiny denim shorts and tight halter top that ties at the neck. They focus on my navy-blue-and-white deck shoes, and the corner of his mouth quirks slightly.

I wonder if he's about to make fun of my shoes, but his almost-smile fades when a husky moan echoes from above us.

"*Yes*." Brooke's throaty voice makes Reed and me cringe.

A male growl follows the request. Callum apparently has no problem getting busy when his sons are close by. I find that disgusting, yet at the same time, I can't bring myself to hate him, not after his confession that he's still grieving for his wife. Loss makes us do crazy things.

Reed bites out a curse. "Let's go."

His steel grip captures my arm, making it impossible to do anything but follow him toward the stairs that lead below deck.

"Where are we going?"

He doesn't answer. He pushes open the door and marches into the luxurious main room, which is furnished with leather couches and glass tables. Reed bulldozes past the full kitchen and dining area toward the cabins in the back.

He knocks on an oak door. "East. Wake the fuck up."

There's a loud groan. "Go away. My head is pounding."

Reed walks into the cabin without knocking. I peek behind his broad shoulders and see Easton sprawled on a massive bed, holding a pillow over his head.

"Get up," Reed orders.

"Why?"

"Need you to keep Dad occupied." Reed laughs sardonically. "Well, he's occupied enough at the moment, but I want you up there in case that changes."

Easton pushes the pillow off his face and sits up with a groan. "You know I've always got your back, but listening to that woman is my idea of a nightmare. Those squeaky noises she makes when Dad—" He stops midsentence when he notices me behind Reed.

I can't see Reed's face, but whatever his eyes are conveying causes Easton to heave himself out of bed. "Gotcha."

"Keep the twins away, too," Reed says.

His brother disappears without another word. Rather than stay in Easton's cabin, Reed walks next door and gestures for me to follow him inside.

I stay put, crossing my arms. "What do you want?"

"To talk."

"Then talk here."

"Get in here, Ella."

"No."

"Yes."

I drop my arms and walk into the cabin. Something about this guy…he issues a command and I obey. I fight it at first, sure. I always fight, but he always wins.

Reed closes the door behind me and runs a hand through his windblown hair. "I've been thinking about what we talked about before."

"We didn't talk before. *You* talked." And my pulse speeds up because now I'm remembering what he'd said.

If I have to fuck you so you don't ruin my family, I'll do it.

"I want you to stay away from my brother."

"Aw, are you jealous?" As Callum would say, I'm poking the tiger, but I don't really care. I'm tired of this guy telling me what to do.

"I get it, you're used to a certain lifestyle," Reed says, ignoring my taunt. "I bet guys were lining up to drill you at your old school."

My heart stops when he grabs the bottom of his shirt.

"You have needs." He shrugs. "Can't fault you for that, and yeah, I haven't made it easy for you to make friends at Astor Park. Not a lot of guys have the balls to go against me and ask you out. They think you're hot, though. They all do."

Where on earth is he going with this? And why—oh my God, why is he taking off his shirt?

I gape at his bare chest. He has a six-pack that makes me drool, and his oblique muscles are tight and delicious. Heat spreads through my body. I clench my thighs together to try to stop the throbbing between them, but it just makes it worse.

He grins at me. Oh yeah, he's fully aware of the effect he has on me.

"My brother's a good lay." His eyes gleam. "But he's not as good as me."

Reed undoes the button of his cargo shorts and tugs on the zipper. I can't breathe. I'm frozen in place as he yanks the shorts off and kicks them away.

My legs start to shake. Everywhere I look I see smooth golden skin and tight muscle.

"Here's the deal," he says. "My brother and father are off-limits to you. If you have an itch that needs scratching, you come to me. I'll take care of it."

He rests his large palm between his pecs, then drags it lower.

All the oxygen is trapped in my lungs. I can't do anything but follow the trajectory of his hand. It slides over his abs and stomach, stops just above his groin, then shifts lower to delve past the elastic of his boxer briefs.

Reed's fingers close around his very obvious hard-on and someone moans. I think it's me. It must be me, because he smiles.

"You want this?" He pumps himself slowly. "You can have it. Lick it, suck it, fuck it, anything you want, baby. As long it's just with me."

My heart beats even faster.

Reed tips his head. "Do we have a deal?"

It's the calculated note in his voice that snaps me out of my trance. Horror and indignation rush to the surface, and I stumble backward, bumping my shins on the bed.

"Screw you," I choke out.

He looks unimpressed with my outburst.

I lick my lips. My mouth is dryer than the Sahara and yet I've never felt more alive. All my stripping, all my dodging of

Mom's handsy boyfriends, hasn't prepared me for this. Maybe there *were* guys lined up to sleep with me, but I was focused on working, caring for my mom, and then just surviving. I can't even remember the face of a single guy I went to school with last year.

The image of Reed standing here—buff, golden, and naked with his dick in his hand—will be burned into my memory forever.

He has everything a girl could want: the hard body, the handsome face that will still look good years from now, the money, and that extra something. Charisma, I guess. The ability to slay you with a single look.

The apple is dangling in front of me, juicy red and delicious, but, like the fairy tale, Reed Royal is the villain disguised as a pretty prince. Taking a bite out of him would be a huge mistake.

And I might be attracted to him, but I refuse to let my first time to be with someone who despises me. Someone who's trying to protect his perfectly capable brother from my innocent destruction.

But I don't want to leave without a taste either, because I'm not that strong…or stupid.

He may hate me, but he *wants* me. His grip on his dick doesn't ease up. If anything, his muscles bunch harder as if he's anticipating my touch.

This is what Valerie was talking about the other night when we were dancing. I didn't respond to the crowd, but Reed's hot eyes tracking my every move made me feel real. I know that if I was in Reed's head right now all I'd see would be *me*.

I saunter to the chair in the corner where a folded robe is wrapped in its sash. I pull the sash off and then run the strip of terry cloth through my fingers.

"Anything I want?" I ask him.

His eyes close momentarily and then snap open with so much need my knees nearly buckle.

"Yes. Anything." His response sounds as if it's wrenched out of him. "But just me."

"Why are you so desperate?" I taunt. "You had sex with someone just last night."

He makes a disgusted sound in the back of his throat. "I didn't have jack last night. You're the one who made out with East."

"And you weren't rocking the Range Rover so hard the tires were coming off?" I say sarcastically.

"That was Wade." My confusion must show because he clarifies. "The quarterback of Astor Park, friend of mine. The bathroom was full. He couldn't wait."

Something like relief floods me. Maybe this is the only way his pride lets us be together. Maybe I could have him. Maybe this is my good thing. My reward. I decide to test it.

"I want to tie you up."

His jaw hardens. He probably thinks that this is my kink—something I've tried out a dozen times before.

"Sure, babe, anything you want."

He's not giving in; he's baiting me. I kick myself for believing for a single moment that I'm anything more to Reed than a convenient warm body.

I approach him with growing resolve. "This is nice, isn't it?"

He watches me warily as I gesture for him to hold out his wrists. And for all my pretend nonchalance, I can barely stifle a gasp when his hand brushes against my bare midriff. Note to self: wear more clothes around Reed for my own self-preservation.

I'm not a Boy Scout or sailor. I know one knot—the shoelace one. I wrap his wrists twice and we both suck in a breath when the sash strikes the front of his boxers not once, but twice. "You're killing me," he says between gritted teeth.

"Good," I murmur, but my hands are shaking so hard I can barely get my simple knots tied.

"You like this? Me at your mercy."

"We both know that you're never at my mercy."

He mutters something under his breath about me not knowing shit, but I ignore him. I look around for a place to tie him to. The great thing about boats is that everything is bolted down. There's a shiny brass loop next to the chair and I lead Reed over to it.

Pushing him down in the chair, I kneel between his legs with the sash in my hands. He sits there like a God, a modern-day King Tut surveying the slave girl at his feet.

The throbbing between my legs is almost painful. All I can hear is a tiny, devilish voice asking me what the harm would be.

This guy wants me so bad that he hasn't lost an inch of his erection. Under the cotton, it's waiting for me to touch it just like he'd ordered—or begged. I've never had my mouth around a dick before. I wonder what it feels like.

Before I can stop myself I reach out and tug his boxers down far enough to free him. He hisses when I touch him. Oh wow. The softness surprises me. His skin is like velvet.

"You're..." Perfect, I want to say, but I'm afraid he'll make fun of me if do. I run my fingertips over him and take a deep breath. Need pulses in my blood.

"Is this what you want?" Reed asks. It's supposed to be a taunt but comes out as a plea.

I stare at his hard-on, intimidated by it. There's a pearl of liquid on the tip and...I lick it. But one taste isn't enough. I go back for seconds, lapping the tip like it's the hottest day in July and he's an ice cream cone about to melt all over my fingers.

"Goddammit." His fisted hands come to rest on the top of my head. "Suck it. Dammit. Suck it like I know you can."

His cruel words break through the fog of desire. I rear back.

"Like you know I can?" My defenses are so low that the vulnerability I've tried to keep from him seeps out.

"Like you..." He falters for a moment, unsettled by the hurt in my voice, but something causes him to rally. "Like you've done a thousand times before."

"Right." I release a shaky laugh. "Then you need to be secured for this, because I know tricks you haven't ever dreamed of."

I pull hard on the sash and tie it to the ring in the floor. I tie it tight. He watches me with glittering eyes. I want to punch him, really make him hurt. But he can endure physical pain, so the only thing I can do is make him believe that I'm going to ruin his precious family in ways that can't be rebuilt. Like the way he's breaking me apart into so many tiny pieces.

I climb onto the chair, my knees on either side of his strong thighs.

"I know you want me. I know that you're dying for me to get back on my knees." Curling my fingernails into his scalp, I jerk his head back so he can see my eyes. "But it will be a cold,

cold day in hell before you ever see me kneel again. I wouldn't touch you if you paid me. I wouldn't touch you again even if you begged me for it. Even if you vowed you loved me more than the sun loves the day or the moon loves the night. I'd screw your father before I'd screw you."

I push him away and climb off. "You know what? Maybe I'll go do that right now. I remember Easton saying your dad likes them young."

I saunter to the door with confidence I don't really feel. Reed jerks against his bonds but my simple knots hold him tight.

"Get back here and untie me," he growls.

"Naah. You're gonna have to figure that one out yourself." I step to the door and place my hand on the knob. Turning back, I plant a hand on my hip and taunt, "If you're better than Easton, then by way of experience, your dad has to be spectacular."

"Ella, get your ass back here."

"No." I smile at him and leave. Behind me, I hear him yelling my name. The sound gets fainter and fainter until his voice is just a bad lingering memory.

On the deck, Callum is tossing back booze while Easton is sleeping next to him in a lounger.

"Ella, are you okay?" Callum hurriedly gets to his feet and comes over.

I smooth down my hair and pretend to be unfazed. "I'm fine. Actually…I was just thinking about Steve and, well, I'd like to know more about him if you're willing to share."

Callum's whole face lights up. "Yes, definitely. Come over and sit down."

I bite my lip and look at my feet. “Could we go somewhere private?”

“Of course. How about my stateroom?”

“That would be perfect.” I beam.

His mouth drops open slightly. “God, that smile is all Steve. Come on.” He drapes an arm around my shoulder. “Steve and I grew up together. His granddad, who formed Atlantic Aviation with my granddad, was a sailor. Steve and I would sit and listen to his PawPaw’s stories for hours. I guess that’s where we got the urge to enlist.”

Easton’s head pops up as Callum leads me toward the stateroom. He stares at me, then at Callum’s arm. I brace myself for a snotty comment, one that I probably deserve this time. Instead he looks like I kicked him in the stomach—or lied to him—which is almost worse.

I LET CALLUM RATTLE ON about good ol’ Steve for about ten minutes before I interrupt him.

“Callum, this is interesting and I appreciate you sharing with me, but…” I hesitate. “I have to ask you a question that’s been bothering me from the moment I stepped foot in your house.”

“Sure, Ella. You can ask me anything.”

“Why are your sons so unhappy?” I think of Reed’s perpetually sullen face and swallow hard. “Why are they so angry? We both know they don’t like me and I want to know why.”

Callum scrubs a hand down his face. “You just have to give it some time. They’ll come around.”

I fold my legs up underneath me on the bed. There’s only one chair in the stateroom, so Callum sat on it while I took the bed. It's awkward to be in here sitting on a mattress while talking to my new father figure about my newly discovered but deceased father.

"You said that before, but I don't think they will," I say quietly. "And I don't get it. I mean, is it the money? Do they really resent you giving me money?"

"It's not the money. It's…shit—I mean, shoot." Callum stumbles over his words. "God, I need a drink." He laughs a little. "But I'd bet you wouldn't let me have one."

"Not now." I cross my arms. Callum wants me to be tough with him? I can do that.

"Straight up, no shit. That's how you want it, right?"

I have to smile. "Right."

He tilts his head back to stare at the ceiling. "At this point, my relationship with the boys is so broken I could bring Mother Teresa home and they'd accuse her of trying to get in my pants. They think I cheated on their mother and caused her death."

I make an effort to keep my jaw closed. Okay. Wow. Well, that explains some of it. I take a breath. "And did you?"

"No. I never cheated on her. I was never even tempted, not once during our marriage. When I was young, Steve and I ran a little wild, but once I married Maria I never looked at another woman."

He sounds sincere, but I feel like I'm not getting the whole story. "Then why are your kids always in a foul mood?"

"Steve was…" Callum looks away. "Hell, Ella, I wanted time for you to learn to love your father, not tell you all the crappy things that he did because he was lonely."

I grasp at every straw I can in order to force Callum to spill whatever it is he's trying so hard to hide. "Look, I'm not trying to be mean, but I don't know Steve and now that he's gone, I won't ever know him. He's not a real person to mean, not like Reed or Easton or you. You want me to be a Royal, but I'm never going to be one if everyone in the family doesn't accept me. Why would I ever come back after graduation to a place where I don't feel wanted?"

My attempts at emotional blackmail are a success. Callum instantly starts speaking, and I'm genuinely touched at how badly he wants me to be part of his family.

"Steve was a bachelor for a long time. He liked to brag a lot, and I think when the boys were younger they thought their Uncle Steve was the epitome of manhood. He'd tell them stories of our wilder days and I never stopped him. We spent a lot of time jetting around on business trips and Steve took advantage of that. I promise you I didn't, but... not everyone believed that."

Like his kids. Like his wife.

He shifts in his chair, obviously uncomfortable with this story. "Maria became depressed and I didn't recognize the signs. Looking back, I realize that her distance and moodiness were symptoms of a serious issue, but I was too busy trying to keep the business in the black during the recession. She was getting more and more pills with only the boys to keep her company. When she had the overdose and I was halfway around the world in Tokyo pulling Steve out of a whorehouse, they blamed me."

Maybe they were right to blame you, I think.

"Steve wasn't a bad guy, but you...you're...*evidence*, I guess. Evidence that he led me around by the nose into things that eventually killed their mother." His eyes plead with me for understanding, even forgiveness, but I'm not the one who can give him that. "When he got the letter from your mom, Steve changed. He was a new man overnight. I swear to you, he would have been the most attentive, doting father. He wanted kids and was over the moon when he discovered you. He would have started looking for you immediately but he'd had this trip planned for a long time with Dinah. It was hang-gliding in a place that apparently doesn't allow it, but Steve managed to bribe some local officials to let them make a run. He was going to look for you the minute he came back. Don't hate him."

"I don't hate him. I don't even know him. I…"

I trail off, because my thoughts are a jumbled mess. Somehow in the Royal boys' minds, their mother's death and Steve's involvement are all tangled up, and I'm a convenient—and living—target. There's nothing I can do that will change their opinion. I see that now. Still, I asked for the truth, and I won't blame Callum for this.

"Thank you," I say in a wobbly voice. "I appreciate you being straight with me." I could be completely virtuous and they'd still hate me. I could be Abby-like and…a thought pops into my mind and out of my mouth before I can stop it. "What was Maria like?"

"Sweet. She was sweet, kind. Just a smidge over five feet and the soul of an angel." He smiles, and in that instant I know he loved Maria. I've seen that kind of true love glow only once before—in the eyes of my own mother. She didn't have all her shit together, but she loved me.

Maria inspired the same love in her sons. That Abby is her replica and the opposite of everything I'm made of shouldn't bother me, but it does, because as much as I hate admitting it, the truth is I want Reed to feel that way about *me*.

Which is about the stupidest sentiment I have ever conjured up.

CHAPTER 19

REED DOESN'T LOOK AT ME the entire trip back to shore or when we arrive home. His brooding silence speaks loudly enough. He's furious and going to stay that way for a good long while.

I beg off dinner citing sunstroke, because there's no way I can endure an entire meal with Reed either ignoring I exist or needling me at every opportunity.

I know I brought this on myself, but when even Easton scowls as I'm heading up to my room, I wonder if I made a mistake.

"I thought you weren't going to screw my dad," he hisses as I pass by him in the hall.

"I didn't. I just wanted Reed to think I did." When Easton still looks doubtful, I let out a sigh. "All Callum and I did was talk about Steve." *And your mom*, but I figure Easton wouldn't appreciate that in his current mood.

He's not pacified one bit by my confession. "Don't play games with my brother. You've got him worked up and now he's gonna have to get it out of his system."

I blanch. "What do you mean?" I ask but dread the answer. He's running to Abby? That makes me want to puke all over Easton's deck shoes.

"Never mind." He waves me off. "You two should either screw or stay away from each other. Staying away from each other is my vote."

"Noted." I start to open my bedroom door but Easton grabs my arm.

"I'm serious. If you need someone, just come to me. I don't mind you so much."

Ugh. I'm done with these Royal boys. "Gosh, Easton. That's so generous. Does your pity sex offer have an expiration date? Or is it a coupon I can use whenever I feel like it?"

I stomp into my bedroom and slam the door in his confused face. It's early, but I decide to go to bed because I have to be at the bakery before the sun rises and then school, and there isn't a person in this house that I want to talk to right now.

I crawl under the covers and force myself to fall asleep, but I drift in and out, rousing at every door slam and foot stomp outside my bedroom.

In the late night hours, I hear furious whispering in the hall. The same furious whispering I heard the other night. Easton and Reed are arguing about something. I check the time. It's about the same time too—just after midnight.

"I'm going," Reed says flatly. "Last time you were pissed I wouldn't let you come and now you're whining when I invite you?"

Oh, that's a guaranteed button pusher.

"Hey, excuse me for worrying that your head's so far up your ass, you won't see a fist coming," Easton snaps back. Yup. Buttons pushed.

"At least I'm not panting after Steve's daughter."

"Yeah right," Easton says derisively. "Because that's why I found you nearly naked and tied to a chair. Because you don't want Ella at all."

They move off far enough down the hall that I can't hear Reed's full response but it sounds something like, "I'd rather bang Jordan than stick my dick in that trap."

My anger has me tossing the covers aside and shooting out of bed. Those two have secrets that they don't want me to know about? Well, if I'm in a war here at the Royal house, I need all the ammunition I can get.

I rush to the closet and throw on the first thing I touch, which turns out to be a miniskirt. Not the perfect creeper clothes, but I don't have time to waste. I jump into the skirt and pull on a T-shirt, then push my feet into my sneakers and creep out of my bedroom as quietly as possible.

I tiptoe down the back stairs. There's no one in the kitchen but I hear faint noises outside. A car door slams. Shit. I need to hurry. Luckily, the twins leave clothes, keys, wallets, and all kinds of junk down in the mudroom all the time.

I race across the kitchen to the connected mudroom and grab the first hoodie I find. There are keys and a wad of cash in the front pocket. Perfect. Ducking down beneath the window in the door, I peek out and see the taillights of Reed's Range Rover blinking down the drive.

I wrench open the door and haul ass to the garage. When the button on the key fob lights up the twins' SUV, I heave a sigh of relief and climb inside.

It's tricky to secretly follow someone in a car on a dark night down a quiet street, but I manage to pull it off, because Reed doesn't stop or whip his vehicle around to angrily confront me. He leads me into the heart of the city and then down several side roads until we arrive at a gate.

Reed parks his SUV. I cut the engine and shut off the lights. In the moonlight, I can barely make out the two brothers as they get out of the Rover and then clamber over the fence.

What the heck am I getting into? Are they dealing drugs? That would be nuts. The family is loaded. The hoodie I'm wearing has five hundred dollars in twenties and fifties balled up, and I'd bet the entire wad that if I went through each one of the pockets of the jackets hanging in the mudroom, I'd find loads of cash in every one of them.

So what could they be doing?

I run over to the fence to check if I can see anything, but all I can make out is a row of long rectangular-shaped structures—all roughly the same size. But no Reed or Easton.

Ignoring the inner voice that's telling me it's beyond stupid to climb a fence and rush into the dark, I do it anyway.

When I get closer to the buildings, I realize that they aren't buildings at all, but shipping containers, which means I must be in a shipyard. My deck shoes are soft on the bottom and make no noise, so when I come upon Easton handing a stack of cash to some hoodie-clad stranger, neither of them hear me.

I duck backward, using the container as a shield while peeking around the corner like an inept spy in a terrible action movie. Beyond Easton and the stranger, there's a makeshift circle set in the center of an empty space at the end of four shipping crates.

And inside that circle is Reed, stripped down to a pair of jeans.

He pulls one arm across his body and then switches to stretch the other arm. Then he bounces on the balls of his feet as if he's trying to loosen himself up. When I spot the other shirtless guy, all the pieces fall into place. The secret late night trips out of the house. The unexplained bruises on his face. Easton must be betting on his brother. Hell, Easton might be fighting, too, if I remember the argument between the two of them last week.

"I thought someone was following us, but Reed wouldn't listen."

I jerk around to find Easton standing right behind me. Then I go on the defensive before he can give me shit about following them. "What are you going to do, tell on me?" I mock.

He rolls his eyes, then pulls me forward. "Come on, you sneak. You're the cause of this. You might as well see it through."

I let him drag me to the edge of the circle, but I do protest. "I'm the cause of this? How do you figure?"

Easton pushes people aside and muscles us up to the front. "Tying Reed to a chair buck ass naked?"

"He had underwear on," I mumble.

Easton ignores me and keeps talking. "Leaving him hornier than a sailor after a nine-month stint at the bottom of the ocean? Please, sis, he's got so much adrenaline in his body right now that it's either fight or," he looks down at me with speculation, "screw, and since you won't screw him, it's this. Hey, big bro," he calls out. "Our baby sis came to watch."

Reed spins around. "What the hell are you doing here?"

I resist the urge to hide behind Easton's big frame. "Just here to cheer on the family. Go—" Royals, I start to say but then wonder if these guys are using aliases or something. I lift my fist, "Go, family!"

"East, if you put her up to this, I swear I'm going to beat your ass into next Sunday."

Easton holds up his hands. "Dude, I told you someone was following us but you couldn't hear anything over all your bitching about how you were going to teach someone," he tilts his head in my direction, "a lesson."

Reed scowls. He clearly wants to pick me up and throw me out into the dark. Before he can do anything, the other shirtless guy with thighs like tree trunks claps him on the shoulder.

"You done having your family reunion? I want to get this fight over with before the sun rises."

The anger in Reed's blue eyes dissolves into amusement. "Cunningham, you won't last five seconds. Where's your bro?"

Cunningham shrugs his massive shoulders. "He's getting his dick sucked by some casual. Now don't be scared, Royal. I won't hurt you too bad. I know you have to show your pretty face at Astor Park tomorrow."

"You stay here." Reed points at me and then at the ground. "Move and it'll be way worse for you."

"Because it's been so good up until now," I crack.

"Quit talking and start fighting," someone from the crowd yells. "If I wanted to watch a soap opera, I would've stayed home."

Easton punches Reed hard in the shoulder and Reed punches him right back. Both blows would have felled me but the two laugh like maniacs.

Cunningham backs up to the center and gestures for Reed to come after him. Reed doesn't hesitate. There's no dancing around, taking each other's measure. Reed launches himself at

Cunningham and for a good five minutes, the two exchange blows. I flinch at every contact Cunningham makes, but Easton just laughs and cheers Reed on.

"Easiest money I ever make, betting on Reed," he crows.

I fold my arms around my waist. Callum said he was in a dark place, but does he realize his sons are there, too? That they come out here and take blow after blow to rid themselves of whatever emotions that haunt them?

And what does it say about me that my palms are dampening and so are other parts of my body? That my breath is quickening and my heart is starting to race?

I can't take my eyes off Reed. His muscles are gleaming in the moonlight, and he's so incredibly beautiful in this animalistic form that something primal inside me responds in a way I don't know how to deal with.

"Getting you hot, isn't it?" Easton whispers knowingly in my ear.

I shake my head no, but my entire body screams *yes*, and as Reed strikes his final blow, one that swings Cunningham all the way around and drops him face-first to the concrete, I know that if he crooks his little finger at me, I won't be able to turn him away. Not this time.

CHAPTER 20

I DRIVE BACK TO THE mansion with Easton in the passenger side because Reed mutters that he doesn't trust me to get back on my own. I want to point out that I got to the shipyard fine all by my lonesome, but my mouth is cemented shut. Obviously Reed isn't to be messed with tonight.

He fought two more guys after Cunningham, and he kicked both their asses, too. Easton counted his winnings on the ride back and they totaled up to eight grand. It seems like a drop in the bucket compared to how loaded they already are, but Easton informs me that money is always sweeter when you've bled for it.

Reed didn't bleed, though. I don't think he'll even be bruised or sore tomorrow. That's how wild and powerful he'd been when he'd slammed his fists over and over again into those guys tonight.

In the driveway, I kill the engine, but I stay in the car because Reed hasn't gotten out of his yet. Easton doesn't stick around—he just tucks his cash in his pocket and ducks out of the SUV, heading for the side door without a backward glance.

It isn't until I see Reed slide out of the driver's seat that I do the same. We stand ten feet apart and our gazes lock. His hard eyes and tight jaw send a wave of exhaustion crashing over me. I'm so tired, and not because it's nearly two a.m. and I've been up since seven.

I'm tired of the hatred that rolls off Reed's body every time he sees me. I'm tired of fighting with him. I'm tired of the games and the tension and the unending hostility.

I take a step toward him.

He turns his back to me and disappears around the side of the house.

No. Not this time. He can't run away from me. I won't let him.

I hurry after him, grateful for the motion-activated lights that surround the house. They guide my way to the backyard and then beyond it, down the path leading to the shore.

Reed has a twenty-foot head start, and the advantage of having lived here all his life. With total ease, he navigates the rocks lining the beach until he reaches the water's edge.

I'm still making my way through the boulder-strewn sand when I see him kick off his shoes and socks and wade into the water. He doesn't seem to care that the bottoms of his jeans are getting soaked.

It's late, but not pitch-black. The moon is out, illuminating his gorgeous face. His shoulders are down, and he rakes both hands through his hair when I finally come up beside him.

"Haven't we tortured each other enough today?" His voice comes out weary.

I let out a heavy sigh. "It has been a pretty eventful day, huh?"

"You tied me to a chair," he mutters.

"You deserved it."

We go quiet for a moment. I slip out of my shoes and take a step forward, then squeal when the freezing-cold water soaks my feet. Reed grunts out a laugh.

"Is the Atlantic always this cold?" I blurt out.

"Yeah."

I stare at the water and listen to the waves crash against the shore. Then I sigh again.

"We can't keep doing this, Reed."

He doesn't answer.

"I mean it." I latch my hand on his arm and twist him around to face me. His blue eyes are expressionless, which I guess is better than the usual dose of contempt. "I don't want to fight anymore. I'm tired of fighting."

"Then leave."

"I already told you, I'm here to stay. I'm here to go to school and graduate and then go to college."

"So you say."

I let out an aggravated groan. "You want me to say something else? Fine, I've got plenty to say. I'm not hooking up with your father, Reed. And I'm never going to, because one, that's gross, and two, that's *gross*. He's my guardian, and I appreciate everything he's done for me. That's it. That's all it'll ever be."

Reed shoves his hands in his pockets and says nothing.

"All Callum and I did on the boat today was talk. He told me about my father, and honestly, I still don't know how I feel about all that. I never even met Steve, and from what I've heard about him, I don't know if I would have liked him. But I can't change the fact that he's my father, okay? And you can't keep holding it against me. I didn't ask for Steve to knock up my mom, and I didn't ask your dad to barge into my life and bring me here."

He scoffs. "You're saying you'd prefer to still be taking your clothes off for money?"

"Right now? Yeah," I say frankly. "At least I knew what to expect from that life. I knew who to trust, and who to stay away from. And say what you want about stripping, but no one, not a single person, ever called me a slut or a whore the whole time I was working the clubs."

Reed rolls his eyes. "Because it's such a respectable profession."

"It's a living," I shoot back. "And when you're fifteen and trying to pay your dying mother's medical bills, it's *survival.* You don't know me. You don't know anything about me, and you haven't even tried getting to know me, so you're not allowed to judge. You're not allowed to talk shit about something you have no clue about."

His shoulders go rigid again. He takes another step forward, causing water to splash my bare ankles.

"You don't know me," I repeat.

He tosses me a dark look. "I know enough."

"I'm a virgin, did you know *that*?" The words pop out before I can stop them, and he jerks in surprise.

He recovers quickly, a cynical look playing across his face. "Sure, Ella. You're a virgin."

"It's the truth." Embarrassment heats my cheeks, though I'm not sure what I'm embarrassed about. "You can keep thinking I'm a slut, but you're wrong. My mom got sick when I was fifteen—when the hell did I have time to screw around with boys?"

He laughs harshly. "Next thing you're going to tell me, you've never kissed a guy, right?"

"No, I have. I've done…some stuff." My cheeks are scorching now. "But not the big stuff. Not the stuff you keep accusing me of."

"Is this the part where you ask me to make a woman of you?"

My skin prickles with insult. "You're a real asshole sometimes, you know that?"

He frowns.

"I'm only telling you this because I want you to realize how unfair you're being," I whisper. "I get it, you've got issues. You hate your dad and you miss your mom and you like to beat people up for shits and giggles. You're messed up in the head, that much is obvious. I don't expect us to be friends, okay? I don't expect anything from you, actually. But I want you to know that I'm done with this…this feud we've got going. I'm sorry about the way I acted earlier. I'm sorry I tied you to a chair and let you think there was something between me and Callum. But as of this moment, I'm done fighting. Say whatever you want to me, think whatever you want about me, keep acting like a jerk, I don't care. I'm not playing the game anymore. I'm done."

When he stays silent, I wade out of the water and make my way back to the house. I've said my piece, and I meant every word. Seeing Reed beat the crap out of someone tonight really put everything in perspective for me.

The Royal brothers are even more screwed up than I am. They're hurting and they're lashing out and I'm the most convenient target, but fighting back only makes it worse. It only fuels their anger toward me. I refuse to engage anymore.

"Ella." Reed's voice stops me as I reach the upper deck.

I halt near the pool, and swallow hard when I glimpse the remorse in his eyes.

He reaches me, his voice thick with gravel as he says, "I—"

A loud voice slurs from behind us. "What are you kids doing out here so late?"

I smother my irritation as Brooke appears at the patio doors. She's in a white silk robe, with her blonde hair flowing over one shoulder. In her right hand she's clutching a bottle of red wine.

I notice that Reed cringes at the sound of her voice, but when he speaks, he sounds cold and indifferent. "We're in the middle of something. Go to bed."

"You know I can't sleep without your dad cuddled up beside me."

Brooke manages to make it down the steps without tripping. She comes up to us, and I sigh when I glimpse her alcohol-glazed eyes. Callum is a pro when it comes to drinking, but this is the first time I've seen Brooke drunk.

"Where's Callum?" I reach a hand out to steady her.

"He went to the office," she whines. "On *Sunday* night. He said there was an emergency he had to handle."

I can't help but feel a pang of sympathy. It's so obvious that Callum is not at all invested in his relationship with Brooke, and equally obvious that she wants so badly for him to love her. I feel bad for her.

"I didn't realize banging your secretary was considered an emergency," Reed says mockingly.

Her eyes laser toward Reed. I take a protective step toward him. "Let me take you inside," I tell Brooke. "To the living room. I'll get you a blanket and—"

She jerks out of my grip. "Are you the lady of the house now?" Her voice is reaching shrilly levels. "Because you're a fool if you think that you'll be anything to these Royals. And you—" she turns with a wild light in her eyes toward Reed, "—you'd better stop talking to me like that."

The retort that I was sure Reed would spit back never comes. I cast a questioning glance toward him, but he's gone. His expression is closed down, almost vacant.

"I'm going to be your mother someday. You should learn to be nicer to me." Brooke takes an unsteady step forward and strokes her manicured nails down his cheek.

He flinches and then pries Brooke's hand off him. "I'll be dead first."

He shoves past her and heads for the French doors. I hurry after him, leaving Callum's girlfriend on the patio.

This time I'm the one calling after him. "Reed."

He stops in front of the stairs in the kitchen. "What?"

"What…what were you going to say before Brooke interrupted us?"

His head turns. Blue eyes hard with malice peer back at me. "Nothing," he mutters. "Absolutely nothing."

Behind me I hear a crash. I want nothing more than to chase after Reed, but Brooke can't be left alone, drunk by the pool.

I hurry back to her side, where I find her staggering precariously close to the edge of the water. "Come on, Brooke."

I tug on her arm. This time she follows docilely, leaning her slight weight against me.

"They're all terrible," she weeps. "You need to stay away from them, just to protect yourself."

"It's going to be okay. Do you want to go upstairs or is the living room all right?"

"With the ghost of Maria staring at me?" Brooke shudders. "She's here. Always here. When I'm in charge, we're moving. We're razing this house to the ground and eradicating Maria."

That sounds unlikely. I lead her, half carrying, half dragging her into the living room where, yep, there's a portrait of Maria over the fireplace. Brooke holds her fingers up in the sign of the cross as we pass in front of it.

I have to swallow a laugh at the ridiculousness of this. The living room is actually a long room that runs along the front of the house. There are two seating areas so I pull Brooke to the second set that is closer to the window and farther away from the portrait of Maria.

She gratefully sinks onto the sofa, bending her knees and tucking her hands under her cheek. Her tears have smeared her makeup and she looks like a tragic doll, like one of the strippers who's so sure that the rich man who gives her the hundred-dollar tip is going to return and sweep her away. Of course, he doesn't. He's just using her.

"Brooke, if being with Callum hurts you like this, why do you stay?"

"Do you really think there's any man out there who *won't* hurt you? That's what men do, Ella. They hurt you." Her hand shoots out to grip my wrist. "You should get away from here. These Royals will ruin you."

"Maybe I want to be ruined," I say lightly.

She lets me go, pulling her hand back, retreating inside herself. “No one wants to be ruined. We all want to be saved.”

“There has to be at least *one* decent guy out there.”

That makes her laugh. Hysterically. And the laughter just keeps going and going.

I leave her to it, heading upstairs with the sound of her giggles tickling my back, this woman who honestly doesn’t believe she can find a man who doesn’t hurt her.

Why that conviction feels like she scraped a knife down my spine, I don’t know.

CHAPTER 21

REED DOESN'T DRIVE ME TO work the next morning. He's already left for football practice when I step out of the house, and I'm not surprised. I'm pretty sure that the last thing he expected to get from me last night was a truce offering. Which means he's probably on his way to school right now, obsessing about whether or not my apology was just another trick.

It wasn't, though. I'm sticking to the decision I made yesterday. I'm done antagonizing the Royals.

I take the bus to the bakery and work alongside Lucy for the next three hours, then walk over to school and duck into the bathroom to change into my uniform.

When I exit the ladies' room, I bump into the girl Easton was supposedly dating before. Claire, I think.

The second she sees me, her mouth pinches in a tight line. Then she brushes past me, leaving one hiss of a word in her wake.

"*Slut*."

That single syllable is like a fist to the stomach. I falter, wondering if I'd misheard her, but as I walk down the hall and every junior girl I pass glowers at me, I realize something's up. From the guys, I get grins and smirks. It's painfully obvious that for some reason, I'm a hot topic today.

It isn't until Valerie finds me at my locker that I'm brought into the loop.

"Why didn't you tell me you made out with Easton Royal?" she demands in a hushed voice.

My calculus book almost slips from my fingers. Wait, this is about *Easton*? But we were in my bedroom when we kissed, and there's no way Reed would have blabbed about that. So how the heck does everyone know—

The club. Crap. The memory whizzes into my head at the same time Valerie starts to laugh.

"I knew I should've kept a closer eye on you that night," she teases. "But we weren't even drinking! That means you made out with him *sober*! Do I need to hold an intervention for you?"

I sigh. "Maybe?"

The girls Val had introduced me to at Jordan's party—The Pastels, she'd called them—walk by. All three of them turn to look at me and whisper amongst themselves.

"It was a stupid move," I admit. "I didn't really think it through." No, all I was thinking about that night was Reed and the way he looked at me when I was in the cage. "Does everybody know, then?"

She grins. "Oh, they know. It's all anyone's been talking about this morning, and the first bell hasn't even gone off. Claire is *pissed*."

I bet she is. And if Claire's mad, I can only imagine what Jordan will have to say about it. A "casual" like me putting my grubby hands all over one of her precious Royals? She's probably freaking out right now.

"What about you?" I ask the only person who matters. "Are you pissed?"

Valerie snickers. "Because you stuck your tongue down Easton's throat? Why would I care about that?"

It's the answer I'd hoped for, and I cling to it as we part ways in the hallway and go off to our morning classes. It doesn't matter that everyone is whispering, or that chicks glare daggers at me whenever I enter a classroom. Valerie's opinion is the only one that matters to me.

Still, by the time lunch rolls around, I'm ready to pull my hair out. Every girl that passes me in the hall looks ready to murder me. Easton makes it worse by going out of his way to pay a visit to my locker and give me a prolonged full-body hug. He pretends not to notice all the stares we're getting, but I'm excruciatingly aware of them.

"You're Ella, right?"

I've just shoved my textbooks in my locker when a guy with spiky blond hair and a striped rugby shirt approaches.

His question is ridiculous, because he damn well knows who I am. These kids have all gone to school together since kindergarten probably, and there isn't a single soul at Astor Park Prep who doesn't know about the new "Royal."

"Yeah." I paste on an indifferent look. "And you are?"

"Daniel Delacorte." He sticks out his hand, then awkwardly lowers it to his side when I don't shake it. "I've wanted to introduce myself for a while, but…" He shrugs.

I roll my eyes. "But it was against Reed's rules?"

He nods sheepishly.

God, these people are the worst. "So why are you introducing yourself now?"

That earns me another shrug. "A couple friends of mine were at the club on Saturday night. They said they saw you with Easton."

"So?" I anticipate some kind of insult, but I don't get one.

"So the rules have changed. Nobody was allowed to ask you out before because of Reed. But you were with Easton the other night, so things are different now."

Wait, he's asking me out?

I narrow my eyes at him. "What, you're not going to call me a slut for making out with Easton at a club?"

His lips twitch with humor. "If I called every girl who's made out with Easton a slut, there'd be no one left in the school."

I can't help but laugh.

"I'm serious," Daniel insists. "Drunken make-outs with Easton Royal are like a rite of passage at Astor Park."

"Are you speaking from personal experience?" I ask politely.

He flashes a grin. The guy's cute, I'll give him that. "Luckily, no. Anyway, I just came over to ask if you wanted to go out for dinner sometime."

A jolt of suspicion travels through me, and Daniel must sense it because he quickly says, "It doesn't have to be a date. We could make it a friend thing if that makes you more comfortable. I just want to get to know the girl who's got all the Royal panties in a twist."

I'm still hesitating, so he lets out a hasty breath. "Can I see your phone?"

Although I'm not sure why, I stick my hand in my back pocket and pull out my phone, passing it over to him.

His fingers move briskly over the touchpad. "There. You've got my number now. So how about this? Think it over, and if you decide you want to do dinner, shoot me a text."

"Um. Okay. Sure."

Daniel smiles again and gives me a little salute before striding off. I watch him go, my gaze focusing on his cute butt. He's got the toned body of an athlete, and I suddenly wonder if he's on the football team. I hope not, because that means Reed will probably hear about Daniel asking me out when they're at their afternoon practice.

But I underestimated the grapevine at this school. The news of Daniel's invitation comes out literally five minutes after he issued it. I'm two steps from the cafeteria when I get a text message from Valerie.

Daniel Delacorte asked u out????

I respond with *yeah.*

Did u say yes?

I said I'd think about it.

Don't think 2 hard. He's one of the nicer ones.

Another text quickly pops up. *Captain of the lacrosse team.* She adds this as if that makes a difference to me.

Rolling my eyes, I enter the cafeteria and track Val down at our usual table in the corner. She grins the moment she sees me, tucks her phone away, and says, "Okay. Tell me everything. Did he get down on one knee? Did he give you flowers?"

For the next hour, she barrages me with questions about a guy I only spoke to for two minutes. Truthfully, it's a nice distraction from this morning's whisper fest, and it stops me from obsessing over what Reed will have to say when he finds out.

CHAPTER 22

I DON'T SEE REED UNTIL after school, and when I do, he's not racing over to demand that I stay away from Daniel. Instead, he's bracing himself against the driver's side door talking to Abby. And the soft blonde is leaning against Reed's Rover with one hand on his hip. The whole scene makes me want to gag.

"They look cozy."

I turn to see Savannah next to me. We haven't spoken at all since the day she gave me a tour of the campus, so I'm surprised to find her there. "I guess."

"Heard Daniel Delacorte asked you out today." She smooths a hand over her stick-straight hair.

"Apparently it's a slow news day at school," I joke. "But yes."

"Don't do it," she says abruptly. "You'll regret it if you do."

After dropping that bomb, she steps off the curb and hurries to her car, leaving me open-mouthed and confused.

Before I can make sense of the warning, a low slung convertible sports car moves into my line of vision. Daniel smiles up at me from the driver's seat.

"Nice car." I peer at the interior. It's black and full of shiny dials. "Sounds like a beast."

"Thanks. Gift from the parents when I was sixteen. I was a little concerned when I heard it had four hundred horsepower. I wondered if my dad thought I needed to overcompensate for something."

I grin. That he has the ability to make a joke about himself makes me warm up to him. "And do you?"

"Ella," he tsks jokingly. "You're supposed to reassure me that I have nothing to worry about in the man department."

"How would I know?" I tease.

"Here's a secret." He leans across the console and gestures for me to come closer. "We males have very fragile egos. It's best to always compliment us so that we don't turn into psychopaths."

"You have nothing to worry about in the man department," I dutifully reply.

"That's my girl." He nods in approval. "Want a ride home?"

I straighten and scan the lot for Easton, the twins or even Durand, but it's empty of Royals except for Reed, who doesn't see me. His attention is on the angelic faery girl who reminds him of his mother.

Daniel tracks my eyes straight to the couple. "Abby and Reed," he muses. "That's a couple destined to be together."

"Why do you say that?" I sound annoyed and I am, but I wish I hid it better.

"Reed's picky, not like Easton. I've seen him with one girl the last two years. I think she's it for him."

"So why aren't they together?"

We both watch as Reed's head dips close to Abby's, as if they're about to kiss.

"Who says they're not?" Daniel's observations are careless, unintended to hurt me, but the pain spreads inside me anyway. "You give more thought to my proposal?"

My eyes shift away from Reed toward Daniel. Daniel is the quintessential rich boy. Kind of like what I thought the Royals would look like: blond hair, blue eyes and a face that probably adorns paintings in old English museums. The Royals are almost thuggish compared to his easy elegance. Any girl would be thrilled to be asked out on a date by Daniel, and I think it says something bad about me that I can't summon up any excitement for him.

"I'm kind of a mess right now," I inform him. "There's better—more together—fish in the pond."

He studies me for a moment. "I can't figure out if you're trying to let me down gently or if you aren't giving yourself enough credit. Either way, I'm not giving up."

I'm saved from making a response when a loud horn blasts behind us. We turn to see that Reed has maneuvered his Rover so close to Daniel's sports car that the fenders are nearly kissing. The juxtaposition between the two vehicles is almost laughable, with the Rover towering over the smaller two-seater convertible. It looks like the Rover is just waiting to drive right over the top of Daniel's car.

Daniel leans back into the driver's seat and puts his car in gear. With a mischievous glint in his eyes, he tilts his head toward Reed. "Someone is overcompensating but I don't think it's me."

With that, he peels away, leaving a space that Reed quickly occupies. Daniel's wrong. Reed has nothing to overcompensate for. His oversized SUV matches him perfectly.

"You going out with him?" Reed asks the moment I close the passenger door.

"Daniel?"

"Did some other guy ask you out, too?"

I wish he wasn't wearing sunglasses. I can't see his eyes. Is he mad? Frustrated? Pleased?

"No, just Daniel. And I'm thinking about it." I search his profile. "Any reason not to?"

A muscle in his jaw flexes. If he gives me the smallest opening, I'd take it. *Come on, Reed. Come on.*

He offers a brief glance before returning his eyes to the road. "I think we called a truce last night, right?"

I want it to be more than a truce, and the thought surprises me. A ceasefire is one thing, but admitting to myself—and to him—that I want to act on the attraction between us? That feels like a dangerous mistake.

"Yeah, something like that," I murmur.

"Then I'd be a dick if I told you not to go out with him."

No, I think, *you'd be telling me you cared about me.* "I don't think looking out for someone's well-being violates the spirit of our truce," I say lightly.

"If you're asking if he's going to hurt you, I'd say no. Haven't heard of him bragging in the locker room about girls he's hooked up with. I think everyone considers him a decent guy." Reed shrugs. "He's with the lacrosse team. Those guys tend to stick together so I don't know him too well, but well enough, I guess. If I had a sister, I wouldn't object to her dating him."

That's not my question! I shout at him in my head. Out loud, I poke at him from a different angle. "Are you and Abby getting back together?"

"We were never together," he says roughly.

"You looked kinda cozy just now. Daniel said you two are meant to be a couple."

"Did he?" Reed sounds amused. "Didn't know Daniel had that kind of interest in my love life."

"So Abby is part of your love life?" I'm a glutton for punishment with all these questions.

"What exactly are you asking?" He turns left and I can't see his face because of it.

Too embarrassed to press the topic, I slump back into the seat. "Nothing."

After a beat, Reed sighs. "Look, I'm going away to college next year. And unlike Gideon I'm not coming back every other weekend. I need time away from this town. This family. Abby and I had a nice time, sure, but she's not my future and I'm not going to dick her around—or anyone else, for that matter—just to get my nut off."

And there's my answer. Even if he is attracted to me—though I notice he was careful not to say it—he's not going to do anything about it. He's leaving as soon as possible. I should admire that kind of honesty, but I don't. Some silly part of me wants him to declare that if he wanted me bad enough, no principles would ever prevent him from having me. God, I'm a sick puppy.

I turn away from him and watch the city pass us by as Reed navigates home.

Finally, tired of the silence, I blurt out, "Why do you fight? Is it for the money?"

He releases a sharp bark of laughter. "Hell no. I fight because it makes me feel good."

"Because you won't let yourself sleep with Abby? So you have to go out and pound a few guys to get rid of whatever is building up inside of you?" The words slip out before my brain catches up.

Reed stops the Rover and I look around, surprised to see we're already home. He pulls off his sunglasses finally and stares at me.

My throat goes dry. "What is it?"

He reaches out and fingers a lock of my hair. His knuckles are inches away from my breast and it takes superhuman effort not to lean into his touch, not to press his hand fully against me.

"Do you really think it's Abby who's keeping me up at night?"

"I don't know." I hesitate. "I don't want it to be."

I hold my breath, waiting for him to answer, but all he does is drop my hair and grab the door handle.

Without turning back to look at me, he says, "Daniel's a good guy. Maybe you should give him a chance."

I SIT IN THE CAR after he leaves so I can regain my composure. Neither of us explicitly stated it, but I know it's out in the open now. I laid my feelings out there and he told me to keep them. He did it in a nice way, but a clean knife still makes a painful wound.

Brooke is sitting poolside when I enter the house. She seems to have recovered from last night's drinking session. She's babbling away to Reed, who stands next to her lounger, stiff as a board, as her hand runs up and down his bare calf. I've seen her touching Gideon like that, too, and I wonder why the boys put up with that. I know they can't stand her. If there was one thing that Callum could do to repair his relationship with his sons, it would be to jettison Brooke.

Lonely and irritated, I seek out Easton, who's slumped on his bed watching a car show where they take it apart and put it back together so it looks like a cartoon vehicle.

"So we're trucing, huh?" He grins when he spots me.

"Is that even a word?" I ask as I walk into his room.

"It sounds like a word, so I guess it has to be."

"Douchetard sounds like a word, too, but I'm pretty sure you won't find it in the dictionary."

"You calling me a douchetard?"

"Naah. You're just a regular old douche."

"Aw, thanks, little sis."

"You know we're the same age, right?" I roll my eyes and climb onto the bed next to him. Easton rolls over to make room for me.

"I've always been older and wiser than my years."

"Uh-huh. Sure."

"Seriously, though. Reed says we're all cool now. Is this for real, or are you playing another game?"

"I was never playing a game to begin with," I grumble. "And yeah, I think it's for real." He looks more relieved than I expected. "Anyway, I wanted to ask you something. What do you think of Daniel Delacorte?"

"Why do you want to know?"

"He asked me out after he heard you kissed me. Apparently that was like the kiss of approval."

Easton waggles his eyebrows at me. "I'm magical, aren't I?"

"You're something." I throw a pillow at his head, which he catches and tucks under his chest. "Why did you kiss me?"

"I was horny. You were there. I wanted to kiss you." He shrugs and turns back to the television. Felt good. Wanted to. It's so simple for Easton. He's driven by his base urges. Eat, drink, kiss, repeat.

"Why'd you kiss *me*?" he counters.

My reasons seem more complicated. I wanted to make Reed jealous. I wanted to prove to myself and everyone else in that club that I was desirable. I wanted a warm, affectionate touch from someone—anyone. I guess my reasons aren't so different from Easton's, after all. "I wanted to."

"Want another go at me?" He pats his cheek in invitation.

Laughing, I shake my head.

"How come?" He's unfazed by my rejection.

"Because…just because." I avert my eyes.

"Nuh-uh, you're not getting off that easy. I want you to say it. Tell your big brother about your crush on your other big brother."

"You're imagining things. I'm not crushing on Reed," I lie.

"Bull."

"I'm not," I insist, but Easton sees right through me.

"Shit, Ella, I need a smoke every time you two are within five feet of each other." He grins, but almost immediately sobers. "Look, I like you. Didn't think I would but I do, and because I like you, I feel the need to warn you that we Royals are pretty fucked up. We're good in bed, but out of it? We're like a stage four hurricane."

"And Daniel?"

"He's a good guy. Isn't a slut like me. Guys on the lacrosse team like him. His dad's a judge."

"Any rumors about him?"

"Not that I know of. You planning on hooking up?"

"Savannah said—"

"You can't listen to a word she says," Easton interrupts.

I eye him suspiciously. "Why not?"

"She and Gid had a thing last year."

My jaw falls open. Seriously? Savannah and *Gideon*? I think back to the campus tour, to Savannah's blunt explanation of how the Royals run the school, but I don't remember her showing any emotion when she said it. Except...she *had* been staring at him during Jordan's party. Staring hard, like she was trying to mentally erase him from her sight.

"Savannah was this awkward middle-schooler," Easton continues. "Braces. Kind of weird hair. Don't know what she did to it. Maybe a different cut or something. Anyway she comes into tenth grade totally changed. Gid took one look at her and slapped his name on her ass. But sometime around Uncle Steve's death, things changed. He dropped her hard and she's been a Bitter Betty ever since."

"Damn," I whistle. Savannah and Gideon. I can't even picture them as a couple.

"Told you. Stage four hurricane." He makes a wrecking motion with his hand, then sighs and turns back to the TV.

CHAPTER 23

DANIEL IS WAITING AT MY locker the next morning. Even though Reed and Easton both gave me their approval, I'm still torn about Daniel. But I need to move on from Reed. That much is clear.

Daniel barely has a chance to say hello before I lay down the law. "I need to tell you up front that I'm the opposite of a sure thing," I explain awkwardly. "Right now I'm dealing with big changes in my life and I can't handle anything heavy."

"I got you," he promises. He leans down and plants a soft kiss on my cheek. "You're sweet. I can wait."

I'm sweet? Other than my mom, nobody has ever called me that. I think I kind of like it.

DANIEL MEETS ME AT MY locker every day after that, sharing something funny and then leaving me with a kiss on the cheek. Easton teases me about it at night, but every time I look at Reed for a response, his face is impenetrable. I have no idea how he feels about all the attention I'm getting from Daniel, but at least our truce is still intact. Even Callum has noticed the difference in the Royal mansion. When he walked past my bedroom the other night and saw me and Easton watching TV together, I swear his eyebrows almost jumped off his face.

On Friday I bring Daniel an apple cruller, which he told me was his favorite pastry at the French Twist. And this time, the kiss he gives me is directly against my lips—soft and dry but surprisingly not unpleasant.

A loud bang at the end of the hall scares me and I jump back, nearly dropping his gift.

"Easy there." Daniel plucks the pastry from my hand. "You can't be damaging the food. That's a serious violation of the Geneva Convention. I'll have to haul you in for punishment." His eyes are twinkling.

"Are you trying to go out with me for my access to baked goods?" I ask in mock suspicion.

"Oh man." He slaps a hand to his heart. "You found me out. Am I in trouble?" His antics draw a smile from me. "Ohh, I got you to smile and that's bad because, sweetheart, that smile is a killer. I think my heart stopped." He taps his chest. "Have a listen."

Daniel's so obviously corny and lighthearted, I decide to play along. I lean my head against his chest and listen to the easy, even thumps of his heartbeat.

Beside me, I hear a gagging noise. When I straighten, I see Easton sticking his finger down his throat. He rolls his eyes at us and keeps walking. At his side, Reed doesn't look up. He looks so hot in his untucked uniform shirt that I have to force myself to look away.

Daniel laughs. "So you coming to the game tonight?"

"I think so." I lock my knees so I don't turn around to see what Reed is doing. "But I probably won't get there until the second half. I work until seven on Fridays."

"How about the party after?"

"I'm going with Easton," I admit. We agreed last night that he'd take me to the post football party. Val is staying home because she has a Skype date with Tam. Which sucks because I always have more fun when she's around.

Throughout the entire discussion between me and Easton about the game and whose car we'll take to the party, Reed stood there like a statue. He didn't say a word, and I just wanted to smash his mute button to pieces and force him to talk to me. But that would probably destroy the truce.

I can't decide what I like more. The calm Royal household with the voiceless Reed or the one where he's yelling at me to stay away and threatening me with his penis.

"I gotcha. We can hang, right?" Daniel asks.

"Right."

As he flashes one of his million-dollar smiles and saunters off, I wonder why I don't just say yes to him.

THE PARTY IS AT ONE of the lacrosse players' mansions. Farris somebody. I don't know him. He's a senior like Reed and supposedly a hardcore science geek. He and another science guy are mixing drinks that they're serving in glass beakers. They fully committed to the act by putting on white lab coats that hang open to display washboard abs, demolishing any nerd stereotype.

I choose the strawberry daiquiri even though the bartender/chemist tries to foist a weird-looking green thing into my hand.

Easton turns it all down. "I drink beer," he declares. "All the hops inside me will protest if I introduce something fruity into my system."

After I take my beaker, Easton leads me away. "That stuff can be real strong so be careful tonight," he warns.

I take a sip. "It tastes like a smoothie."

"Exactly. These guys are masters at getting everyone hammered without anyone realizing it."

"Okay. One drink is all I'll have." I'm touched that Easton is looking out for me. I've never had that before. I sweep the room looking for Reed, but I don't see him anywhere. Pathetically, I check with Easton. "Is Reed coming?"

"I don't know. Probably, but…I saw him with Abby again tonight after the game."

I chug half the beaker in response.

Easton searches my face. "You gonna be okay?"

"Peachy," I lie.

"If you need anything, I'm only a phone call away." He holds up his cell. "But for now, I need to get laid, little sis." He pops a kiss on my cheek and heads out toward the pool.

Daniel sidles up the moment Easton disappears. His eyes twinkle playfully. "Jeez, I thought the chaperone would never leave. Come on, I'll introduce you around."

He wraps an arm around my shoulder and takes me from group to group. Kids at school who haven't given me the time of day are suddenly nodding, smiling, and making conversation as we talk about the game we won tonight. The opponent next week, who we'll crush. The hobbit chem teacher no one likes and the art teacher everyone does.

The experience is almost dreamlike. I'm not sure if it's because Daniel is by my side, or if news of the Royal truce has trickled down to the little people, but everyone is nice. Their smiles are bright, and the laughter—the shared giddiness—is infectious. My cheeks ache from smiling so much.

"You having a good time?" Daniel murmurs into my hair.

I lean against him. "I am. I really am," I say in surprise. Reed is off somewhere and this time it's probably him and Abby rocking his Range Rover and not Wade, who I saw inside with a girl perched on his knee. But so what? Nice Daniel is here with his solid arm across my shoulders and his warm body snugged up to mine. A strange sluggishness creeps over me. The alcohol is stripping down my defenses, just like Easton warned, and a prickle of alarm zips up the nape of my neck.

"Let me get you another drink," Daniel offers.

"I think..." I stare up at him, unsure of what I'm thinking.

"She needs to use the bathroom."

I frown at the intruder. Savannah Montgomery. What's she doing here? Before I can protest, she drags me off to the closest bathroom and shuts the door.

I watch as she turns on the faucet and dips a hand towel under the stream of water.

"What the hell is going on right now?" I demand.

She turns with a cloudy expression. "Look," she says bluntly, "I don't like you much—"

"Gee, thanks."

"—but I wouldn't let even my worst enemy be sucked in by Daniel."

My confusion triples. "What's wrong with Daniel? Reed and Easton vouched for him. They said he's a good—"

"You want some advice?" she cuts in. "Don't take a Royal's word for anything."

That bitterness Easton had mentioned is now painfully obvious. It's in the tight set of her jaw, the harshness of her words.

"I get that you don't like them," I say softly. "I heard about you and Gideon—"

She interrupts again, her green eyes burning with disgust. "You know what? I changed my mind. You and Daniel are perfect for each other. Have a great night, Ella."

With that, Savannah throws the wet towel at me and it strikes me across the face, soaking the front of my T-shirt. Bewildered, I hang the towel up and pluck the wet fabric away from my chest. What the hell just happened?

Daniel is waiting outside the bathroom, concern etched into his face. "What's wrong? You and Savannah get into it?"

"Not exactly. I don't know what happened back there other than she got mad and soaked my shirt." I point to the wet Astor Park T-shirt I borrowed from one of the twins and tied in the back to make it fit.

"Do you need another shirt? I can grab one from Farris' room." He points upward.

"No, that's okay. It'll dry." I flap the fabric. It's thin enough that it should dry fairly quickly.

He nods. "Look, I don't want to say anything bad about her, but Sav isn't a real happy person these days. Don't let it rub off on you."

"Yeah, I get that."

"They're setting up a dart game in the other room. You interested?"

"Sure, why not."

He hands me a water bottle. "Don't know if you want this since you're already soaked, but I thought you might like it. Those drinks Farris mixes are potent."

"Thanks." I twist the bottle open, noting that the seal hadn't been broken. Daniel clearly falls in the good guy category, and I'd be really stupid not to at least give him a chance.

His arm bumps against my shoulder as we walk down the hall.

"You know, Daniel..." I take a breath. "I think we should go out."

"Yeah?" He beams.

"Definitely."

"All right then." He pulls me to his side and kisses me on the temple in another nice, reassuring move. "But first, let's go kick some ass in darts."

The dartboard is a bar-sized thing in the pool house at the back of the Farris property. The sight of two other girls already lounging on a leather sectional eases my mind that Daniel hadn't immediately assumed my agreement for one date meant I'm ready to get down.

"This is Zoe and Nadine. They're from town."

Zoe lifts a limp wrist. "We go to South East High."

"Didn't we just play your team tonight?"

"Yup," she confirms. "And now we're celebrating."

I have to laugh. "But you lost."

"Then I guess we're getting consoled." She and Nadine giggle again.

"Good thing we have Hugh here."

Hugh is a wiry guy, a few inches taller than me, who takes a drag of whatever it is he's smoking and merely nods.

Daniel winks at the girls. "Well, Ella and I have a date with the dartboard. You three want to join us?"

"Nope. We'll just watch. Hugh likes watching, don't you, Hugh?"

Hugh blows smoke in their faces, which makes them laugh even harder. Not hard to guess these girls are drunk or stoned.

"You want red or yellow?" Daniel holds up two darts.

"Red."

He hands me the red darts, then pulls me over to the dartboard. Before I can throw mine, I feel a prick in my upper arm.

"Ouch!" I slap my hand over my arm. "What was that?"

He holds up his yellow dart, looking sheepish. "I poked you with my dart."

"Jeez, Daniel, that hurt. Not even funny." I rub the sore spot.

He frowns at the point of his dart. "I'm sorry. I must have pricked you too hard."

I force myself to relax. "Just…don't do it again, okay?"

He draws me into his arms. "It won't happen again."

I let him hold me for a minute because the contact feels really good. When he releases me, I have to catch myself on a nearby table. My balance is off. I must be still experiencing the effects of the drink. We play one round and then another. My aim is terrible and I hit the wall more than I hit the dartboard. Daniel makes a few jokes about how he hopes I never have to compete in the Hunger Games.

By the third round, my mouth is strangely dry. I reach for my water bottle, but my hand misses and knocks it over. "Oh crap. Sorry."

I hear the girls giggle behind me. I fall to my knees and look for something to mop up the floor with. My shirt. My shirt is absorbent and already wet. Besides, the fabric is really bothering me. Actually, all of my clothes are starting to irritate me. My bra feels too tight and the elastic of my underwear is digging into my skin. The threads of the hem of my skirt scratch my thighs every time I move. I should take off my clothes.

"That's a good idea," Daniel agrees.

I must have said that out loud. "My clothes *are* bothering me," I confess.

"Yes, let's take off our clothes!" one of the girl shouts from the sofa. I hear a rustling of fabric and then more giggles.

"My head is stuck," one of them chirps.

"Why don't you two help each other out?" Hugh suggests.

I push to my feet, bracing myself against Daniel's shoulder. Zoe tugs Nadine's top off and throws it at Hugh. He drops it to the floor and strolls over to the sofa.

"I should go," I tell Daniel. I have a good idea what's going to happen between the three of them, and I don't really care to watch.

Daniel tugs me against his body again, wrapping an arm around my waist. His physical response to the scene unfolding in front of me is unmistakable.

"Where's Reed?" I turn abruptly. The tingling between my legs makes me think of him. "I need him."

"No you don't. You've got me." Daniel grinds himself slowly against me.

"No." I jerk out of his grasp. "I'm sorry, Daniel. I don't think…I'm not…" I raise a hand to my head and shakily push it through my hair. Need is pulsing through my blood. I can hear my heartbeat, loud and fast, in my ears. I force myself to concentrate. "I need Reed."

"Jesus, you stupid bitch. Just close your eyes and enjoy it."

His voice isn't nice anymore. It's cold and annoyed. He yanks at the bottom of my shirt. I bat at his hands but my movements lack coordination and he's got my top off before I can protest.

"How's it going over there?" I hear Hugh say. His voice is close. Very close.

"She's just rolling. I gave her some molly. She thought I pricked her with a dart." Daniel sounds delighted with his trick. I try to swing out a fist but my arm is too heavy.

Hugh pauses. "Dude…You think you should be doing that with Ella Royal? I thought we were going to stick with out-of-towners after the thing with Savannah's cousin. No good to shit where you eat."

Daniel snorts. "The Royals can't stand her. She's not going to say anything. She's trash. Trumped-up nobody made me work for a week."

He cups my face and it feels so good. I wish Reed was here and that it was his hand.

I moan his name.

"What'd she say?"

Daniel laughs. "I think this chick banged both Easton and Reed." He roughly fondles my boobs and the contact draws another groan from me.

"Shit, she's horny," Hugh gloats. "Awesome. Can I have her when you're done?"

"Sure. Let me do my thing and then she's all yours."

"How loose do you think she is? Heard she's had a lot of action."

"Don't know yet. Can't get her damn legs open." He pushes me down onto a chair and thrusts a knee between my legs.

"Why not give her a little coke? That'll wake her up."

"Yeah, good idea."

The pressure disappears as Daniel gets up and stalks over to the counter. I watch with alarm as he rummages through a drawer.

"Where does Farris keep that shit…I thought it was here… Oh, maybe the fridge."

I hear muffled voices from outside the pool house. "Ella… seen her…Daniel…pool…"

"Reed." I force myself to get to my feet. "Reed." I stumble past the two girls who are busy kissing each other.

"Hey, hold up." Daniel slams a drawer shut and races over to me, slapping his hand on the door before I can pull it open. "Where you going?"

"I need to leave," I insist and grab for the doorknob.

"No you don't. Come back here."

We fight for the door. Daniel has something sharp and shiny in his hand. "Hugh. A hand please," he calls.

I pound on the door. "Reed! Reed!"

Daniel curses and Hugh yanks me away, but they're too late. The door bursts open and Reed appears. His blue eyes immediately become enraged when he spots the three of us.

I lurch toward him. Daniel, in his surprise, lets me go and I fall on the floor.

"What the *fuck* is going on?" Reed growls.

"Shit, man, she's trashed," Daniel says with a hasty laugh. "I had to bring her here so she wouldn't embarrass herself."

"No, no," I protest, trying to sit up but it's all a muddle. I can't find the words to explain myself. I can only look up at Reed in despair. He'll hate me now. He'll really believe I'm a slut. All the fight drains out of me. I'm done.

More people arrive and five sets of big feet line up before my eyes. The number of people here to witness my humiliation grows. I drop my head to the tiled floor hoping that it opens up and swallows me whole.

"You have two options." Reed starts speaking. His voice is strong and calm, as if he's giving a morning address to the student body. "You can either apologize and tell the truth, and only one of us will beat your face in. Or you lie and we all take turns making your body into a science project. Choose your words carefully."

Is he talking to me? I think he might be. I raise my head to protest that I did nothing wrong, but when I look up I see a wall of Royal bodies. All of the brothers are there. Every single one of them, including Gideon. Their arms are crossed and their faces are thunderous. But none of them are looking at me.

I peer over my shoulder where Daniel is, his hands at his sides and a syringe dangling between his fingers.

He clears his throat. "Reed, I didn't do anything—"

"Guess you've made your choice."

"A really stupid one, too," I hear Easton mutter.

Dismissing Daniel from his gaze, Reed leans down and lifts me into his arms. He folds me against his chest, one arm holding my bottom, the other wrapped tightly around my shoulders. This guy has been my enemy, the source of so much emotional pain. But right now, I cling to him as if he holds the only comfort I will ever find in this world.

INSIDE THE RANGE ROVER, I begin to cry. "Reed, something is wrong with me."

"I know, baby. It's going to be okay." He lays a cool hand on my leg and the sensation is mind-blowing.

"I need you to touch me." I try to drag his hand upward.

He groans. His grip tightens on my leg, just for a second, but then he pulls away.

"No," I protest. "That feels good."

"Daniel shot you up with ecstasy, Ella. You're in a drug-induced state of horniness and I'm not taking advantage of you."

"But—" I argue, reaching for him.

"No," he barks back. "Now, please. For the love of God, will you please be quiet and let me drive."

I scuttle back, but the prickling sensation on my skin doesn't stop. I rub my legs together to ease some of the ache and I find that helps a little. I'd rather have the touch be from Reed, but my own hands are providing relief and so I take it. I run my hands over my thighs, down my calves. My skin feels like it's alive and I reach under Reed's borrowed shirt to massage away the ache.

"Jesus, Ella, please. You're killing me here."

Embarrassed, I try to stop. "I'm sorry," I apologize in a small voice. "I don't know what's happening."

"Let's just get you home." He sounds exhausted.

The rest of the car ride is agonizing. It takes all my mental energy to keep from touching myself.

Reed whips the car down the lane and then jumps out of the Rover before the engine dies down. He jerks open the door and I tumble out into his arms. We both moan—me in relief, and him in frustration.

Other car doors slam and the other brothers join us with Sawyer running ahead to get the door.

Gideon speaks up. "She's going to have a long night. One of you needs to help her."

"In what way," Reed grinds out.

"You know." Gideon's voice is low.

"Fuck."

"You want me to do it?" Easton asks.

I curl into Reed. His grip around me tightens. "No. No one but me."

My head is foggy as he carries me up the stairs and deposits me on the bed. When he moves away, I reach for him in dismay. "Don't leave me."

"I won't," he promises. "I'm just getting a washcloth."

I start crying again when he disappears into the bathroom. "I don't know why I'm so weepy."

"You're drugged to hell. Molly. Coke. God knows what else he gave you." Reed sounds disgusted.

"I'm sorry," I whisper.

"I'm not mad at you." He presses the cold cloth against my forehead. "I'm mad at myself. I did this. Well, Easton and I. I brought this on you. I'm Reed the Destroyer." He sounds sad. "Didn't you know that?"

"I don't like that name."

He sits next to me, drawing the cloth around and around my face, down my neck and onto my shoulders. It feels heavenly. "Yeah, and what would you call me instead?"

I open my mouth and say, "Mine."

CHAPTER 24

WE BOTH STOP BREATHING.

"Ella," he starts, but he doesn't finish. He just watches as I sit up.

I pull the wet cloth from his hand and toss it onto the floor. His borrowed shirt follows shortly after.

"Ella," he tries again.

But I'm done with him trying to be noble. I need him right now.

I climb onto his lap, winding my legs around his hips. "Ask me why Daniel was so angry with me before."

Reed tries to untangle my legs. "Ella—"

"Ask me."

There's a beat, and then his attempts to push me off him stop. His hands come to rest on my thighs, and a full-body shiver races through me. "Why was he so angry with you?" Reed asks hoarsely.

"Because I wouldn't stop saying your name."

His eyes flare.

"Because it's you. It's always been you and I'm tired of fighting it."

Cloudiness fills his expression. "My brother—"

"You," I repeat. "Always you."

I lock my hands at the nape of his neck, and he groans. "You're not thinking clearly."

"Not 'cause of the drugs," I whisper. "Haven't been thinking clearly since I met you."

Another groan leaves his lips. "I feel like I'm taking advantage of you."

I tug his head down to mine. "I need you, Reed. Don't make me beg."

And just like that, he gives in. One hand comes up to tangle in my hair while the other pulls me roughly against him. "You don't ever have to ask again. I'll give you anything you want."

His mouth slants over mine, softly at first. Just featherlight touches, as if he's memorizing the shape of my lips with his own. And then, just when I'm about to plead for more, he sweeps his tongue inside my parted lips and kisses me so deeply that I feel dizzy.

We tumble back onto the mattress. His hands find my hips and they move me against him. His mouth is fused to mine, hungry and demanding. I pour everything I have into the kiss. All my love, my loneliness, my hopes, my sadness.

Reed takes it and gives me everything in return. We tangle up in each other's arms, and his mouth finds the pulse points behind my ear and at the base of my throat, as he kisses me like he can't get enough.

He pushes one thigh between my legs and even through my panties and his jeans, I find the relief I need. Almost. It's still not enough, and I make my unhappiness known in the form of an agonized moan.

He raises himself up on his elbows and peers down at me, his eyes at half-mast, lips swollen from our kisses. He is the hottest guy on the planet, and he's mine. At least for tonight.

"More," I beg.

He grins, then rolls over on his side and slides one hand between my legs.

A shockwave rocks my body.

"Better?" he whispers.

Not even close. I squirm, and another grin tugs at the corners of his mouth before his gaze smolders again. His palm moves in a small circle, and the heel of his hand presses into the spot that's aching for him.

My body is like a live wire, seconds away from exploding. Literally seconds, because all it takes is another rub of his palm and pleasure bursts inside me. I gasp and tremble, stunned by how incredible it feels. Maybe it's the drugs, but I like to think it's Reed. His low murmur of encouragement as I rock against his hand. The proof of his excitement pressing against my hip.

His lips find mine again, and I kiss him with renewed urgency, because the need is rising again, faster than either of us expected. I reach for him, pulling on his shoulders until he's on top of me.

Our mouths collide and he groans when I arch upward to rub against him. The hardness of his body is the only thing providing me relief. He's huge and ready, but when I reach between us, he pushes my hand away.

"No." His voice is tortured. "This isn't about me. Not tonight. Not when you're..."

Drugged, I think he wants to say, but I don't feel high anymore. Or at least not high on anything other than *him*.

His mouth latches onto my neck, kissing and sucking it as he rocks his body against mine. The pleasure builds, but his jeans are getting in the way. I don't want this to just be about me. I want—

He swats my hand away again and then moves off me altogether. But he doesn't go far. Heat prickles my skin as he kisses a path across my breasts. Warm lips brush my nipple. When his tongue comes out for a taste, I see stars. When his mouth closes over me, I stop breathing.

Each teasing lick makes me hotter and hotter. Under his grip, I thrash, my body straining for something elusive. He shifts again, taking my other nipple into his mouth. And then he moves lower, his lips gliding down to my stomach.

"Oh my God," I whisper. My nerve endings hum with need. "Reed," I beg.

"It's all right, baby, I've got you. I know what you need."

My heart stops when he moves between my legs. I can feel his hand trembling as he slides the thin panties down my legs. A sharp intake of breath is all he gives before his mouth lowers onto me.

I cry out from the unfamiliar sensation. It feels good. *So* good. His tongue finds a sensitive spot, causing my hips to buck up. A loud moan flies out. I dig my teeth into my bottom lip to try to stay quiet, but Reed is driving me crazy. I almost pass out, grabbing the back of his head to pull his hair.

He peers up with smoky eyes. "You want me to stop?"

"*No*."

He keeps going. His tongue is magic, flicking against me in a relentless rhythm. He makes a husky noise as if my response is as wonderful as all the things he's making me feel.

His fingers trace a path up my inner thigh. He lifts his head to ask for silent permission. I give it to him with an anxious nod. I want this so bad.

His eyes close as he slides one finger slowly inside me. He grits his teeth. "You're so fucking tight."

"Told you so," I manage to choke out.

He laughs. "Yeah, you did." He pulls out and glides a hand over my thigh. "I'm going to make this feel so good for you."

"I already feel good," I protest, drawing up my legs.

A cocky, familiar grin shines up at me. "You haven't seen anything yet."

He settles back between my legs, and his shoulders push me open so far that I should be blushing, but all I can feel is anticipation. With one arm looped around my thigh, he eases his finger back inside me.

The muscles in my legs tighten. My fingers dig into his skull but he doesn't stop kissing me even as the pleasure crashes over me in waves that drag me under. Once I go limp, he climbs up and lies beside me, drawing me toward him.

His lips find my neck again and he breathes deeply.

"Why did you have to come here?"

I'm confused by the question. "I...you know why. Your father—"

"I mean why now." His frustrated words heat my skin. "Maybe another time, away from this place, you and me would have a different story."

"I don't understand what you're saying."

"I'm saying this can't happen again." He lifts his head, and I see his misery. "I need to go away. I need to leave this goddamn place and remake myself into something better. Someone…worthy…" His voice trips on that last word.

"Worthy," I echo in a whisper. "Why do you think you're not worthy?"

He's silent for a moment. His palm absently caresses my shoulder. "It doesn't matter," he finally says. "Just forget it."

"Reed…"

He sits up and shrugs out of the spare T-shirt he'd put on in the car. The other shirt, the one he ripped off his back and put on me when we were leaving the party, sits discarded on the floor, along with the rest of my clothes.

"Close your eyes, Ella," he says roughly, settling beside me again. He's shirtless now, but still wearing his jeans. The denim scratches my bare leg when I swing it over him. "Just close your eyes and go to sleep."

My voice is muffled against his bare chest. "You promise you won't leave?"

"I promise."

I snuggle closer, losing myself in the warmth of his body and the steady beating of his heart beneath my ear.

When I wake up the next morning, Reed is gone.

CHAPTER 25

"YOU DOING GOOD, LITTLE SIS?" Easton eyes me from the kitchen table as I stagger into the kitchen feeling like I'd been run over by an eighteen-wheeler.

"No. I feel awful." I pour myself a glass of water at the sink, chug it, then pour another one.

Easton's tone is lined with sympathy. "You crashed hard, huh? Happened to me, too, the first time molly walked into my life."

"Molly?" Callum's curious voice says from the doorway. "Got a new girlfriend, Easton? What happened to Claire?"

I can see Easton fighting back laughter. "Claire and I are dunzo. But this Molly chick is pretty cool." He shoots me an impish grin.

My head is pounding too hard for me to even crack a smile. Callum's gaze shifts to me, and he's visibly startled. "Ella, you look terrible." Suspicion darkens his face as he swings back to his son. "What kind of trouble did you get her into last night?"

"Just the usual liquid trouble. Turns out Ella can't handle her liquor."

I give him a grateful look behind Callum's back. I guess the Royal truce also includes covering for each other. Not that I willingly took drugs last night. My hands curl into fists as I remember Daniel's lust-glazed eyes and the way he'd groped me.

"You got drunk last night?" Callum's mouth is tight as he turns back to me.

"A little," I confess.

"Oh, come on, Dad, don't get all parental on us now," Easton pipes up. "You gave me my first beer when I was twelve."

"Eleven for me," Gideon says, striding into the kitchen. He's shirtless, and there's a noticeable scratch mark over his left pec. He glances at me, his sympathy obvious. "How you feeling?"

"Hung over," Easton answers for me, then glances pointedly at his brother when their dad isn't looking.

Callum still isn't happy with me. "I don't want you drinking excessively."

"You jealous she might dethrone you as Excessive Drinking Champion of the Royal family?" Easton cracks.

"That's enough, Easton."

"Hey, just pointing out the hypocrisy, Dad. And, apparently, the double standard. You don't give a shit when any of us get wasted, so why can't Ella?"

Callum looks from his sons to me, then shakes his head. "I guess I should be happy that you all are sticking up for each other now."

Footsteps echo in the hall, and my breath lodges in my throat when Reed enters the kitchen. Black track pants ride low on his hips, and his muscular chest is bare and slightly damp, as if he's just come out of the shower.

He doesn't look at me as he heads for the fridge.

My spirits plummet, though I'm not sure what kind of reaction I expected. Waking up alone was a clear message. And what he'd said yesterday—*this can't happen again*—only makes that message clearer.

"Oh, Ella," Callum says suddenly. "I forgot to tell you. Your car is arriving tomorrow, so you'll be able to drive yourself to work on Monday morning."

Although I'm relieved that Callum can finally say the word "work" without frowning at me, I'm also hit with a rush of disappointment. At the fridge, Reed's back stiffens. He knows what this means, too. No more carpooling for us.

"That's great," I say meekly.

"Anyway." Callum glances around the kitchen. "What's everyone's plans for today? Ella, I was thinking you and I could go to—"

"I'm going to the pier with Valerie," I interrupt. "We're having lunch at this seafood restaurant right on the water that she keeps raving about."

He seems disappointed. "Oh, all right. That sounds like fun." He turns to his sons. "Anyone want to hit the driving range with me? It's been ages since we've all gone."

Not a single Royal brother takes him up on his invitation, and when Callum trudges out of the kitchen looking like a lost puppy, I can't help but frown.

"You guys can't even try to make an effort?" I ask them.

"Trust me, we make an effort." It's Gideon who answers, and his ugly sneer catches me off-guard.

When he stalks off, I look at Easton. "What's up his ass?"

"No clue."

For once, Easton is as clueless as I am, but Reed must know something we both don't, because he scowls and says, "Lay off Gid."

Then he walks out, too. He hadn't looked at me, not even once, and the pain that squeezes my heart is a thousand times worse than any hangover.

LUNCH WITH VALERIE IS FUN, but I beg off early because my head still feels like it's being stabbed with rusty knives. She laughs and tells me that the bigger the hangover, the better the party must have been, and I let her believe the same thing Callum believes—that I drank a little too much and now I'm being punished for it.

I don't know why I don't tell her about Daniel. Val is my friend, and she'd be the first person in line to beat the bejeezus out of Daniel for what he did to me. But something holds me back from telling her. Maybe it's shame.

I shouldn't feel ashamed. I *shouldn't*. I didn't do anything wrong, and if I'd had even the slightest suspicion that Daniel was such a psycho, I never would have gone into the pool house with him. Ever.

But each time I think about last night, I picture myself ripping my clothes off and whispering Reed's name while Daniel's slimy hands ran all over my body. I picture that and I'm flooded with shame.

And I can't even distract myself by thinking about what happened afterward—the good part, when I was whispering Reed's name for other reasons. I can't think about it because it makes me sad. Reed wanted me last night, and he gave me as much of himself as he'd been willing to give, but now he's taken it away again.

Valerie drops me off at the mansion and speeds off in her housekeeper's car. She told me at lunch that her boyfriend is coming home next weekend, and I'm looking forward to meeting the guy. The amount of time she spends talking about Tam, I feel like I already known him.

It's another beautiful afternoon, so I decide to change into my bathing suit and lie by the pool for a while. Hopefully the sunshine will make me feel human again. I grab a book and get settled on a lounger, but I only have about twenty minutes of solitude before Gideon strides out in his Speedo.

Of all the Royal brothers, Gideon is probably the one with the least amount of body fat. He has a swimmer's frame, and Easton told me he got a full ride to college on a swim scholarship. The twins insist that he'll be winning gold at the next summer Olympics, but it's a good thing there are no Olympic officials around today, because they'd reject him in a heartbeat. His strokes are uneven, and his pace is alarmingly slow.

But maybe I'm worried for nothing. I mean, I've only seen him swim one other time. Maybe he's just taking it easy today.

"Ella," he calls as he heaves himself out of the pool nearly an hour later.

"Yeah?"

He walks toward me, dripping water all over the deck. "There's a party on the beach tonight. At the Worthington estate." He rubs his towel over his chest. "I want you to stay home."

I arch a brow. "You're in charge of my social calendar now?"

"Tonight I am." His tone brooks no argument. "I mean it. Stay away from the party."

After last night, I have no interest in going to another party ever again, but I still don't appreciate being told what to do. "Maybe."

"No maybe about it. Stay home."

He disappears into the house, and not even five minutes later, Easton walks out and looms over my chair. "Brent Worthington is having a—"

"A party," I finish. "Yeah, I know all about it."

He rubs a hand over the stubble on his jaw. "You're not going."

"You've been talking to Gideon, I see."

His expression reveals that he has, but then he tries a different approach, flashing me that boyish grin of his. "Look, there's no reason for you to go out, little sis. Take the night off, relax, watch some soap operas—"

"Soap operas? Who do you think I am, a fifty-year-old housewife?"

He snickers. "Fine, then watch some porn. But you're not coming with us tonight."

"Us?" I echo. "Is Reed going?"

Easton shrugs, and the way he avoids my gaze raises my hackles. What the hell do they have planned for tonight? Panic tugs at my belly. Is Daniel going to be there? Is that why they want to keep me away?

I don't get a chance to ask the question, because Easton is already dashing off. Sighing, I pick up my book and try to concentrate on the chapter I'm reading, but it's no use. I'm worried again.

"Hey."

I look up and find Reed approaching. For the first time today, he actually meets my eyes.

He lowers his broad body into the chair next to mine. "How you feeling?"

I tuck my book at my side. "Better. My head isn't pounding anymore, but my body still feels kinda weak."

He nods. "You should eat something."

"I did."

"Then eat more."

"Trust me, I'm stuffed." A grin springs to my lips. "Valerie shoved an insane amount of shrimp and crab legs down my throat at lunch."

His lips twitch.

Smile, I beg silently at him. *Smile at me. Touch me. Kiss me. Anything.*

The smile doesn't surface. "Listen, about last night..." He clears his throat. "I need to know something."

My forehead creases. "Okay."

"Did you...was it..." He lets out a breath. "Do you feel like I took advantage of you?"

"What? Of course not."

But the intensity in his eyes doesn't waver. "You need to be straight with me. If you feel like I took advantage, or did anything you didn't want me to do...you have to tell me."

I sit up and lean toward him, cupping his face with both hands. "You didn't do anything that I didn't want you to do."

His relief is obvious. When I sweep my thumbs over his jaw, his breath hitches. "Don't look at me like that."

"Like what?" I whisper.

"You know what." Groaning, he moves my hands off his face and rises unsteadily to his feet. "It can't happen again. I won't let it."

Frustration jams inside me. "Why not?"

"Because it's not right. I'm not…I don't want you, okay?" A sneer forms. "I was being nice to you last night because you were hopped up on E and you needed some relief. I was just doing you a solid, but that's all it was. I don't want you."

He marches away before I can answer. Or rather, before I can call him a big fat liar. He doesn't want me? Bullshit. If he didn't want me, then he wouldn't have kissed me like he was a starving man and I was his only source of nourishment. If he didn't want me, he wouldn't have worshipped my body like it was the greatest gift he'd ever received, or held me in his arms until I fell asleep.

He's lying to me, and now my concern levels are at an all-time high. Not just concern, but determination, because clearly Reed Royal has secrets I can't even begin to decode.

But I will. I'm going to find out everything. Why he keeps everyone at a distance, why he feels unworthy, why he's pretending there isn't something between us when we both know there is. I'm going to learn all his secrets, dammit.

Which means…I guess I'm going to another party tonight.

CHAPTER 26

I need reinforcements or, at the very least, intel. From what Gideon said, the Worthingtons live down the shore and close enough that you must be able to hear some noise at the Royal property. They also must have kids close in age to the Royal brothers. But that's about it.

Good thing I know someone who's gossip central.

Valerie answers on the first ring. "You need more seafood? I told you that the best cure for a hangover is food."

The thought of even one more piece of shellfish in my stomach makes me want to barf. "No thanks. I was wondering if you were done Skyping with Tam and wanted to come over and spy on the Royals with me."

Valerie sucks in a breath. "I'll be right over."

"Hey," I interject before she hangs up. "Do you have a car?"

"No. And you can't ask one of the brothers to pick me up, can you?" she says glumly.

"Don't worry. Durand will pick you up. Hell, once I tell Callum I want to have a friend over, he'll volunteer."

"Oh, Callum. Nice. He's hot for an old guy."

"Gross, Valerie. He's like over forty."

"So? He's what they call a silver fox. You know who's into those?"

"I have no idea. One of the Pastels?"

"Oh hell no. Those girls wouldn't know what to do with an adult male, let alone one with a few decades under his belt. Jordan's older sister! She's twenty-two and constantly bringing home old guys. The last one actually had gray hair and I swear he was older than Uncle Brian. I can't decide whether she's super kinky and these are the only guys who know what they're doing, or if she has daddy issues."

"My insult to Jordan at her party might have hit a little too close to home then?"

"Probably didn't help," Valerie says cheerfully.

"I'm hanging up now because I'm seriously thinking of vomiting up my lunch over this discussion." I lay the phone down and try to scrub any thoughts of Callum doing kinky things from my brain.

Fortunately, Durand is available and Valerie is brought to the Royal estate in quick order.

"Wow, this place is so…" She gropes for the right word as she gapes at my bedroom.

I supply several. "Juvenile? Girlie? An homage to Valentine's Day gone wrong?"

She falls backward on the pink ruffled bedspread. "Interesting."

"That's one word for it." I settle into the white fur-covered vanity chair and watch Valerie bat at the sheer curtains that hang around the four-poster bed. "Want something to drink? I actually have a mini fridge in here." I open the glass door of the beverage cooler situated under the counter of the vanity.

"Sure. I'll have diet whatever. Besides the pink, this is a great room. Television, posh bed." She touches the bedspread. "Is this silk?"

I have my hand in the fridge when she drops that bomb. "I'm sleeping on a silk blanket?"

"Technically you sleep under it. I mean, you don't have to but you're supposed to sleep on the sheets and under the coverlet." Valerie looks all concerned as if my upbringing was so bizarre I might not know about sheets. Sadly, she's not *that* far from the truth.

"I know that, smart ass." I pull out a Diet Coke and shove it in her hand. I pop one open for myself. "It's just weird. I went from sleeping bag to silk blankets or—excuse me—coverlets," I correct myself before Valerie can. But enough about bed stuff. I need intel. "Tell me everything you know about the Worthingtons," I order.

"The telecom Worthingtons or the real estate Worthingtons?" she asks, her mouth still around the opening of the pop can.

"I have no clue. They live close to here and are having a beach party tonight."

"Oh, then the telecom Worthingtons. They live about five houses down." She holds up her can. "Do you have a coaster?"

I throw her a notebook, which she uses to set her can on.

"Brent Worthington is a senior. He's super uptight, although more about name recognition than money. His girlfriend Lindsey's parents had to declare bankruptcy a couple of years ago and pulled Lindsey from Astor Park because they couldn't afford the tuition, but Brent never broke up with her because Lindsey is a DAR."

"What do the Dars do?" I ask.

Valerie laughs and shakes her head. "No, that's not a last name. Daughters of the American Revolution. She can trace her family tree back to one of the original three boats that came over from England."

"That's a thing?" I gape.

"Yup. So what's going on?"

"The Royals are going there tonight and told me to stay away."

"Why? Those parties are pretty bland as far as high school events go. They lock all the doors in the house because Brent doesn't want anyone having sex in the rooms. There's one bathroom that people are allowed to use and it's right off the patio. The pool house is locked, too. Brent has it catered and likes for everyone to show up like they're about to go yachting. He even wears his country club sports coat and all of the girls wear dresses. No exceptions."

Sounds terrible. If the Royals had given me this rundown, they wouldn't have even needed to warn me away. But they did, so that means something is happening that they don't want me to see or be a part of.

"Would Daniel Delacorte be invited?"

She considers it and then nods slowly. "Yeah. His father is a judge. I think Daniel plans to be one, too, and you can't have too many judges as your BFFs, right?"

It occurs to me then and there that this is why the rich get richer. They form these bonds in high school, maybe even earlier, and when they get older, they just continue to scratch each other's backs.

"Did something happen between you and Daniel the other night? I know you were hung over but Jordan said you were so trashed Reed had to carry you out of Farris's house. He didn't...do something?" She looks worried.

I don't want to tell Valerie about the awfulness of that night, but if she's going to be involved, then she deserves something. "He thought I was easy. I'm not. And the Royals don't like it when their maybe, not really, but kind of sister is messed with. Let's leave it at that."

She screws up her face. "God, what a douche. But why am I here if the Royals are already exacting revenge?"

"I don't know if they are, only that three of them told me I wasn't to come to the Worthington party tonight no matter what."

Valerie's eyes light up. "I love that you don't care what the Royals think." She hops off the bed and throws open my closet door. "Let's see what Worthington-approved dresses you have."

I drink the rest of my Coke as Valerie rifles through, and discards, item after item.

"You need more clothes. Even the Carringtons stuff my closet full of anything I want. It keeps up appearances, you know. I didn't realize Callum was that stingy with you."

"He's not," I answer, stung on Callum's behalf. "I had to go shopping with Brooke and the places she took me were too expensive."

"Everything around here is expensive." Valerie waves her hand. "Think of it as an extension of your uniform. Besides, if you look bad, then people will think the same thing I did—that Callum is being cheap with you. Ah ha!" She pulls out a navy sundress with tiny cap sleeves and a deep V-neck edged in white lace. I don't remember seeing it, which means Brooke must have picked it out when I wasn't looking. "This is nice. It has a deep neckline that says I'm sexy without saying I charge fifty bucks and I'd like my cash up front."

"I'm bowing to your better judgment." In my former line of work, you'd need a neckline a heck of a lot deeper than that to get fifty bucks up front. I cross the room and start to change. It's getting late and I want to make sure I head over to the party before the fireworks start.

"You okay if I borrow this dress?" Valerie drapes a white lace number against her body.

"Knock yourself out." She's an inch shorter than me and given the length of the skirt, the hem should hit her around mid-thigh. "Out of curiosity, how many dresses do I need?" Two seems plenty.

"A couple dozen."

I whirl around, but Valerie looks dead serious. "You're joking."

"I'm not." She hangs the dress back in the closet and starts poking up her fingers one by one. "You need afternoon dresses, boating dresses, clubbing dresses—both the country club and the night club kind"—my head is spinning— "garden party dresses, official school party dresses, after school dresses, wedding dresses, funeral dresses—"

"Did you say funeral dresses?" I interrupt.

Valerie points her finger and winks. "Just making sure you were paying attention." She laughs when I roll my eyes, and starts undressing. "You do need a lot more clothes than you have. Appearances are important, even to the Royals." Her voice is muffled as she pulls her shirt over her head. "Example—say even the most minor negative thing about Maria Royal and all her sons go crazy. Reed almost got locked up for assault after some kid from South East High called her a pill-popping suicide case."

"He accused Maria of killing herself?" I exclaim, shocked by that.

Valerie looks around as if expecting to see Reed jump out at her. Then she lowers her voice and says, "It's a rumor, and one the Royals don't like. They even sued Maria's doctor for malpractice."

"Did they win?"

"It was settled and the doctor left the practice and the state so…yes?"

"Wow."

"Anyway," Valerie continues, "they're fiercely protective of their mom, and I'd guess it would be important that people outside of the family believe they're treating you right."

A pang hits me. Is that what Reed is doing? Just making sure he upholds the family reputation? No, it can't be. All the things we did in here, on that silk blanket and under it, were private and had nothing to do with any Royal reputation.

I check the clock and realize I need to hurry. I change in a rush, but when I look in the mirror, I see a problem. "Val, this neckline is too low." I turn so she can see that the white bow of my bra is showing.

She shrugs. "You'll have to go without. Wear Band-Aids if you're worried about nipping out."

"I guess." Although being in the same zip code as Daniel without wearing a bra kind of skeeves me out.

It takes us another half hour to fix our hair and makeup. I actually do Valerie's face. She's astonished at the amount of makeup I've accumulated.

"You might need dresses, but your makeup kit is the bomb dot com," she exclaims.

"Thanks but you need to shut up now so I don't get lipstick on your teeth." I wave the lipstick brush at her threateningly and she closes her mouth obediently.

Once we're ready, we wait around for the Royals to leave. There's a general slamming of doors and scuffling of feet in the hall. At least one set stops at my door.

There's a deafening bang that makes me wince, followed by Easton's voice. "You okay in there? We'll be home earlyish."

"Don't care," I call back, pretending to be pissed. "And don't knock on my door again. I'm mad at you. All of you."

"Even Reed?" Easton jokes.

"All of you."

"Ah come on, sis, this is for your own good."

Suddenly I don't have to fake my anger. "You Royals wouldn't know what was good for me if it was shoved in your face by a Playboy Bunny."

Valerie gives me two thumbs up in encouragement.

Easton heaves a big put-upon sigh. "Of course I wouldn't be able to see anything if a Playboy Bunny was in front of me. I'd be too busy ogling her tits to pay attention to anything else."

Valerie can't stop herself from laughing.

"Don't," I hiss. "You'll only encourage him."

"I hear you and yes, I am encouraged," Easton calls out from behind the door. "We'll be home in a couple of hours. Wait up and we'll all watch a movie."

"Go away, Easton."

He shuffles off.

"Easton's adorable. If I wasn't so in love with Tam, I'd pursue Easton hard," Valerie admits.

"I don't think catching him is the problem," I reply dryly.

"No? Then what is?"

"Keeping him."

CHAPTER 27

CARRYING OUR SHOES, VALERIE AND I walk down the shoreline toward the Worthington place. "What stops people from crashing the party?" I ask curiously. "Can't anyone just walk down this beach and then up into the house?"

"They'd know you didn't belong just by the clothes you were wearing. Plus, the only people who have access to this beach live on it, and unless you can afford a ten million dollar pad, you won't be on this sand."

"Will we be turned away?" The thought hadn't even occurred to me because I've never encountered parties like this before.

"Nope, because you're Ella Royal and even though I'm a poor relation, my last name is still Carrington."

We don't even get far enough in to be confronted by Brent Worthington, because the five Royal brothers are clustered together at the edge of the property. They're cooking something up, just like I knew they would. And it's definitely a scheme to get back at Daniel, because who else could they be targeting?

If anyone deserves to get revenge, it's me. I stomp right up to their group and they don't even notice.

"Hey big bro, what's going on?" I poke Gideon in the back.

Reed swivels around and chastises me first. "What are you doing here? I told you to stay home."

"So did I." Gideon looks down at me with a tight-lipped frown.

"Me, too." Easton tosses in his two cents.

"And you two?" I look pointedly at the twins, both of whom are dressed in identical khaki shorts and white polo shirts with an alligator over their left pec. They blink innocently at me. There's no way to tell them apart tonight, which might be exactly what their girlfriend enjoys. I'm going to have to mark one with lipstick before the night is over. "Well, newsflash, I'm not a dog. I don't just sit and stay because you order me to. Why was I supposed to stay away anyway? Are the drinks drugged here, too?"

Behind me, Valerie gasps, which sends five annoyed glares in my direction.

"No," Gideon says, "but if something bad goes down, Dad wouldn't be as angry if you were home and tucked in your bed."

"Or making out with Valerie," Easton pipes up. "But in bed and at home were the important things," he adds hastily when it's his turn to get a number of condemning stares.

"You being here might tip off Daniel that we're planning something," Reed says, his scowl deepening.

Valerie steps to my side. "If the plan was to not be suspicious, then Easton should have his tongue in someone's mouth, Reed should be whispering sweet nothings to Abby"—

gag me—"Gideon should be doing college stuff and you two," she waggles a finger between the twins, "should be pranking people because damn if I can tell you apart."

Easton covers a laugh with a fake cough while the twins pretend to be looking anywhere but at Valerie. Reed and Gideon exchange a long look. When it comes to the Royal brothers, these two are in charge. At least for tonight.

"Since you're here, there's no point in making you go home, but this is Royal business." Gideon gives Valerie a pointed look.

She's quick. "Suddenly I feel very thirsty. I think I'll go shake down the hosts for a glass of champagne."

After Val leaves, I rub my hands together. "So what's the plan?"

"Reed is going to start a fight and beat the ever loving shit of out Daniel," Easton informs me.

"That's a terrible plan."

They all turn to me again. Being the single focus of five Royals is kind of overwhelming.

I focus on Reed and Gideon, the two that I need to convince. "You think you're just going to goad Daniel into a fight?" Both brothers shrug. "And I'm sure you think it's going to work because all of you would fight to defend your name. But this guy has no honor. He's not a fair fighter. He's the type of guy who drugs a girl because he wasn't confident or patient enough to win her over. He's a coward." I wave a hand over Reed's insanely ripped body. "Reed has twenty pounds on him and fights regularly."

"She knows about the fighting?" Gideon interrupts. Reed gives an abrupt nod and Gideon flicks both hands at us as if he's done with our high school asses.

"He's still going to want to defend himself," Reed argues.

"I bet you a hundred bucks he'll laugh and say that he knows you're going to win. Then if you try to push it, you'll look like the bad guy."

"I don't care."

"Fine. If all you want to do is beat him up then just go and do it." I point to the back lawn, which is getting crowded.

"Reed can't throw the first punch," Easton interjects.

Puzzled, I look from one brother to another. "Is this some kind of fight club rule?"

"No. Dad caught Reed fighting a few months ago. Said if he caught him doing it again he'd ship the twins off to military school."

Wow, that's diabolical. I know that Reed wouldn't care about going to military school—or at least not care that much, but he'd hate it for the twins. Callum is constantly surprising me.

"So you can't hit anyone ever?"

"No, I can't throw a punch unless I'm defending myself or a family member from imminent harm. Those were his exact words," Reed says through clenched teeth. "If you have a better idea, spit it out."

I don't and they all know it. Gideon shakes his head and even Easton looks disappointed with me. I stare at the dark blue sky, then at the ocean, up at the house, and then back at the brothers. An idea sparks.

"Do the Worthingtons have a pool house?"

"Yeah," Reed says warily.

"Where is it?" The Royals' poolhouse is made almost entirely of glass so you can see the ocean from one side and the pool from the other. I tug on Reed's arm. "Show me."

Reed helps me up over the rocky ledge and onto the back lawn. He points to a dark structure standing just to the edge of the concrete deck around the large, rectangular pool. "Worthington keeps it locked."

"So no one can have sex in there. Valerie told me." This is all so perfect.

I run my eyes over the twins.

"If this involves me dressing up as a woman, I'm out." Sawyer holds up a protesting hand. At least I think it's Sawyer by the fading burn on his wrist.

"Let me get Valerie. It's going to take two of us. And I'll need both of the twins. The rest of you pretend like you're at a party. When the time is right, Sawyer will come out and let you know. You'll need to gather as much of the crowd as you can by the pool. Maybe get your cameras ready."

"What do you have planned, little sis?" Easton sidles up to me.

"Hell hath no fury like a woman scorned or a girl drugged against her will," I say mysteriously and run off to look for Valerie.

I find her chatting up Savannah halfway between the shore and the pool, which is some kind of perfect serendipity. "Hey, can I talk to you guys for a minute?"

Valerie has to drag Savannah, but I manage to sequester the two of them off to the side.

I address Savannah first. "Look, I want to apologize for not listening to you the other night. I was lonely and wanting someone I couldn't have, so I thought I'd hang with Daniel. That was a mistake."

She presses her lips together, but either my genuine regret or our mutual hatred of Daniel breaks down her icy barriers. "I accept your apology," she says stiffly.

"Oh, Sav, get the stick out of your ass," Valerie chides. "We're here to get Daniel back. Right, Ella?"

Savannah quirks an interested eyebrow in my direction and I nod enthusiastically. "Here's the plan."

After I explain the details to them, Valerie hoots. But Savannah looks skeptical.

"You really thing he's going to fall for this?"

"Savannah, the guy drugs girls for sex. He's not going to turn this offer down. It's a power trip for him and we're going to feed into that."

She lifts an elegant shoulder. "All right. I'm in. Let's take this jackass down."

DANIEL IS SITTING ON A lounge chair next to the pool with a Heineken in one hand and the thigh of a young-looking girl in the other. She has to be a freshman. A renewed sense of righteousness washes over me. Daniel has to be stopped. Like Savannah said, it's time to bring him down.

"Hi, Daniel." I adopt the most submissive tone I can muster.

His head jerks up and he scans the crowd looking for the Royal brothers. When he doesn't see them, he leans back, pulling the girl closer to his side, almost as if she's a shield. "What do you want? I'm busy."

I scuff the toe of my ballet slipper in the stamped concrete. "I wanted to apologize for the other night. I...I overreacted.

You're Daniel Delacorte and I'm…" I fight back my gag reflex, "…a trumped-up nobody."

The girl shifts uncomfortably. "Um, I think I hear my sister calling for me."

She slips out from under Daniel's hand. When he protests, I jump in. "I just need Daniel for a minute and then he's all yours."

Daniel smirks. "Just a minute? I last a lot longer than that."

The girl titters and runs away. I get it. It's awkward as hell watching someone humiliating herself. The minute she's out of earshot, Daniel's careless smile turns into a glower. "What are you playing at?"

"I want another chance." I lean forward so that my cleavage is on display for him. "I made a mistake. If you'd just told me what you wanted, I wouldn't have overreacted." God, I can't believe I have to say this crap to him.

His eyes drop to my gaping neckline and he licks his lips like an awful pig. "The Royals didn't seem really happy."

"They were mad because I made a scene. They want me to shut up and stay out of sight."

"Yet you're here."

"Their dad makes them bring me."

He frowns. "So you want to get back at them? Is that it?"

"Honestly? Kind of," I lie, because I think sticking it to the Royals might be something that will appeal to him. "I'm tired of those jerks forcing me to act like something I'm not." I shrug. "I like to party and I like to have fun. I was trying to be all proper for their sake, but…that's not who I am."

Daniel looks intrigued.

"So let's stop pretending. Whatever you want, I'm down for and not just me." I point to some vague area behind me.

"You know Valerie, right?" He nods, his gaze dropping back to my chest. "I told her about your friends, Zoe and Nadine. And she's interested. We thought…" I trail off and brace my hand next to Daniel's knee. I bring my lips close to his ear. "We thought we could show you what Astor Park girls can do. We're both dancers, you know."

"Yeah?" His eyes light up.

"And you can do whatever you want with us," I tease.

He seems more than interested now. "Anything?"

"Anything…and everything. Feel free to bring your camera. You might want to keep mementos."

"Where?" His hand slips between his legs. Ugh, is he feeling himself up right in front of me? I clamp my lips together so I don't ralph all over his lap.

"The pool house. I picked the lock. Meet us there in five minutes."

I waltz away without looking back. If I've misjudged Daniel, this isn't going to work and I'll have to eat crow to the Royal brothers. But I don't think I'm wrong. Daniel Delacorte has an opportunity to degrade two "trumped-up nobodies" and take pictures of them that he can show to all his pervy buddies. No way is he passing up that golden opportunity.

As I let myself into the small structure, Valerie pops up from one of the two chairs that she and Savannah dragged away from the floor-to-ceiling windows. Like the Royals' pool house, this one is nearly all glass so that the view from the house to the ocean is unobstructed, but there are shades and the two girls have drawn them all.

"I like what you've done with the place," I joke.

Valerie tosses me something, which I catch reflexively. A robe tie. "Thanks, we were going for minimalist. Savannah and I thought that it would display our artwork better if there weren't any distractions. You okay with the sash?"

Thinking back to the yacht and Reed, I tell her, "That'll work." I wrap the length around my waist. "Where's Savannah?"

"I'm in the bathroom," she hisses out.

A sharp knock on the door signals Daniel's arrival.

"Showtime," I whisper and then open the door.

CHAPTER 28

"I HALF THOUGHT YOU MIGHT be setting me up, but I just saw the Royals drinking. Reed looks ready to go balls deep into Abby tonight." Daniel runs his eyes insolently over me and then shifts to Valerie. "And you, Val. I never suspected you were such a dirty girl. But maybe I should've guessed."

Because you're both low class and trashy, I finish for him silently.

Valerie's mouth twists in a noticeable sneer. Since she isn't doing a good job of pretending to be hot for Daniel, I hurry over to distract him.

"What do you want to do first?" I stroke a hand over his shoulders and steer him toward the table in the middle of the room. It must have been too heavy for Valerie and Savannah to move.

"How about the two of you go down on each other?" he suggests.

"No lead up? Just straight to the action?" With a harder hand than necessary, I push him down onto the table. "I think you need a lesson in anticipation. Let us dance for you a little."

Leaning back against his arms, he gives us a superior nod of his chin. "Fine. But I want to see your hands on each other and lots of skin."

Valerie gathers herself and steps forward. "How about we give you a massage? You ever have one of those?"

"A massage? Sure, I get them at my dad's club all the time."

"But from two girls with a happy ending?" She wiggles her fingers. "Like Ella said, let's not rush things. We can give you a massage and then you can watch us do our thing. After all, you should get off first."

Daniel ponders this offer for a moment and then agrees. "Yeah, that sounds right. You bitches can wait your turn." He winks at the end to signal we're supposed to take his bitches comment as a joke. Neither of us laugh and it takes superhuman effort not to punch his smug face.

"Let's help you out of your clothes," I say sweetly.

Fortunately, Daniel doesn't suspect a thing. He'd be mistrustful of Reed or Gideon, but not two trashy girls who, if not for their rich relatives, would probably be selling their bodies on the streets anyway. That's how his mind operates, which is why our little charade is possible. Because he's Daniel Delacorte, son of a judge, lacrosse player, a guy with a sterling reputation who nobody would ever suspect of being such a douche. I don't doubt for a second that Savannah's cousin is probably from a less successful branch of the family.

Valerie and I steel ourselves to put our hands on his body, but to our relief he doesn't need help. He drops his shorts, pulls down his boxers and has his T-shirt over his head before we can take our next breath.

"Someone's eager," Valerie mutters under her breath.

Daniel licks his lips. "Where do you want me?"

She places her hands on her hips and pretends to consider the question. "How about there?" She points to a nest of pillows situated right in front of the windows.

Daniel strides over and kneels down on the soft cushions. "Don't forget to keep your teeth to yourself. Maybe cover them with your lips."

That's the last instruction he's ever going to give me, I think, and then I nonchalantly swipe a fruit bowl off the table and hit him over the head with it.

He rears up with a shout. "What the hell!" Stunned, he clamps one hand to the back of his head.

"I told you the bowl was too weak," Savannah says, bursting out of the bathroom. Before Daniel can leap away, she whips up a bottle of hairspray and sends a stream of stinging solvents straight into his face.

"Mother*fucker*! You three are dead meat!" Daniel roars. He stumbles to his left and bangs into the windows.

The three of us laugh.

"I don't want to kill him, just maim him," I remind Savannah. "How about the candlestick?" I swing the heavy silver weapon and strike Daniel in the shoulder. Savannah brings the matching one down on the top of his head, and Daniel slumps over.

Valerie picks up one sash and tosses me the other one. "You're right, Ella. This guy is a creep."

As quickly as possible, we truss him up like a turkey. With Daniel momentarily dazed, it's easy for us to secure his hands behind his back, tie his ankles together and then loop a length of sash between the two sets of bindings.

"Too bad we don't have tape." I pick up a banana from the floor and toss it in the air. "We could tape this to his ass."

"That'd be awesome," Valerie crows.

Savannah scowls. "I have something to stick up his ass." She stomps over, draws back her leg and delivers the harshest kick I've seen outside a movie. Apparently smashing a five-pound candlestick into his skull didn't quite lessen her anger toward him.

The impact of her delicate foot to his butt is surprisingly hard. It jolts Daniel from his stupor, and he releases a yowl of pain. An ugly smile stretches across Savannah's face. Valerie and I watch as she bends close to whisper something to him, something that makes him shudder.

Then she straightens up and runs a hand over her hair, smoothing all the strands to lie flat against her pretty head. "I'm ready. I don't want to spend another minute with this piece of garbage."

"Hold up," Valerie says. We turn to see her throwing an apple up in the air.

A grin slowly spreads across my face. "Are you thinking what I'm thinking?" I ask. The plan is so evil. I love it.

Savannah starts laughing and is almost laughing too hard to help us pull open Daniel's mouth and shove the apple inside, but one dazed, naked boy is no match for the three of us.

"Let's go." I run to the door and find Sawyer there. "We're ready."

"So are we," he answers with a grin. "Did you kill him? Because that yelp back there sounded bad."

"I think Savannah wanted to but we held her back."

"I've always liked that chick," Sawyer says.

I lean back and gesture for the girls to exit. Savannah and Valerie slip out the sliding doors leading to the beach. Once they're down at the shore, I hit the lights and the button for the remote control curtains. The Worthingtons made this whole thing easy for us. As the lights flicker on and the curtains part, Sawyer and I haul ass after the girls, who we find standing with Sebastian.

Once we arrive, Seb places a hand on the shoulders of Valerie and Savannah. "Can't believe we're missing the show," he says glumly.

I'm bummed too, but we decided it wasn't a good idea for me and the girls to be part of the crowd during Daniel's unveiling. If any of his buddies figure out we were behind it, they might turn on us. The twins are down here serving as our bodyguards in case that happens.

We stand and wait, straining for the sounds that will mark the reveal of Daniel—tied up and on display like a pig at a luau.

The first noises we hear are a chorus of gasps. There's a shout that we can't make out and then a moment of silence. After what seems like a long time to me, but must feel like an eternity to the naked and bound Daniel, there's a shout of "Oh my God!" and "Holy shit, is that Daniel Delacorte?" Other voices join in until it seems like every guest is commenting on the scene before them.

There's clapping, whistling, and screaming, and for some reason I start shaking. I tremble so hard I have to lean against Sawyer. He puts an arm around me and rubs a hand against my side.

"I-I don't know why I'm so weak," I stutter.

"You're coming off an adrenaline high." He digs around in his pocket and then hands me a roll of mints. "That's all I got. Sorry."

"S'okay," I mumble and shove two in my mouth. I concentrate on chewing the candies, and whether it's the tiny shock of sugar that helps or just focusing on something other than the stunt I just participated in, my shaking stops and I start warming up. "Where's the rest of the Royal crew?"

Sebastian gives me an amused glance as if he knows exactly which Royal I'm curious about. "Witnessing Daniel's humiliation with the rest of Astor Park and making sure the right story is being spread."

"What story is that?"

"The truth. He got beat up by a girl."

"Three girls," I correct.

"It's a better story when it's only one girl," Sawyer pipes up.

"But don't you want to take credit, too?"

"Publicly? Naah. It'd get back to Dad and then he'll be on our asses about the military school thing again." Sawyer grins. "But we'll know we did this, and that's all that matters."

A commotion at the top of the embankment catches my attention. The three other Royals are coming. Sawyer grabs me by the arm and herds me down the beach. Valerie shouts after us that she's catching a ride home with Savannah, and I give her a quick wave as I race off with the twins. Their brothers aren't far behind us.

"You should have seen the look on his face—" Gideon starts.

"Man, his dick is teeny weeny," Easton crows. "Was that shrinkage or is he really that small—"

"The bruise on his forehead looked nasty. Did that come from you?" Reed sounds impressed.

Three Royal brothers converge on us, all talking at once.

"Whoa, whoa, whoa." I raise my hands. "I can't handle all of you at once."

"You did good." Gideon surprises me by ruffling my hair.

"It was perfect," Reed drawls, and the approval in his eyes makes me feel warm and gooey inside.

Easton picks me up and whirls me around. "You're a boss, Ella. Remind me never to piss you off."

A racket of shouts and curses has us turning back toward the Worthington place. Easton lets me slide to the ground as we see a crowd form on the top of the ridge. There's a splash—did someone just get pushed into the pool?

"He just dunked Penny Lockwood-Smith into the pool!" someone from the party yells before erupting in laughter.

"Here he comes," Gideon says with a sigh.

He is Daniel, who's charging through a line of people. Even in the dark blue of the night, we can see that he's furious.

"Don't let him bite you," Easton murmurs in my ear. "He might have rabies."

Daniel stops at the edge of lawn and scans the shoreline. When he sees us, he roars, points, and then leaps down onto the sand in one jump. It's an impressive athletic move.

"Look at him go," I marvel.

"He is on the lacrosse team," Sawyer reminds me.

"I'm going to kill you. All of you! Starting with you, you gutter trash."

Reed's face breaks out in a grin as he turns to the rest of us. Figures that this would be the moment he unleashes one of his rare smiles. "That sounded like a threat, right?"

Easton nods. "I think Ella's in imminent danger. You know Dad wouldn't like that."

Happy as I've ever seen him, Reed pushes me behind him as Daniel runs down the sand, clad in only his khaki shorts. Small pinpoints of light pop up as a number of the partygoers decide that this scene should be immortalized. The Royals shuffle me backward and I have to force my way between the twins to see what's going on.

And I'm just in time, too, because as soon as I stick my head out between the mountain of Royal muscle, Daniel launches himself at Reed with a growl. Reed takes one step forward and smashes his fist into Daniel's jaw.

Daniel drops like a stone.

CHAPTER 29

WE'RE ALL IN HIGH SPIRITS as we head back to the mansion. I shoot Valerie a quick text to make sure she's cool driving home with Savannah, and she assures me it's fine. It turns out the Carringtons live around the corner from the Montgomerys.

Easton walks beside me. The twins are up ahead, still laughing about the scene we'd left back at the Worthington house. Their voices float toward us.

"He knocked him out cold in one second flat." Sawyer is chuckling.

"New record for Reed," Sebastian agrees.

Reed and Gideon trail behind us. Every time I turn around, their heads are bent close in conversation. It's obvious those two have secrets that Easton and the twins don't know about, and that bothers me, because I was really starting to buy into the motto about Royals sticking together.

We reach the house but I halt at the steps leading up to it. "I'm going to walk along the water for a bit," I tell Easton.

"I'll walk with you."

I shake my head. "I kinda want to be alone. No offense."

"None taken." He leans in and smacks a kiss on my cheek. "That was some first-class vengeance tonight, little sis. You're my new hero."

After he's gone, I leave my shoes on a rock and walk barefoot along the soft sand. The moon lights my way, and I haven't taken twenty steps when I hear footsteps behind me. I don't need to turn around to know it's Reed.

"You shouldn't be out here alone."

"What, you think Daniel is going to jump out from behind a boulder and attack me?"

Reed reaches me. I stop walking and turn toward him. As usual, his gorgeous face makes my breath hitch.

"He might. You humiliated him pretty good tonight."

I have to laugh. "And you knocked him out. He's probably at home right now icing his face."

Reed shrugs. "He had it coming."

I stare at the water. He stares at me. I can feel his gaze burning into my face, and I shift my head again, smiling wryly.

"Let's hear it."

"Hear what?"

"Some more lies. You know, how last night was just you doing me a favor, you don't really want me, yada, yada." I wave my hand.

To my surprise, he laughs.

"Oh my God. Was that a laugh? Reed Royal laughs, folks. Someone call the Vatican because an honest-to-God miracle has occurred."

That gets me another chuckle. "You're so annoying," he grumbles.

"Yeah, but you still like me."

He goes quiet. I think he's going to stay that way, but then he curses under his breath and says, "Yeah, maybe I do."

I feign amazement. "*Two* miracles in one night? Is the world ending?"

Reed grabs a chunk of my hair and gives it a tug. "That's enough outta you."

I step closer to the water, but it's even more freezing than usual. I squeal when it touches my toes, then dart back.

"I hate the Atlantic," I declare. "The Pacific is *way* better."

"You lived on the west coast?" He sounds grudgingly curious.

"West, east, north, south. We lived everywhere. Never stayed in one place for long. I think the longest was a year, and that was in Chicago. Or I guess Seattle was the longest—two years—but I don't count that because my mom was sick and we didn't have a choice but to stay put."

"Why did you move around so much?"

"Money, mostly. If Mom lost her job, we had to pack up and go where the money was. Or she'd fall in love and we'd move in with her latest boyfriend."

"She had a lot of boyfriends?" His voice is harsh.

I'm honest with him. "Yeah. She fell in love a lot."

"Then she wasn't really in love."

I look over quizzically.

"That's lust," Reed says with a shrug. "Not love."

"Maybe. But to her, it was love." I hesitate. "Did your parents love each other?"

I shouldn't have asked because he goes stiffer than a board. "My dad claims they did. But he sure as shit never acted like a man in love."

I think Reed is wrong. Just hearing Callum talk about Maria, you can tell that he loved her deeply. I don't know why his sons refuse to see that.

"You guys all miss her, huh?" I move the subject somewhere safer, but it doesn't erase the tension in his face.

Reed doesn't answer.

"It's okay to say it. I miss my mom every day. She was the most important person in my life."

"She was a stripper."

His mocking reply makes my shoulders tighten. "So?" I come to Mom's defense instantly. "Her stripping paid our bills. It kept a roof over our heads. It paid for my dance classes."

Sharp blue eyes focus on me. "Did she force you to strip when she got sick?"

"No. She never knew about it. I told her I was waiting tables, which was true. I did do that, and I also worked at a truck stop, but it wasn't enough to pay all her medical bills, so I stole her ID and got a job at one of the clubs." I sigh. "I don't expect you to understand. You've never had to worry about money a day in your life."

"No, I haven't," he agrees.

I'm not sure if I move first, or if he does, but we're walking again. A few feet of distance stretch between us at first, but as we walk, we get closer and closer until our bare arms are brushing with every step. His skin is warm, and my arm prickles each time we make contact.

"My mother was kind," he finally reveals.

That's what Callum said, too. I think of the woman that Steve married—Dinah, the awful shrew who has naked pictures of herself all over her home—and I wonder how two friends could have married such dramatically different women.

"She cared about people. Too much, maybe. She was a sucker for a sob story. She always went out of her way to help people."

"Was she good to you? And your brothers?"

Reed nods. "She loved us. She was always there for us, giving advice, helping with our homework. And every day she'd spend alone time with each of us. I guess she didn't want any of us to feel neglected or like she had a favorite. And on the weekends we'd all do stuff together."

"Like what?" I ask curiously.

He shrugs. "Museums, the zoo, kiting."

"Kiting?"

He rolls his eyes at me. "Flying a kite, Ella. Don't tell me you've never done that."

"Nope." I purse my lips. "I did go to a zoo once, though. One of my mom's boyfriends took us to this shitty petting zoo in the middle of nowhere. They had a goat and a llama and this little monkey that threw poop at me when I walked by."

Reed throws his head back and laughs. It's the sexiest sound I've ever heard.

"And then it turned out the zoo was a front for a drug dealing operation. The boyfriend was just there to buy weed."

Neither of us comment on the drastic differences in our childhoods, but I know we're both thinking about it.

We keep walking. His fingers graze mine. I hold my breath, wondering if he's going to take my hand, but he doesn't, and the disappointment is too much to bear.

I stop in my tracks and meet his eyes. Not a good idea, because I know he can see the longing on my face. It causes his gaze to grow shuttered, and I bite back my frustration.

"You like me," I announce.

His jaw tics.

"You want me."

Another tic.

"Dammit, Reed, why can't you just admit it? What's the point in lying?"

When he doesn't answer, I whirl around and march off, my bare feet kicking up sand. Suddenly I'm yanked backward, and my shoulders collide with a solid male chest, stealing the breath from my lungs.

Reed's chin comes down to rest on my shoulder, his lips millimeters from my ear. "You want me to say it?" he whispers. "Fine, I'll say it. I want you. I fucking want you."

I feel the hard length of him pressing against my butt and I know he's not lying. As a thrill shoots up my spine, Reed twists me around and his mouth crashes down on mine.

The kiss is hot enough to turn the Atlantic into lava. My lips part and he slides his tongue past them, devouring my mouth in greedy strokes that leave me breathless. I cling to his broad shoulders, then slide my hands down to his trim waist.

He groans and cups my bottom, rotating his hips so I can feel every inch of him. Then, after one more drugging kiss, he releases me and staggers backward.

"I'm leaving for college next year," he says hoarsely. "I'm leaving, and chances are I'm never coming back. I'm not selfish enough to start something I can't finish. I'm not gonna do that to you."

I don't care, I want to say. I'll take him any way I can, even if it's for a short time, but I don't voice the words, because I know they won't sway him.

"Let's go back to the house," he mumbles when my silence drags on.

I follow him without a word, my lips still tingling from his kiss, my heart still aching from his rejection.

I'M JUST DRIFTING OFF TO sleep when my bedroom door creaks open. I groggily lift my head. Within seconds I'm wide awake.

Reed climbs into bed beside me. He doesn't say a word. The room is too dark, so I can't see his expression, but I can feel the warmth of his body as he slides closer. The heat of his palm as he strokes my cheek before grasping my chin and tilting my head toward his.

"What are you doing?" I whisper.

His voice is pained. "I decided to be selfish."

Happiness explodes in my chest. I wrap my arms around his neck and pull him closer. His lips hover over mine, but he doesn't kiss me.

"Just for tonight," he tells me.

"That's what you said last night, too."

"This time I mean it." And then he kisses me, and any protest I might have expressed gets lost in the hurried joining of our mouths.

He groans when my tongue touches his. Strong hips rock against me, his hard-on rubbing my thigh. I move so that we're on both on our sides, face-to-face, mouths fused together.

"Fuck," he chokes out, and then his hand slips under my shirt. Into my panties.

His fingers tease me, pressing against sensitive spots that make me moan against his lips. We touch each other, running our hands over all the bare skin we can find, neither one of us coming up for air as we practically eat each other's faces off.

It isn't long before the knot of tension inside me breaks apart in a million little pieces. Pleasure soars through my body as I gasp into his mouth. Reed trembles against me, and this time I'm the one swallowing his groan of pleasure.

Afterward, we lie tangled up together, kissing for what feels like hours. I never want him to go. I want him to stay in this bed forever.

But just like last night, he's gone when I open my eyes the next morning.

I wonder if I dreamed it, but when I roll over, I smell him on my pillows. His shampoo, his soap, the spicy aftershave he wears. He was here. It was real. The loss hits me hard, and not even the sunshine streaming in from the curtains can ease the disappointment I wake up with.

But then the disappointment is replaced with a jolt of panic, because a high-pitched shriek suddenly rings out through the mansion. I think it came from the front parlor, and I jump out of bed, throwing open my door just as another shriek assaults my eardrums.

"You are *not* getting away with this!" Brooke is screaming. "Not this time, Callum Royal!"

CHAPTER 30

I REACH THE RAILING AT the same time Easton pops out of his bedroom. His dark hair sticks up in all directions, and his eyes are bloodshot as he comes up beside me. "What the hell," he mumbles.

We both look down at foyer, where Brooke and Callum are facing off. It's comical almost, because she's more than a head shorter than him thus posing the least threatening picture on the planet.

"It's my right to be there!" Brooke shouts, jamming the center of Callum's chest with one sharp fingernail.

"No, it isn't. You're not a Royal and you're not an O'Halloran. It's not your place."

"Then tell me, what *is* my place? Why do I put up with all your bullshit then? You treat me like I'm your mistress instead of your girlfriend! Where's my ring, Callum? *Where the fuck is my ring*?"

I can't see Callum's face, but I don't miss the tension in his shoulders. "My wife's body is barely even cold!" he roars.

Beside me, Easton tenses up, too. I reach out and take his hand, and he squeezes my fingers tight enough to bring a sting of pain.

"You expect me to just remarry like it's no big deal—"

"Two years!" Brooke interrupts. "She's been dead for two years! Get over it!"

Callum stumbles as if she's struck him.

"I won't let you string me along anymore. I *won't*." Brooke lunges forward and grabs the front of his dress shirt, bunching it between her fingers. "I am done with you, you hear me? *Done*!"

With that, she shoves his chest and spins toward the door, her high heels slapping the marble floor.

Callum doesn't go after her, and when she realizes it, she whirls around and points a finger at him. "If I walk out right now, I am never coming back!"

His voice is colder than ice. "Don't let the door hit you on the ass on your way out."

Easton snickers.

"You…you…you *monster*!" Brooke shrieks. She flings open the door with so much force that a gust of air blows through the foyer and I feel it from the second floor.

Her blonde head and minidress-clad body disappear through the threshold. She slams the door with equal force.

Silence crashes over the foyer. I see a flash of movement in the corner of my eye, and I turn around to find the other Royals standing behind us. The twins look sleepy. Gideon looks shocked. Reed's face is impassive, but I swear I see a glimpse of triumph in his eyes.

Easton doesn't even try to hide his glee. "Did that really just happen?" he asks us, shaking his head in amazement.

Callum hears his son's voice, and his head tilts up to the railing. He looks stricken, but not devastated that his girlfriend just stormed off.

"Dad," Easton calls out, grinning from ear-to-ear. "You the man! Come up here and gimme a high five."

His father's expression turns weary. Instead of answering Easton, Callum flicks his gaze toward me. "Since you're awake, Ella, why don't you come down to my study? We need to have a little chat." Then he exits the foyer.

I bite my lip, hesitant to follow him. I suddenly remember what he just said to Brooke—how she's not a Royal or an O'Halloran—and my anxiety grows. I have a feeling they were fighting about Steve. Which means that indirectly, it was also about me.

"Go," Reed murmurs when I don't move from the railing.

As usual, I instinctively obey his command. It's like he has a hold on me and I'm not sure I like it. But I'm helpless to stop it.

I walk downstairs on wobbly legs and find Callum in the study. He's already hit the liquor cabinet, pouring himself a glass of scotch when I walk in.

"Are you okay?" I ask quietly.

He waves the glass in his hand, causing liquid to splash over the rim. "I'm fine. It's fine. I'm sorry you had to wake up to that."

"Do you think it's really over with you two?" I can't help but feel bad for Brooke. I've seen a bitchy side to her, definitely, but she's also been nice to me. Or at least I think she has. Brooke Davidson is a tough nut to crack.

"Probably." He sips his drink. "She wasn't entirely out of line. Two years is a long time for a woman to wait." Callum sets the glass on his desk and runs a hand through his hair. "The reading of the will is scheduled for two weeks from tomorrow."

I look blankly at him. "The will?"

"Yes. Steve's will."

I'm still confused. "Didn't that already happen? I thought you said there was a funeral."

"There was, but the estate hasn't been settled yet. Dinah and I started probate after Steve's death, but the reading itself was put off until you could be located."

I bet Dinah must have loved that. "Do I really have to be there? Doesn't Dinah inherit everything because she's his wife?"

"It's a lot more complicated than that." He doesn't elaborate. "But yes, you need to be there. I'll be there, too, as your legal guardian, and so will Dinah and our lawyers. She left for Paris last night, but she'll be back in two weeks, and then we'll get everything straightened out. It'll be painless, I promise."

With Dinah O'Halloran in attendance? Yeah right. Pain*ful* is more like it.

But I just nod and say, "Okay. If I have to go, I'll go."

He nods, too, and picks up his drink again.

CALLUM TAKES OFF SHORTLY AFTER to play golf. He claims that walking the eighteen links helps clear his mind. I worry about how loaded he plans to get and then remind myself that he's the adult and I'm the seventeen-year-old, so I bite my tongue.

One by one the Royals leave. Gideon heads off before lunch to go back to college. He always looks happier leaving than arriving.

Soon it's just me. I heat up leftover quiche and then consider going for a walk on the beach.

It's only been a month at the Royal household, but that month has been full of, well, life. Stuff is always happening. It's not always *good* stuff, but I haven't been alone, and until now, in this moment of solitude, I realize I don't like being alone. It's nice to have friends and family around, even if the family is super dysfunctional.

I wonder if that's the reason Gideon keeps coming back.

"Did you save some of that egg thing for me?" Reed's voice makes me jump.

I slap a hand over my heart to keep it from leaping out of my chest. "You scared me. I thought you left with Easton."

"Nope." He crosses the room to peer over my shoulder. "What else is in the fridge?"

"Food," I answer.

He tugs on my hair playfully—at least I hope it's playfully—and goes to investigate his options.

Door in one hand, he stands in front of the fridge—leans, really, with the other hand braced on the cabinet—until the entire room is cold with refrigerated air.

"Problem?" I take a break from eating so I can admire the sexy line of his body and the way his muscles bunch and flex as he rummages for food.

"Don't suppose you'd make me a sandwich?" he says from somewhere in the interior of the refrigerator.

"That'd be a no."

He slams the door shut and joins me at the table, ripping the plate and fork from underneath my nose and then shoveling half the quiche down his throat before I can even protest.

"That was mine!" I reach over and try to wrest it back

"Sandra would want you to share with me." He holds me off with one hand…again.

Damn. I need to start a weightlifting program. I try one more time to grab the plate back, and this time Reed doesn't fend me off. He pulls me in and the surprise move makes me lose my balance. I end up tumbling into his lap with my legs splayed on either side of his broad thighs.

My attempts to wriggle free are put to an end when he clamps one hand around my butt and pulls me against him. When he kisses me, I can't help but respond eagerly, wanting him to make those husky noises that tell me how hot I get him.

"You left this morning," I say when he releases my mouth. I wish I could stuff the words back in, because I'm afraid he's going to say something hurtful.

"Didn't want to," he replies.

"Why'd you leave?" All my pride is left on the floor, but my weakness doesn't turn him off.

He runs his fingers through my hair. "Because I'm weak when it comes to you. I don't trust myself to be in your bed all night. Hell, I should be thrown in jail for half the things I just think about."

His words fill me with giddy pleasure. "You think too much."

He makes some indecipherable noise—impatience, cynicism, humor—and then kisses me again. Soon the kissing isn't enough. I reach down to tug at the bottom of his shirt. His hands are all over me too—inside my T-shirt, down the elastic waistband of my shorts. I strain toward him, seeking the release I've discovered only Reed can provide.

A scuffling noise outside the kitchen breaks us apart.

"Did you hear something?" I whisper.

Reed stands up in one smooth and powerful gesture, still holding me in his arms, and walks out into the hall. It's empty.

Setting me on my feet, he gives my butt a little smack. "Why don't you go put a swimsuit on?"

"Um, why would I want to do that?" I just want to go back to the table and sit on his lap while he kisses me senseless, but he's already moving outside.

"Because we're going for a swim," he calls over his shoulder.

With a sigh, I trudge upstairs. When I reach the top, I see Brooke coming out of my room. Or, at least, that's what it looks like.

I halt in my tracks, anger and suspicion forming a tight pretzel in my gut. What the hell was she doing in my bedroom?

Oh shit! My money is in there.

What if she took it?

I scan her quickly but she doesn't have a purse and her clothes are so tight that there's no way she can hide a stack of cash on her. Still, she doesn't belong here, and I make my displeasure known as I march toward her.

"What are you doing here?" I demand.

She saunters my way. "Well, if it isn't little orphaned Ella, the new princess of Castle Royal."

"I thought you told Callum you were leaving and never coming back," I say warily.

"Don't you wish." She sneers and flicks her long blonde hair to one side. Whatever warm feelings she may have had for me are long gone.

There's no point in engaging, so I sidestep her and move in front of my bedroom door. "Stay out of my room. I'm serious, Brooke. If I catch you up here again, I'm telling Callum."

"Right. Callum. Your savior. The man who swept you out of the gutter and brought you to his palace." Bitterness fills her eyes. "He did the same thing for me. He saved me too, remember? But guess what, sweetie—we're disposable. We're all fucking disposable to him." She waves a perfectly manicured finger in my face. "Your life is transformed, isn't it? Like some princess out of a fairytale. But fairytales aren't real. Girls like us, we'll always turn back into a pumpkin after the ball."

I notice that her eyes have started to glisten with unshed tears. "Brooke," I say gently. "Let me call you a cab, okay?" My heart softens toward her. She's hurting and needs help. I don't know what I can do for her, though, other than a safe ride home.

"He'll tire of you, too," Brooke continues as if I hadn't even spoken. My response doesn't matter. She just needs an audience. "Mark my words."

"Thanks for your insight," I say dryly. "But I think it's time for you to go."

I try to steer her toward the stairs, but she flinches away, stumbling against the opposite wall. A peal of maniacal laughter tumbles from her cherry red lips. "I've had the Royals in my palm for a lot longer than you have, honey."

I'm done listening to her. She just wants to whine and badmouth the Royals. My patience evaporates, so I just duck into my room, slam the door shut, and run to the bathroom. With a shaking hand, I feel inside the cabinet. When my hand brushes across the taped wad of bills, I sag with relief.

I need to move my cash to somewhere only I have access. ASAP.

"WHAT'S WRONG?" REED ASKS THE moment I step onto the patio.

I can't answer him immediately because my tongue is attached to the roof of my mouth. I don't know how I'm supposed to function when Reed stands there in only a pair of board shorts that look like they're about to drop off his hips. His chest is a wall of lickable muscle, and it's hard to concentrate. My argument with Brooke fades in importance when the hottest guy on the planet is standing there on display for me.

"Ella?" he prompts, with humor in his voice.

"What?" I shake myself. "Oh I'm sorry. It was Brooke. She was coming out of my bedroom. Or at least I think it was my bedroom."

Callum's room is on the other side of the house. The sweeping staircase bisects the two wings and the boys' rooms are on one side and Callum's room is on the other. Guest rooms are on the first floor. There was absolutely no reason for Brooke to be on our side of the house.

Reed frowns and starts to move toward the door.

"She left," I tell him. "I saw her car heading down the drive before I came out here."

"We need to change the gate code," he mutters.

"Mmm-hmm." I can't stop staring.

Before I can blink, Reed lifts me in his arms and throws me in the pool.

I land with a huge awkward splash, spitting up water as I kick up to the surface. "What was that for?" I yell, pulling wet strands of hair away from my face.

He grins wickedly. "You looked like you needed cooling off."

"You're one to talk!" I swing myself onto the tiled surround and lunge for him.

He skates away easily. There's no point in chasing him. He's bigger and faster than me, so I have to resort to trickery.

I pretend to bang my foot against a lounger.

"Ouch!" I holler and stagger over to the pool's edge where I bend down and clutch my foot.

Reed comes over immediately. "You okay?"

I lift my supposedly hurt foot up for his inspection. "I stubbed my toe."

He leans down and I push him into the water.

He surfaces immediately, whipping his head around to get the water out of his eyes. Then he grins. "I let you do that."

"Sure you did."

I watch with fascination as the water clings to his body. He beckons me toward him. "We're both wet so you might as well get your pretty ass in the pool."

"Why? So you can dunk me?"

"I won't dunk you." He holds up two fingers. "Scout's honor."

I squint at his spread fingers. "I think that's the Vulcan greeting, not a Scout's pledge."

He slaps a hand hard against the surface and a huge wave of water sprays over me. "Smart ass. The Vulcan greeting is four fingers. Now don't make me come out there."

"I'm only getting in because I want to, not because you ordered me to."

Reed rolls his eyes and sprays me again.

I back up and then run hard, launching myself high in the air and then curling into a ball to drop right beside Reed. I hear him hoot with laughter as I sink into the water.

We spend about ten minutes trying to drown each other.

In the process, I might have tugged his shorts down a little too far and he might have grazed my bikini top with his hand. My body responds immediately to even that light caress.

The next time I dive for his hips, he wraps his hands around my wrists and hauls me up to the surface. He drags me backward until he's sitting on the ledge that surrounds the pool and I'm standing in front of him, still in the water.

"You think you can depants me, huh?"

"I was just swimming." I blink. "I'm innocent, officer." I raise my still shackled wrists.

Reed flicks a finger over my breast. "You don't look innocent."

In retaliation, I run my foot along his calf and smile smugly as he shifts uncomfortably against the tile.

"It's cold out here," I say. "Anyone would nip out."

"If you're cold, I should warm you up." He takes his free hand and nudges aside my bikini top until I'm fully exposed.

I think I've always closed my eyes before when he's touched me here, and it's shockingly erotic to watch him, in broad daylight, take me into his mouth. He gives me a gentle little bite and then licks the sting away before opening his mouth and sucking my nipple.

Holy hell.

"I, ah, I think I'm going to drown in here." I gasp.

He lifts his head and gives me a wicked look. "We can't have that." Then he boosts me out of the pool and drags me to the pool house.

BREATHLESS, WE TUMBLE ONTO THE couch, then Reed rolls onto his back and pulls me on top of him so I'm straddling his thighs. We're both soaking wet, but I don't care that my hair is dripping water all over his bare chest. I'm too busy moaning because his hands are tugging on my bikini top and his hips are rocking up against me.

He pulls at the strings around my neck and back, and my bikini falls off. Heat instantly floods his gaze. "I wanted you from the second I saw you," he confesses.

"Really?" I tease. "You mean when I walked into your house for the first time and you stood up at the railing glaring at me?"

"Oh yeah. You came in dressed like a hobo, with that flannel shirt buttoned all the way to your neck and your eyes blazing up at me. It was the hottest thing I've ever seen."

"I think we have different definitions of *hot*."

He laughs.

Speaking of hot, his chest is on fire, burning my palms as I stroke his pecs. When I lean down to kiss him, he responds so eagerly that it takes my breath away. Our lips fit perfectly. I run my hands over his chest and his breath sucks in. The muscles there quiver beneath my fingertips.

I love knowing that I'm the one turning him on. I'm turning on *Reed Royal*, the guy who scowls instead of smiles, who keeps his emotions under lock and key, hiding them from the world.

He's not hiding anything right now. His desire for me is written all over his face. I can feel it when he presses against me.

I bend my head to kiss him again and he makes me gasp by sucking on my tongue. Then he makes me moan by using his thumbs to toy with my nipples.

Breathing hard, I lean into his palms, and a frustrated noise leaves his mouth.

"I'm being selfish again," he mutters.

"I like it when you're selfish," I breathe.

He gives a strangled laugh, then rolls us over again and slips one hand inside my bathing suit bottoms.

"I wanna make you feel good." His lips find mine, and a zing of pleasure races through me. I close my eyes and ride the incredible waves of sensation until we're both breathing hard enough to fog up every pane of glass in the pool house.

"Reed." His name shudders out as my surroundings fade. My brain shuts down. All I can do is let the soaring pleasure take over.

When I crash back to earth, he's grinning at me, looking mighty pleased with himself.

I narrow my eyes, wanting to smack him for having the power to make me lose control like that, but that's a stupid thought, because oh my God, that felt good.

But it wouldn't hurt to level the playing field a little. I shove him so that he's flat on his back again. Then I start kissing his chest. Every glorious inch of it.

Reed's breathing grows unsteady. When my lips travel down to the waistband of his trunks, he tenses up. I lift my head to check his expression. It's tight with anticipation.

My fingers shake as I toy with his waistband. "Reed?"

"Mmm?" His eyes are closed now.

"Can you teach me how to…um…" I mumble out a vague, "…you know."

His eyes snap open. To my annoyance, he looks like he's trying not to laugh. "Ah. Yeah…sure."

I bristle. "Yeah, sure? I don't have to if you don't want—"

"I want." He answers so comically fast that I'm the one laughing now. "I really, really want." He quickly eases his board shorts down.

My heart pounds as I bring my mouth close to him. I want do to this right, but because I can feel him watching me, self-consciousness makes me want to run.

"You've really never done this?" he says hoarsely.

I shake my head. For some reason, he looks really upset by that. "What's wrong?" My forehead creases when his expression grows even more tortured.

"I'm such an asshole. All the stuff I said to you on the yacht… You should hate me, Ella."

"But I don't." I rub my hand along his knee. "Teach me how to make it good for you."

"It's already good." His eyes are hazy, and he cups the back of my head, gently threading his fingers through my hair. His other hand reaches for one of mine and he slowly wraps my fingers around him. "Use your hand, too," he whispers.

I give a little pump. "Like that?"

"Yeah, like that. That's…good…"

Feeling bolder, I take the tip of him in my mouth and suck. He almost jerks off the couch. "That's even better," he growls.

I smile against him, enjoying the noises he's making. I might not have experience but I hope my enthusiasm makes up for it because I really want to make him feel good. I want him to lose control.

He keeps stroking my hair and I get my wish sooner rather than later. He comes apart beneath me, trembling wildly, and when I crawl up his body afterward, he holds me tight to him and says, "I don't deserve this."

I want to ask him what he means, but I don't get the chance. Loud pounding on one of the glass doors interrupts us.

"Little sis! Big bro! Banging time's over." It's Easton, and he's laughing hysterically as he hammers his fist against the glass.

"Get lost," Reed calls back.

"Love to, but Dad just called. He's on his way home and wants to take us out for dinner later. He'll be here in five."

"Damn." Reed sits up and shoves a hand through his hair. Then he looks at our naked bodies and grins. "We should get dressed. Dad'll shit a brick if he finds us like this."

Will he? For the first time since this thing with Reed started, I let myself think about how Callum would react if he knew. My heart sinks to the pit of my stomach, because I think Reed might be right. I've been in Bayview only a month and Callum is already super protective of me. Hell, he was protective of me before he even knew me.

Callum won't like this.

My gaze fixes on Reed's bare butt as he stands up and yanks his trunks up his hips.

No, Callum will *hate* this.

CHAPTER 31

"Ella!" Callum calls from the base of the stairs thirty minutes later. "Come down, I've got something to show you!"

I roll over and pull a pillow over my head. I don't want to leave my bedroom. I came up here to change for dinner, but really, I've just been lying in bed reliving every awesome thing that happened in the pool house.

I don't want to go downstairs and see Callum and worry about what he'd say or how he'd feel if he knew what Reed and I had been doing. I just want to stay in this pink cocoon and hug my memory tight. Because what we did in the pool house was good and right and nothing is going to ruin that memory for me.

But the insistent call for me to get downstairs is hard to ignore, especially when Easton is now outside my door, pounding on the wood. "Come on, Ella. I'm hungry and Dad won't let us leave for the restaurant until you come down."

"I'm coming." I fling myself out of the bed and shove my feet into the deck shoes, which are becoming my favorite pair of footwear. They are so fricking comfortable. I wonder for a second if wearing boat shoes outside of a boat is a huge faux pas but then decide I don't really care.

When I reach the second floor landing, all the Royals are waiting for me down below, wearing varying degrees of smiles, from a sly one on Reed's face to a huge, ear-to-ear one on Callum.

"Can one of you stare at the ceiling?" I grumble. "You're making me self-conscious."

Callum makes an impatient gesture. "Come outside and we'll all stare at what's in the driveway."

Against my will, I feel a swell of excitement. My car—or at least the car that Callum got for me to drive—must have arrived. I try not to run down the stairs but Easton is tired of waiting. He takes the stairs two at a time and then drags me down to the foyer and the rest of the Royals push me outside.

In the center of the driveway, at the foot of the wide tiled steps, sits a two-seater convertible. The interior is covered in cream leather and dark shiny wood. The chrome on the steering wheel gleams so brightly that I almost have to shade my eyes.

But none of that is as shocking as the color. Not pink. Not red. But a true royal blue—the same blue that adorned the plane that flew me here, the same one on Callum's business cards.

My eyes fly to Callum and he nods. "Had it painted in our California factory. It's Royal blue and the formula is patented by Atlantic Aviation."

Reed presses a hand at the small of my back and I stumble forward down to the car. It's so beautiful and clean and new that I'm afraid to even drive it.

"You ready to go for a ride?"

"No, not really," I confess.

They all laugh, not at me, but in genuine, good-hearted amusement. My heart lurches. Is this really my family? The thought makes the few barriers I had left crumble away.

Callum hands me the keys along with a piece of paper. "This is the title to the car. No matter what happens, this is yours."

Meaning that if I decide to leave, for whatever reason, he expects me to take this car with me. Which is nuts because I'm scared to even sit in it.

"Come on, let's take this baby for a spin." Reed opens the passenger door and slides in.

With all of them watching expectantly, I have no other choice but to walk around to the driver's side. Reed explains how to move my seat forward, tilt the wheel down and operate the radio—the most important feature.

And then with a literal press of a button, the engine roars to life and we're off.

"I hate driving," I admit as I steer the car down the quiet two-lane road that leads to the Royal residence. My fingers are clutching the wheel hard and I can't seem to bring myself to drive more than twenty-five miles an hour. The homes along this tree-lined boulevard are either gated or the driveway is so long you can't see anything but a blacktop lane swallowed up by trees and bougainvillea.

The car is small enough that Reed can easily stretch his arm to rest it on the back of my seat. He threads his fingers through the ends of my hair. "It's a good thing you have me then, because I like driving."

"Do I?" I ask quietly, almost glad that I have to stare at the road instead of into his blue eyes. "Have you, that is?"

"Yeah, I think you do."

And for the rest of the ride, it feels like I'm flying.

"Looks like you enjoyed yourself," Callum greets us when we return.

"Best ride ever," I declare. And then because I'm giddy with happiness, I throw myself into his arms. "You've been too good to me, Callum. Thank you. Thank you for everything."

Callum's stunned by my outburst of emotion but hugs me back quickly. The boys separate us, complaining about their empty stomachs and we all go out to a steak place down the road where the Royals eat enough for five families.

When we get home, I run upstairs to add *the drive* to my mental catalog of wonderful things that have happened in my life. I place it right after *blow job*.

That night, so late even the mice have tucked their babies in, Reed slides into my bed.

"I was having the best dream," I mumble as he curls his body around my back.

"What was it?" he says roughly.

"That you showed up in my bedroom and held me all night long."

"I like that dream," he whispers in my ear and then he does just that—holds me until I fall asleep.

He's gone again when I wake up, but the smell of him is on my sheets.

Downstairs, I find him leaning against the kitchen table.

"Don't you have practice?" I ask lightly, not willing to believe that he still wants to drive me to work.

"Can't have you on the road this early in a new vehicle. You need to break it in some more before you handle it while you're half asleep."

I try to downplay the way my excited heart is bouncing around the walls of my chest. "Hey, I was sleeping innocently until a big bear came in and decided that my bed was just right."

He tugs on my hair. "I think you got the wrong fairytale here."

"What would be the right one? *Aladdin* because you plan to take me on a magical carpet ride?" I waggle my eyebrows.

Reed bursts out laughing. "Is that what you think of my dick? That it's magical?" I blush so furiously that he laughs even harder. "Damn, you really are a virgin, aren't you?"

Cheeks still flaming, I flip up my middle finger. "That's what I think of you and your magical, uh..."

"Dick," he supplies between laughs. "Come on, virgin, just say it—dick."

"Oh, you're a *dick*, all right." I glare at him all the way to the car.

Reed manages to gain control of himself as he buckles up. He leans over to kiss me, and that's all it takes for my irritation to fade.

I'm practically floating on air during my morning shift at the French Twist, and my good mood stays with me throughout the school day. I run into Reed in the hall a few times, but other than a few secretive looks and a wink from him, we don't speak. I don't mind, because I'm not sure I'm ready to advertise to everyone at Astor Park that I'm kinda sorta involved with my kinda sorta stepbrother.

At lunch, Valerie and I are shocked when Savannah gestures for us to sit with her and her friends. I guess Operation Take-Down-Daniel-Delacorte was a success in more ways than one, though Savannah still doesn't seem entirely comfortable around me.

After school, I lie on the south lawn doing my homework until Reed and Easton are done with their team meeting, and then Reed drives me back to the mansion, keeping his arm around me during the whole ride.

When we get home, we discover that Callum has gone on a business trip to Nevada, which means we'll have the house to ourselves until Saturday. Hell yeah.

THAT EVENING, REED WALTZES INTO my bedroom while I'm reading.

"Sure, come on in. I don't mind," I say sarcastically. I roll over on my back and watch as he sets a huge bowl of popcorn on my nightstand.

"Thanks. Don't mind if I do. Want something to drink?" He peers into my mini fridge. "Don't you have anything without the word *diet* in here?"

He walks over and leans out in the hall. "Bring the beer. Ella just has diet shit."

I hear a faint, "Got it," echo from the end of the hall.

I scoot up against the headboard. "I'm afraid to ask what's going on."

"We're watching the game."

"We?"

"You, me, and Easton. We," he explains and then climbs on the bed. I move over so he doesn't sit on top of me.

I look around dubiously. The bed is big enough to hold Reed and me, but Reed, Easton and me? "I don't think we'll fit."

"Sure we will." Smirking, Reed lifts me up and drops me between his legs, pulling me snug against his chest.

Easton arrives moments later, taking my abandoned spot. He doesn't even blink at the cozy position he finds us in. Reed places the popcorn bowl between us and flicks on the television.

"Where are the twins?" I ask. My bed feels crowded with two giant Royals on it, but add the twins and it would be like stuffing double D's into an A-cup bra.

"They're going over to Lauren's house," Easton answers before shoving a handful of popcorn in his mouth.

"Both of them?"

"Don't ask questions you don't want to know the answer to," Reed hints and I promptly shut up.

Even if I had more questions, I don't think I'd be able to get any answers. Once the game is on, it's like I'm not even there. Reed and Easton cheer, groan and high-five each other. I spend my time admiring all the tight asses on the screen and smirking at all the innuendo-laden commentary, like how the one guy with the ball really needs to jam the hole and how the other team isn't getting enough penetration in the backfield.

Neither of the guys appreciate my observations. I settle in between Reed's legs and just enjoy the company. Occasionally, Reed reaches over and rubs my back or runs his hands through my hair. They're careless, offhand gestures as if we've been a couple for years, and I drink it up like a thirsty kitten. There are way worse ways to spend my night, I muse.

The score is pretty lopsided and somewhere along the line I doze off, full of popcorn and bored by the game. I wake up to the sound of Easton's phone blowing up. He leaves to answer it and Reed stretches out beside me like my own personal heater.

"Who was that?" I mumble, feeling groggy.

"Who knows. Were you sleeping?"

"No, just resting my eyes. What's going on with the game?"

"The Lions are killing the Titans."

"Are those real team names or are you just making stuff up?"

"Those are real team names." He sounds amused. A warm finger skims across the waistband of my shorts. I stretch, feeling a newly familiar heat seep into my bones.

"Are we done watching football?" It's more of a suggestion than a question.

Reed's blue eyes get stormy. He climbs over me, caging me between his arms and legs. "Yeah, I think we're done with that."

His head descends slowly and I lick my lips in anticipation—

"—what the hell, did the Lions just score?" Easton bursts in.

Reed sighs and heaves himself off me.

"See how nice it would be if people started knocking," I whisper as Easton grabs the remote from the bed and turns up the volume on the game.

Reed just folds his arms and grunts. We both watch as Easton begins to pace.

The team wearing blue and silver and sporting lions on their helmets is marching down the field. The opposing team with a flaming T on their helmets isn't doing a very good job protecting its scoring area. For the next twenty minutes, the blue and navy team scores one touchdown after another until the score is tied.

Easton is beside himself. By the time the whistle blows, he's as white as the sheer curtains hanging on the windows.

"What's going on?" Reed demands. "How much did you put on this game?"

I inherited addiction issues from my mommy. Oh, Easton.

Easton shrugs, trying to act like it's no big deal. "I got this, big bro."

Reed's jaw works as if he's fighting not to yell at Easton. Finally, he says, "If you need anything, hit me up."

Easton gives us a weary smile. "Yeah, of course. Gotta make a phone call now. Don't do anything I wouldn't do," he says with forced cheeriness.

"Does Easton have a gambling problem?" I ask once Easton's door closes down the hall.

Reed exhales in frustration. "Maybe? I don't know. I think he gambles and drinks because he's bored, not because he's addicted. But then I'm not a psychiatrist, am I?"

I flounder for something to say, but can only come up with, "I'm sorry."

He shrugs. "Nothing you or I can do about it."

By the fierce set of Reed's jaw, I can tell he doesn't believe that for a minute.

"I'm going to bed." Reed pushes away from the mattress.

I curl my legs underneath me, fighting the urge to beg him to stay. "Okay," I say in a small voice.

His brows scrunch together. "I don't think I'd be good company tonight."

"That's fine." I rise from the bed and head toward the bathroom. Am I hurt that he doesn't want to stay with me tonight? A little.

He grabs my wrist as I walk by. "I'm just worked up and…I don't want to pressure you into anything."

"Is this an *it's not you, it's me* speech? Because that's the absolute worst. No one wants to hear that."

A reluctant smile tugs at his mouth. "No. It's a *you're too hot for your own damn good* speech and I'm having a hard time, literally, keeping my hands off you."

I round on him and poke a finger into his rock-solid chest. "Who says I want you to keep your hands to yourself?"

He grabs my finger and hauls me up against him. "You really ready, Ella? Ready for it all?"

I hesitate and that's all the answer he needs. Dipping his head close to mine, he runs his nose along my cheek. "You aren't and that's okay because I can wait, but sleeping next to you is torture for me. Your body pressed up against me…and I wake up—" He breaks off but I know what he's saying because it's true for me, too.

I'm suddenly aching in spots I didn't realize could ache. "We could do other stuff." I lick my lips, thinking of the pool house.

He groans and buries his face in my neck. "There's no rush. Seriously. We're going to take our time and do this right." With another deep breath, he sets me away from him and strokes a strand of hair out of my eyes. "We okay?"

There's no point in disagreeing. I know Reed well enough that once he's made up his mind about something, it takes a long time to change it, which means I'm spending the night alone.

"We're okay." I rise on my tiptoes to kiss his cheek but Reed turns his face so our lips meet.

The long, tender kiss he gives me goes a long way toward easing any hurt feelings. The feel of his hard frame against my body doesn't hurt either.

And the last hints of rejection are brushed away when Reed slips into my bed later that night. Silently, I pull his arm around me and fall into a deep and welcome sleep.

CHAPTER 32

ON THURSDAY, VALERIE ACCOSTS ME at lunch. "What is going on with you and Reed?"

I try to look as innocent as possible when I answer, "What do you mean?"

"Apparently yesterday he walked by you on the way to Bio and flicked your hair," she announces.

I stare at her and then burst out laughing. "And that's some sort of big declaration by Reed Royal?" I ask incredulously.

She nods. "Reed does *not* do PDA. Even when he was supposedly dating Abby—"

I crinkle my nose at this. I don't like hearing those two names in the same sentence.

Valerie ignores me and continues, "—he avoided her. There was no kissing her up against the locker. No holding her hand. Sure, she went to his football games, but he's on the field so it's not like they were making out during the games or anything." She looks thoughtfully into the distance as if envisioning them. I hold back a gag. "I think the only time people ever saw them together was at a party. So yeah, the fact that he intentionally reached out to touch you is huge."

I stare at my tray of locally-sourced organic chicken breast and farm-fresh vegetables so that Valerie doesn't see that it's huge to me, too. The graze of his fingers against the base of my neck on Tuesday morning stayed with me for hours.

When I get myself under control, I glance back at Valerie. "We're enjoying a truce," is all I admit to.

She shoots me a worried look but doesn't press because she's a friend.

Impishly, I reach across the table and grab her hand, pressing it to my chest. "You're first in my heart, Val."

"I better be, bitch." She honks my boob and I slap her hand away.

Giggling, she sticks a carrot in her mouth. After we're done with lunch, she tells me that the Moonglow club is having another eighteen-and-over night. "You in?"

I hesitate, because my first instinct is to text Reed and find out what he's doing, but then I realize that not only would I give myself away to Valerie but that no matter what is going on between Reed and me, I need a life separate from his. So I nod firmly. "I'm in."

She bumps my shoulder companionably as we walk back toward our lockers.

"Are we dancing in the cage?" I ask with a grin.

"Is the Pope Catholic?"

"Am I going to need another outfit?"

She shakes her head in mock dismay. "It's like it's your first day of school all over again. Have you learned nothing since you've been here? Of course you need a new outfit."

Valerie and I make plans to go shopping later.

"I'll pick you up after work," I tell her, remembering my brand new set of wheels cooling at home.

She stops abruptly and grabs my arm. "What do you mean you'll pick me up? Did you get a car?"

I nod. "A convertible. Callum gave it to me."

She whistles long and low but loud enough that it turns the heads of everyone within about ten feet from us.

"Did you bring it to school?" She claps her hands together. "I want to see it!"

"Ah, no." I stall, trying to think of a plausible excuse for why I rode with Reed this morning. "I caught a ride with Reed. He's got football practice in the mornings so it makes more sense for us to carpool."

Valerie rolls her eyes. "How long are you two going to pretend that you're not going out?"

I suppress a smile. "For as long as anyone will buy it." And that is as close as I'll come to admitting she's right.

VALERIE PREDICTABLY LOVES THE LITTLE car. And I use some of my stash to buy an outfit for tonight. She takes me to an ordinary mall where the prices are high but not so high that I feel like I'm wearing an entire paycheck to the club. At the Royal mansion, I do her hair and makeup and my own, creating dramatic nightclub looks.

"I look hot," Valerie declares as she examines herself in the mirror. "Let me take a selfie for Tam."

"I can take it for you."

She hands me the phone and I snap a couple of photos, which she sends off immediately to her boyfriend. Those two seem to have such a great relationship, even though he didn't show up a week ago like he'd promised. Val didn't seem too upset about it.

"How do you do it?" I think of Reed in college and wonder if I'd be able to handle him being around so many pretty older girls.

Valerie takes a shot of me before answering. "I have to trust him. I send him lots of pictures."

"Nudes?"

"Yep. Naughty photos, too, mostly of my chin down…just in case." She makes a face. "Not that I don't trust him, but if someone steals his phone or something."

"Right." I hesitate. "Was Tam your first?"

"Are you judging me?" she asks curiously.

"No, absolutely not!" I wave my hands in the air. "No judgment."

She peers at me in disbelief. "Wait. Have you never had sex before?"

I lower my head and admit, "No, never."

"Never?" She draws back. "Wow. Now I'm rethinking your relationship with Reed because there's no way that dude is going without."

"I-I-I—" I stutter, at a loss for words.

She slaps a hand across her mouth. "I did not mean that. If he's with you, then I guarantee he's not sleeping around. When he dated Abby, I never saw him hook up with another girl."

"Yeah, okay." I feel a little numb. It never even occurred to me that he might be sleeping with someone else. Is that why he's not pressuring me?

Valerie squeezes my shoulder. "It was a stupid comment. I didn't mean anything by it. Honest. I tried to be funny and it came off wrong. Forgive me?"

"Of course." I hug her, but in the back of my mind, doubt has crept in.

A few minutes later, we step out of my bedroom in our teeny dresses, high heels, and big hair. Easton is leaving his room at the same time and lets out a long whistle. "Where are you two going?"

"Moonglow. They're having another rave," I explain.

He quirks an eyebrow. "You tell Reed about this?"

"No. Should I?" I hadn't seen Reed since this morning.

"All right. See you later," Easton says and jogs down the stairs.

"Later where?" I yell after him.

"Where do you think?" He snorts. "I tell Reed you're wearing a Band-Aid and cage dancing and you're going to have one hot-headed Royal on your hands."

"So I guess that's a yes that Reed and Easton will be there tonight," Valerie surmises.

I don't make any attempt to hide my satisfied smile.

VALERIE AND I ARE ESCORTED to the cages almost before we can clear the entrance. I guess they remember us. We put on a show for two songs until I hear my name being called. I look down through the bars and see Easton with his hands cupped around his mouth yelling my name.

When he catches my attention, he points toward the bar. I follow the line of his arm to Reed, who's leaning against the bar top in virtually the same pose as that first night Valerie and I danced here. Only this time he doesn't disappear.

He waits.

He waits for me to climb down from the cage.

He waits for me to walk all the way across the room.

He waits for me to reach him.

And all the while his blazing eyes track each step that brings me closer.

I halt a hand's width away. "What are you thinking about?" I ask huskily.

He looks pointedly at my chest and then the length of my legs exposed by the short, tight black skirt. "You know exactly what I'm thinking about." He inhales deeply. "But since we're in public, I can only *think* about it"

I lift a hand to his shoulder, and this guy who doesn't like public displays of affection takes it and brings it to his mouth. His hot breath gusts against my palm and then, with a hard jerk, he brings me flush against him.

"You're driving half the guys in here crazy," he growls against my hair.

"Only half?" I joke.

"The other half are in love with Easton," he informs me. He dips his hand underneath my hair and runs it all the way down to the small of my back. A small tug brings me sharply between his legs. We both suck in a breath when we make contact.

"Wanna dance," I manage to croak out.

He tosses back whatever he's drinking, slams the empty glass on the bar, and takes my hand. "Let's go."

On the dance floor, we press tight against each other. One of his strong thighs finds its way between my legs and he bends his knees so that I'm virtually riding him. Then he runs his fingers across the newly exposed skin at the backs of my thighs.

I twine my arms around his neck and hang on, trusting him.

"I almost exploded in my pants watching you dance," he rasps in my ear.

"Yeah? You like watching Val and I dance together?" I tease. Every guy's fantasy, I think.

"There was someone else up there with you?" He smooths a hand over my hair. "I only saw you."

I nearly melt into a puddle of goo. "Keep talking like that and you might get lucky."

His breath hitches and his fingers tighten against my flesh. "You want to get out of here?"

Heated, anxious, totally desperate for him, I nod helplessly.

"Let me find Easton and let him know we're taking off." He squeezes my hand and leans forward to brush his lips against my temple. That innocent kiss lights me up.

"I'm going to the bar to get a glass of water." I'm beyond parched.

"Okay, I'll be back in a sec."

Reed is swallowed up by the crowd while I move in the opposite direction and attempt to flag down a bartender. Val is still up in the cages, dancing her pretty booty off.

A cute guy with floppy brown hair stands in front of me. He's wearing a button-down shirt rolled and cuffed over a pair of plaid shorts. He looks vaguely familiar and I wonder if he goes to Astor Park.

"Ella Royal, right?" he asks.

I've given up on trying to get anyone to call me by my actual last name. I hold a tenner between my fingers and one of the bartenders acknowledges me with a tip of his chin. "Water," I mouth. The girl nods and I stuff the tip into the jar. It's a lot of money for water, but I'm thirsty and I figure it's the fastest way to get served. "Yeah, I'm Ella. Are you from Astor Park?"

"Scott Gastonburg." He leans an elbow on the counter. "Can I ask you a question?"

"Sure." I take the glass from the bartender and yell my thanks.

"I'm just wondering whether you started with the twins and are moving up the Royal age ladder, or are you just jumping around?"

I jerk around so fast the water spills all over my hand. "Screw you."

He holds out his hands. "I'm more than willing, baby, but my last name's not Royal."

I resist the urge to throw the entire contents of the glass in this asswipe's face. "Go to hell." I slam the glass on the bar top, then turn around and bump into Reed.

He takes one look at my face, then at Plaid Shorts' insolent expression, and immediately sizes up what's going on.

His eyes narrow and he shoves me behind him. "What'd you say to her?" he demands.

"It's nothing." I tug on Reed's arm. "Nothing. Let's just go."

Scott either lacks any self-preservation instincts or has a lot of liquid courage, because he grins and says, "Ellie here just offered to screw me but I reminded her I wasn't a Royal. I'm not even a cousin, but hey, I'm willing to take her off your hands once she's done with you guys."

Reed's fist flies out so fast I don't have a chance to react. By the time I realize what's going on, Scott is on the ground and Reed is pounding on him. Even over the heavy bass, I can hear the crack of knuckles against bone.

"Reed! Reed! Come on!" I yell and pull at his shoulders, but he's too focused on rearranging all of Scott's features. Others try to help me, although I think some of them are actively cheering on the fight.

Finally three bouncers push through the crowd and yank Reed away, leaving Scott lying on the floor—blood streaming from his nostrils and one eye swollen shut.

"You're going to have to leave," one of the black T-shirt clad bouncers snaps.

"Fine." Reed jerks out of the bouncer's grasp and grabs my wrist. I know what he wants before he opens his mouth.

"I'll get Easton," I assure him.

Reed nods. He points to one of the bouncers, a blond guy who looks like he eats steroids for breakfast and small children for dinner. "You, stay with her. Anything happens to her again," he stresses that word, "this place will be shut down and turned into a kiddie playground before end of business tomorrow."

I don't wait for the bouncers and Reed to come to an agreement. It's time for Reed to get out of here. He's filled with adrenaline and I can see he needs to exit this bar before the urge to get into another fight overtakes him.

"Easton's over by the bathrooms," Reed shouts as the bouncers escort him toward the entrance. I've lost track of Val, but I've got to get to Easton.

As I hurry away, I hear whispers. The people nearest to the fight have started gossiping.

"What just happened?"

"I think we just saw the proclamation of another Royal decree. Say anything bad about Ella Royal and you'll be drinking your meals from a straw for the next six months."

"She must be awesome in bed," someone remarks.

"No sex like trashy sex," another voice says. "Those bitches will let you do anything."

My ears burn and I'm tempted to repeat Reed's violent actions on every one of those smug faces, but I can't stop because I catch sight of Easton in the hallway near the bathrooms.

I push through the crowd, but Easton doesn't go into the men's room. Instead he walks to the end of the hall toward the exit door.

"Excuse me," I mutter as I duck around the line of girls waiting to use the ladies' room and past a couple making out in a not-so-dark corner.

"Easton," I call, but he doesn't stop. I know he hears me, because I can see his body twitch in acknowledgment. But he just keeps going.

I race down the hall, emerging from the door several seconds after him. I instantly skid to a halt.

He's in the back alley with two other guys, and it doesn't look like they're enjoying a smoke break.

Oh no. What has Easton gotten himself into?

The two guys have dark brown hair, slicked back away from their faces. They're wearing white T-shirts and jeans that hang down low and I'd bet if they turned around I'd see their boxers. Not that I would want to. A metal chain hangs from one of their belt loops.

"Go inside, Ella." Easton's voice is harder and colder than I've ever heard from him before.

"Now hold up," says the chain guy. "You can pay your debt off with her if you want." He grabs his crotch. "Lend the bitch to me for a week and we'll call it even."

My life before the Royals was filled with seediness, and I recognize a shake down when I see one.

The Monday night football game runs through my mind.

"How much?" I ask Mr. Chain.

"Ella—" Easton starts.

I cut him off. "How much does he owe you?"

"Eight grand."

I nearly faint, but beside me, Easton tries to shrug it off like eight grand is pocket change. "I'll have it next week. All you have to do is sit tight."

If it was pocket change he wouldn't be here in the back of the bar being threatened, and Mr. Chain knows it. "Yeah right. You rich kids live on credit, but not with me. I don't carry your broke asses on my books for longer than a week because I gotta pay the bills. So pony up your cash or you get to be this week's warning to all your pussy friends that Tony Loreno isn't anyone's pawn broker."

Easton's shoulders set in a hard line as he slightly adjusts his stance. Shit. He's preparing for a fight, and we all know it.

Tony reaches inside his pocket and fear spikes in my chest.

"Stop." I dig into my purse for my keys. "I've got your money. Wait here."

"What the hell, Ella?" Easton barks out.

No one waits. They all follow me to my car.

CHAPTER 33

AS I HIT THE KEY fob to unlock the trunk, I scan the parking lot for Reed's Range Rover. I don't see it anywhere, which means he probably parked in one of the spots along the other side of the building.

Relief floods my stomach, because Reed stumbling onto this little showdown would be the worst thing that could happen right now. He already beat the crap out of one guy tonight and I know he wouldn't hesitate to do it again, especially to back up his brother.

"You better not be reaching for a weapon in there," Tony hisses out, hovering behind me.

I roll my eyes. "Yeah, buddy, I keep an arsenal of assault rifles in the trunk of my car. Chill."

I lift up the felt square that covers the compartment for the spare tire and reach for the plastic baggie I stashed underneath the jack. There's a heavy feeling in my chest as I pull the stack of cash from the bag and count out eight grand worth of bills.

Easton doesn't say a word, but he watches me with a frown. He frowns even harder when I slap the bills into Tony's hand.

"There. You guys are square now. Pleasure doing business with you," I say sarcastically.

Smirking, Tony stands there and counts the money. Twice. When he starts to do it a third time, Easton growls.

"It's all there, jackass. Get the hell out of here."

"Watch yourself, Royal," Tony warns. "I still might make an example of you just because I feel like it."

But we all know he won't. A beating would only draw attention to us and to his "business" dealings.

"Oh, and you can place your bets somewhere else from now on," Tony says coldly. "Your money's no good to me anymore. I'm tired of seeing your ugly face."

The two guys stalk off, Tony tucking the cash in his back pocket, and yep, I can see his boxers hanging out of his pants.

When they're gone, I spin around to Easton. "What is *wrong* with you? Why would you ever associate with creeps like that?"

He just shrugs.

Adrenaline surges through my blood as I stare at him in disbelief. We could have been hurt. Tony could have killed him. And he's standing there like he doesn't give a shit about any of it. The corner of his mouth is even quirked up as if he's trying not to smile.

"This is fun for you?" I yell. "Almost getting killed gives you a boner, is that it?"

He finally speaks. "Ella—"

"No, just shut up. I don't want to hear it right now." I shove my hand in my purse and grab my phone, then text Reed to let him know Easton's riding back with me and that he should meet us at home.

I'm still holding the plastic baggie in my other hand, so I toss it into the trunk, trying not to think about how empty it is. Eight grand gone, plus another three hundred from my shopping trip with Val today. Until Callum gives me next month's ten-grand allowance, I only have seventeen hundred dollars in my escape fund.

I hadn't planned on running, not after all the positive changes in my life, but right now, I'm tempted to take the money and go.

"Ella—" Easton starts.

I hold up my hand. "Not now. I have to find Val." I dial her number, hoping she hears it inside the club.

Fortunately, she answers. "Hey, is everything okay?"

I glare at Easton. "It is now. Can you meet us outside at the car? The club isn't going to let us back in."

"On my way."

"Ella," Easton tries again.

"I'm not in the mood."

He clamps his mouth shut and we wait in tense silence for Val to appear. When she does, I force Easton to sit in the cramped back. Val opens her mouth to object but decides, wisely, that it's pointless.

The drive to her house is in complete silence.

"Call me tomorrow?" she says as she climbs out. Easton follows her out of the car.

"Yeah, and I'm sorry about tonight."

She gives me a forgiving smile. "Shit happens, babe. No biggie."

"Night, Val."

She waves her fingers and disappears inside the Carrington mansion. Quietly, Easton slides into the passenger seat. I clutch the steering wheel in a death grip and force myself to focus on driving, but it's hard to do when I'm seconds away from smacking the guy beside me.

About five minutes into the drive back home, my breathing finally steadies, and Easton's voice drifts over to me.

"I'm sorry."

There's genuine regret there, and I turn to look at him. "You should be."

He hesitates. "Why do you have money hidden in your car?"

"Because I do." It's a stupid answer, but that's all he's getting from me. I'm too pissed off to offer anything else.

But Easton proves that he knows me better than I think. "My dad gave it to you, didn't he? That's how he convinced you to come live with us, and now you're keeping it hidden in case you need to skip town."

I clench my teeth.

"Ella."

I jump when his warm hand covers mine, and then his head moves to rest on my shoulder. His soft hair tickles my bare skin, and I force myself not to run a comforting hand through it. He doesn't deserve comfort right now.

"You can't leave," he whispers, his breath fanning over my neck. "I don't want you to go."

He kisses my shoulder, but there's nothing sexual about it. Nothing romantic in the way his hand tightens over my knuckles.

"You belong with us. You're the best thing that ever happened to this family."

Surprise filters through me. Okay. Wow.

"You're ours," Easton mumbles. "I'm sorry about tonight. I really am, Ella. Please…don't be mad at me."

My anger melts away. He sounds like a lost little boy, and I can't stop myself from stroking his hair now. "I'm not mad. But dammit, Easton, the gambling needs to stop. I might not be there to bail you out next time."

"I know." He groans. "You shouldn't have had to bail me out tonight. I promise I'll pay you back, every last cent. I…" He lifts his head and presses a kiss to my cheek. "Thank you for doing that. I mean it."

Sighing, I turn my eyes back to the road. "You're welcome."

AT THE HOUSE, REED IS already waiting in the driveway. He glances from me to Easton in suspicion, but I head inside before he can question what went down tonight. Easton can fill him in. I'm too tired to rehash it.

I walk into my bedroom and strip off my dress, replacing it with the oversized T-shirt I sleep in. Then I duck into the bathroom to remove my makeup and brush my teeth. It's only ten o'clock, but that scene with Tony left me drained, so I shut off the light and climb into bed.

It's a long time before Reed comes to my room. An hour at least, which tells me that he and Easton must have had a really long talk.

"You had my brother's back tonight." His husky voice finds me in the darkness and the mattress shifts as he slides in next to me.

I don't resist when he wraps his strong arms around me and rolls me over so that my head is resting on his bare chest.

"Thank you," he says, and he sounds so touched that I shift in discomfort.

"I just paid off his debt. No big deal," I answer, downplaying my role in tonight's events.

"Fuck that. It *is* a big deal." He strokes the small of my back. "Easton told me about the money in your car. You didn't have to give it to that bookie, but I'm so grateful that you did. I tore Easton a new asshole tonight for getting involved with that guy. His other bookie is legit, but Loreno is bad news."

"Hopefully he stops using bookies altogether after tonight." I'm not convinced he will, though. Easton feeds off the thrill he gets from gambling or drinking or screwing everyone he can. That's just who he is.

Reed tugs me on top of him and we both laugh when the sheets get tangled up in our legs. He kicks them away, then brings my head down and kisses me. He strokes me over my shirt as his tongue chases mine into my mouth, and then he says, "Are you pissed that I threw down with that creep tonight?"

I'm too distracted by his wandering hands to understand the question. "You beat up Tony?"

"No, that dickweed Scott." Reed's features harden. "Nobody's allowed to talk to you like that. I won't let them."

Reed Royal, my very own dragon slayer. I smile and bend down to kiss him again. "Maybe this says something about me, but I think it's hot when you go all caveman on me."

He grins. “Just say the word and I’ll knock you over the head with a club and drag you into a cave.”

I burst out laughing. “Aw, that’s *so* romantic.”

“Never said I was good at romance.” His voice thickens. “I’m good at other things, though.”

He totally is. We stop talking as our lips meet again, and then we lie there kissing, while his hands run up and down my body. When his finger slides inside me, I forget all about the club and the bookie and Easton’s plea for me never to leave. Hell, I forget my name.

Reed is the only thing that exists. Right here, right now, he’s the center of my universe.

THE WEEKEND PASSES QUICKLY. CALLUM comes home on Saturday morning, so Reed and I are forced to sneak off to fool around in the pool house. And on Saturday night, Valerie and I go out for dinner and I finally cave and tell her about all the dirty things I do with Reed Royal. She’s thrilled about it, but points out that we’re still not doing the dirtiest thing of all and proceeds to tease me about being a prude.

But I don’t mind the slow pace Reed has set. A part of me is definitely ready to cross that final hurdle, but he keeps holding back, almost as if he’s afraid to go there. I don’t know why he would be, considering we’re getting each other off on a daily basis in other ways.

On Monday, Reed drives me to work, and to my dismay, the school day flies by. Today is the will reading, but no matter how hard I beg my watch to tick slower, the final bell rings before I’m ready and then I’m walking down the front steps toward the waiting Town Car.

Callum doesn't say much as Durand drives us into the city, but when we reach the gleaming building that houses the law offices of Grier, Gray, and Devereaux, he turns to me with an encouraging smile.

"It might get rough in there," he warns. "But just know that Dinah is all bark and no bite. For the most part, anyway."

I haven't seen Steve's widow since our first meeting at her penthouse, and I'm not looking forward to the reunion. Neither is she apparently, because she sneers the moment Callum and I enter the fancy office.

I'm introduced to four lawyers and ushered to a comfortable sofa. Callum is about to sit beside me when one of the lawyers shifts his body and a familiar figure steps out from behind it.

"What are you doing here?" Callum snaps. "I specifically ordered you not to come."

Brooke is unfazed by his tone. "I'm here to support my best friend."

Dinah steps up beside her and the two women link arms. They could be sisters, with their long blonde hair and delicate features. I suddenly realize I don't know anything about their history, and I probably should have asked Callum about it a long time ago, because obviously the two of them are super tight.

If we're choosing sides, then I guess Brooke and I are occupying opposite corners. My loyalties are with the Royals. By the disdain in Brooke's eyes, she knows it. I guess she thought I'd be with her. That she, Dinah, and I would team up against the evil Royal males and now I'm betraying them.

"I asked her to come," Dinah says coldly. "Now let's get started. We have early dinner reservations at Pierre's."

We're about to sit down to hear her dead husband's will and she's worrying about missing her dinner reservations? This woman is really something.

Another man separates himself from the group. "I'm James Dake. Mrs. O'Halloran's attorney." He offers his hand to Callum, who looks at the hand and then at Dinah in disbelief.

I'm not familiar with this sort of thing but it's easy to see that Callum is confused and unhappy about Dinah bringing both Brooke and another lawyer.

Callum reluctantly lowers himself on the couch, while Brooke and Dinah sit on the one opposite us. The lawyers seat themselves in various chairs, while the one behind the desk—the Grier of Grier, Gray and Devereaux—shuffles some papers and clears his throat.

"This is the last will and testament of Steven George O'Halloran," he begins.

The gray-haired lawyer spits out a bunch of legal gibberish about bequests to various people I've never heard of, money left in trust to a few charities, and something called a life estate being granted to Dinah. Dinah's lawyer frowns at this so it must not be good for Dinah. There are also substantial gifts to Callum's boys, in case, and the lawyer coughs before he recites the line, "Callum has pissed away his fortune on booze and blondes before I kick off."

Callum merely smiles.

"And to any legal issue surviving my death, I leave…"

I'm too busy trying to figure out what 'legal issue' means to focus on the rest of Grier's sentence, so I jolt in surprise when Dinah lets out an outraged screech.

"*What*? No! I will not stand for this!"

I lean in to Callum for an explanation of what the lawyer said, and I'm stunned by his answer. Apparently *I'm* the legal issue. Steve left me half of his fortune, somewhere to the tune of…I feel faint when Callum tells me the number. Holy crap. The father I never even met didn't leave me millions. He didn't leave me tens of millions.

He left me *hundreds of millions.*

I'm going to pass out. I really am.

"And a fourth of the company," Callum adds. "The shares will be transferred into your name when you're twenty-one."

Across the room, Dinah shoots to her feet, wobbling on her impossibly high heels as she swings around to glare at the lawyers. "He was *my* husband! Everything he had is mine and I refuse to share it with this gutter brat who might not even be his child!"

"The DNA testing—" Callum starts angrily.

"*Your* DNA testing!" she shoots back. "And we all know the lengths you'll go to when it comes to protecting your precious Steve!" She spins toward the lawyers again. "I demand another test, one that's conducted by *my* people."

Grier nods. "We would be happy to accommodate that request. Your husband left several DNA samples that are being stored at a private lab in Raleigh. I took care of the paperwork myself."

Dinah's lawyer speaks up reassuringly. "We'll get a sample of comparison from Miss Harper before we leave. I can supervise the process."

The adults keep talking and bickering among themselves, while I sit there in stunned silence. My mind keeps tripping over the words "hundreds of millions." It's more money than I could have ever dreamed of, and a part of me feels guilty for inheriting it. I didn't know Steve. I don't deserve half of his money.

Callum notices my stricken face and squeezes my hand, while Brooke's lips curl in distaste. I ignore the waves of hostility rolling toward me and concentrate on drawing air in and out of my lungs.

I didn't know Steve. He didn't know me. But as I sit here battling my shock, I suddenly realize that he loved me. Or at least, he'd *wanted* to love me.

And my heart aches that I never got the chance to love him back.

CHAPTER 34

HOURS AFTER THE WILL READING, I'm still numb. Still shocked. Still sad. I don't know what to do with the ball of pain in my stomach, so I just curl up on my bed and let my mind go blank.

I don't let myself think about Steve O'Halloran and how I'll never, ever know him. *Really* know him.

I don't think about Dinah's threats as Callum and I were leaving the law office, or the angry words Brooke hurled at Callum when he refused to take her dinner so they could "talk." I guess she wants him back. I'm not surprised.

Eventually Reed walks into my room. He locks the door, then joins me on the bed and pulls me into his arms.

"Dad said to give you space. So I gave you two hours. But that's over now. Talk to me, babe."

I bury my face in his neck. "I don't feel like talking."

"What happened with the lawyers? Dad wouldn't say anything."

He's determined to make me talk, dammit. Groaning, I sit up and meet his concerned eyes. "I'm a multi-millionaire," I blurt out. "Not just a regular old millionaire, but a *multi*-millionaire. I'm freaking out right now."

His lips twitch.

"I'm serious! What the hell am I going to do with that kind of money?" I wail.

"Invest it. Give it to charity. Spend it." Reed pulls me toward him again. "You can do whatever you want."

"I...don't deserve it." The meek response slips out before I can stop it, and the next thing I know, all my emotions rush to the surface. I tell him about the will reading, and Dinah's reaction, and my realization that Steve actually considered me his daughter even though he never knew me.

Reed doesn't comment, not once during my long-winded speech, and I realize that's what I wanted from him. I don't need advice or reassurances, I just need someone to listen.

When I finally go quiet, he does something even better—he kisses me, long and deep, and the strength of his body pressed against mine eases the anxiety in my chest.

His lips travel along my neck, the line of my jaw, my cheeks. Every kiss makes me fall harder and harder for him. It's a terrifying feeling, and it lodges in my throat and triggers the urge to run. I've never loved anyone before. I loved my mom, but it's not the same thing. What I'm feeling right now is...all-consuming. It's hot and achy and powerful and it's everywhere, overflowing in my heart, pulsing through my blood.

Reed Royal is inside me. Figuratively, but oh God, I need it to be literally, too. I need him and I'm going to have him, and my hands are frantic as they claw at his zipper.

"Ella," he groans, intercepting my hands. "No."

"Yes," I whisper into his lips. "I want this."

"Callum's home."

The reminder is like a splash of cold water to the face. His dad could knock on my door at any second, and probably will, because I know Callum sensed how upset I was when we got home.

I curse in frustration. "You're right. We can't."

Reed kisses me again, just the soft brush of his lips before he slides off the bed. "Are you gonna be okay? Easton and I were supposed to go out for beers with some of the guys from the team tonight, but I can cancel if you need me to stick around."

"No, it's fine. Go. I'm still digesting this money thing and I probably won't be good company tonight."

"I'll be back in a couple hours," he promises. "We can watch a movie or something if you're still up."

After he's gone, I curl up again and end up falling asleep for two hours, which is totally going to mess up my sleep schedule. I wake up when my cell phone rings, and I'm startled to see Gideon's number on the screen. I have all the brothers' numbers, but this is the first time Gideon has ever called me.

I answer the phone, still a bit groggy. "Hey. What's up?"

"You home?" is his terse reply.

I'm on guard almost immediately. It's just two words, but I hear something in his voice that scares me. He's angry.

"Yeah, why?"

"I'm five minutes away—"

He is? On a Monday? Gideon never comes home from college during the week.

"Can we go for a drive? I need to talk to you."

My brows knit together. "Why can't we talk here?"

"Because I don't want anyone overhearing us."

I sit up in bed, but I'm still not comfortable with his request. Not that I think he's going to murder me on the side of the road or anything, but asking me to go for a drive is strange, especially for Gideon.

"It's about Savannah, okay?" he mutters. "And I want it to stay between you and me."

I relax slightly. But the confusion lingers. This is the first time Gideon has mentioned Savannah to me. I only know about their history because of Easton. Still, I can't deny I'm insanely curious about it.

"I'll meet you outside," I tell him.

His huge SUV waits in the driveway when I descend the front steps. I hop into the passenger seat and Gideon drives off without a word. His profile is like stone and his shoulders rigid. And he doesn't say a single word until he pulls into a small plaza five minutes later and kills the engine.

"Are you having sex with Reed?"

My mouth falls open, and my heart starts pounding, because the furious look in his eyes is unexpected.

"Um. I…No," I stammer. It's the truth.

"But you're together," Gideon presses. "You're hooking up?"

"Why are you asking me this?"

"I'm trying to figure out how much damage control I'm gonna have to do."

Damage control? What the hell is he talking about?

"Shouldn't we be talking about Savannah?" I ask uneasily.

"This is about Savannah. And you. And Reed." His breathing sounds labored. "Whatever you're doing, you need to stop. Right now, Ella. You need to end it."

My pulse is even more off-kilter. "Why?"

"Because no good will come of it."

He drags a hand through his hair, which causes his head to tilt back a bit, drawing my attention to the red mark on his neck. It looks like a hickey.

"Reed is screwed up," Gideon says hoarsely. "He's as screwed up as I am, and, look, you're a nice girl. There are other guys at Astor. Reed'll be off to college soon."

Gideon's words tumble out, a bunch of disjointed sentences that I can't make sense out of. "I know Reed's screwed up," I start to say.

"You have no clue. No clue at all," he interrupts. "Reed and I and my dad, we have one thing in common. We ruin women's lives. We drive women to the cliff and then push them over. You're a decent person, Ella. But if you stay here and continue with Reed, I..." He breaks off, his breathing heavy.

"You what?"

His knuckles whiten as he grips the steering wheel tighter but offers no other explanation.

"You what, Gideon?"

"You need to stop asking questions and start listening," Gideon snaps. "End it with my brother. You can be his friend, like you are with Easton and the twins. Don't start up a relationship with him."

"Why not?"

"Goddammit, are you always this fucking difficult? I'm trying to save you from getting your heart broken and offing yourself with a bottle of pills," he finally explodes.

Oh. His outburst makes sense now. His mother killed herself… Oh God, did Savannah try something, too?

Reed and I have things sorted out, but I don't think Gideon is ready to hear that. And I suspect he isn't going to let up until I agree to his crazy demands. Well, fine. I'll agree then. Reed and I are already sneaking around behind Callum's back. It'll be easy enough to hide it from Gideon, too.

"Okay." I reach out and rest a soothing hand on his. "I'll end it with Reed. You're right, we're messing around, but it's not serious or anything," I lie.

He runs a hand through his hair again. "You sure about that?"

I nod. "Reed won't care. And honestly, if it upsets you this much, I'm sure he'll agree that it's not worth it." I squeeze Gideon's hand. "Chill, okay? I don't want to ruin the dynamic we have going on in the house. I'm cool about ending it."

Gideon relaxes, his breath coming out in a long rush. "Okay. Good."

I take my hand back. "Can we go home now? If someone drives by and sees us parked here, the rumor mill at school is going to explode tomorrow."

He chuckles weakly. "Truth."

I fix my gaze out the window as he starts the engine and pulls out of the parking lot. We don't talk on the ride back, and he doesn't get out of the car when he drops me off.

"You heading back to school now?" I ask.

"Yeah."

He speeds off, and for some reason I don't believe that he's returning to college. At least, not tonight. I'm also more than a little freaked out by his outburst and his insane request for me to stay away from Reed. Speaking of Reed, his Rover is parked near the garage, and the sight fills me with relief. He's back. And all the other vehicles are gone, even the Town Car, which means Reed and I will be alone.

I hurry inside and take the stairs two at a time. At the landing, I veer right, toward the east wing, where every door is open except for Reed's. The twins and Easton are nowhere to be seen, and my bedroom is empty too when I peek in.

I haven't been in Reed's bedroom before—he always hangs out in mine—but tonight I'm not going to wait for him to come to me. Gideon really shook me up, and Reed is the only one who can help me make sense of his brother's strange behavior.

I reach his door and lift my hand to knock, then smile ruefully because God knows no one in this house ever knocks on *my* door. They just waltz in like they belong in my room. So I decide to give Reed a taste of his own medicine. Childish as it is, I kinda hope he's jerking off in there, just to teach him a lesson about the importance of knocking.

I throw open the door and say, "Reed, I—"

The words die in my throat. I stumble to a stop and gasp.

CHAPTER 35

THE CLOTHES LITTER THE FLOOR like an obscene breadcrumb trail. I follow the path with my eyes. High-heeled shoes tipped over on their sides. Running shoes bracketing them. A shirt, a dress, under—I close my eyes as if I can erase the images but when I open them again, it's unchanged. Lacy black things—things I would never wear—look as if they were dropped just before their owner climbed into bed.

My gaze flickers upward, past strong calves, over knees, beyond a pair of hands loosely clasped together. Up the ladder of his bare, ridged abdomen, pausing at a new scratch on his left pectoral, about where his heart is supposed to be, stopping to meet his gaze.

"Where's Easton?" I blurt out. My mind rejects the scene. I superimpose a different story than the one laid out in front of me. A story where I've stumbled into Easton's room, and Reed, in a booze-induced haze, stumbled into the wrong room, too.

But Reed just stares stonily back at me, daring me to question his actions.

There's no way that Reed is going without, I hear Val whisper in my ear.

"The guys you were meeting for beers?" I toss out desperately. I give Reed every chance to spin an account different than the one I see before me. *Lie to me, dammit!* But he remains stubbornly silent.

Brooke rises like a ghostly specter from behind him, and the earth stops. Time stretches out as she slides her hand up Reed's spine, over his shoulder and then brings her manicured fingers across his chest.

There's no question she's naked. She kisses Reed's neck, all the while looking at me. And he doesn't move. Not one muscle.

"Reed…" His name is no more than a whisper, a painful scratch against my throat.

"Your desperation is sad." Brooke's voice sounds wrong in this room. "You should leave. Unless…" She stretches out a bare leg and drapes it outside of Reed's hips, which are still covered in the cotton of his sweatpants. "Unless you want to watch."

The pain in my throat gets worse as she remains wrapped around him and he makes no effort to move away.

Her hand drifts down his arm and when it reaches his wrist, he moves—a tiny, almost imperceptible flinch. I watch with alarm as her fingers glide across his abs, and before she can take hold of what I'd started to believe belonged to me, I turn abruptly and leave.

I had been wrong. Wrong about so many things that my mind can't catalog them all.

When we were moving around so often, I thought I needed roots. When Mom had her umpteenth boyfriend who leered at me too long, I wondered if I needed a father figure. When I was alone at night and she was working long, tiring hours waiting tables, stripping and God knows what else to keep me fed and clothed, I longed for siblings. When she was sick, I prayed for money.

And now I have all of that and I am worse off than before.

I run to my bedroom and stuff my backpack full of my makeup, my two pairs of skinny jeans, five T-shirts, underwear, stripper gear from Miss Candy's and my mother's dress.

I keep the tears at bay because crying isn't going to get me out of this nightmare. Only putting one foot in front of the other.

The house is deathly silent. The echoes of Brooke's laughter when I told her that there was one good and decent man out there bounces from one side of my skull to the other.

My imagination conjures up visions of Brooke and Reed. His mouth on her, his fingers touching her. Outside the house, I stumble to the corner and vomit.

Acid coats my mouth but I push on. The car starts immediately. I shove it into gear and, with shaking hands, navigate down the driveway. I keep waiting for that movie moment when Reed runs out of the house, screaming for me to come back.

But it never happens.

There's no rain-filled reunion and the only moisture are the tears I can't hold back any longer.

The monotone voice of the GPS directs me to my destination. I shut off the engine, pull out the title to the car and shove it in my Auden book. Auden wrote that when the boy falls from the sky after calamity after calamity, he still has a future somewhere and that there's no point in dwelling on one's loss. But did he suffer this? Would he have written that if he had lived *my* life?

I rest my head on the steering wheel. My shoulders shake from my sobs and my stomach heaves again. I lurch out of the car and stagger on shaky legs to the entrance of the bus station.

"You all right, honey?" the ticket counter attendant asks, looking worried. Her kindness wrenches another sob from me.

"My-my grandmother passed," I lie.

"Oh, I'm so sorry. Funeral then?"

I jerk my head in a nod.

She types into her computer, the long nails clicking against the keyboard. "Round trip?"

"No, one way. I don't think I'm coming back."

Her hands pause above the keys. "Are you sure? It's cheaper to buy a round trip ticket."

"There's nothing here for me. Nothing," I repeat.

I think it's the anguish in my eyes that gets her to stop asking questions. She silently prints out the ticket. I take it and climb into the bus that cannot take me far enough and fast enough from this place.

Reed Royal has broken me. I've fallen from the sky and I'm not sure I can get up. Not this time.

STAY CONNECTED

WILL ELLA RETURN TO THE Royal mansion full of its royal problems, or has Reed lost her for good? And are you curious to find out who says this in BROKEN PRINCE?

> "You look gorgeous and hot and if I stay in here any longer, your virginity will be on the floor somewhere next to yesterday's panties."

Sign up for the newsletter to be the first to know when BROKEN PRINCE is on sale! We promise to only send an email when it's really important. Stay connected with us by liking Erin Watt's Facebook page for updates and fun teasers!

LIKE US ON FACEBOOK:

https://www.facebook.com/authorerinwatt

FOLLOW US ON GOODREADS:

https://www.goodreads.com/author/show/14902188.Erin_Watt

ABOUT THE AUTHOR

Erin Watt is the brainchild of two bestselling authors linked together through their love of great books and an addiction to writing. They share one creative imagination. Their greatest love (after their families and pets, of course)? Coming up with fun--and sometimes crazy–ideas. Their greatest fear? Breaking up. You can contact them at their shared inbox: authorerinwatt@gmail.com

CPSIA information can be obtained at www.ICGtesting.com
Printed in the USA
BVOW08s1418080516

447254BV00004B/100/P